The

PRIVATE

Serials

Edited by
Hot Tree Editing

The Private Serials

© *Copyright Anie Michaels 2015*

TABLE OF CONTENTS

PRIVATE *Affairs*

PRIVATE *Encounters*

PRIVATE *Getaway*

PRIVATE *Property*

Part One

PRIVATE

Affairs

Chapter One

Thwap.

That was the noise which brought me out of my fuzzy, morning fog. Putting my coffee mug down, I looked at the granite countertop to see the envelope that had just been tossed there. I looked around to see if he was anywhere near me still, but all I caught was his back as he walked out of the front door. I sighed and glanced at the rectangle staring back up at me. My name was scrawled across the front, hastily written, slanted and sloppy.

Lena

I was hoping we could just ignore the significance of this day. Hoping we could just continue to live in comfortable silence and not draw any more attention to the marriage that was so completely and utterly failing.

Every day I woke up wondering which emotion would rule me. Would I be sad? Sad that the man I'd once loved was more like a roommate than a partner? Would I be angry? Angry he'd physically and emotionally abandoned me, both of which he'd vowed never to do? Would this be the day I was happy? Happy that I wasn't tied emotionally any longer to a man who obviously couldn't fulfill his obligations as my husband? Most days I managed to make the rounds and visit every emotion humanly possible, slowly fading from one to the next.

Today, unusually, I was filled with sorrow. Reminded by the greeting card sitting on my counter, today I grieved the loss of my marriage. For seven years we'd been married, and if I was really being honest with myself, we'd only been happy for about two of those.

I picked up the envelope and slid my finger beneath the lip, trying to open it without tearing the paper. I pulled the card out and read the sentiments pre-printed inside. None of the words meant anything to me; didn't evoke any emotion, because they were empty. He bought this card because he thought he had to. He hadn't even written anything on the inside. No personal note, no words to make me believe or hope that perhaps there was still something of our marriage to salvage. Nothing. I put the card down and exhaled slowly.

Seven years ago I married my college boyfriend and I remembered being replete with love and excitement. I met Derrek during my sophomore year at a frat party. I hadn't been a part of the Greek system and felt overwhelmingly out of place, having been dragged there by my roommate, Samantha. I stood in the corner of the room, holding up a wall, slowly sipping on some sugary, fruity drink in a red cup.

While I looked around the room, trying not to seem as uncomfortable as I felt, I noticed a guy staring at me. Our gazes locked and I was immediately stunned by the deep blue of his eyes. Being caught off guard by their beauty, I hadn't noticed them coming closer, or who they belonged to. When they were suddenly right in front of me, returning my gaze, I was forced to acknowledge the person they were attached to. Not surprisingly, the most beautiful eyes I'd ever seen belonged to the most beautiful man I had ever encountered. How convenient.

He was smiling, his full lips sliding over his white teeth, as he leaned against the wall next to me.

"I've never seen you here before," he said, still smiling. His voice was deep and playful. Nothing about him was off-putting. Everything about him screamed perfection.

That should have been my first indication to run the other way. Instead, I leaned in a little closer.

"That's probably because I've never been here before," I answered, talking loudly to be heard over the music and other party noises.

"Well, welcome then."

"Thanks."

He reached his hand out to me. "My name's Derrek. It's nice to meet you."

"Lena," I said, taking his hand. His grip was firm, but not overpowering. He held on to my hand longer than necessary, his smile never wavering as he slowly shook it. When he finally dropped my hand, it had immediately felt colder and a little empty.

He spent the rest of the evening chatting with me. He was very attentive, never paying attention to any other girls, only saying a few words to his friends who occasionally passed by. He seemed to be fully interested in spending the night talking to me, which was more flattering than I ever expected. At one point, the music and laughter in the house made it difficult to hear each other, so he'd asked if I wanted to go for a walk. My stomach fluttered at the thought of spending time with him completely alone, but something about him, which I couldn't exactly pinpoint, made me comfortable.

"Let me go and tell my friend I'm leaving," I said, smiling at the thought of going with him.

"Great. I'll meet you out front when you're ready."

Samantha had given me the obligatory best friend lecture about going for walks in the dark with strangers, and she'd been right; I was about to break every rule we college girls had been warned against. But I had a cell phone with a good battery charge and I also had pepper spray on my keychain. I was confident I would be fine.

And it turned out that I would be fine – for a while.

We walked around campus all night, continuing our conversation from the party and talking about so much more. By the time the sun came up, we were holding hands and strolling toward my dorm. We walked up the concrete stairs and stopped by the door. Both of us made some comment about how much fun we'd had, and I thought my heart would melt when he leaned in and kissed my cheek.

After that night we were inseparable. We found ourselves in an instant relationship. It had seemed so natural, and everything about it was perfect. We had similar backgrounds and our lives almost seemed to mirror each other's.

Both of our fathers had started their businesses from the ground up, and both had become immensely successful CEOs, so both Derrek and I were familiar with the lifestyle of the upper class. We'd played different roles, but they complemented each other. Derrek was being groomed to one day take over his father's role in the company, while I was expected be a wife to someone just like him. I hadn't planned on becoming someone's arm candy – I would have my own life and my own career – but I was expected to make a good match for someone important one day. My parents would not have been happy if I had married a starving artist. I was expected to marry someone who would fit nicely into the life my parents had made for me, and honestly, up until a few years after I was married, I had no problem with that notion.

But there I was, seven years into my marriage, and I was anything but happy.

I pulled myself out of the memory of meeting Derrek and slowly walked to the garbage, dropping the anniversary card on top of all the other trash inside. I didn't understand why he'd given it to me, other than perhaps he was trying to stave off an argument. But we hadn't argued in forever. To argue, one had to communicate, even if it was angry, loud, harsh communication. The most we said to each other over the past few weeks had been stilted, forced conversations pertaining to upholding our appearances. We still went to functions together, still played the part of a happily married couple, but when we came home, we separated.

I always found myself alone in our king-sized bed, and he always found himself asleep on the pull-out couch in his office. We could go days without seeing each other if we tried, and sometimes I did try. I tried to pretend as if he wasn't there, as if I wasn't trapped in some loveless marriage any longer, but even that was depressing. If I wasn't married to Derrek, I was living an empty life in an even emptier house.

Something needed to change, and in that moment, I decided, perhaps, it had to be me.

I had loved him once, a long time ago, when careers and expectations hadn't been on our radar. When we'd been young and, in many ways, free. When love hadn't been a means to fulfill the wishes of our parents, but had been born out of our inability to stay away from one another. Truth be told, I still loved him; loved the idea of him, of us. But that need for him had disappeared. I wanted it back – desperately.

I made the decision in that moment to try to fix us. To do whatever was needed to make my marriage work again, and not just be a roommate to my husband. I wanted to be his wife again.

Chapter Two

When I heard the front door open that evening, it signaled Derrek was home from work and also signaled the beginning of my attempt to win my husband back. My heart nearly stopped and I had to talk myself down from the proverbial ledge. I was nervous to be alone with my own husband, apprehensive about putting myself in the line of fire. But something needed to change;

something had to give. I'd been ambitious my whole life – a doer. If I saw a problem at my job, I fixed it. In all other aspects of life, if something needed attention, I focused until I was the victor. I was determined to make my marriage work and not be miserable for the rest of my life.

"Derrek, is that you?" I heard his footsteps falter. He'd been making a hasty retreat to his office, as he did most evenings upon arriving home. My question caught him off guard.

"Yes. It's me."

"Would you come to the dining room, please?" There were a few seconds of silence, and then I heard footfalls coming closer. When he entered the room I tried not to be discouraged by the expressions that crossed his face. At first, I saw annoyance, more than likely that I'd asked something of him. Then the annoyance gave way to surprise, which eventually turned back into annoyance. I watched as his gaze floated over to the table, taking in the lit candles, the use of our wedding china, the beautiful meal I'd made, and the bottle of expensive wine airing.

"Lena, what is all this?" he asked, as his hand made a sharp jab toward the table and then fell to his side.

"This is the anniversary dinner I made for us," I said with a shaky smile, trying so hard not to sound desperate or false. I attempted to sound like this was something he should have been expecting – his loving wife preparing a delicious meal to celebrate seven years of marriage.

"Lena…" he said, with defeat heavy in his voice. I could fill in the blanks, say the words he was thinking; I'd thought them for so long, too. *This is ridiculous. I don't know what you expect from me. What are we doing? How long can we keep this up without ruining our lives?* I knew what was running through his mind, but I needed to stop him from uttering the words, because once we said them, once they were out in the open, we could never cover them up again.

"Please, Derrek, sit down. I made your favorite. Beef roast. Just sit." I was begging my husband to have a meal with me.

He sighed heavily, but set his briefcase on the ground near the entryway and sat down at the head of the table. I smiled to myself because this was the first hurdle, and we'd already jumped it and landed on the other side unscathed. I walked to his chair, hoping to catch his eyes admiring me in the dress I bought to impress him.

I was nearly thirty, never had children, and worked very hard to maintain my body. My dress was black, tight, and just a little short. I watched his eyes, hoping they'd roam over me, hoping that seeing him appreciate my form would spark some sort of fire within me.

He never looked at me. He was focused on his plate.

"Did you have a good day at work?" I asked innocently, like it was a question I asked him every evening.

"I suppose. I was busy. Lots of meetings."

"Oh, well, hopefully you'll be able to relax tonight."

I picked up the platter of roast and carried it to him, stood there as he picked up the fork and started serving himself. I took him in, looked over his profile. His hair looked a little messy, which was abnormal for him. He was usually put together, always immaculately pristine. His hard day of work must have stressed him out more than he let on. It looked as if he'd run his hands through his hair all day, undoing any styling he'd invested in this morning before he left the house.

My eyes wandered still lower, along the thickness of his neck. The muscles that ran from his chin down to his shoulders flexed as his jaw clenched. He looked nervous, and I saw his pulse beating rapidly along his throat.

"Are you feeling all right?" I asked, genuinely concerned.

"I'm fine, Lena. Let's just get on with this." I was startled by his rudeness. He was often cold toward me, removed and stiff, but never rude.

I was turning away from him, moving to grab the bowl of roasted potatoes, when my eye spotted something down inside the collar of his shirt. Before I could stop it, my finger involuntarily moved to his collar and pushed it aside gently and I saw more of what had caught my eye to begin with.

"Did you hurt yourself?" I asked, and at the same time, he swatted my hand away from his neck.

"No, I didn't hurt myself. Lena, this is ridiculous. I have things to do."

My mind swirled with different thoughts and feelings as I tried to process everything that was happening. One thing became abundantly clear in that moment: he was hiding something from me. What I had first spotted and assumed was a bruise along his collarbone, I realized, like a bucket of cold water dumped on me unexpectedly, was a hickey.

He stood abruptly, the sound of the chair legs scraping against the travertine tile floors sending shivers down my spine, like nails on a chalkboard. I'd always hated those tile floors.

"Where are you going?" I asked hurriedly, trying to catch him before he made it all the way out of the room. Although, I could guess where he was headed – his office. If he was home and awake, he was usually hiding in there. He knew I had no business being in there, and so that was how he escaped me.

"Like I said, I have things to do." He continued out of the room and I set the platter down, following him.

"What could be more important than having a meal with your wife on your anniversary?" I shouted at him as I followed him through the house, my voice echoing off the walls. I heard him sigh loudly again, but he still walked away from me.

"Lena, don't do this." He had entered his office and sat down at the big chair behind his desk.

"Don't do what? Make you dinner? Ask to spend time with you? Why can't we *try* to be normal or maybe even happy, just for one night? We used to be happy, Derrek. We used to be in love and happy. I just wanted to try and get a little happiness back tonight."

He was silent for a moment, shuffling papers around on his desk, avoiding my eyes. He moved those papers around, stacking them on one corner of his desk, and then moved them to another corner. He tapped on his keyboard, stared at the screen of his computer like the answers to all the world's problems could be found there. One thing he wouldn't look at was me.

"You can't ignore me, Derrek. I'm your wife."

"I'm aware of that fact," he mumbled, sounding angry.

"What was that mark I saw under your shirt collar, Derrek?"

"I don't know what you're talking about."

"I think you do."

"Lena, please…" He pinched the bridge of his nose. "I don't understand what's gotten into you."

"I spent all day trying to think of how I could surprise you for our anniversary, trying to think of ways to get back that spark we use to have between us, and you come home with a hickey under your shirt."

"You're being ridiculous," he said under his breath.

"Am I?"

"Yes."

"Then take off your shirt."

He paused, obviously not expecting me to say those words. I hadn't asked him to take off any piece of clothing in months. Perhaps even over a year. I'd have to really think about it to come up with a solid answer.

"Lena, please, let's stop deluding ourselves," he finally replied, finally lifted his eyes to look me straight in mine.

"I don't think I'm deluding myself. I know what I saw."

"Our marriage, the part of our relationship where we have meals together or spend time alone together, is over. It's been over for a long time now. You know it. I know it. I'm content with the way things are now."

"What do you mean, 'it's over'?" I gasped.

"We haven't behaved like a married couple for years now, Lena. Out in the public eye, we continue to hold up the image of our marriage, but here – in this house – our marriage fell apart long ago."

I agreed with him, knew what he was saying to be true, but I didn't think it was a lost cause, didn't think it was doomed. He sounded like it was dead and gone. I just felt like it needed some work – could be resuscitated.

"So let's fix it," I cried.

"We can't. It's too late."

"So, what? You want a divorce? You're going to leave me?" The image of that hickey flashed into my mind. "You're having an affair?"

"I am *not* having an affair." His voice was cold and stone-like. His affirmation was almost like a gust of chilling wind; it hit me hard and made me shiver. "I am, however, going back to the office. It's abundantly clear I won't be able to get any work done here tonight."

I watched as he stood again and walked right past me, walking back toward the dining room. He retrieved his briefcase and walked toward the front door. When I heard it open and then subsequently slam shut, I felt the loud sounds vibrate through me, and felt a little crack form in the façade I'd been wearing for what seemed like forever. It seemed as if, in one thirty minute window, we'd moved from pretending our marriage was fine to acknowledging its failure, but I was still left wallowing in confusion.

I walked slowly to the dining room, mindlessly clearing the table, just going through the motions while my mind reeled.

What were we to do? Just continue on this path of sharing a house but sharing nothing besides? My hands dipped in and out of the warm, soapy water, washing the dishes, rinsing them, and then setting them on the rack to dry. We had a dishwasher, but washing them by hand calmed me.

I didn't want a marriage of convenience, but from his words, it seemed like Derrek had thrown in the towel and wanted nothing to do with me. Well, aside from a companion to accompany him to work functions and parties. He wanted to hold up the appearance of our marriage, but drop the charade at the door.

I saw a tear drop into the dishwater. Not realizing I was crying, the tear caught me off guard. Once I saw the first one fall, however, the rest were not far behind.

This was not where I wanted to be, wasn't how I envisioned my life to be at twenty-nine. When I married Derrek, I was sure we'd be happy forever. Sure, I suspected we'd have difficult times, trying times, but I thought we'd work together to get past them. I never would have imagined that one day Derrek would tell me our marriage was over, that the real part – the loving part – had been lost.

Then there was the hickey he denied.

Of everything that happened, the hickey was the least of my worries. Well, it would have been if he'd owned up to it. We couldn't work past a problem if he didn't admit to it, and I would gladly, at this point, look past any transgressions on his part if he'd just agree to be my husband again.

I cried because he didn't want me and I cried because I still wanted him. I wanted my marriage. I wanted the future I'd signed up for so many years ago, and I didn't think it was fair that someone else could make those decisions for me. Didn't I get a say in how our future played out?

My hand slammed down on the counter, suds spraying out around my wet hand.

"Shit," I cried through a whisper. Perhaps I shouldn't have ambushed him with this dinner. Perhaps I should have approached him on a different night, some other time when the pressure wasn't so high. I should have let our anniversary pass by and tried to talk to him when he was more relaxed and not so obviously stressed. All those thoughts just made me cry harder. I never wanted to have to walk on eggshells around my husband. I also cried harder because I could remember a time when I didn't have to, when I could go to him with any problem I was having or any emotion I was feeling.

Once the dishes were clean and the dining room was put back in order, I ambled up the stairs and readied myself for bed, not expecting to see Derrek for the rest of the evening. And I was right. He never came home that night.

Chapter Three

I woke to the sound of my phone buzzing against the wood of my bedside table. I hadn't set an alarm and wasn't expecting to be woken up, so I startled a bit. The buzzing stopped, and before I could reach over to see what had caused it, I must have fallen asleep again because I was awoken by the buzzing a second time. This time, however, the damage was done and I was awake. A groan escaped me as I rolled over to see who was trying to contact me. I pressed the button on the phone to light up the screen and saw two text messages from Samantha.

Hey, woman. How did the surprise anniversary dinner go?

You're either still asleep because you're exhausted from all the sex you and your husband had last night, or because you cried yourself to sleep. Either way, we need to talk. Text me back.

I sighed at her intuitive mind. Couldn't I have just been asleep because I was sleeping? Maybe I went for a run last night and was exhausted from that. I wasn't really surprised that she'd clued in to what had really happened, but I was more upset that now I was probably going to have to talk to her about it. Talking about it to someone else made it real. I wasn't trying to delude myself into thinking I had a perfect marriage, but admitting to my best friend that last night had put some sort of nail in my marriage coffin would be the most real and heartbreaking conversation I might ever have. It occurred to me I would have this real and heartbreaking conversation with my best friend and not my husband, and that, perhaps, was the most depressing and telling thought of all.

I pressed the buttons on my phone to send a message back to her.

Same time, same place?

It only took a few seconds for her to respond.

See you there.

    Years ago, Samantha and I had found a tiny little coffee shop equidistant between our houses, and we'd started meeting there for coffee weekly, or whenever one of us called upon the other. It was nice, all those years, to have something steady and reliable to hang on to – something to look forward to. Sometimes, we didn't have anything new or exciting to talk about and we just reminisced, laughing about things that happened in college or since. Other times, I held her hand as she told me about her break-ups, or we listened to each other's work problems, trying to ease the anxiety of navigating the working world as young and independent women.

    I met Samantha when we'd been assigned as dorm roommates our freshman year of college. She and I couldn't have been any more different. She was outgoing, brave, and brought energy with her wherever she went. Her vitality was contagious, and as soon as we met, I felt the fever she carried with her for life. I had spent my entire life protected from the adventurous spirit she exuded, and when I got a taste of it, I grabbed ahold of her and never let her get away. She taught me how to let go, how to feel free even if I really wasn't. When I was with her, I could sometimes pretend I didn't have my father to answer to, or a life waiting for me that I wasn't sure I wanted to live.

    When I was twenty-four, my father passed away suddenly, and even though I was internally conflicted over my feelings toward his death, she was there for me every step of the way. I didn't have to explain to her that I was devastated my father was dead, but relieved that I no longer had to worry about living up to his standards for me. His death saddened and freed me all in the same moment. She knew it, understood, and never judged me. Not once.

Samantha had spent many hours listening to me talk about my marriage. She knew everything about it – the good and the bad. She also had very strong feelings about it.

She hated Derrek.

It hadn't always been that way; he hadn't always been the spawn of Satan in her eyes. All through college, Derrek and Sam got along really well. We spent countless Saturday nights at his frat house and the two of them never had one argument. She was my maid of honor in our wedding. She was so happy for us – so supportive. However, when the marriage began to change, began to fall into the dark place it seemed to reside in now, she always questioned why I stayed with him.

I hated complaining to her about him or our relationship, because it did nothing but further tarnish him in her eyes, but I had no one else to turn to. In my family, we didn't talk about problems. It was understood that you were to always keep up appearances. If you had an issue, you resolved it quietly. You didn't bring attention to it. You swept it under the rug. I had been trained my whole life to stay silent, until Sam.

It was comforting to walk in to our usual coffee shop and see her sitting at a table waiting for me. I went straight for her. She stood when she saw me and opened her arms for me without question, knowing I'd be here with bad news instead of good.

"What happened, Lena?"

I let myself take the comfort from her, allowed her arms to pull out some of my anxiety. I sighed into her shoulder, trying to keep the tears at bay. I didn't want to cry anymore.

"I don't know, Sam." I pulled away and sat in the chair opposite her, giving a sad smile to the cup waiting for me. If Sam made it to the coffee shop first, she always bought my drink, and vice versa. "Thank you for the coffee." She smiled at me, but said nothing. "I made the dinner, put on the dress, and was all ready for him when he came home from work." I dove right into the story. I knew Sam wasn't going to stand for pleasantries and chit chat.

"Did he appreciate it?" she asked, not even blinking.

"No. Actually, he seemed put out by it. Like having dinner with me was an inconvenience to his evening schedule."

"That bastard."

"It gets worse."

"I'm not surprised." She raised her eyebrows, waiting for me to continue.

"When I mentioned I wanted to work on our marriage, that I wanted to get back to the happy couple we had been when we got married, he basically told me our marriage was over and that I should get used to the status quo. He said that our marriage fell apart a long time ago and that it was too late to fix it." Samantha said nothing, but I could tell she was holding her rage inside for my benefit. She knew what I had been hoping for, knew I wanted my husband back. So, out of love for me, she was reining in all the expletives I knew she wanted to unleash, because she knew it wouldn't help me, wouldn't make me feel any better. I loved her even more for it.

I looked down at my coffee cup, slowly twisting it around and around, watching it circle in my fingers, while I continued.

"He wants to hold up the façade of our marriage, you know, still make appearances together in public, but pretty much indicated he was done with me in private." My voice faltered on the last few words, my throat constricting with that painful pinch that was always followed by tears, aching. But I pushed it back. I wouldn't cry any more. "He only wants to be my husband when other people can see us."

Sam was quiet for a few moments more, and then she adjusted in her seat and tilted her head to the side. "Why would any man want to continue a marriage without the *benefits* of marriage? I mean, let's be real. He's a man. I can understand him wanting to stay in the marriage if you were going to try and fix it and work on the intimacy, or I can understand him cutting his losses and wanting out in order to find that intimacy in other places. But what hot-blooded man chooses to stay in a sexless marriage and wants it to remain that way?"

I didn't look up at her and I didn't say anything, afraid to tell her what I'd seen under his shirt collar. Being a terrible husband, being absent and emotionally unavailable, was bad enough. If I told her what I saw, she'd likely be unstoppable in her rage and find him to take her anger out on him. She would also try to pressure me into leaving him, and I knew I couldn't do that. I also knew she'd never be able to understand why. The mistake I'd made before our marriage had even begun would keep me tethered to him.

I sighed loudly and shook my head. "I couldn't fathom the thoughts running through his mind. Perhaps in a few days I can try to talk to him again. Maybe I just caught him at a bad time."

"Your wedding anniversary was a bad time for him to talk to you?" she asked snidely. I didn't take offense. I knew she wasn't angry with me.

"He's stressed at work," I mumbled.

"Don't make excuses for him, Lena."

"Sorry."

"Don't apologize either!"

"What do you want from me?"

"I want you to take a stand! Don't let him walk all over you and don't let him make all the decisions! It's your marriage, too, Lena. It's your life just as much as it is his."

I heard her words, felt them sink into me, and then I felt them fall away. I was conflicted. Before I could stop them, the words were falling out of my mouth. "I think he's cheating on me," I whispered.

Sam didn't blink, didn't breathe. She just looked at me as she formulated her thoughts. "Why do you think that?"

"Last night, when he came home, I saw something inside his shirt near his collar. At first, stupidly, I thought it was a bruise. But I eventually realized it was *not* a bruise. It was a hickey."

"Did you ask him about it?"

"I tried, but he changed the subject and left."

"Hmm. Suspicious," she said, warily. I nodded. We were both quiet for a few minutes. I replayed the whole evening in my mind, running through each and every thing I could have done differently. But no decisions I'd made or words I could have said differently changed the fact that he'd come home with that mark on him. A mark another woman had put on him.

"Why don't you leave him, honey?" Sam's words were a quiet whisper, as if her voice could have scared me away. She was treading lightly, not wanting me to turn away from the direction the conversation was heading.

"I can't," I whispered, just as quietly.

"Yes," she said, placing her hand over mine. "You can." I shook my head slightly, feeling my hair sway back and forth over my ears.

"No," I whispered again. I tipped my head up to look her in the eyes again. "I can't, Sam. Really. It's complicated."

"How can I help?"

I shrugged. My next words were drowning in tears, choked out on sobs. "I don't know." *I don't know.* Those three words were the answer to a lot of questions I had running through my mind. Was there any hope left for my marriage? Would I spend the rest of my life tied to a man who didn't want to be with me? Would I feel this lonely forever? Would I go the rest of my life without feeling a man's hands on me again? My head fell into my hands as I tried to cry discreetly in the coffee shop. I heard Sam move and then heard her next to me before I felt her arms come around me. I leaned into her and let the tears come, but stifled the sobs, tried to hold at least those in.

"What are you going to do?" Sam finally asked after I'd calmed down a little.

"Well," I said, wiping my eyes. "I guess I'm going to find out if he's really cheating on me."

"The hickey isn't enough proof for you?"

I shook my head again. "Listen," I started, unsure of how I could explain something to her I'd never explained to anyone. Unsure of how to say the words I'd never uttered to a single soul. "I can't just go on a hunch," I said quietly. "I need actual proof."

"For peace of mind?" she asked.

I nodded. "Sure."

She tilted her head to the side again, her eyebrows narrowing at me. "What's going on, Lena?"

"I'm sorry. I can't go into any more detail than that. All I'm saying is, if anything is going to change, I need actual, physical proof he's cheating. Me spying what I think is a hickey on the inside of his collar isn't going to cut it."

"Well, then," Sam said with resolution in her voice. "We'd better get a rental car, some black turtlenecks and ski masks, and brush up on our stakeout skills."

"What?" I said, half laughing.

Sam had a sneaky smile on her face when she answered me, rubbing her hands together. "We're going to stalk your husband."

Chapter Four

I sat in the passenger seat of a black Toyota Corolla, quietly crunching on Cheetos, my eyes glued to the front doors of my husband's work. Cheetos, in hindsight, might have been a bad snack choice when wearing all black, and I struggled to keep the neon orange cheese powder from making its way into the fibers of my new turtleneck. I heard a giggle and looked over at Sam, sitting in the driver's seat.

"What's so funny?"

She took a bite of the licorice in her hand and waved the red rope between us. "We might be some of the worst stalkers ever."

She wasn't wrong, although, we had gotten most of the basics down. Black car? Check. The cover of night? Check. Black clothes to blend into said cover of night? Check and check. But we also might have indulged and turned our rental car into a snack wagon, using our stakeout as an opportunity and excuse to eat gas station fare, which we never really had a valid reason to buy. But under the guise of our stalker outfits, it seemed fitting to break a few rules, even if they were self-imposed.

It had taken two weeks from our original conversation about my husband's possible affair for me to agree to Sam's crazy idea. At first, although it was tempting to see if we could find out what was going on, I wasn't really ready to know. I went home from our coffee shop date and pushed the idea of his affair out of my mind. I had gone back to plan A. If I tried to be the perfect wife, perhaps he would come around and want to be my husband again.

So I baked and cleaned and was waiting to be the doting wife when he came home from work. Only, sometimes he never came home from work, and most of the time, when hc did come home, it was so late that I was either crashed on the couch in the living room, or had long given up and was asleep in our bed upstairs. On top of that, hc often left for work before the sun came up and I would wake to a house just as empty as it had been when I'd fallen asleep.

I counted eight days in a row in which I didn't once lay eyes on my husband.

I saw proof of him and his presence around the house: a coffee mug in the sink, wet towels in the laundry room, opened mail on the counter. But I never saw him and I hadn't spoken to him since our anniversary. He wouldn't answer when I called him at work, and I was sent directly to voicemail if I called his cell. After about the first five days of silence from him, I stopped trying to reach him at all.

Finally, I decided to take some sort of action, so I called Sam and told her to greenlight her plan. Three nights later we were sitting in a black rental car, watching the doors to my husband's building, waiting for him to exit so we could follow him. It shouldn't have been fun and it shouldn't have felt like an adventure, but it sort of did. It was impossible not to laugh when trapped in a car with my best friend, especially when she was trying her hardest to keep the mood light, trying to entertain me. I knew what she was doing – trying to keep my mind off the idea that we were, in fact, trying to catch my husband in the act of cheating – and I let her do it. I let her make me laugh so hard I cried. I let her rap along to the radio even though she didn't know all the words and made a horrible rapper. And I let her tell me the horror stories of her most recent travels into the world of dating at twenty-nine.

Suddenly, everything lost its humor as I watched Derrek walk out of the building. Both Sam and I went quiet, watching and waiting. When his car pulled onto the road,

Sam gave me a look, silently asking me if I still wanted to go through with our plan. I nodded. She started the engine and pulled out, only a few cars behind his.

I had never tailed a car before and found it was a delicate balance between staying close enough to follow, but far enough away so that you melted into the background. After a few minutes, it became clear he was not headed to our home. I wasn't surprised at all by this fact, but I was, admittedly, a little saddened. I came out with Sam to find out if he was cheating, but now that we were actually in the midst of possibly finding proof, I realized I might not be ready to deal with the reality proof would bring with it.

"You okay, Lena?"

"Yeah," I said. I took on the role of navigator, keeping my eyes on his car and telling Sam which way to turn or which lane to move into so she could focus on just driving. His car took us more than forty-five minutes away from his work. We were a good distance out of the city, far away from our home, and unfamiliar with the area.

"Where in the world is he going?" I asked, knowing Sam didn't have the answer. I hadn't expected to leave the city. I imagined him pulling up to a corner and propositioning a prostitute, or pulling in to a seedy motel to meet up with some random woman. I had never imagined him leading us to suburbia. The further we got away from the city and closer we got to housing developments, the more nervous I became. My body was clued into what was happening and sending me all kinds of signals to run away. My fight or flight instincts were kicking in, and my body was telling me to fly.

But his car kept driving so we kept following. An hour after he'd left his building we watched as he pulled into the driveway of a house. We stopped down the block and turned off the headlights, watching with suicidal fascination. I wanted to look, but I knew on some unconscious level it was going to hurt. Whatever we saw was going to open me up and rip me to shreds, but I couldn't look away.

He opened his car door and climbed out, stretching up toward the sky, obviously tight from the long drive. He grabbed his briefcase from the backseat and walked toward the two-story, cookie-cutter house. When he was halfway up the path to the house, the door opened and my mouth gaped as a small child ran toward him. Derrek dropped his briefcase and crouched down, opening his arms. When the child, a girl if her long hair was any indication, made it to him, he picked her up, hugging her tightly. Then, as if my world couldn't fall apart any more, a woman came out of the house, a smaller child held to her hip. She stood on the front porch, watching Derrek and the little girl, a warm smile on her face.

Derrek picked up his briefcase, never putting the little girl down, and walked toward the door and the woman. When they met, he leaned into her and pressed a kiss to her mouth and lingered there, their kiss obviously deep and heated. Then, he bent down a little and pressed a kiss to the forehead of the small child she held. They all turned and went into the perfect house.

"Holy shit." Sam's voice was quiet and confounded. "Holy," she said louder and turned to me. "Shit."

"Sam, please drive away now," I muttered.

"Holy *shit!*" she said as she put the car in drive and made a U-turn, taking us out of the neighborhood without driving past the house. "What in holy hell did we just see, Lena?"

"I think we just found the answer to our question, Sam. Derrek is definitely cheating on me."

"Yeah, no shit." She looked at me with worried eyes. "Sorry, Lena. That just came out. Are you okay?"

No. No, I wasn't. I was currently longing for the orange, Cheeto-dust-filled laughter I'd had about an hour earlier, before I knew for sure my husband was cheating. Only, he wasn't just cheating. No, what he was doing was so much more than cheating. He had a whole other life – a family – an hour outside the city.

Suddenly, I was questioning my own sanity. Questioning whether I had an accurate or firm grip on reality. I had spent the last seven years of my life married to Derrek, hadn't I? We shared a house and a life and a history, right? How, if what I had seen minutes before was true, if he did in fact have a whole other life, hadn't I noticed? How could I have not realized what was going on around me? How did you keep an entire family hidden?

"I'm so confused," I whispered.

"No fucking shit, Lena. What the hell is going on?" Sam sounded frantic, like her grip on reality was also in question.

"Derrek seems to be leading a double life," I said, sounding astonishingly calmer than I was feeling. "Although, truth be told, in order to be leading a double life, both lives have to be *real* lives. Obviously, he's focusing more on his other life than the one he's leading with me."

"Do you think those were his children?" Sam pondered.

"What other conclusion are we to jump to? What other plausible explanation can there be?"

"Does he have a sister? Could those be his nieces or something?"

"I think I'd rather him be leading a double life than think about him kissing his sister like that. Plus, no, he doesn't have any siblings." I took a deep breath in. I knew he was cheating; there was no other explanation. And I knew why the deception was taken to this level. I felt my stomach bottom out and saliva start to pool in my mouth. "Sam, pull over," I cried, my hand coming to cover my mouth. Luckily, we were still in suburbia, so she was able to veer the car to the curb quickly. I opened the door, stumbled out, and I threw up onto the sidewalk. I retched and heaved until there was nothing left in my stomach, and I immediately regretted the neon orange Cheetos.

"Here," Sam said as I climbed back into the car, handing me a bottle of water left over from our snack attack earlier.

"Thanks." I took a sip.

"You all right?" she asked softly.

"Sam, do me a favor and don't ask me dumb questions. I'm not okay. This is not okay."

"Well, what are we going to do now?"

"Can you please just take me home?"

When we finally made it back to my house Sam was reluctant to leave me there alone, but I made her drive away, needing some time to myself.

"If he comes back tonight and you need someone, call me, Lena. Okay?"

"Sure," I said, unconvincingly. Sam reached across the console and wrapped her arms around my shoulders, hugging me close.

"I'm so sorry, Lena. If I thought we were going to see him, see that, I wouldn't have ever pushed you to do this." Her voice was a quiet whisper, and I could hear the remorse and guilt lacing her words.

"It's not your fault, Sam." She didn't respond, just squeezed me a little harder. "I'll call you tomorrow."

When I entered the house, I pushed the door shut behind me and stood in the foyer, listening to the silence. The darkness wrapped around me, the quiet flooding the black space. I'd lived in this house for six years, but never had it felt this huge, empty, or cold.

I took a deep breath and made my way back to my bedroom, walking the entire way in the dark. I didn't need any light. I knew the hallways well enough, and every once in a while I'd pass a room with windows and the moonlight granted me a little visibility. But I didn't want to see the house. I didn't want to see the pictures hanging on the wall. I didn't want to see the couch in the living room Derrek and I made love on multiple times. I didn't want to see his clothes still hanging in the closet.

I walked back to our bedroom and went to my side of the bed, trying to keep my eyes from wandering to his. I slid my shoes off my feet, leaving them to rest on the floor by my bedside table, then peeled off my ridiculous black outfit, and crawled into bed. The cool sheets felt good on my skin, overheated from the events of the evening, my blood running hot from what I'd seen. I rolled toward the window so I wasn't facing Derrek's side of the bed, and I placed my hands underneath my cheek, and gazed out into the darkness.

I spent the entire night awake, resting in that bed, replaying what I'd seen in my head. At one point, I felt a single tear slide down the side of my face and onto my hands, but I hadn't realized I was crying and it didn't last long.

My feelings fluctuated from being angry with Derrek, to being disappointed in myself. One moment I was mad at him for cheating on me, and the next I was angry with him for not just asking for a divorce before he built a whole new family, a whole new life. I was angry with myself, too, perhaps even more than I was with Derrek. I'd done this to myself, set myself up for this, made myself a victim.

When the sunlight started streaking through the window, I decided to get out of bed and start my day. I wasn't surprised Derrek hadn't come home. He'd looked like he was pretty settled where he had been. I listened all night for the sounds of him coming into the house, but everything was silent. Most of me was glad he hadn't come home, for I hadn't quite figured out what my plan of action was.

I went into our large closet that resembled more of a dressing room than a closet. I found my favorite jogging outfit, pulled it on, and sat on the bench to lace up my jogging shoes. Standing in front of the vanity, I swiped raven hair back from my face and affixed it in a tight ponytail at the back of my head.

When I left the house, I put the passcode into the security system and shut the door behind me. I stopped on the driveway to stretch a little before I took off. There was a treadmill in the gym inside the house, but I never ran on it. Derrek bought it a few years ago and I thought it was silly. I would much rather run outside than on an endless loop facing a wall. When I felt sufficiently warmed up, I started with a small jog up the street. I had a particular route I liked to take and if I ran the loop twice, it was equal to about four miles.

About halfway into my run, I started to feel the freedom I was searching for, the endorphin rush that catapulted me into a space in my mind where I could think clearly.

Derrek no longer loved me; that thought made itself abundantly clear. Surprisingly, once I'd thought it, I realized I had known it for a while. He tolerated me, at best. And although I didn't know if I was still in love with him, I knew things were far from where they'd started. But with all the new information, I knew my plan to try and resurrect our relationship was no longer an option. I needed a new plan.

So I kept running. I reached the four-mile mark and just kept going, hoping for more of that clarity I sought on my runs. Around mile six I stopped, breaths ragged and panting in and out at a rapid pace, with sweat dripping down my forehead. I was bent over, hands on my knees, thoughts racing through my brain.

I was exactly where I thought I'd safeguarded myself against being. This was what I had thought I was planning against. And he was pushing me out. Well, fuck that and fuck him. My house was just a few blocks up and I sprinted the entire way there. When I made it to the front door, I entered the passcode on the doorknob and after hearing the beep indicating the alarm system had been deactivated, I opened the door and stormed in.

I went straight for his office, my feet loudly stomping down the hallway. When I reached the office, I flung open the door and wasted no time heading to his desk. Pulling open drawers, I swept everything out, throwing all the contents on the floor. Not looking for anything in particular, just looking to make a mess, needing to take my anger out on *something*.

When all the drawers were empty, I moved on to the filing cabinet, finding that tossing papers over my shoulder and up in the air relieved almost as much tension as running. Taking something of his and destroying it was liberating and admittedly, made me feel better.

When I found myself ankle deep in forms and documents, breath heaving, hands shaking, I decided I'd done enough damage. I had visions of myself throwing his desktop out of the bay window behind me, but truth be told, I wasn't normally a destructive person and knew that would be going a little overboard.

I did, however, pull back his plush desk chair, rolling it over piles of papers, hearing the wheels crackling over my husband's hard work, and sat down. I wiggled the mouse to wake up the computer and then opened up a browser and went straight to Google. I typed in the words 'private investigator'. I was flooded with results and went back to narrow down my search. I clicked in the text box again and added the word 'Portland'. I hit enter and new results popped up. I scrolled down the page, my eyes gliding over all the information, and I realized I had no idea what I was looking for. One private investigator was just the same as the next, right? I found one listing that said 'PDX Investigates'. I clicked on the link and was brought to a professional looking webpage that claimed the company was licensed and bonded. I had no clue what that meant, but it sounded official enough to me.

Standing, I then jogged to my bedroom, grabbed my cell phone, then jogged back to the computer and dialed the number.

"PDX Investigates. This is Todd. How can I help you?"

"Uh, hi, Todd. My name is Lena and I'm looking for some help. I need someone to find out some information for me about my husband."

"What kind of information are we talking about?" Todd asked, sounding busy and a little annoyed.

"Well, I'm pretty sure he's cheating on me and I'd like someone to help me find out for sure. I need irrefutable proof."

"Sure. We offer a free consultation, but if you decide to hire us to help, the rate is two hundred dollars an hour with a two thousand dollar retainer. Depending on how complicated your case is, we would either bill you monthly for the balance should you exceed your retainer, or refund you what's left if we wrap it up easily."

"All right, that sounds fine." I had no idea what sounded fine. I had no idea what private investigators charged, but at that point, I didn't really care, either. I just needed to move in a new direction and this was the one that made the most sense. "When is your earliest availability for the consultation?"

"One of our agents has an opening tomorrow afternoon. Does one o'clock work for you?"

"Sure. That will be fine."

"Great. Do you need the address to our offices?"

"No, I've got them right here on the computer."

"Great, we'll see you then."

The line disconnected and I felt my breath leave me suddenly. What had my life come to? Hiring private investigators to spy on my husband? I never imagined that this was where I'd be seven years ago when I told Derrek,

"I do" through laughter and smiles. I'd been so excited to marry him that I couldn't even contain myself long enough to make it through the vows. I'd smiled and laughed through the entire ceremony, happiness bubbling over. I was nowhere near smiling and laughing now. But I wasn't crying, so I thought that was a step in the right direction.

I took in a deep breath and, even though I didn't think I should have to, I started picking up all the papers I'd strewn across the room. I bagged them all up and put them in the big trash bin in our garage. I couldn't find it in me to care if he needed them or not, more than likely – since he never really spent time here anymore – he wouldn't even notice they were missing.

The next day, I was just about to leave for my appointment at PDX Investigates when my phone rang, showing an unfamiliar number. It wasn't often I received calls from strange numbers, so I answered with a slow and suspicious, "Hello?"

"Is this Lena Bellows?" As soon as I heard the deep and gravelly voice on the other end of the line, I knew I'd never spoken to this man before. I would remember a voice like his, remember the way just him saying my name made shivers run down my spine. I took note of my reaction, but pressed forward with the conversation.

"Yes, this is she. Who am I speaking with?"

"My name is Preston Reid, and we have an appointment. I'm with PDX Investigates."

"Oh, all right. What can I do for you?"

"I am out working on something for a client and won't be able to make it back to the office in time for our meeting. I was hoping you could meet me for a drink so we could discuss your case."

"Oh, um, I suppose. I don't see why not. Where did you have in mind?"

"There's a martini bar on Third, on the East side, called Bartini."

Clever. "But it will only be one in the afternoon. Will they even be open?"

"I know the owners."

"All right. I'll meet you there." The line went dead and I realized the men who worked for PDX Investigates needed to be taught how to end a phone conversation. Twice I'd been hung up on. I grabbed my purse and headed for the door.

When I walked into Bartini, I noticed the elaborate Moroccan theme apparent throughout. There were many round tables with deep red tablecloths draped over them, candles – although unlit at this hour – and gold accents everywhere. There were throw pillows placed on bench seats, golden chandeliers hanging from the ceiling, and beautiful, lush fabrics in all manner of jewel tones draped the walls in lieu of wallpaper or paint. As I was admiring the décor, a man who worked there led me to a table and told me Mr. Reid would be there any minute. He asked me if I would like a drink and, despite the hour, I told him I'd take a vodka martini, wet, and with an olive.

I pulled out my phone to pass the time and noticed a text message from Derrek.

I have to go out of town for a few days on business. Don't expect me home until Sunday evening.

I stared at the message in confusion, as if it were written in braille. Why in the world, after two and half weeks of not seeing each other or even speaking, really, would he send me this message? My blood began to run a little hot at the thought of him shacking up with his other family all weekend, trying to brush me aside with the cover of a business trip. I didn't even bother answering, but placed my phone on the table as my drink was delivered.

I brought the glass to my lips, closing my eyes as the vodka and vermouth slid over my tongue. It had been a while since I'd indulged in a real drink and in this moment, it couldn't have tasted any better. I picked up the skewer that held one green olive and placed it in my mouth, my teeth gliding the olive off and onto my tongue. In that same moment, I saw the door open and I halted, the skewer paused, trapped between my teeth.

A man walked in and part of me hoped and prayed he was there to see me. The other part, the part that wasn't prepared to deal with the type of masculine beauty he possessed, hoped and prayed he would walk right past me. My breath snagged in my lungs as his eyes met mine and he started toward my table.

Dark hair and dark eyes. Eyes so dark, they could have been chocolate. His chestnut hair was shaved short on the sides, but was longer on the top, just long enough to slide through his fingers when his hand ran through it. I watched as his big hand came to his forehead and then moved through locks that looked as though they might feel like silk. He was wearing a black leather jacket that looked soft and worn. Although the jacket fit well enough, it hugged his biceps and the sight of the muscles hidden beneath the supple leather made my stomach flip. He wore a black button-up shirt beneath the amazing jacket, the top two buttons undone, and only part of the hem tucked into his faded blue jeans, ending with black leather shoes to match the jacket.

And he came right for me.

He stalked toward me with his eyes zeroing in on mine. I didn't stand when he stopped next to me, did not move a muscle except the ones in my neck that made it possible for my eyes to remain locked on his. My head tilted up, captivated by him, and I couldn't even find the words to utter a greeting.

"Lena?" he asked, one eyebrow raised. There was that voice again. The voice matched the man: hard, dark, rough. My poor body couldn't handle the combination of all the parts which made up that man, especially when they were coming at me all at once, assaulting me. My stomach flipped – bottomed out. My heart pounded and my mouth went dry.

"Yea…yes…that's me," I muttered, right after I pulled the skewer from my teeth, which I'd managed to leave hanging there like an idiot. Still not standing or reaching out my hand to shake his. Just staring. He was the one who broke our eye contact, looking at the chair opposite me before he placed himself in it.

"I'm Preston. Thanks for rearranging your schedule and meeting me here instead," he said, nodding at the waiter who appeared a moment later to take his order. "Scotch. Neat." The waiter gave a nod and disappeared again.

"It was no problem," I said in response, surprised I was able to put together a complete sentence. I had never been affected by a man this way before – not even Derrek. Instantly, but just for one tiny second, I felt guilty for the primal and guttural reaction I was having to this man – I was a married woman, after all. But just as quickly as the guilt came on, it slinked away and left me feeling slightly smug. I could, and would, admire this man as long as he was in front of me. And I would enjoy it too.

"So, tell me. How can I be of service to you?" He placed his forearms on the table, clasped his hands together, leaned forward, aimed his coffee colored eyes at me and waited for my response.

"Well," my voice shook, "I am hoping you can do a little investigating for me. I need someone to catch my husband with whomever he's cheating on me with." I lowered my voice a little when the waiter dropped off his drink. I watched as Preston brought the glass to his lips, only just then noticing how full and lush they were, fascinated as he let the smallest sip of scotch past them. I saw his eyes narrow slightly, guessing the burn of the scotch was coating his throat, but other than the small reaction, he looked like someone who drank straight scotch regularly.

Preston reached into his jacket and pulled out a small notebook and pen. He started scribbling notes on a clean sheet and looked back to me.

"What's your husband's name?"

"Derrek Bellows."

"What makes you think he's cheating on you?"

"Is that relevant?" I put my guard up. I didn't feel like explaining how my husband found me inadequate to the beautiful man sitting across from me. His hand lifted his glass to his mouth again and he took another sip.

"The way I see it," he stated, not looking me in the eye, but looking at his glass. "You called *me*. You need *my* help. I don't care why your husband is cheating, it makes no difference to me." His eyes moved up slowly and locked with mine. "But if you want my help, you're going to have to trust me and tell me whatever it is I want to know." He paused and for just one brief moment, his eyes glanced at my mouth. Immediately, they were back, focused on my eyes, but it didn't go unnoticed. "I could walk out of here and take any number of cases. I could find any number of people who won't question me or act suspiciously when I ask perfectly reasonable questions. So," he stated finally, "I'll only ask one more time before I get up and leave you to find someone else willing to put up with your doubts. What makes you think he's cheating on you?"

I took in a deep breath, but never moved my eyes from his.

"I'll tell you whatever you want to know, but first, you have to understand that what I'm about to say, I've never told another living soul. It's a secret I thought, without a tiny sliver of doubt, I'd take to my grave. I have to believe this is confidential."

"I'm in the business of secrets, sweetheart."

I tried to ignore the arousal that pooled in my core at him calling me sweetheart, tried not to give any weight to the fact that my heart thundered in my chest, and tried to mumble my next statement with my voice unaffected.

"Marrying Derrek was the worst mistake I ever made. I was young. I was foolish, and I stupidly believed in our 'happily ever after'. I can pinpoint, to the second, when my idiocy imploded, and I will forever feel the ripples and after-effects of that one moment in time."

He lifted his glass again, this time taking a gulp of his scotch, draining it, then nodding to the waiter again, signaling he'd like another.

"Go on, Lena."

Chapter Five

"The night before our wedding, literally minutes before Derrek left our condo to spend the evening with his buddies, Derrek handed me a packet of papers and told me he needed me to sign them. I looked at them, glanced at them really, and saw he'd handed me a prenuptial agreement." I stopped to take a sip of my martini, hoping Preston didn't notice my hand was trembling slightly. I looked back to him and saw he was patiently waiting for me to finish my admission. So I took a deep breath and dove into the story.

"We'd never spoken about having a prenup, not once. So I was obviously caught a little off guard and had a few questions about why and how. Looking back on that evening, I think I acted well within reason – a bride is handed a prenup out of nowhere the night before her wedding, it's her prerogative to flip out a little. Derrek was telling me just to sign it and get it over with, that he had to go, had things to do, but I couldn't just *sign* a prenup. The discussion elevated to a full-on fight, with both of us screaming at each other, both of us using the same piece of logic to argue our very different opinions." I took in another deep breath and then pushed it out, trying not to let the emotions of that one evening so long ago seep into my reality now.

"I kept asking him, 'If you don't ever see us getting divorced, then why should I have to sign this?' And he kept asking me, 'If you don't ever see us getting divorced, then why *don't* you sign it?'" I shook my head at the memory, looking down at my hands resting on the tabletop. "It was a cyclical fight, one that we fought for over an hour, yelling at each other. The fight only ended when I picked up the pen and signed the papers, stupidly, without reading them thoroughly." A small laugh escaped my lips, surprising even me. "Thinking about it now, the fight was probably part of his plan. He needed to distract me somehow, get me riled up about something, push me so far that I'd do something so entirely stupid, and it worked. Here I am. Trying to fight against that stupid piece of paper I signed so long ago – a young bride hoping for a fairytale."

"What did the contract say about cheating?" Preston's voice was soft, which surprised me, causing me to look up into his eyes, and his face matched his voice. Softness.

"The prenup states, which I didn't find out until two years later when I finally grew a brain cell and looked at it, that if I divorced him for any reason, other than adultery, I would leave the marriage with exactly what I came into it with. Which, to be clear, was absolutely nothing."

Preston was quiet for a moment, his thumb running back and forth over the side of his glass. "So you think he's cheating, and you need me to get proof so you don't walk away empty handed?"

"I already have proof," I stated quickly. "What I need you to find is solid proof. Irrefutable proof." I leaned closer to him. "I refuse to walk away with nothing. I've spent the last seven years supporting him, helping him build his business, being the picture-perfect wife, and I'll be damned if he gets to keep everything."

"Careful," he said quietly. "You'll start to sound like the bitter, jilted wife."

"Maybe I am the bitter, jilted wife."

"What does the contract say about you?"

"What do you mean?"

"I mean, what are the stipulations regarding your extramarital affairs?"

"Same. If he walks away for any reason other than adultery, he forfeits everything to me. Except, if I cheat on him, I'm on the line for punitive damages. I'd be left with nothing except a bill for one hundred thousand dollars."

"And what if you can prove he's cheating?"

"Half. Of everything."

"So, he cheats you get half. You cheat you owe one hundred grand."

"That pretty much sums it up."

"So, have you?"

"Have I what?"

"Cheated?"

"That's none of your business, and has no bearing on what I'm hiring you to investigate."

"Yeah, but I'm interested as fuck."

Hearing him say 'fuck' sent shocks of electricity through my veins – another primal reaction to him I desperately wanted to ignore. But I wanted to hear him say that word over and over again, wanted to watch his lips caress that word. I crossed my legs under the table, trying to relieve some of the pressure that was starting to build there. He watched me squirm and I might have seen his eyes shift from curios to aroused.

"Well, you'll have to live in your curiosity, because my sex life is none of your concern."

"Fine, have it your way, sweetheart," he said as he took another sip of his scotch. "You say you've already got proof of his infidelity. So why, exactly, am I here?"

"All I've got is my word, and if I've got nothing and he's got everything, he'll be able to hire lawyers to tear me and my word apart."

"And what's your word?"

"Pardon?"

"You say you've got your word? What does your word say? What's your proof?"

"I saw him."

"Saw him?"

"Yes. Derrek hasn't been coming home lately, been staying out late or not coming back to the house at all. So a few nights ago, my girlfriend and I followed him when he got off work. We tailed him to a house about an hour out of the city where he was met by a woman with two small children. The children looked to be very familiar with him and he looked very familiar with the woman as he kissed her right on her porch."

"You're right," he stated flatly.

"Right about what?"

"That story would never get you anywhere."

"It's not a story, it's the truth, but you're not telling me anything I didn't already know. I need more proof."

"You think the children are his?"

I thought about the little girl running and jumping into his arms and him lifting her over his head, his beautiful smile pulling across his face at her laughter. A lump caught in my throat and I nodded. "Yeah, I think they're his."

"So, he isn't just cheating on you, he's got a whole other fucking life."

My core clenched again at the word 'fucking' passing over his lips. My body's reaction to him was ridiculous, and even though I tried my hardest to fight it, I felt my cheeks flushing, my skin heating. My body should have been reacting to his proclamation, the fact my husband had another life, another woman at his side. Instead, my thighs were clenching together trying to calm the pulsing between them.

"That's what I'm hiring you to find out," I whispered. He was quiet for a moment as he stared at me over the table. His face was unreadable. I had absolutely no idea as to what he was thinking. But his stare was heavy and with every second his eyes burned into me, I felt my pulse race faster.

"The retainer's two thousand," he finally said, coldly. I swallowed then blinked.

"That's fine." I reached into my purse and pulled out my checkbook.

"You can't write a check. Your husband would figure you out in a heartbeat. Can you get a hold of cash?"

I hadn't even thought about that. I racked my brain for ways to come up with two thousand dollars without Derrek getting suspicious. I'd have to ask Samantha.

"I can have cash for you in the next couple of days. Is that all right?"

"That's fine." Suddenly, he picked up my phone and started touching the screen.

"What are you doing?"

"I called you from my work number. Odds are you won't be able to reach me there, so don't even bother. I'll give you my private cell number and you call me when you've got the money. Until then, I'll start working on this." He handed my phone back to me. "But if you find something out, anything you think might be useful, don't hesitate to call me."

"Okay," I said softly. "So, that's it? You just go on your merry way and I sit around while you prove my husband is a cheating bastard?"

"Was there something else you wanted from me?" His face was stoic as he said those words and his eyes bore into me, asking a question heavy with so much meaning. I tried to swallow but found my mouth and throat dry, goose bumps rising on my arms.

"No," I whispered, some part of me knowing I was telling possibly the biggest lie of all. A quiet moment passed where our eyes held each other's. Then, so quickly, it was over. He stood and pulled his wallet out of his back pocket, tossing two twenty dollar bills on the table, then folded his wallet and put it away again.

"I'll be in touch." Those were his last words before he turned and walked right out the door. I let out a loud breath and collapsed against the back of my chair, not realizing I'd been upright and tense. I brought a shaky hand to my forehead and brushed my hair back, smoothing away nothing because I knew my hair was perfect. My hands were just looking for something to do besides the very thing they wanted to do, which was slide down my thighs and give attention to the ache that was still pulsing in my core.

I hoped, if only for my sanity, that Preston Reid was as good at his job as he was good looking. The less time I spent around him, the better. He was bad news, but I was beginning to suspect that my body liked bad.

Chapter Six

The next day, after my body had calmed down, I called Sam and asked her over for lunch. Once she arrived, she wasted no time expressing her anger toward me.

"I told you to call me, Lena."

"And I did. You're here, aren't you?" I didn't bother looking at her as I spoke; I was busy building us sandwiches. I knew she'd be over her tiff in a few minutes anyway. She just needed a few to harp on me and all would be well again.

"Two days later! I texted you a million times. I even came by earlier today but you didn't answer the door."

"I was out."

"Yeah, I figured," she said snidely.

I turned and handed her a plate with a BLT and some macaroni salad. "Let's go sit on the deck." I motioned with my head toward the sliding door that would lead us outside to a wrought iron table and chairs. Once seated, Sam dove right back in.

"So, what's happened since you discovered your husband is the biggest asshole on the planet?" She finished her sentence and took a big bite of her sandwich, her eyes locked on mine.

I laughed because I loved how much she hated Derrek, and because of how ready she was to simply kick his ass.

"I've got a plan in place. Actually, that's one of the things I need to talk to you about." I paused and tried to work up the nerve to ask my best friend for a loan. A loan she would know I didn't need, so it had to come with an explanation.

"Yesterday, I hired a private investigator to look into Derrek and his other life."

"Why do you need a private investigator? We *saw* him, Lena. We already know he's cheating."

"I know, Sam, trust me. I know. But I want more. I need to know how long it's been going on, how deep it goes. I know it might seem masochistic, but I just need to know." I shook my head a little and looked down at my hands in my lap. I couldn't tell her about the prenup. I was so ashamed that it even existed and I didn't need her pity. I looked up at her. She already had a sad look on her face, and I knew it was sadness for me, and that was more than enough pity. "There's one other thing, though." I took in another deep breath. "I went to pay him with a check and he refused, saying that if I used a check, Derrek would catch on. For the same reason, I can't really withdraw the money from our bank account, so I was hoping–"

"How much do you need?"

"Two thousand," I said, as I winced.

"Done. I'll go to the bank today."

I sagged in my chair with relief. "Oh, my gosh, Sam, thank you so much. I promise I will get you the money. It just might take a week or two."

"Don't worry about it. Honestly, I'm glad to help." She paused for a moment, then tilted her head to the side and narrowed her eyes. "I can't believe you hired a private investigator. How did you even find one?"

"Google," I said with a laugh. "It wasn't difficult at all."

"So, you just call them up and tell them what you need?"

"Well, basically, except we met in person to discuss specifics."

"Oh." Then her face scrunched up and she sat back further in her chair. "I can't believe you met a P.I. without me." She frowned and I laughed.

"I didn't think it was a group activity."

"It totally was. It's like something out of an action movie. Your life just got so exciting and I want to be there to watch everything unfold." I raised an eyebrow at her. "You know what I mean! I'm not glad your husband is a cheating bastard, but I am happy to watch him go down in flames."

I could understand her point of view. Even I was looking forward to watching Derrek's other world crumble. "Well, the next time I have reason to call a private investigator, I'll be sure I conference you in."

"So, what's he going to do? How is he going to earn his two grand?"

I bit my bottom lip, then opened my mouth to reply, but promptly shut it again when I realized I didn't have an answer. "You know what? I'm not quite sure. I didn't really ask him what his plans were."

"See, just one of the reasons you should have brought me with you. I would have asked all the pertinent questions."

"Okay," I said with a small laugh. "I'm beginning to see the error of my ways." We continued eating our lunch with our usual light conversation, only sometimes venturing to talk about Derrek and what we'd seen, or Preston and what we thought he might be up to. Our imaginations were more than likely a lot more interesting than the actual happenings. But when Sam focused on something, she really focused. She seemed to be convinced that Preston was more like a James Bond than the image of a normal cop deciding to branch out on his own, which was what I believed to be more likely. Although, Preston was devastatingly handsome, so I gave Sam that tick in the Bond column.

We had just started clearing the table when the doorbell sounded throughout the house. I put down the dishes in my hand and walked toward the front door. When I opened it, I was immediately confused and stammered my greeting.

"Preston…Mr. Reid…What are you…How did you…"

"Good afternoon, Lena." His voice was flat and all business.

"How do you know where I live?"

At that, he smiled. It was a sardonic smile, as if he were laughing at me, but it was still breathtaking. "I'm a private investigator, sweetheart. It's my job to acquire information."

Why in the world did he keep calling me that? It was not only unprofessional, but also flustered me and left me mumbling like an idiot.

"What…why…?"

"I was hoping I could take a peek in your husband's office. See if there's anything in there that might aid my investigation."

"Right. Of course. Come in, please." I stepped back, opening the door to let him in. He walked past me and I tried so very hard not to notice that he smelled divine. Clean, with a hint of spice, from an aftershave perhaps. It wasn't overpowering, but just strong enough to penetrate my thoughts and make me want to smell that scent forever.

He stopped just a few steps in, waiting for me to lead him back to Derrek's office, and just then, Sam walked into the foyer.

"Oh," she said with surprise. Her eyes roamed all over Preston and I watched as she came to the same conclusion any straight woman with a pulse would – he was absolutely beautiful.

He was still sporting his black leather jacket, but he was dressed a little more casually underneath it than he'd been the day before. He wore a dark blue Henley t-shirt, coupled with the same faded jeans, but instead of his leather shoes, he had on black Converse.

"Who are you?" Sam asked, a little breathless, her eyes still taking in all of him.

"Sam, this is Mr. Reid, the private investigator I hired." Her eyes slowly made their way to mine, one eyebrow raised, a conspiratorial smile flashing across her mouth.

"Well, now I see why you didn't want me to come with you."

I glared at her, but tried my best to ignore her comment. "You can follow me, Mr. Re–"

"Preston, please. Call me Preston."

"All right. This way, Preston. Derrek's office is down the hall." I made my way back to the office, trying not to think about the fact that Preston was behind me, in my house, and that we were essentially alone together. And I definitely tried not to think about the way he smelled.

I entered the office and stood in front of the desk as I watched him do his P.I. thing. He looked around the room and I had no idea what it was he thought he'd find, but he was intent. He walked to stand behind Derrek's desk and opened up the first drawer on the right side, then frowned. Next, he bent a little lower, opened the drawer beneath it, and then frowned again.

"The drawers are empty," he said with confusion.

"Oh. Yes. I might have thrown some things away," I said, trying not to sound as embarrassed as I was.

"You *might* have thrown some things away?" His voice had a smile to it, but he was busy opening and closing empty drawers.

"The night we followed Derrek and saw him with his other family, I came home and needed to relieve some stress."

"So you threw away some papers?" His question came with a chuckle.

His words made my spine straighten. He was laughing at me.

"First, I threw them all over the room, *then* I threw them in the garbage."

He was trying to keep the smirk from his face, I could tell. "So you came home, emptied his drawers in a fit of rage, scattering his documents all over the room, and then you cleaned up your mess?"

He was definitely laughing at me.

I narrowed my eyes at him.

"What are you getting at?" I sneered.

He came from behind the desk and walked toward me. For just a moment, his eyes were on mine, but then they moved to the wall behind me where Derrek had his diplomas displayed. He passed me, but left no room between us, his arm brushing my shoulder, but then I felt him turn sharply so he was just behind me, pressed up against me slightly. I stiffened when I felt his front graze my back. I lost the ability to breathe when I felt his breath against my ear as he spoke.

"I'm just saying," he practically growled. "There are better, more gratifying ways to release your aggression." I felt him move away, but the absence of him made no difference to the storm that was now brewing inside my traitorous body. I was stunned silent, my heartbeat pulsing through me, pumping blood to areas suddenly awakened by his breath on my skin. For the second time in just as many days, I found myself pressing my thighs together, trying to stave off the physical reaction I was having to Preston. My breath shuddered out of me, not quietly, and I winced, thinking he had heard and could tell I was affected by him. Although, it wouldn't take a rocket scientist to figure out I was aroused; my entire body seemed to be quivering.

I tried to be angry at him, tried to be appalled that he, the supposed professional in our arrangement, would be hitting on me, a married woman. But even though the notion was there, the intention to find his actions repulsive, I couldn't move past my acute arousal.

"I think," I managed to say, although I sounded completely unsure of my words and not at all as forceful as I imagined I would in my mind, "I think you need to leave."

"Why's that?" His voice was still behind me, but I turned to see him inspecting the certificates on the wall.

"What if Derrek returns? How will I explain a strange man in his office? In his home?"

He turned back around, but didn't look at me. He moved again, heading to the big chair behind the desk and sat down, powering on the computer. "You obviously have no faith in me and my ability to do my job. Why in the world did you even hire me?"

"Your company was just the first one I came to," I answered honestly. He nodded but didn't speak immediately. He pressed some buttons on the computer then spoke again.

"You hired me to investigate your husband and his extracurricular activities. He is currently in Bend. Whether he's there for business or pleasure, I'm not sure."

"Then shouldn't you be there trying to *investigate* that?"

His eyes snapped to me and his voice was smooth but dark. "Would you like to pay me six hundred dollars, each way, to follow your philandering husband on a ski weekend?" He paused and watched me. I tried not to give away that no, I did not want to pay him twelve hundred dollars to drive to Bend, but I wouldn't give him the satisfaction.

Instead, I turned and left the room, throwing over my shoulder, "Let me know if you need anything else." I continued back into the kitchen, where I found Sam leaning her hip against the counter, one hand to her mouth, unconsciously biting her nails.

"Holy shit, Lena," she said loudly when I walked in. "You did not tell me your private investigator is the most attractive man I've ever seen in person."

"Keep your voice down!" I whispered to her. The very last thing I needed was Preston Reid hearing us talk about how attractive he was. "And he is *not* the most attractive person you've ever seen," I countered.

She scoffed at me. "He abso-fucking-lutely is the hottest man I have ever encountered."

"You had your eyes on him for all of ten seconds," I said as I moved past her, trying to busy myself with cleaning the kitchen, needing a distraction.

"I only needed three," she replied. "What are you going to do?"

"What do you mean?"

"What are you going to do about the man in your husband's office who exudes sexual prowess?"

"Sam, you're being ridiculous. I've hired him to investigate my cheating husband, that's all."

"So you're not even going to try to see him naked?"

"What? No! I'm married."

"You're married to a man who has another woman on the side with whom he has two children." This was information I already had, but hearing someone else say the words so callously hurt.

"That doesn't mean I'm going to jump the first attractive man I come across."

"So you think he's attractive?" Sam asked, her voice more amused than it should have been.

"Excuse me, Lena?"

Both Sam and I twisted when we heard Preston's voice shoot through the room, and saw him standing in the entryway, the smirk on his face alluding to the fact he'd heard our conversation.

Shit.

"What can I help you with?" I asked.

"I need to look in your bedroom."

"My bedroom? What for?"

"You really don't understand how this whole investigative thing works, do you? I just need to look around, see if there's anything that piques my interest."

"You think he left clues to his affair in our bedroom?"

He shrugged in response.

I sneered at him again, but then moved to lead him to my bedroom.

"I'm going to head to the bank real quick to get you that money, Lena," I heard Sam call out as I walked down the hall.

"All right," I called back. I turned back to Preston. "She's going to loan me the retainer, so if you're still here when she gets back, you can have your money."

"She seems like a good friend."

"She is," I said, facing forward again.

"Does she know? About the prenup, I mean?" he asked gently.

"Preston, like I said yesterday, you're the only person I've ever told about that." I sighed and stopped outside my bedroom door, motioning with my hand. I didn't want to spend time in my and my husband's bedroom with another man. It didn't seem right – it felt cheap and wrong. But it also felt exciting and, for that, I decided not to go in. "I'll be in the kitchen if you need anything," I said quietly, and then left him to do his private investigating.

In the kitchen, I continued to clean what was left from our lunch and then, for the second day in a row, decided to indulge in a drink. Not feeling like putting in too much effort, I simply grabbed some orange juice from the refrigerator and poured some in a glass, then added a generous portion of vodka. I sat down on one of the barstools that lined the long side of the island and listened for sounds of Preston rummaging through my marriage.

I couldn't imagine what he thought he would find in our bedroom that I might not have seen, might not have caught on to. He wouldn't find any evidence of a loving relationship; that was for sure. There would be no sexy underwear in the hamper, no rumpled sheets on the bed. No, I imagined from his perspective he would see a very sterile room and pity my husband for having such a frigid wife.

I was halfway through my drink when I heard him come back into the kitchen.

"I think I'm about through here. Sorry for the intrusion."

I got the feeling he was referring to more than just interrupting lunch.

"It's no problem. Find what you were looking for?"

"Not sure yet," he said, seriously, his eyes locked on to mine. I simply couldn't handle his eyes on me, not when they were full of words that I felt he wanted to say but held back. No, it was time to say goodbye to Preston Reid.

"Sam isn't back yet, but I'll be sure to get you the money soon. I could drop it by the office later today if that's more convenient for you."

"No, don't take it to the office. I'll be in contact. I'm not worried about the money."

"All right," I said. "Let me walk you to the door." I stood and made my way past him, leading him back into the foyer. I reached for the door handle but stopped when I heard his voice again.

"Was staying with him this long, suffering through what seems like a loveless marriage, really worth the money you're fighting for now?"

I stared at him, trying not to let my face give away the array of emotions his question sent spinning around in my head.

"I didn't realize, until just recently, I was in a loveless marriage." I looked him straight in the eye, my face expressionless, steeled to look void of anything. Without removing my eyes from him, I turned the doorknob and opened the door. He obviously took my silence as the only farewell he would be getting and he walked through.

I tried not to notice that even though he had plenty of room, he passed so close to me that I felt his shoulder brush me again. I also tried to ignore what his scent did to me, as well as the jolt that zipped through me when my body touched his.

Chapter Seven

The next night, I laid in bed and listened for Derrek to return. Preston hadn't said whether Derrek had gone to Bend alone. I wasn't even sure he knew, but I had spent over a day imagining the happy couple enjoying a short weekend getaway. Perhaps he'd taken his youngest to her first skiing lesson, watching her wobble and fall in the soft snow, her nose turning pink from the cold.

I had always told Derrek I wanted children, and he'd always gone to great lengths to convince me that we had time. He wanted to focus on his job and he needed me to help him with that aspect of our life. I wasn't, by any means, past my prime, and still had a few good baby-making years left in me. But knowing he'd started a family with someone else, that he'd taken my ability to start a family hostage, left my heart pumping in an empty chest. I was angry, but more so, I was hurt.

I'd always imagined having a few babies. I'd daydreamed about holding the warm bundles in my arms, snuggling them, kissing them, but now I was left with nothing. Well, nothing besides a cheating husband who planned to keep me around for a reason only God could understand. That wasn't true either – he kept me around so he didn't lose his precious money.

My eyes widened as a new thought occurred to me. Did the other woman know about me? I wanted to believe that she didn't, that she couldn't. I hoped she was just as blind to his transgressions as I had been. I didn't want to think one woman could do that to another. At this point, the sisterhood was the only thing in which I had any faith left.

I heard the door open and I stopped breathing, as the sound of my breaths was interfering with my ability to hear the faint sounds of him entering the house. I listened as he closed the door and then I heard some rustling, which I figured was him setting his things down. When I heard his footsteps head down the hall toward his office, I let out my breath quietly. My lungs were burning and my heart was pounding. I took in a few gulping breaths to try to let my lungs relax, and then, before I knew what I was doing and could stop myself, I pulled the covers back and walked down the stairs toward Derrek.

When I made it to the doorway, I stalled, still unwillingly captivated by how handsome he was. He was standing behind his desk, pulling the tie loose from around his neck. He was wearing gray suit pants with a shiny black belt, a white button up shirt that looked wrinkled, as if he'd been wearing it for a while, and the tie he was pulling from his neck was black as well.

"You're home," I said softly. I hadn't intended to speak to him. Hell, I hadn't intended to walk down here at all. But I was also acutely aware that I wasn't fully in control of my mind, body, or mouth at the moment.

"It would seem so," he said, without meeting my eyes.

"Where did you go?"

"Out of town on business." His words were cold, stale, and stone-like. I tried to read into them, tried to figure out whether he was lying and discern if he'd really been away for pleasure. His eyes still weren't meeting mine as he sat down in his chair and put his thumb and forefinger up to the bridge of his nose, pinching it.

"Did you get a lot done?" My voice was calm and smooth. Part of me was still hoping he'd been away on business.

"Lena…"

He didn't want to talk.

"Will you be coming to bed?" I had no idea why I asked that question. There were two reasons why that question was completely unnecessary. One: I already knew the answer was no. I already knew he wouldn't be coming to our bed. He would probably never be in that bed again, and I knew that. And two: I didn't want him in our bed. I was almost sure I didn't want him in our bed. What I wanted was to go to sleep and wake up, having the last five years of my life be a sick and twisted nightmare. I wanted to wake up to the husband who I loved, the husband who honored our vows, and didn't sneak away for weekend getaways with other women and his love children.

He didn't want to talk. So he didn't. He never answered my question, just clicked his computer on and continued to ignore me, pretending to be interested in whatever had appeared on his screen.

Watching him completely shut me out flipped some sort of switch inside my body. The very last piece of me that was holding out for some sort of understanding, some sort of resolution that included saving my marriage, faded away right into the darkness that filled every room of our house.

I turned and walked back up the stairs and climbed into my cold bed, falling into sleep as I contemplated how I was going to move forward. Unfortunately, all of those thoughts circled around Preston Reid.

The next day, I went to work as if it were any other day of the week. I had a comfortable position at a lucrative and expanding marketing firm in Portland. Derrek would have preferred me to sit on the board of a charity, or spend my time doing more social activities, making connections, networking with wives of powerful men, but I always stood firm on having my own career.

I was halfway through the day, mindlessly tending to all the catch-up from the weekend, when I heard my phone vibrating in the top drawer of my desk. I pulled the phone out and slid my finger across the screen, revealing I had a new text message. It was from Preston.

I need you tonight.

I read the words and tried to keep my pulse under control. Then I admonished myself for allowing my body to react so powerfully to his words. I gaped at my phone and felt my core pulsing with every heartbeat, which was rapid and ferocious. I swallowed, but still didn't move, uncertain of what my next move even was. Before I was forced to make a decision, my phone vibrated again.

I can be at your house to pick you up around five.

What in the world was he talking about? I was still trying to recover from his first text, also trying to keep my mind from running away with those words and turning them into something completely inappropriate.

What, exactly, do you need me for?

I felt my breathing even out as I waited for a response. There was no hope to focus on anything else until he responded. After what seemed like a millennium, his answer came.

Lena, there are many things I need you for. The list is long, involved, and dirty. But tonight, I need you for professional reasons. However, if you wish to rearrange the parameters of our relationship, I am open to that discussion.

Holy shit. He was flirting with me. Well, if one could call that flirting. He was flat out propositioning me. My hand, of its own accord, came to the base of my neck, trailing across my collarbone. I thought about my options for a moment, and even though I tried, desperately, to keep my mind on the task at hand – finding inarguable proof that Derrek was cheating – my mind wandered to Preston's dark eyes and luscious lips. My fingertips trailed down my sternum and then back up my neck, the tickling sensation making goose bumps appear wherever my skin was bare. Then my phone buzzed again and I jerked my eyes to the screen.

Sweetheart, are you with me?

Oh, God.

I'm here.

I replied without meaning to.

Will you be ready at five?

I swallowed hard and my fingers moved over the screen.

I'll be ready.

At five sharp, I watched as a very sleek, very sexy, black Lotus pulled into my driveway. I continued to watch as the driver's door opened and Preston unfolded himself from it. He was still wearing that sexy jacket and I wondered if he ever went anywhere without it, or even took it off. He had a dark blue t-shirt stretched over his chest, just tight enough to hint at what was beneath it, and a pair of black jeans. He walked toward my front door and I forced myself to stop peering at him through the living room blinds.

I stood and brushed my hands down my front, making sure I looked presentable. When I heard the doorbell ring, I continued to the door, opening it right after I took a calming breath. In through the nose, out through the mouth.

When the door was open, we both just stood there, neither one of us able to hide the fact that our eyes roamed the other.

"You're not dressed appropriately." He spoke first, his eyes still running up and down my body.

I looked down at my outfit. "What do you mean?" I was wearing jeans and a soft, white, short-sleeved sweater.

"I mean," he said, stepping into my house, forcing me to step back and allow him entrance, "you can't wear that. Go change into something dark, like black. We can't have you standing out."

"Where are we going?"

"We're going to follow Derrek home from work. I'm hoping he'll head to his *other* home."

Well, that stung.

I nodded out the door to his black car with very dark tinted windows. "I don't think anyone will be able to see me through your windows."

The corners of his mouth turned up slightly, not a full smile, but a hint of one. He turned and walked further into the house, forcing me to follow.

"Who says we'll stay in the car?"

I guess he had me there. "I'll be right back," I mumbled, grudgingly. When I returned, I looked much the same as I did when Sam and I did our stakeout. I was in black jeans, but instead of the turtleneck, I wore a black, V-neck cotton tee. The jersey knit hugged my chest and I purposefully chose it over the frumpy turtleneck. If I had to look at Preston in his leather jacket and blue, clingy shirt, he would have to endure my tee that gave a slight view of my cleavage. He looked at me when I reentered the room, but quickly motioned toward the front door.

"Let's get a move on. We don't have much time."

The ride to Derrek's work was silent, and I was okay with that. I spent my time trying to figure out what all the buttons did inside Preston's Lotus. It looked how I imagined the inside of a space shuttle might: flashing lights, switches, buttons everywhere, and even my ass was warm. He parked across the street from the main door, just like Sam had, and we sat and watched, waiting for him to come out. I was in the middle of wishing we had snacks when Derrek walked out. My breath caught in my throat as we silently watched him walk to his car, and I managed to exhale when he pulled out into traffic. Preston pulled out after him, but we didn't talk as he tailed him.

Preston was noticeably better at following a car than Sam and I had been. He didn't need me to tell him where to go, or which direction Derrek's car was heading, as he seemed to manage both the tailing and driving aspects fairly well on his own. So well, in fact, I began to wonder why he'd even brought me along.

"Why am I here?"

"What do you mean? You want to get your proof, right?"

"Yeah, but I'm obviously not needed. I haven't said one word and you haven't asked me one question. I'm not aiding your investigation one bit. So why did you bring me?"

"Where did you meet him?" he asked, keeping his eyes on the road and presumably Derrek's car.

"What?"

"Your husband. Where did you meet him?"

"How is that going to help your investigation?"

He shrugged. "It won't. You just seem a little uptight so I thought I'd give you what you want – a little interaction."

I eyed him, trying to decide whether I was going to answer his question. I finally rolled my eyes and gave him the answer. "I met him at a frat party my sophomore year of college."

"Hmm," was his response.

"Hmm?"

"I could totally see Derrek as a frat guy, but you, well, you don't strike me as the kind of girl who hangs out with them." As he said this, his head swiveled toward me and his eyes were gleaming, a slight smile pulling up the corners of his mouth.

"I wasn't, really," I said, turning away from him again. "Sam dragged me there and I was holding up a wall, drinking alone, when Derrek approached me."

"And then he swept you off your feet?"

It was my turn to shrug. "I suppose. I mean, it's not like we were engaged the next day or anything, but I never dated anyone else after I met him that night."

"How old were you?"

"Nineteen."

"That's not a lot of time to cram in a lot of dating experience."

"I hadn't had any." The words came tumbling from my mouth and I wanted to reach out and grab each and every one before he'd had a chance to hear them. I cringed inwardly. Preston cleared his throat and shifted in his seat, obviously uncomfortable with my careless and inappropriate confession, and then suddenly, I realized I wasn't familiar with my surroundings any longer. "I don't think he's heading to the same house as he did the other night."

"What makes you say that?" he asked, and I couldn't help but think he was glad for the sudden change in subject.

"This isn't the same route. Last time, we left his building and made our way straight to the freeway. He's definitely heading somewhere different."

"Do you remember which freeway he took?"

"Yes. He took I-84, headed East."

Before I knew what was happening, Preston slid his souped-up Lotus around the next corner, hanging a right so sharp I was forced to lean to my left, and centrifugal force had me leaning right into Preston's shoulder. My hands reached out to the sides, trying to find purchase on any surface that would keep me upright.

"What the hell, Preston?" I shouted as the car straightened out. My heartbeat was thundering and I looked to him, searching for an explanation.

"If I get us to the freeway, can you direct me to the house again?"

"You mean his other house with his other wife and children?" My question was snide. How could I forget the house my husband shared with another woman or the path there? Both were branded into my mind.

"Yeah. Can you get me there?"

I blinked at him, my eyes narrowing, eyebrows scrunching together. Somehow, in the last thirty seconds, he'd gone from somewhat aloof, asking me pointless questions, to this high-strung man making demands and full of tension.

"Yea...yes, I think I can get you there," I stammered.

Again, we were thrust into silence as he navigated his way to the interstate. When we'd been driving for nearly thirty minutes, I recognized our exit and then proceeded to direct him back to the house.

We pulled up and drove by slowly. The house was dark and seemed empty. It was only early evening and it seemed unlikely that someone was inside, considering how dark it was. Preston kept driving, but at the next intersection, he made a U-turn and then pulled over a few houses down the road. We sat in silence and I stole glances at Preston, waiting for his next move.

"What are we doing here?" I whispered. No one could hear me but him, but it felt like a situation that warranted whispering.

"Investigating," he said slowly, his eyes still on the house.

"But no one's here," I whispered in response.

"That's where the private comes into play." This he said with a small smile, and damn it if I couldn't help a smile coming across my face as well. I let the smile settle. It caused a little bit of tension to roll away, and I relaxed into the lush seats of his fancy car. For a few more minutes we sat in the quiet car. Preston's eyes were locked on the house and then finally he reached down an unbuckled his seatbelt.

"What are you doing?"

"*We're* going into the house."

"Oh, no, we're not," I stated loudly, a little surprised he would even consider it.

"The proof you're so desperate for might be inside that house, Lena. Do you think he's just going to hand it to you? You think he's just going to give up and hand you half of a fortune he feels one-hundred-percent entitled to? You hired me to find you proof, and this is how we're going to get it. Now, get out of the car and follow me."

My mouth gaped open for a moment, then I snapped it shut. He was right. We wouldn't get the proof I needed sitting in his car. I unclicked my seatbelt and opened the door, shutting it softly behind me, not wanting to draw attention to us. I met Preston at the front of his car and gasped when his hand folded around mine and laced our fingers together. He tugged gently on my hand, pulling me into his side, and he pushed our clasped hands behind me, pressing them into my lower back.

The front of me was fully pressed against his side and his warm fingers were wrapped around mine. I was sure he could hear my heartbeat pounding through my body, and I instinctively pressed my free hand into his chest, trying and failing to push him away. He was too close. He felt too good. I was tugged a little closer and felt his lips on the shell of my ear.

"Don't pull away, sweetheart." His breath floated over my skin and I bit my lip to hold in a moan, still fighting my body for control, fighting the reaction I was having. "If anyone is watching us, we simply look like a couple taking an evening stroll." His mouth lingered and I relaxed. I told myself I was playing along, not wanting to draw attention. Really, I took the opportunity to feel him. My hand on his chest moved slightly, running along the valley between his pectoral muscles. His body was hard and warm, my fingers grazing along his front. His hand gently squeezed mine behind my back, silently reassuring me. My hand moved up over his shoulder, slowly cresting and ending up behind his neck, my fingers running over the softness of the close-shaved hair at the nape. He exhaled and I felt his forehead press into my temple.

"We're going to go in the house and you're going to keep watch, yeah?"

I nodded, but left my hand on his neck. I felt Preston's head tilt slightly, and then his lips were pressed against the sensitive skin just below my ear. My lungs quit working and all the synapses in my body fired at the same time, and I felt my stomach flip. His mouth was on me and it was glorious.

Then he was gone.

He kept a hold on my hand, pulling me toward the house I'd seen Derrek go into just days before. As we walked up the drive, Preston pulled something from his back pocket and when we reached the front door, he let go of my hand and crouched down. I did my duty and looked around, watching for anyone who might see us, and I heard the sound of the doorknob jiggling and metal scraping against metal. When I heard the door open, I turned and saw Preston slowly making his way inside.

My heart thundered so fiercely in my body, I wasn't sure I was going to survive. Never in my life had I done anything illegal, so breaking into someone's house was not something I was used to. When I stalled on the front porch,

Preston came back for me, wrapping his hand around mine once again, and tugging me into the house, shutting the door behind me.

"Lena, breathe. Everything is going to be fine. No one is here."

I took his advice and dragged in a breath, doing my best not to pass out in the entryway. I nodded at him, but couldn't see his expression in the darkened house. He gave my hand a squeeze, but then let it go and moved away from me.

"Where are you going?" I whispered, this time the whisper totally justified.

"I'm going to investigate." I didn't have to see his face to know he was smiling. "You stay here and keep watch. If you see or hear anything suspicious, let me know."

"Okay."

He disappeared, the darkness swallowing him, but I could still hear him throughout the house. I stood at the door, peering out the windows next to it, watching for anything that might cause alarm. Minutes passed and my heart slowed and my body started to relax. A car came down the road and my breath caught, but when it slowly drove past, I relaxed again.

After a while of nothing exciting, I saw a person walking on the sidewalk across the street. They came from the right and when they were directly across from the house, they stopped and turned toward it and seemed to just stare. They were too far away for me to see clearly, but I knew the person was facing the house and not moving. When they didn't continue on their way, I panicked and went to find Preston.

"Preston," I whisper-shouted into the blackness. Not being familiar with my husband's other home, I was fumbling in the darkness, trying not to run into furniture or walls. "Preston!" I whisper-shouted again. I was walking down a hallway, peering into dim doorways, trying quietly to whisper his name.

I came to another door and noticed a figure moving inside the room.

"Preston?" I whispered.

"Yeah?" he said. I turned into the room and saw a beautiful four-poster king-sized bed. I halted just a few steps in, realizing I was in a bedroom. Most likely, *their* bedroom. A wave of nausea came over me, but was pulled away from it when a warm hand wrapped around my upper arm. "What is it?"

I blinked, trying to acclimate, trying to see him. "There's a person across the street watching the house."

He didn't respond right away, but his hand never left my arm.

"What did they look like?"

"I couldn't see them very well, what with the darkness and all," I said, with more snark than I probably needed. His hand ran down my arm to grasp mine and he led me to the side of the window. He pulled me next to him so our backs were both pressed against the wall and then he leaned over and peeked through the edge of the curtains. After a few seconds, he moved back next to me.

"There's no one out there now."

"Okay," I said, whispering still, suddenly very aware I was in a dark bedroom with Preston Reid. My pulse fluttered and I tried to remind myself I was in the bedroom my husband shared with his mistress. I tugged my hand from his grasp and started walking toward the hallway to resume my post at the front door.

Two things happened in the next few seconds. The first thing was I heard the front door opening down the hall. The unmistakable sound of the key in the deadbolt caused all my blood to freeze in my veins, along with the air in my lungs. The second thing that happened was me being swiftly lifted fully off my feet, with a strong arm wrapped around my waist, and hauled into a walk-in closet. My mouth opened, ready to scream, but then I remembered we were on a stealthy B&E, and clamped my mouth closed before any sound came out.

I was whisked into the closet and taken all the way to the back. Preston pushed aside shirts and sweaters, bringing us both behind the clothes, then fixed the hangers, trying to hide us. I found myself in the corner, my back pressed up against a wall, and Preston pressed up against my front. He was warm and tall, and magnificently hard. I felt all his muscles pressing against every single inch of my body, and my hands came to rest naturally on his chest, my eyes searching for his in the dark.

"Preston—" I started to object to his body pressing so deliciously into mine, but I felt his finger press into my lips, effectively shushing me. Something about his finger on my mouth sent my body into overdrive, and I squirmed against him, my traitorous body searching for more contact.

"No talking, sweetheart," he said, so quietly I wasn't even sure I'd heard it. But I felt his breath and the way his chest moved when he said 'sweetheart.' If I wasn't completely paralyzed already, I then heard Derrek's voice ringing through the house.

"Jessica, it's not a big deal. Just grab your purse and let's go."

Then I heard *her* voice.

"I'm sorry. I thought I had everything, but Elise threw the biggest fit when I was trying to leave the house and I must have just forgotten."

"It's really fine. I'm not mad. But if we don't leave soon, we'll actually be late instead of fashionably late."

Their voices were getting closer and closer until I realized they were in the bedroom and the only thing separating us was a row of neatly hung blouses and a closet door. At the realization of their nearness, Preston pressed into me further and my eyes fluttered closed when I felt his lips just barely touch mine. He didn't kiss me. He wasn't kissing me. Our lips only just barely grazed against one another, allowing our breaths to intermingle. When I realized he wasn't *going* to kiss me, I opened my eyes. His hands were over my head, pressed up against the wall I was leaning into. My hands were still on his chest, and one of his thighs had parted my knees and was pressed against me.

"Here it is, honey," I heard the woman, *Jessica*, say brightly.

"Great," Derrek replied. "I'm just going to change my tie. Sadie had some sort of muck on her hands when she grabbed it earlier."

My eyes grew wide when I realized Derrek was heading into the closet. When the door opened, a dim light spread across the large closet, coming from the bedroom. I gasped silently and then, even though I would have bet it not possible, Preston moved even closer to me. His hands slid further up the wall and he dipped his face down to rest in the crook of my neck, his front pressing against me even harder, and my hands slid around his back and up to grip his shoulders.

The sound of the closet door closing again came very quickly, as if Derrek had grabbed a tie and left almost immediately. Preston made no move to back away as we listened to the voices drift away down the hall and then, finally, we heard the front door open and close again. Only after we heard the deadbolt lock again did Preston move. But he didn't move away fully, just far enough so that we were back to the kissing-but-not-kissing stance.

"Lena," he whispered against my lips. I melted instantly. Simply liquefied. His hands came away from the wall, but only came to cup the sides of my face, but he was still not kissing me. I let him hold me like that for a few moments, let the feeling of his hands on my skin wash over me. I hadn't been touched by a man in months, and being touched by Preston was proving to be the most heavenly experience of my life, even if it was just his hands on my cheeks. I reveled in it, soaked it in.

Then, reluctantly, I let reality back in and pressed my hands against his chest again, urging him away from me.

"Preston, we can't do this," I said, no longer worried about the level of my voice, but still speaking quietly. He made no move to let me go, didn't move back even a centimeter. "Please, let me go," I begged quietly. I heard him inhale deeply, then he stepped away and all of a sudden, I was free of him, and I tried not to notice how cold I instantly was. I didn't say anything, just pressed past him and made my way back to the front door to keep watch. I figured Derrek and Jessica probably wouldn't be returning, but I needed an excuse to get away from him.

A few minutes later, he came out of the darkness and appeared by the door.

"Anyone else come by?" he asked coolly, as if he wasn't just pressed up against me in a dark closet.

"No."

"Let's go, then." He reached out, unlocked the door and walked out into the night.

I followed him out of necessity. "Aren't you going to relock the door?"

"Nope."

"But they'll know someone was here."

He shrugged. "Or they'll just think they forgot to lock it. Either way, I don't care."

"Hey," I nearly shouted. "You might not care what they think, or if they know someone was here, but I do, and last I checked, I wasn't paying you to cause problems."

"Last I checked, you haven't paid me *anything*."

I narrowed my eyes at him. "You know what I mean. If you cause suspicion, Derrek could catch on to everything." Preston, with his hands planted on his hips, looked down at the ground, and even from fifteen feet away, I could tell he was angry. I wasn't the resident lock picker; there was no way I could make it look like no one had been there. I needed him to snap out of it. "Please, Preston. Don't jeopardize me this way."

He sighed but walked toward the door again. I turned, watching him crouch and fiddle with the lock. I heard it click into place and he stood, walking back to his car without a glance at me. When he reached his car, he coldly said as he slid into the driver's seat, "Get in." It wasn't a request; it was a demand.

The part of me that had liquefied before heated again at his words, and I tried to keep my breathing even. He was obviously being a jerk, but again, my body didn't care.

I spent the car ride back to Portland trying to dissect my attraction to him. I wasn't even sure attraction was the right word. I wasn't attracted to him. I was pulled to him. Drawn to him. It didn't make any sense, not to me, anyway. He was almost the exact polar opposite of everything I'd ever told myself I wanted. Well, as far as I knew. I realized I didn't know much about him. All I really knew was he wore that black leather jacket like a second skin, he never looked bad in a pair of jeans, and his brown eyes were mesmerizing. Oh, and my body craved the proximity of his.

We said absolutely no words all the way back into the city, and when he pulled into my driveway, I opened the door and climbed out without breaking the silence. I drew in a sharp breath when I heard his door open and his footsteps coming in my direction. I did not, however, give him the satisfaction of turning around. I continued up the path to the door, only stopping to input the code in the keypad on the door.

"Lena." Just my name falling from his lips turned my stomach inside out. I shook it off, literally shaking my head from side to side, trying to give him a clear indication that I didn't want to hear what he had to say. Not surprisingly, he didn't listen. Instead, his hand wrapped around my elbow and he turned me, and then pulled me into his front, our faces only inches from one another again. One of his hands found its way to my cheek again and I resisted the urge to lean into it, to let myself *feel* something from a man again.

Everything I was trying to accomplish, Preston was single handedly and slowly going to ruin. I had only one goal at that moment and that was to prove my husband was a cheating, lying bastard, get what was owed to me, and move on with my life. Preston Reid was threatening to me in more ways than one.

"We need to talk," he tried again.

"No," I said immediately. "You need to go home and finish this job on your own. Get me my proof and then we can just go our separate ways." I remembered that his money was on my kitchen table. "I'll go inside and get your money. Give me one moment."

"I don't want your money."

I halted at his words and turned to him, trying to be brave and act like I wasn't affected by him.

"I hired you to do a job, so you'll take the money. Unless you think I should hire someone else?" My eyes found his and even in the dim light from the streetlamps, I could still see the dark brown irises looking back at me. I thought, for just an instant, I saw panic flash through them, but just as quickly as the emotion flitted across them, it was gone.

"No. You don't need to hire anyone else. I'll get you your proof."

"Okay," I whispered. I opened the door and walked in, heading into the kitchen to find the envelope Sam had brought me with the two thousand dollars cash inside. I grabbed it from the counter and turned to walk back outside, only to find Preston inside my house, leaning against the doorframe of the kitchen. "Here," I said softly as I held the envelope out toward him.

He took the few steps toward me and when his eyes met mine, I was a little surprised to see sadness there. He took the money and tucked it into his back pocket. His chin tipped up in a nod that said 'Thanks.' I found manners winning out and I couldn't stop myself before I offered, "Would you like something to drink? Scotch, perhaps?"

"Neat," was his short response, and it rolled through me like a wave, his dark voice deep and gravelly.

I nodded and said, "I'll be right back." When I made it to the liquor cabinet in the formal living room, I leaned against the bar, gripping the edge tightly, trying to rein in the heat coursing through my body. This was ridiculous. The very last thing I needed right then was some wild, gravitational pull to a man who wasn't my husband. I didn't even want my husband. But what I really didn't need was some seriously sexy man tempting me into wagering my future life away. But I'd offered him scotch, so I'd get him scotch. Then I'd make him leave.

I set the tumbler down in front of him, noticing he'd made himself comfortable at the head of my dining room table. I sat in the chair to his right and sipped from my tumbler.

"You spend a lot of time in this big house all by yourself?" His question caught me off guard, but also offended me a little. I didn't like him insinuating that I was often alone. I could have many friends I spent time with, or a ton of hobbies that kept me out. Zumba. Pottery. Cooking class. Then I remembered I was the jilted wife who hired him to tail her husband and his mistress. I wasn't the poster child for happy, satisfied women.

"I have things I do. I jog sometimes. I see Sam often. I'm not a shut-in."

He looked at me over the rim of his glass as he sipped his scotch. After a beat, he pulled the glass from his mouth and placed it slowly on the tabletop. "That's not what I meant," he said, his voice low again.

"Well, then please, elaborate."

"I meant does your husband leave you here alone often?"

His question threw me again, and I didn't know how to answer it. I suspected if I told him the truth, it might elicit a reaction from him I didn't want to deal with. Then again, I suspected if I lied to him, he'd know. In fact, the more I thought about it, the more I thought he already knew the answer to his question.

"Sometimes," was the answer I settled on.

"Sometimes?"

I shrugged, offering him nothing else.

"I don't like the idea of you being here alone."

His words cut right through the pretense I had been trying to build for the last hour and a half. Sliced right through the wall I'd put up. It had been years since a man had shown any kind of concern for me. I'd been on my own for so long, I couldn't have anticipated what it would feel like when a man, whom I apparently desired, showed concern for me. For whatever reason, Preston cared.

Before, in the closet, I could have written the whole ordeal off as physical – no, sexual – chemistry, but when he said things like that, basically telling me he cared about my well-being, there was no going back.

"I have an alarm," was my brilliant response.

"A man shouldn't leave his wife in a bed, alone, by herself, for any reason." He paused, perhaps waiting for me to interject, but I had no argument. I agreed with him. "Why do you put up with it?"

"I don't anymore."

"Hmm." His voice rumbled, even though he didn't really speak any words. "If you were mine, you'd never get a chance to even feel the sheets getting cold."

As if he'd reached inside, grabbed my breath, and dragged it from my body, I gasped.

"There wouldn't be a thing in this world that could keep me from my bed, were you in it."

He'd slayed me twice. A combo hit. TKO.

"Preston," I whispered, simply unable to piece any more words together than that. He didn't say another word, just slammed the rest of his scotch, got up, and walked out my door. I gaped after him, not sure what I was supposed to do. How does one recover from words like that?

Eventually I stood up, bringing both our empty glasses to the kitchen, placing the tumblers in the dishwasher. I walked to the foyer and punched in the passcode on the security panel, activating the alarm. I went upstairs and decided to take a long and very hot shower.

I spent most of my time in the shower replaying the entire evening, wondering how I'd gotten myself into such a strange situation. It might have been the longest shower I'd ever taken, and it took all the self-control I had not to slide my hand between my legs and replay the words he'd said to me over and over in my mind. I wasn't stupid enough to deny the fact my body wanted him – badly. But when everything else was said and done, I was still a married woman, and I wasn't sure I was ready to be a married woman who crossed those lines. And touching myself while thinking about another man wasn't something I thought was right to do, even if I desperately wanted to.

When I finally made it to bed, I pulled the covers back, bracing myself for cold sheets, then went to the window to close the curtains. Right before they closed all the way, I noticed the black Lotus sitting on the street just a few houses down.

Chapter Eight

When I woke up the next morning, Preston's car was gone. I tried not to think about him sitting in the Lotus all night keeping watch over my house because he cared about me. Nothing good could come from the warmth I felt in my chest when I thought about it, so I tried not to. It wasn't easy, especially because he came back every night for the rest of the week and kept watch over me.

Derrek hardly came home at all, and when he did, it was only for a few moments. He'd grab something and leave again, or pick up some mail he'd been expecting. Once or twice, he said something to me, but mostly, he wasn't even looking for me, only speaking to me if he happened to encounter me.

It took everything in me to not question him about Jessica, or let him know I knew what a scumbag he was, but I knew I had to bide my time. Eventually, I hoped I'd be able to tell him everything I wanted to. Right before I walked out the door forever.

On Thursday, after Derrek had come home and so brazenly packed an overnight bag, not even trying to convince me he was going away for business, I lost a little of my self-control and decided to call Preston for an update on the investigation. Surely, he'd have found something by then. I dialed his number and after a few rings, he answered with his deep voice, sending involuntary shivers up my spine.

"Reid," he said in greeting, his voice clipped but still sexy.

"It's me, Lena."

There was a pause, but then he spoke. "Is everything all right?"

"Yes, of course. I was just wondering if you've made any progress on the case." I heard a faint clicking in the background. "Are you in your car? Should I call you back?"

"No, it's fine. Bluetooth."

"Oh. Well? Any news?"

"Listen, Lena, I've been working on it, but another case has been taking up a lot of my time. It'll be a few more days before I can really get anything to you."

"Oh," I said, with more disappointment than I intended. Surely, I couldn't expect to be Preston's main focus. Of course he had other jobs he was seeing to. Then I heard my phone beep and when I pulled it away, I saw a text message from Derrek. "Can you hold on one second, Preston? I just got a text."

"Sure."

I pulled the phone away from my ear again and activated the screen.

We're going to a Gala tomorrow night. One of the charities the company supports is throwing a fundraiser. Formal. I'll be there at seven to pick you up.

"Shit," I said as I finished reading it. I put the phone back up to my ear just as Preston started speaking.

"Lena? Is everything all right?"

I sighed. "No, not really. Derrek says we have to go to a fundraiser tomorrow night. I hate those enough to begin with, but having to pretend to be his happy wife for an evening really doesn't sound like my idea of a fun time." I rubbed the little bundle of wrinkles between my eyebrows, the skin bunching there from the tension rolling through my body.

Preston was silent at the other end of the line, but the silence also allowed me to hear his car turning off, signaling he'd arrived wherever he was headed.

"Anyway, sorry to bother you. Take your time with the case. I'm just anxious to get out of here."

"Lena," he whispered my name like it hurt him to do so. His voice was pained and thick, soft but strained. "Don't go."

"What?" My reply was whispered, just like his voice.

"Don't go. Don't. Make up some excuse, but don't go with him."

My mouth opened to say something, but then closed again, my mind not coming up with a reply.

"Preston, I have to go. I'm his wife," I finally uttered. I heard him inhale and I winced, feeling like I'd hurt him somehow with my words.

"You're only his wife on paper," he said, sounding angrier, harsher.

"That's the only part that matters right now."

"His money can't be so important to you that you'd basically sell yourself. That's what you're doing, Lena. You're selling yourself if you go with him. You're pretending to be his wife for money. What does that make you?"

Now it was my turn to be angry. "What, exactly, are you trying to say?" I turned out of the living room, headed to my bedroom and walked to my window, pulling the curtains back just slightly. Just enough to see his black Lotus in its usual spot a few houses down.

"I don't want you with him." This statement was spoken in a voice still firm and a little angry, but also pleading.

His words evoked so many emotions from me it was hard to nail one down. The overwhelming feelings were happiness and warmth. Preston cared enough about me to want to keep me from Derrek. Whether this was out of just macho dominance or genuine concern, it didn't matter. It'd been years since someone cared about me and I wanted to wrap myself up in it. But all of that happiness was tamped down by my need to get out of my marriage intact. I couldn't let my emotions ruin my plans.

"Preston, I don't want to be with him, either," I said as I looked at his car. I strained to see his form through the windows, but he was too far. The urge to lay my eyes on him was overwhelming. Just to see him. That was all I needed. "Will you do me a favor?" I whispered.

"Anything," he replied, making my eyes close and the breath steal away from me.

"Can you get out of your car for just a moment?"

He didn't answer, just opened his car door and got out, walking to the front of it, staring right at me in my bedroom window. I bit down on my lips to keep myself from asking him to come in, because I knew, without a doubt, if I invited him in the game would be over.

"You're always gone when I wake up. How long do you stay out there?"

"Until I know for sure you're safe." His answer was both infuriating and beautiful.

"Goodnight, Preston."

"Sleep tight, sweetheart."

The next night, I found myself wasting a fantastic dress on Derrek. I turned in the mirror to check the back of the dress. Yup. What a waste.

From the waist up, the dress was all black lace. It had a tight collar neck with capped sleeves. The lace came down the back, but in the front there was a rather large keyhole. It was big enough to show decent cleavage, but not distastefully. The lace went down to my hips where it met a soft, pink flowing material that floated out around me whenever I moved, swishing in a way that made most girls smile. It was the kind of material that made you want to move to see and feel the fabric swirl around you. It had a high-low hem, so the front came to just above my knees, but the back floated all the way to the ground. The lace was used in the bottom half of the dress as detail, and swirled daintily around my hips and curves.

My dark hair was up in a sophisticated twist with a few tendrils left down to curl around my face. My makeup was soft and natural. The only jewelry I wore were the diamond solitaire earrings my father gave me for college graduation and my wedding ring.

I heard the front door open and took a deep breath in, trying to ready myself to spend an evening pretending to be happy with my husband. I heard him walking toward the bedroom and my eyes moved to the door. He walked briskly through the door, glancing at me, then moving back toward the dresser, where he stopped and opened the top drawer. I noticed he was in a tuxedo and I wondered, briefly, where he'd gotten ready. Then I laughed softly because I realized exactly where he'd dressed. I also noticed he spared not even three seconds to admire me in this dress, in which I looked fantastic. But just as quickly as his eyes passed over me, the thought flitted from my mind. I didn't need or want him to desire me. I wanted out. Unfortunately, I was forced to spend the next few hours with him.

"Are you ready to go?" he asked as he put new cufflinks in.

"Yup," I said, popping the P at the end of the word.

"Great, the town car is outside waiting for you."

I wasted no time walking outside, only stopping to grab my coat. As I walked down the path to the waiting car, I saw the black Lotus drive slowly past my house and my heart rate spiked, knowing Preston was inside the car. The car continued down the road, turning at the corner, and then disappearing. I took in a sharp breath when I heard the front door close behind me and heard Derrek's voice.

"Lena, we don't have all night. Let's go." He was being impatient. Fantastic. I climbed in the car, hoping Preston didn't follow us. I didn't need this kind of drama tonight. I just wanted to get the event over with and go home, hopefully without Derrek, and hopefully with Preston in his car down the road. It was selfish of me, I realized, but I also didn't care. What I didn't need was Preston making a scene. I hoped he was smart enough to realize that and keep his distance.

An hour later, we were fully surrounded by Derrek's co-workers and employees. There were many other people in attendance and occasionally Derrek would pull me away to meet people he was trying to network with. I played my part: smiled, nodded, and pretended to be interested in their conversation. I also withheld from shooting glares at Derrek when his hand rested on the small of my back, or he leaned over and placed soft kisses on my neck behind my ear. In the past, these gestures would have left me swooning, my heartbeat pulsing through my veins, my need for him building, the anticipation of our night in bed filling my mind. Instead, I tried not to roll my eyes when he touched me. At one point, I found myself fantasizing about Preston kicking my door down and rushing to find me in bed, waiting for him, naked.

I was pulled from my daydream, and caught completely off guard, when Derrek interrupted me with an introduction that sounded forced and uncomfortable.

"Ms. Fahey, this is my wife, Lena."

I turned to see the woman I was being introduced to was, in fact, my husband's mistress. I deserved an academy award for my performance over the next few minutes. Not only was I able to keep my face from showing any of the discomfort I was feeling as I eyed the woman sleeping with my husband, but I managed to ignore the glare she was not as good at hiding from me. She looked me up and down, obviously sizing up the competition.

"Lena, this is Jessica Fahey. She's the assistant to the CEO." I smiled sweetly at her, secretly pleased that I was already winning the 'Who Can Keep Their Cool' competition. She was losing, miserably.

"It's so nice to meet you," I said, with a smile. "I love your dress." Her dress was hideous.

She tilted her head to the side and tried to smile, but it came off sort of like a grimace. "Thanks. Your wedding ring is lovely," she said, gesturing to my hand.

No way that bitch was gutsy enough to gawk at my wedding ring. She obviously had no idea I knew who she was, or that she was fucking my husband. I played right along, though.

"Oh, thanks," I cried, holding my hand out for her to examine the ring. "It's three carats," I said, sighing, playing up the smitten wife role. I leaned into her and whispered, "Do you want to try it on? I don't mind." She pulled back from me like she'd been bitten. *Oh, I think I touched a nerve.* She looked as if she tasted something sour and then she took a stance as if to lunge at me, but Derrek grabbed her elbow and strode her away from me, saying something about having to discuss a certain account with her.

As he ushered her away from me, I felt a strange sensation, as if I were being watched. The hairs on the back of my neck stood up and my heart pounded in my chest. My head swiveled to the left, then to the right, but I saw nothing out of the ordinary. My eyes found Derrek again and I watched as he tried to calm Jessica down, tried to keep her from causing a scene. She looked near tears and it was obvious my being there was distressing to her. *Join the club, lady.* I couldn't watch my husband comfort his mistress any longer, so I turned to find the restroom.

I walked down the hallway along the far end of the ballroom, guessing I would find the restrooms somewhere close by. My heels were clacking on the hard floors, a sound I had always enjoyed hearing, and I focused on the echo it made. Then, the echo of my shoes was joined by the sound of another set of shoes walking behind me. Before I could process the extra footfalls, I felt a hand on my elbow and I was being pulled through a door to my right.

I was tugged into the room and I stumbled a few steps, trying to regain my balance. The room was lit, but dimly, and all I could focus on was Preston and his face, which looked like a cross between pained and furious.

"What are you doing here?" I asked, my voice urgent but quiet. I did not need to be discovered in a utility closet with a man who wasn't my husband. "And what is your problem? You can't just yank me around!"

"I didn't *yank* you." He was pacing around the room like a caged tiger. As he walked back and forth, he ran his hand through his hair, and I couldn't help but notice he was wearing a tuxedo. This was not a tuxedo he'd rented for an evening. This was *his* tuxedo, and it was tailored specifically for him. Even though most of his body was covered, I'd never been so enraptured by it before. The man wore that tuxedo in a way that made my entire body want to crawl inside of it with him.

"Preston, why are you here?"

"He had his hands on you." He stopped pacing when he spoke, looking directly at me. I swallowed hard, taking in the sharp features of his face, made even more striking by his anger. He took a step toward me and I instinctively took a step backward. He continued in my direction and I retreated until I was pressed against a wall, and he was just feet away. I had nowhere to go so I just tipped my chin up and looked him in the eye, not backing down. "I would have stayed out of sight," he said, stopping inches from me. "I planned to stay out of sight, but then he had to put his hands on you."

I took a deep breath in, but he was so close my breasts pushed against him. I exhaled quickly, enjoying the contact too much, and then tried to respond to him.

"He's my husband," I managed, if only a strangled whisper, his face now just a breath away from mine.

"But you belong to me." I didn't have time to respond to his words before his mouth crashed down onto mine. I fought his mouth, my hands coming to his chest to push him away at first, but then his tongue slid along the seam of my lips, and when I moaned involuntarily, he snuck in. My body couldn't fight him anymore, didn't want to fight him. My mind was quickly ticking through all the reasons kissing Preston was the worst mistake I could make in that moment, but rather quickly, as his hands began to slide up my sides, barely brushing the edge of my breasts, the reasons I shouldn't kiss him morphed into the reasons I never wanted to stop.

When he felt me give in to him, something else inside him snapped, and the kiss went even deeper. His tongue swiped through my mouth and my tongue was desperate to find his. His hands found the sides of my face, angling me perfectly to take even more from me.

Good God.

The man could kiss.

My hands slid up the front of him, running into the buttons of his tux jacket. I undid the buttons and pushed his coat aside, only to encounter the vest, which I hastily unbuttoned as well. Finally, only the thin layer of his dress shirt was between my hands and his chest and I could feel every ripple of muscle the man was hiding. Muscles I'd been imagining every day since I first met him in that bar. I clutched his shirt, my back arching, trying to get as close to him as possible.

As he kissed me, he unleashed a growl and my reaction was instinct. I moaned as wetness pooled between my legs and my hands shook with anticipation. His left hand moved to the back of my neck, keeping my mouth pressed firmly against his, while his right hand slid down my front, over my breast. His hand cupped my lace-covered breast, his thumb pressing gently over my nipple, so hard he could no doubt feel it through my dress.

I moaned again, louder this time, causing our mouths to break apart. My eyes closed and my head rolled back, unable to focus on anything besides sensation. His thumb and forefinger tugged on my nipple through my dress and I mewled again, my clit pulsing, begging for contact. I felt his mouth between my breasts, licking the valley there, as his hand moved lower.

"Preston," I moaned. I knew we shouldn't continue, knew I should push him away, but the rational part of my brain was being held hostage by the part that wanted to fuck him in this room. Wanted to feel him inside of me, wanted all of him, and there was no reasoning with this part. I didn't even try.

"Be quiet, sweetheart," he whispered, the anger gone from his voice. He sounded softer but still gruff. He sounded like he was aroused, and hearing his voice like that, calling me sweetheart, catapulted me into another stratosphere. His mouth left my cleavage and I felt him move lower, my eyes moving to watch him crouch to the ground. As he slid down, his hands grazed down the sides of me, leaving trails of electricity and sparks behind. Everywhere he touched me turned to fire.

When his face aligned with the part of me pulsing and throbbing, I silently begged him to put his mouth on me. I wanted nothing more in that moment than to feel his tongue slide through me. Instead, his eyes moved back to mine and he spoke.

"In another place, in another time, I'd bury my face in you so fast, my only goal to make you scream my name. But not tonight, Lena." With those breathtaking words, his hands softly started at my knees and then moved to the back of my thighs, sliding up and over my ass, then stopped at the top of my panties. I gasped when he pulled them gently down my legs, stopping at my ankles. "Lift."

Without giving it much thought, I raised one foot, watching him carefully maneuver the lacy, beige thong around the high heels, then he gently tapped my other ankle and we repeated the process. He stood slowly, my panties in his hand, and gave me a sexy, sultry smile. I was still lightly panting, my body not used to being this revved up. Then my breath stopped completely when he placed my panties in the front breast pocket of his tuxedo jacket.

"Now these belong to me, too."

"Preston," I started, only to be stopped again by his mouth. With his lips pressed firmly against mine, his hands brushed up the outside of my thighs, bringing my dress up with them until I was bare from the waist down. His left arm wrapped around my waist, holding up my dress and his other hand found its way to my ass, palming it, pulling me closer to him.

I was bare, being pushed against his front, and all I could feel was his erection pressing into me. Without much thought to anything else besides the heat between my legs, I wrapped one leg around his hip, allowing the very center of me to press up against him.

His fingers moved softly over the swell of my ass, over the crease between my hip and thigh, and continued down the front of me until his fingers were teasing the very spot that ached for him. He continued to kiss me as his fingers gently parted me and slowly dipped in, seeming to test me. I reached down between us, my hand covering his wrist, urging him on, hoping he'd give me what I needed.

"Please," I breathed against his kiss, and I cried out as his fingers pushed farther into me. Our foreheads pressed together as we both looked down to see his hand working in and out of me.

"Christ, you're wet," he growled.

With each swipe of his fingers, I felt him graze that spot buried deep inside me that triggered me to gasp and shake all over. He felt it, too, fed off my reaction to his touch, and every time his fingers delved into me, he was searching for that perfect spot.

His forehead pulled away from mine and his lips wandered to my neck, just adding to the pile of sensations I would have to walk away from when it was all over. His tongue on my skin, his breath on my ear, his fingers gently, but firmly, fucking me into bliss – all of it, I would have to leave behind. Any depressing thoughts of Preston's hands never being on me again were promptly shoved to the side when his fingers landed directly on the perfect spot, a place deep inside that, truly, I'd been the only one to find in the past. His teeth nipping at my neck, his arm around my waist, and his fore and middle fingers working me over; all those caused my head to tip back and a stifled cry to leave me. As if that weren't enough, his thumb then found my clit, a power-move I was sure he was saving until that very moment to send me over the edge. His thumb circled it feverishly and I simply crackled. Sizzled. I was aflame. I thrust my pelvis into his hand, wanting everything he could give me, taking everything he was offering, and I might have climbed up him as I came.

The orgasm he gave me went on and on, and perhaps was more than one, but I couldn't tell. I was floating on a cloud, having the best out-of-body experience I could imagine. When I felt myself finally flutter back to the ground, with Preston's fingers still gingerly stroking me, my eyes came back into focus and I looked at him. Before I could get a word out, his lips came to mine again, but this time, the kiss was sweet and slow.

His left hand found its way back to my face, cupping my cheek, and his other hand wrapped around my waist, simply holding me to him. I tightened my leg around him, still needing to be as close to him as possible, knowing he was going to pull away eventually and I'd have to give him up forever.

When he did tear his lips from mine, it was only far enough away to say my name against them.

"Lena," he whispered. "I'm sorry." His words we pained but his touch was still soft. "I didn't want this to happen here."

"It's a little late for regrets," I said, letting my leg drop back to the ground.

"No," he said, gripping me behind my knee and pulling my leg back to his hip. "I could never regret touching you. I just regret doing it here. I wanted you in my bed, Lena. I want you naked, lying down, completely bare and spread for me. Open for me to see and feel. I want every piece of you, and I want to be able to make you scream my name without worry of who might hear. I didn't want to fuck you with my hand in a broom closet."

"Then why did you?"

"He had his hands on you," he repeated his words from earlier.

"He's my husband." I repeated mine.

"I don't care what some stupid piece of paper says, Lena. You've been mine since the very first time I saw you walk into that bar."

My eyebrows scrunched at his words. "You couldn't have watched me walk into the bar. I beat you there. I watched *you* come in."

His thumb came up and traced over my bottom lip. "Will you always underestimate me?" He said the words with a smile, but I felt the word 'always' like it hit me in the gut. We wouldn't have an always. We had a 'right this instant,' and it was closely followed with a 'this is so terribly wrong.' I couldn't help but feel like it was the best wrong I'd ever had.

"I beat you there by about twenty minutes, but I was waiting outside. As I watched you walk in to that bar, I knew everything in my world was about to be flipped upside down, and I followed you in anticipation of that."

"Preston," I said softly. "This," I said, using my hand to motion between us, "It doesn't change anything." I took in a breath, hoping the words didn't hurt as much coming out as it did holding them in. "When I walk out of here, we can't be together again. It's too dangerous. I can't even believe I let this happen, here, with Derrek just in the other room." I put my hands back on his chest, trying to push him away again, but his hands were firmly planted on my thigh and waist, and he wasn't letting go. "I need to deal with my marriage. I need to put that behind me before I can even start to think about being with someone else."

My leg fell back down as his hand moved from my thigh to cup the side of my face, then moved just slightly into the hair pinned back, pulling me closer to him.

"You need to let me worry about Derrek. I'll get what you need. But you can't push me away, sweetheart. You've already let me partway in, and I plan on getting all the way in soon. In every sense of the word."

"What if I don't want you in at all?" I tried to use a voice more forceful and strong, but I was sure I sounded shaky and unsure.

He pressed me up against the wall again and I could feel his cock, rock hard still, between us. I whimpered involuntarily, unprepared to feel him hard and huge against me, and as he leaned down and nipped my bottom lip between his teeth, he ground his hips into me, my traitorous eyes fluttering closed.

"You're a shit liar, Lena. You're dripping for me right now." Even as he said the words, his hand ran over my opening, making me cry out, a sound of pleasure mixed with surprise. He pushed his fingers into me again, slowly, and I couldn't hold back my moan as I exhaled. "Here's what you're going to do." His fingers slid out of me and my eyes snapped open, looking to him for explanation. "You're going to walk out of here," his fingers pushed back in, making my mouth gape open. Then he pulled out and made a slow circle around my clit, eliciting more cries from me. "You're going to walk right out of this gala." He lazily slipped his fingers back in and then out again. "You're going to get a cab home and then wait for me." The warmth of his hand was then absent altogether, and I hated that I missed it.

"You're going to fuck everything up," I said, accepting the fact I wasn't in control anymore, and that even though Preston was, the odds were against me.

"Hardly, sweetheart. I'm going to fuck *you*. But it's not going to be in a closet, and it's not going to be fast or quick. I'm going to fuck you in my bed, slow and hard, and then I'm going to do it again and again until we're both exhausted and sore in all the good places."

I swallowed hard, both completely aroused by his promises, and scared about the reality that waited for me outside this utility closet.

"I can't just leave. Derrek will wonder where I've gone. We're supposed to be putting on a show for everyone, parading our happy marriage for all to see."

"I'll take care of Derrek." My eyebrows rose in doubt. "Trust me," he said, reading me.

"Okay," I whispered.

"Good girl," he said against my lips, before he took them again in a scorching kiss. It was wet and hot and long. It was also full of promises – vows made directly to my body, which I instantly and stupidly believed.

He pulled away from the kiss, his hands trailing down my neck, and he said, "Go now, sweetheart. I'll meet you at your house."

For reasons I couldn't quite understand, I did exactly as he asked. I left the utility closet and walked straight out of the gala, not speaking to anyone except the clerk working the coat check when I retrieved my coat and purse. I walked out of the building, hailed a cab, and rode home. All the while, I was painfully aware I had no panties on.

For most of the ride, my mind flipped and flopped from thinking about how stupid I was being for even entertaining the idea of getting involved with Preston, to then picturing his hand as it thrust inside me, making me come inside a closet. By the time the cab pulled up in front of my house, I had really only come to one conclusion.

I wanted Preston inside me. Desperately. All of him.

So I walked inside to prepare to give myself to someone other than my husband. I had everything to lose and practically nothing to gain, but I couldn't bring myself to care.

END OF PART ONE

Part Two

PRIVATE
Encounters

Chapter One

I watched the city streetlights blaze past the windows of the cab, my mind reeling just as quickly as the buildings flew by. I closed my eyes and all I could see was Preston tucking my panties into his breast pocket, his gaze searing my body. My clit pulsed as I remembered what it felt like when his thumb stroked it. My eyes opened quickly and fluttered to the cab driver, making sure he wasn't watching me. His focus was on the road, which was good, because one look at me and he definitely would have been able to tell my thoughts were dark and dirty.

With just a few more blocks to travel to my house, my phone pinged in my purse.

Pack an overnight bag. I'm coming to get you.

The text from Preston made my insides liquefy, but I wasn't sure if going with him was the smartest decision. My body wanted to leave with him, of that there was no question, but the cab ride had given my brain room to breathe and it was leading me in the direction of not doing more harm to my already crumbling marriage. Not that I was concerned with saving it, but I *was* concerned with getting out unscathed and with the money I was entitled to.

I paid the cab driver, walked up the driveway, and then heard the unmistakable sound of Preston's Lotus coming around the corner. I watched as he passed his normal spot down the street and instead pulled right into the driveway as if he belonged there. That was a problem. He opened the door and got out, walking toward me as he pressed a button on his key fob, making the car's lights flash and its horn beep two short, quick blasts.

He stalked toward me in that ridiculously attractive tuxedo, his eyes locked on mine and giving no indication he planned to move them. In fact, his eyes stayed on mine until he was right in front of me, only breaking the contact when he gently placed his hand around my elbow, turning me, and leading me toward the house. He came to the electronic keypad and with precision, keyed in the passcode.

My mouth gaped open as he hauled me into the foyer.

"How do you know the passcode to my house?" Without stopping, he pulled me up the stairs toward my bedroom, but spoke to me as we walked.

"Again, Lena, knowing things, especially secrets, is my job."

We entered the bedroom and his hand released from my elbow, but he continued to the closet, flipping on the light from the inside.

"Have you been in my house without me here?"

"Pack your bag," was his only response as a duffle bag came flying out of the semi-open door, landing in the middle of the bed.

"Preston," I said firmly, "have you been in my house while I wasn't here?" I watched as he came into view, stepping out from the closet and walked to me. He stopped when there were just inches between us, but made no move to touch me. He looked me right in the eyes.

"A few days ago, I was tailing Derrek and he came here. He went in the house with a briefcase, but came back to his car without it. I thought, perhaps, there was something of importance in there, something I could use against him. So, yes, I came in the house. But I didn't look at anything or anywhere besides his office."

For a reason I hadn't yet fully formed in my mind, it bothered me that there was a level of distrust between Preston and me. I'd, for all intents and purposes, hired him to be sneaky and shifty, but I didn't like feeling as if he was hiding something from me. Admitting this, though, would also be like accepting things were changing between us. It would be like admitting he was no longer just someone I'd hired to end my marriage; he had become someone involved in the actual demise of it.

"Lena," he whispered, stepping closer to me, his hands wrapping gently around my neck, urging me to look up at him. "Don't let your mind run away with you." His thumbs moved over my cheekbones, the soft friction nearly soothing me. "Don't get caught up in the whys and the hows." He bent down and pressed his lips to mine in, easily, the most sensuous kiss I'd ever experienced. I felt that kiss everywhere: my chest, my mind, my heart, and most definitely my core. It wasn't an exceptionally sexual kiss; his tongue just barely grazed the seam of my lips, not wanting in, just tasting. I took a deep breath in through my nose as the kiss continued, and was gifted with the musky scent of his cologne. It was spicy and dry, and it added one more dimension of sexy I would have to try to ignore.

When his hands travelled into my hair and started removing pins as he kissed me, my resolve crumbled slightly. He was trying to take care of me, all the while kissing me. The pins were hidden in the twist of my hair, but he gently took one out, then two, then ran his fingers lightly through the hair that had come undone. He twisted a tendril around his finger and the rest of my resolve collapsed entirely.

My hands reached up and gripped the lapels of his tux jacket, pulling him to me, deepening the kiss. He followed me into it, following me to the depths, his hands leaving my hair but wrapping tightly around my waist, pulling me into him. I gasped when his lips left mine, traveling along my jawline, back toward my ear.

"Not here, sweetheart," he whispered. Then my body ached as he pulled away from me, his eyes finding mine. "I want nothing more than to bury myself in you, show you how badly I've wanted you, how much I want to worship you, but not here."

I nodded and he kissed me chastely on the lips. A quick, poignant kiss.

"Change. Pack. Meet me downstairs." He turned from me and walked toward the door.

"Preston?" I said, my voice stronger than I thought I could manage. He turned and looked back to me. "How long will I be gone?"

"I want to keep you forever, Lena, believe me. But I'll have you back tomorrow." His voice was low and tortured, defeated, as if he would rather do anything than bring me back here. He turned and left the room and I heard his footsteps disappear down the stairs.

I took a deep breath in and then let it out slowly, trying to wrap my mind around my situation without letting it ruin the sensations still coursing through my body. Shaking my head, I moved to the bed and opened the duffle bag, making a mental list of what to pack.

Ten minutes later, I came down the stairs wearing comfortable drawstring lounge pants, a fitted t-shirt, and flip flops. I'd been in a formal dress with killer heels all night and wasn't exactly eager to try and impress Preston with my nightwear.

When I entered the foyer, he turned to me and his smile let me know he didn't care in the slightest what I was wearing. I had finished unpinning my hair and now my raven locks hung loose around my shoulders, and when I stepped up to Preston he wasted no time fingering the tresses.

"You ready to go?" he asked, his finger lost in another tendril of hair. I smiled and nodded, my eyes swimming in his dark ones.

He kissed me, too briefly, then pulled away, saying, "Let's go." He grabbed the duffle bag from me, then clasped my hand in his and walked me out of the house, stopping to turn the alarm on as we left. As we approached the Lotus, I found myself smiling just at the thought of Preston behind the wheel of such a sexy machine. I'd been tamping down my attraction to him since we'd met, but tonight, seeing him in front of his car was overwhelmingly arousing. He opened the door for me and I climbed inside, inhaling the scent of the leather that still lingered, mixed with the distinct smell of Preston.

We pulled out and headed away from the house and it occurred to me I had no idea where we were going. Furthermore, I knew very little about the man in the seat next to me. The only thing I knew for sure was I wanted uninhibited access to him for the night and I would give him the same unfettered access to me. I wanted him in me, on me, around me—I wanted to be claimed by him. But I also hoped in the time we spent together, I'd get an opportunity to know him in more than just a physical way.

"Where are you taking me?"

"To my place," he answered without hesitation.

"And where is that?"

"The West Hills." I knew the area he was talking about. It was a part of Portland known to be affluent: large houses, nice cars, big bank accounts. It wasn't different from the area I lived in, but The West Hills had a reputation. "Don't worry. It's not as stuffy as it sounds. Besides, I'm new to the area." We kept driving and I started to love the way Preston drove the Lotus. It hugged curves and growled in a way that had parts of me dampening. Cars were sexy; I'd always thought so. But cars were exponentially sexier when men like Preston drove them.

His grip on the wheel was relaxed but firm and it allowed his biceps to flex under the fabric of his jacket. When he shifted gears, I could admire his big hands with long, agile fingers. If our encounter in the utility closet hadn't been foreplay enough, watching him handle this car would have done the job beautifully all on its own.

"Have you always lived in Portland?" I ventured a question, hoping to learn something, *anything*, about him.

"I've almost always lived nearby. I grew up in Lake Oswego, moved away for college, but found myself back here after a few years of living in different cities, trying them on. It never really felt right anywhere else, so I'm back for good, it seems." He turned his head to mine and gifted me with a smile I hadn't seen before from him. It was big, bright and beautiful. It caught me off guard a little, but I adjusted as my insides melted from it.

"Where did you go to school?" The question came from me without thought, seeming to be the next logical step in our conversation.

"Stanford. I thought I wanted to be a lawyer, but quickly realized I enjoyed enforcing the law a lot more than defending it. I started in the law school, but eventually got my degree in computer forensics, hoping that would help me in the future."

"California is like another universe," I said thoughtfully. "I've been there a few times, never for any real length of time, but it always felt strange to me, like I was out of place."

"I was out of place there, too. After college, I tried a few different places; Chicago and New York, I even went south to Texas for a bit. But nothing felt like Portland." He smiled at me and I grinned back because I agreed. Then his smile was gone as his eyes flashed into the rearview mirror. His lips moved into a line and a few wrinkles appeared on his forehead. "It appears," he said as he took a sharp right turn I wasn't expecting, which forced me into his side, "we're being followed."

"What?" I nearly shrieked. I turned around, trying to see out the back windshield, but all I saw were headlights. Regular, run-of-the-mill headlights one would normally see if someone were in the lane behind them. "How can you tell they're following us?"

"Because he's made the same last five turns as we have."

"How can you tell it's a man?" I looked in the side view mirror, still trying to see something that would clue me in to what was happening. I heard him chuckle and my head snapped to look at him.

"I've never been tailed by a girl."

I narrowed my eyes at him, not liking the insinuation that a girl couldn't properly follow him. I opened my mouth to give him a snarky remark, but was thrust up against the door as he took another turn with too much speed for my liking. I gripped the handle on the door, my heart jumping into my throat. "He's persistent," Preston said, still taking frequent glances in the mirrors. "Hold on."

I didn't have a chance to ask him what exactly I should hold on to in his tiny sports car before he gunned the gas pedal and tore off down the street in the middle of downtown Portland. It was Friday night in the city and people and cars were everywhere. My feet planted firmly on the floor of the car. One hand pressed against the door and the other hand had found its way to Preston's bicep.

He wove in and out of traffic, breaking a few laws, I was sure, and managed to avoid hitting any of the pedestrians I alerted him to with my screams. Either he was used to driving with a woman yelling at him in the passenger seat, or he was doing a bang-up job ignoring me. Regardless, my heart rate was through the roof and I was getting tired of being thrust from side to side as he flung his Lotus around corners and through parking lots, all in an effort to lose the person who was following him. Eventually, he managed to get the car turned so it was heading north and I started to relax as we made our way from the area of town full of bars and nightlife, entering the part that was more industrial.

I turned and saw the car was still behind us, even after all that fancy driving, and I looked to Preston.

"He's still there. What are you going to do?" I'd never been in a car chase before. In all the movies I'd seen, the car being followed either lost the other car, or it crashed. We hadn't achieved the former and I hoped to avoid the latter.

"Just hang on tight," he said again, making my eyes roll. I resumed my hold on the door and his arm.

He pulled into an empty warehouse parking lot, luring the other car into it behind him, then he gunned it, aiming his car for a small alley that ran along the back of the building. Even for such a small car as the Lotus, it was a tight squeeze, and I found myself closing my eyes in fear, my fingers gripping Preston's arm. Surely, the car following us couldn't make it through the same alley. I felt the car leave the ground, causing the same feeling in my stomach as when you hit the summit of a roller coaster and then quickly fall. Weightlessness. We were airborne. I let out a strangled cry, but was thrust back into silence when the car jolted back onto the pavement.

My eyes popped open, and I was relieved to see we were, indeed, on the ground and in one piece. I looked to Preston and his eyes were focused as he was driving. I turned quickly to look behind us, but didn't see the car any longer.

"I think you lost him," I whispered, the car silent aside from our heavy breaths.

Preston didn't respond immediately, but when he did, all he said was, "Hold on." Suddenly, I flew forward and to the side, only to feel Preston's arm swing out and press me back into my seat. Then we were still for just a second. His hand flew to the gear shift, putting the car in reverse. Preston placed his arm over the back of my seat and looked out the back windshield of the car, lurching backward down yet another alley. I closed my eyes tightly again, fearing we would crash.

Then we were still. The car was off, as were the headlights.

I opened my eyes and felt Preston's hands on my face, turning it toward him.

"Are you okay?" he asked, his eyes roaming over my face, inspecting me.

"Preston," I breathed. My voice was gone and his name was just air.

"Lena, baby," he said, pulling me into him, guiding my face into his neck, his arms wrapping around my shoulders. "It's okay. I'm sorry," he whispered. I breathed into him, trying really hard not to cry, the adrenaline making my heart race and eyes well with tears.

"I'm o-okay," I stammered. Then the car lit up and he pulled away from me. Two headlights were beaming right into the car and I was frozen, aside from the trembling, not knowing what was going on. Preston grabbed my face again and looked at me, speaking clearly and quickly.

"I'll handle this, Lena. Don't get out of the car, okay?"

I nodded, his hands still on my cheeks. Then he pressed a very quick kiss to my lips and went to open his door. He was halfway out when I heard a man's voice.

"Not so fast, Reid. Get back in the car and roll the window down." The headlights went off, shrouding us in darkness again. Preston folded himself inside the car and rolled the window down as asked.

"Shit," he mumbled under his breath. He reached over and gave my knee a quick squeeze. "Everything's going to be fine. I promise," he said quietly.

I heard footsteps coming closer to the car, and even though Preston no longer seemed threatened, I was still trembling and scared. Looking for the person who had chased us, my eyes darted through the darkness. Finally, the outline of a man appeared, coming closer to us with steady, unhurried steps. He was a tall, round man. Easily three hundred pounds, perhaps six-feet tall. He was lucky he'd chased us in his car, because Preston could effortlessly beat him in a foot race.

"Reid, nice evening for a leisurely drive." The man was just outside the driver's side of the car now, looking in at Preston.

"Edgar, I'd say it was a pleasure to see you, but I'd be lying."

I swallowed hard, freaking out a little bit that Preston was mouthing off to the man who had us trapped in an alley.

"You know I like it when you call me Eddie," the man said, placing one hand on the door and leaning down so his head was in view. His face matched his body, round and full.

"What do you want, Eddie?" Preston's voice was low and angry.

"I'm just checking on my assets." Eddie's eyes fell on me. "Hello there, Lena, darling. I hope our little car chase didn't frighten you too badly."

I saw a muscle in Preston's jaw twitch and his grip on the steering wheel tightened.

"Again, what do you want?" His voice was even lower now, nearly a growl.

"I just want to make sure you've thought through all your actions, Reid." Eddie's eyes traveled to me again. "Some of us are starting to doubt your decision-making capabilities."

"I don't answer to you, Eddie, but even if I did, all I'd say is that I am just doing my job."

Eddie chuckled, then sighed. "You've got balls, Reid. I'll give you that." Eddie stood up and thumped his hand on the roof of the car. "This job doesn't go right, you're going to lose a lot more than just your balls, Reid. Don't say I didn't warn you." With those parting words, Eddie walked back to his car. After a moment, his headlights came on, flooding the Lotus with light again, then he backed up and drove away.

Chapter Two

I exhaled heavily when his car was out of sight, then turned to Preston, who was still gripping the steering wheel so tightly his knuckles were white. "What the hell was that all about?" Preston's hands finally loosened on the wheel, but instead of answering me, he just started the car again and put the gear shift in drive. He pulled out of the alley and started driving back into the city. "Preston, why did that guy chase you all over the city and then just walk away like that?"

He let out an aggravated sigh. "Eddie is someone I work with. He was just trying to scare me. I don't want you worried about it."

"How did he know my name?"

"Like I said, I work with him."

"I thought you said you were in the business of secrets. I don't understand why he needs to know my name." Something was off about the way Eddie approached Preston. It made me nervous, as if somehow I was involved in something I didn't want to be a part of and I'd gotten in over my head.

"Listen, he doesn't know why you hired me. He doesn't even know the specifics of the case. Hell, he might not have even known I was working with you until he saw you—you're not exactly unrecognizable."

"What's that supposed to mean?"

"It means, anyone who's anyone in this town would see your face and know your name. You're Lena fucking Bellows, for Christ's sake." He was shouting now, his voice angry and agitated. His hand slammed down on the steering wheel as he yelled, "Fuck!" He took another hard right turn then pulled over on the side of the road. He threw the car in park and then turned in his seat to face me. "Listen, I never intended for you to get involved this way. When I took this job, I thought it would be a slam dunk. I'd be in and out in a matter of days and then move along, just like I always have." His voice softened as he spoke, his eyes imploring me to listen and understand.

"I wasn't expecting to be this drawn to you, Lena. I couldn't have prepared myself for the attraction I felt when we first met. I should have turned the job down, should have walked away, but I'm not that strong." His voice had lost all its roughness and anger from earlier and was now like silk.

Thinking about him walking away caused a sudden and unexpected panic in me. Surely, if on that first day he'd turned me down and left that bar without taking the job, I would have simply found someone else. But after the small amount of time we'd spent together, knowing the way he could make me feel, the power he had over my body, and the promise of something more to come, the thought of him ending whatever it was between us was terrifying. I didn't want him walking away, but I also didn't want to be a part of these strange and dramatic scenes, either. Sexual escapades in closets and car chases weren't my idea of a good time. I wanted quiet movie nights cuddled up by a warm fire. I wanted inside jokes and silly notes left in obscure places. I wasn't sure Preston Reid was the man to give me what I wanted.

"Maybe you should take me home."

"Fuck that, Lena. I'm taking you to my place. You can't spend the night alone in your house and I haven't slept well in nearly a week. I'm not sleeping in my car again." He put the car in gear and we jerked back onto the road. Soft

Preston was gone again and I was in the car with pushy Preston.

"Okay," I sighed. The rest of the ride was quiet. Neither he nor I spoke. When the car slowed again it was to stop at a gated community. He stopped at a keypad, rolled his window down, and entered four digits.

"Fourteen, ninety-two," he said softly. "The year Columbus sailed the ocean blue." He turned toward me slightly, a boyish grin on his face. "It was the only four-digit combination I knew I'd never forget."

"Makes sense," I replied.

"Remember that, you'll need it."

He made his way to a building that had garages all along the first floor and I realized we were at his condo. It hadn't occurred to me that there were anything but giant mansions in the West Hills.

As we neared one of the garages, it began to open, timed perfectly so we didn't even have to stop or slow down—he just pulled right in, effortlessly. Once the car was in, the garage door closed behind us and Preston folded himself out of the car. I followed, grabbing my duffle, trying not to let my nerves get the best of me. More excitement had occurred in the last three hours than I could remember in my whole life, and I was still trying to keep my wits about me. I had to remind myself why, in all reality, I'd come here. To be with him. To let the all-encompassing attraction I'd had to him since that first day take me wherever it led.

Without words, he led me into his house and I took the quiet opportunity to admire his home. It was definitely a man's place. Everything was either black, white, or gray. He led me past the living room and I took a second to look inside. The furniture was black leather, reminding me of the jacket he'd worn every time I'd seen him, apart from that night. There was a glass coffee table in the middle of the room and an enormous flat screen TV hanging on the wall.

I continued to follow him down the hall, which I noticed had no pictures hanging on the walls. Everything was stark and empty. I tried not to think about how his house could be spruced up or what I could add to make it more homey and warm. When I followed him into the next room, I gasped at the most beautiful kitchen I'd ever seen. I had a nice kitchen at my home. It was functional and I used it often, but Preston's was a work of art.

Black granite countertops, a huge island with a six-burner stove built in, stainless steel appliances, and gorgeous dark cabinets. There were twin ovens built into the wall, stacked on top of one another, and a door slightly ajar that looked like a walk-in pantry.

"You like to cook?"

"Not really. I don't have a lot of time to cook."

"Oh." That surprised me. Why would he have such a state-of-the-art kitchen if he didn't cook?

"I bought the condo new, and it was already built this way," he said, reading my mind. "Don't get me wrong, I *can* cook. I just don't find myself home a lot." He walked to the far side of the island and then his eyes looked to me. "Can I make you a drink? Vodka martini?"

I blushed at his remembrance of my drink of choice, my heart speeding up just a little at the thought of him paying attention to such details.

"Can I just have straight vodka? On the rocks?" I needed something to take down quick, not something to savor. He didn't answer me but I watched as he pulled out a tumbler and made my drink, also pouring himself a scotch.

With both tumblers in hand, he walked around the island, heading straight for me. His eyes never left mine as he approached and when he made it near me he came to stand directly behind me, forcing me to turn to him. He placed both tumblers on the granite behind me, one on either side, leaning into me. I could feel the cool, hard edge of the granite biting into my back, coupled with the warm hardness of his chest pressing into my front.

He reached down and took the duffle from my hands.

"Anything breakable in here?"

"No." I quirked a smile at his strange question and then yelped as he tossed it over the island and into the sitting room beyond. Then his hand was in front of me again, holding my drink out for me. "Thank you," I said as I took the tumbler from him. I pressed the glass to my lips, still looking him in the eyes, then tipped the glass back, taking the cold liquid down in one swallow. I winced just a little as it burned, but recovered quickly, enjoying the warmth it spread through my belly.

He smiled down at me, but this was a new and different smile. This smile was nearly predatory, dangerous. My smile disappeared quickly, replaced by my heartbeat thrumming through my veins, both my hands gripping the glass in my hands as if it were the only thing keeping me upright. Leaning back just far enough to bring his glass to his lips, he took a small sip of his scotch, eyes glued to mine.

"Can I try it?" I asked, before I knew the words were coming out of my mouth. I blushed a little, realizing it was a strange request. "I've never had scotch before." His eyes were lidded and dark as they came closer to me, his face tilting slightly as he gently pressed his lips against mine. The kiss wasn't insistent, wasn't pushy; it was soft and cautious. His tongue teased the seam of my lips and when I opened to him, I tasted the scotch. Our tongues melded to one another and the kiss was nutty and peppery. I released a small moan and he pressed into me further.

In the back of my mind, I registered my glass being taken from my hands, the sound of both our glasses being set on the counter, but I was too involved in our kiss to care. When his hands were free, they found my hair, pulling me into him, placing my head just exactly where he wanted it, angling me so he could get everything from the kiss he was searching for. His tongue danced with mine, flicked at the roof of my mouth, slid around the rim of my lips; it was the slowest and sexiest kiss I'd ever participated in.

His face pulled back from mine, both of us breathing hard and fast.

"Lena," he whispered, before his mouth moved down my jaw and lapped at my neck. "Soon, I'm not going to be able to stop myself," he said between nips at the sensitive skin behind my ear. My fingers moved to the soft part of his hair, where it was shaved close, urging him on, praying he never stopped making me feel as if I were about to combust.

"I don't want you to stop, Preston. *Please…*"

His face pulled away from my neck, but we never lost contact as his forehead moved to press against mine.

"Please, what? Lena, you have to tell me what *you* want. This has to be on your terms." His voice was choppy and sounded a little frantic.

I pulled back and held his face between my hands. "Hey, what's going on?"

"I want you so badly, Lena," he whispered, his eyes darting back and forth between mine. "But I also know what's at stake for you. I won't take anything from you, sweetheart."

My mouth gaped a little at his admission. He wanted me. I'd already known that, to some degree. But he wanted to protect me, too. That was something new to think about. Derrek had never really been protective of me and I didn't realize I would appreciate it if he had. But watching Preston physically hold himself back, hearing the concern in his voice, it was moving. I wanted Derrek to pay for holding me hostage in a marriage for so long, a marriage he never intended to work on or make better. I wanted the money I thought I was entitled to, the money I'd helped him make. But being here with Preston felt more important than the money, more important than any other moment I'd spent with Derrek in the last five years. It felt right.

"I want you, too, Preston," I managed, even if it was just a whisper. It felt like the most important whisper to ever move over my lips. He swallowed hard, taking in my words, but still made no move for me. I could almost see his brain working, the thoughts evident across his face.

"That's not good enough." He sighed, sounding sad. "I need to know exactly what you want."

My hands fell from his face, confused, but willing to give him whatever he needed in that moment. "I want you, Preston. I want you to take me into your bedroom." I leaned closer to him, placing a small kiss on his chin. "Take my clothes off." My mouth moved softly up his jawbone. "And I want to feel you inside of me," I whispered in his ear.

"You know what that would mean, right?" he asked against the skin of my neck, his stubble rubbing on me, causing me to shiver. My hands traveled to the back of his neck, pressing the front of my body against his, feeling his hardness pressed against my belly.

"I know what it means to me, for me. I understand what I'm doing."

"No." His voice was low and gravelly. "It means you're mine. From now on, it's only me. You'll be with me and trust me to keep you safe." His hands travelled down my back and ended on my ass, pulling me into him again, making me gasp. "Give yourself to me, sweetheart. But make sure it's what you want."

"I want you," I said firmly, into his ear. "I want all of you to have all of me. Take me, please." Instantly, his hands were on my waist, hoisting me onto the counter. Then he found the hem of my shirt and lifted it over my head, so quickly I barely had time to process what was happening.

"I got to see a lot of you from the waist down earlier. I'm looking forward to exploring the other half of you," he said, his thumbs brushing over my cheekbones. I watched as his eyes slid down my front, and I loved seeing his eyes widen when they reached the black lace, see-through bra I had on. "You're a little minx," he said with a smile, running his forefinger along the lace edge that sat at the swell of my breast. "You came down your stairs looking like you were ready for a nap in this t-shirt and pajama pants. I can appreciate the relaxed look," he said, moving his finger to the other side, causing my breath to hitch. "But you knew what you had on under that shirt."

I opened my mouth on a moan as his tongue traced a path down my chest and into the valley between my breasts. His left hand palmed me and the friction of his skin over the lace rubbing against my nipple was blissful. His mouth moved down my right breast and his hand pulled the lace down, exposing me to him. He leaned back slightly to look at me, his eyes clouded over with lust, but wasted no time taking me into his mouth.

My legs wrapped around his waist, urging him closer to me, his cock pressing up against my center. He felt unimaginably hard and large. My hand went to the closure on his pants, opening them. His mouth was still working my nipple, his teeth gently tugging, his tongue lapping and swirling. I reached past the waistband of his underwear, wrapped my fingers around his cock, and he growled around my breast.

He was like hot steel in my hands, hard and warm. I gripped him and slid my hand from root to tip, using my thumb to trace circles over his head.

"Fuck, Lena," he said, pulling his mouth away from my breast.

"Please," I begged quietly. "I want to be naked in a bed with you." My words were hardly out of my mouth before his arm was around my waist, lifting me from the counter. I wrapped my arms around his neck, my legs around his waist, and enjoyed a front piggyback ride through his house. I used my tongue to tease his neck as he walked, not paying attention in the least to the rest of his house.

When we finally made it to a bed, he climbed on first, crawling on his knees to the middle, his arms still holding me close to him. Then he lowered me excruciatingly slowly, kissing me the entire way. When I was comfortably lying on the bed, he settled his hips between my thighs, the pressure of his middle against my center so spectacularly arousing, I needed everything to be moving faster. He seemed content to savor everything happening between us, but I was eager and craving him.

I reached between us and pushed his pants down over his hips, using my feet to free him completely, then I brought my hands up to push his tux jacket off his shoulders. He broke our kiss to lean up and slide his jacket and vest off.

"You're in a hurry?" He had a smug smile on his face. Usually, I would have made a snide remark about it, but he wasn't wrong. I *was* in a hurry. I reached down to take off my lounge pants, but his hands wrapped around my wrists. "You might be okay with the fast route, but I'll be the one to undress you, Lena. You're like a gift I want to take my time unwrapping."

His mouth trailed down the center of my breasts, leaving light kisses in his wake. When he passed my belly button, he made sure to kiss it deeply and I felt shockwaves roll through me, ending in my center, igniting a whole new flame. I writhed underneath him, panting, and with anticipation prickling across my skin.

"Jesus, Lena. You're so responsive. I've barely touched you."

"Don't stop," I whispered.

His hands gripped the top of my pants and started pulling them down, slowly sliding his fingers down my hips and thighs. Once I was free of them, his mouth was at my ankle and he trailed his tongue all the way up my right leg, alternating between licks and wet kisses. By the time he made it to the edge of my panties, I was moaning and squirming.

His warmth disappeared and my eyes opened, searching for him. He was leaning back, simply looking at me. My first instinct was to be embarrassed by his intense stare, to want to cover up. My hands itched to cover my belly or hide my breasts. But the look in his eyes was enough to send even more heat through my body. He liked what he saw, enjoyed looking at my body; he wanted me.

I let my gaze drift over him and my pulse thundered through my veins at what I saw. Preston Reid, white tuxedo shirt partly unbuttoned, and black boxer briefs. He looked like every woman's fantasy. His dark hair was mussed from my fingers, his briefs tented *thoroughly*; my mouth watered at what he had hidden under that cotton fabric. I simply couldn't take it any longer.

I sat up, feverishly working to unbutton the rest of his shirt. As I moved from button to button, his chest was slowly revealed to me, and even though I could have imagined this moment a thousand times, I never would have gotten it right. My mind could not have comprehended what Preston's naked chest would look like, because I'd never seen anything like it.

He was glorious. He was ripped. He was hard and broad. I wanted to lick every solitary inch of him. So I did. As I slid his shirt off his shoulders, I pressed a wet kiss right between his pecs, and tongued my way down the crease of his abs, my hands finally joining me and grazing over all his hard and powerful muscles. After enjoying the front of him, my hands slid around his waist, slipped under the waistband of his briefs, and palmed his fantastic ass, skin against skin. He was perfect everywhere.

I pushed his underwear down and he lifted up onto his knees, allowing them to fall down his thighs. When his cock finally sprang free, I wasted no time admiring it with both my eyes and hands. I gripped him, watching my hand slide up and down his shaft. He was long, hard, wide and perfect. As I stroked him, he leaned over to his bedside table and opened a drawer, pulling a condom out and handing it to me.

"Put it on me, Lena," he said, his voice low. I took it from him, but didn't open it. I just looked down at it in my hand, contemplating what my next move would be. "Baby," he whispered, using his hand to bring my face to his.

"I want to feel you, Preston." My words were quiet and soft; I wasn't sure I wanted him to hear me.

"Tell me what you need."

"I don't want you to wear this." The words rushed out of me. I paused and then took a deep breath, continuing on. "I've only ever been with one person, and I've been on birth control for ten years." I closed my eyes, thinking about how many times I'd wanted to throw the pills away in the past, but I shook my head slightly, trying to clear my thoughts and focus on the hand gently caressing my cheek. "I don't want anything between us," I breathed out.

"Do you trust me?" he asked, his brown eyes dark and deep.

"Yes," was my immediate response.

"Then lie back, sweetheart."

My pulse throbbed at his command—everywhere. The pulse point in my neck was bouncing; I could hear my heartbeat in my ears, and my clit ached. I lay back, my head landing on feathery pillows, the cool sheets chilling my warm skin.

I watched him kick off his briefs then his gaze roamed over me from head to toe. When his face was over mine, he gave me his sexy smile and I tried to smile back, but lost the ability to keep my eyes open when his hand glided over the crotch of my panties.

"You're soaked," he whispered against my neck. One of his fingers moved the cotton panel to the side and slowly slid into me. I gasped and my hands moved up above my head instinctively. Then another finger joined the first and he started pumping in and out of me, his mouth still assaulting my neck. His other hand moved between my back and the mattress, unhooking my bra effortlessly, and I moved quickly to get it off.

His eyes fell to my bare breasts and his cock jumped against my thigh.

"I need you," I mewled, thrusting my hips up to meet his hand. I cried out when his teeth gently pulled on my nipple, but it wasn't nearly enough. "Preston," I groaned.

In one moment, he was gone, his weight lifted from me, his hand missing from inside me. Then he pulled off my panties and tossed them to the floor. My eyes found his and I watched his face as he moved over me, the tip of him pressing up against my opening. I kept my eyes on his, our gaze never leaving one another's, as he slowly pressed his cock into me. I gasped at the feeling of him, hard and warm, stretching me, feeling fuller than I ever could have anticipated.

"Oh, God," I rasped. "It's so good."

When he was fully seated in me, when I could feel him nudging the deepest part of me, I sighed and his face found the crook of my neck. I wrapped my arms around him, his hot breath against my neck. After a moment, he placed sweet kisses along my shoulder and whispered, "I'm going to move now."

I didn't have time to respond before he slowly pulled out, so I could feel every nuance and ridge of him sliding against me. When he was nearly all the way out, with just the head of him left inside, he moved swiftly back in, causing my breath to fall away, my legs to pull up along his hips, and my back to arch all the way off the bed. It was magnificent.

"Sweet Jesus," he grunted. "Lena, you're perfect."

"Mmmhmm…" was all I could manage as he continued his rhythm of thrusting in and out. His hands moved all over me, from my thighs to my breasts, my neck to my wrists. He was everywhere and I was floating on a cloud, simply chasing all the sensations my body was reacquainting with. It had been a long time since a man had touched me, but my body had never felt this way before. I tried to tell myself it was just because it had been so long since I'd been with a man, but my mind argued it wasn't the feeling of the hands running over my breasts, it was the man the hands belonged to that was eliciting this response from me.

At first, he was slow and gentle. I felt as if we were just getting used to each other, to the way we made each other's bodies feel. But after we were familiar, he took liberties and I let him. He arranged me how he wanted me, praising me every time he found something new that pleased him.

He put one of my ankles over his shoulder and groaned with relief, like he'd been waiting for that very moment his whole life. He placed both of my legs over his shoulders, my ankles resting on their breadth, he couldn't hold back his audible pleasure when he sank into me fully.

"Fuck, I'm so deep. And you're so tight."

Again, all I could do was moan in agreement. He was deep, so deep it nearly hurt, but it was a good pain, and I knew I'd be so happy to be sore in the morning if this was how I'd earned it. I felt the tightening between my legs, throughout my back, arching all the way up to my neck. I knew I was getting close to orgasm, and I reached between us to urge myself over the cusp.

"Touch yourself, baby," he said as he watched my hand disappear. "Rub your clit and make yourself come."

As my fingers found my aching clit, my body bucked against the sensation, my hips jumping up to meet Preston's strokes, and I writhed that way until I finally broke through, falling madly from the high of the orgasm. Tingles made their way through my whole body and I shook with release. My pussy clenched down on his cock, pulsing, gloriously trying to hang on to him. Preston fucked me all the way through my climax, cursing through clenched teeth.

"Fucking Christ, Lena. That was the most beautiful goddamned thing I've ever seen."

I couldn't speak, hadn't found my voice yet, so I just thrust my hips up to him again, not wanting him to stop. I wanted him to find the same euphoria I had, wanted him to use me to get there. I moved my legs down to his waist and wrapped my ankles around it, pulling him into me, and allowing me to meet him thrust for thrust, grinding my hips up to meet his.

His eyes rolled back in his head and I knew he was feeling my pussy wrapped around him, even wetter with my climax, warm and damp, gripping him.

"I want you to come, Preston. Tell me how to get you there," I pleaded with him. He growled in response, and then moved down over me, his hands sliding underneath me, gripping my shoulders, pulling me onto him even harder. I gasped at the new sensation. Then he lost himself in me. He was moving with purpose now, not just to make us feel good, but to find that release. I did everything I could to help, even if it was a selfish ploy. His cock felt magnificent grinding into me, thrusting in and out, reaching every spot inside which ached for him.

He pistoned in and out at a rapid pace, his breath coming faster and faster, and then he bit into my shoulder, just hard enough to cause me to cry out. The speed and angle at which he hit me was just enough to send me spiraling into another trembling orgasm, and I heard him grunting and knew he'd found his release as well.

My core pulsed around him, jolt after jolt of pleasure making me clench around him, all the while feeling him twitch inside me, emptying himself into me; it was the most erotic and glorious feeling I'd ever experienced.

Our sweat-sticky bodies clung to one another, our breath coming in rapid pants, and he melted into me, his muscles going lax, relaxing on top of me. I took his weight gladly, reveled in it, and loved the feeling of him surrounding me in every way possible.

Once we'd both settled, he rolled off me, moving to press his front against me and pulling my back against him. His arm came to rest over the curve of my waist and he searched for my hand. He found it and threaded his fingers through mine, linking them. His foot snagged the comforter from the foot of the bed, which had become a rumpled mess during our exploits. He kicked it up and I grabbed the edge with my free hand, pulling it up to our chests, covering us.

"Sleep," he mumbled against my ear right before he kissed me there. I was too tired to respond, so I let myself drift away.

Chapter Three

I was pulled from a very deep sleep by Preston's fingers trailing through my cleft. At first he was gentle, trying to rouse me from sleep without startling me. But he grew more insistent in his rubbing and I woke fully aroused and panting. My hand gripped his wrist instinctively, my eyes opening to find his as a moan escaped me.

"Good morning, sweetheart," was all he said as my eyes asked a million questions. Then his thumb found my clit and my eyes closed on a groan, and all the questions I had floated away. "That's right," he said with a voice so low and sexy I nearly came just listening to him. "Let me give you what you need and then I'm going to take what I want."

His words skyrocketed me into orgasm. It was a fast, quick, earth-shattering high, but it felt fucking fantastic.

"Good girl," he said with a sly grin. I tried to reply but was interrupted by his hands on my hips. He pulled out and then flipped me onto my stomach. "On your knees, Lena." I would have complied, but found myself being forced into the position by him, and that, unexpectedly, sent a shiver of excitement through me. Him *handling* me, putting me where he wanted me, demanding things of me, turned me on instantly.

His hand was on my back between my shoulder blades and he pressed me gently into the mattress.

"Lena, baby, I want you to hold on to the slats in the headboard for me. Hold on tight and lock your elbows." His hand caressed my back along my spine, all the way down to my ass, as I reached forward and did as he asked. "Last night was fantastic, but today, I'm going to fuck you like I've imagined since I met you."

I took in a shuddering breath, his words having a physical effect on me. I straightened my arms and locked my elbows.

"Keep your arms straight, baby. I don't want to hurt you."

"Okay," I mumbled, half into the pillow that was fluffed up around my face. His hand slid back up my spine and curl around my shoulder, his touch gentle until his grip became firm. Then I cried out, half in surprise and half in ecstasy, as he slammed into me.

"Fuck," he groaned, paused for the moment so deep in me; I could feel his scrotum up against the sensitive skin of my lips. "Are you all right?" His question was quiet and concerned.

"I'm fine," I managed. I wanted to tell him that I was fucking perfect, or so entirely fantastic with him filling me, but *fine* was all I could get out.

He took my 'fine' as an affirmative and began his onslaught of fucking. I immediately understood why he wanted my elbows locked, and I savored all the sensations that came when I used my arms to push my ass into his thrusts. He pounded away, his hands gripping my hips, pulling me farther onto him, muttering obscenities that did nothing but turn me on even more.

"Your pussy was fucking made for me," he said between thrusts. "Your beautiful cunt belongs to me now," was followed by, "Jesus, you feel so fucking fantastic on my dick, Lena." He was filthy and dirty and he was right: my body loved every single second of it and it did belong to him. I was a goner.

He came in a roar, growling through his release. One hand gripped my hip, the other curled over my shoulder, pressing himself so entirely into me, I was gasping.

This time, when he collapsed onto the bed next to me, neither one of us moved toward the other. I was fighting to catch my breath and he was doing the same. I couldn't exactly figure out why I was out of breath—he'd done all the hard work. But taking him like that had been too exhilarating and I'd lost myself in him.

Eventually, he did turn his head toward me, my face still pushed deep into his fluffy pillows.

"Are you okay?" he asked quietly.

"Mmmhmmm," was my response.

"Lena, please, I need some actual words."

I groaned, but then lifted my head from his heavenly pillow and stated, "I'm fantastic, thank you." Then I plopped my head back down and enjoyed the afterglow. He chuckled, but then there was silence and I settled in again.

After a few minutes, the bed shifted and I watched as Preston walked his naked self into his attached bathroom. Luckily for me, I didn't have to move my head at all to watch his entire trip as his gloriously chiseled body gracefully left me. He was exactly what God had envisioned when he created man; I was sure of it. Every muscle moved in accordance with the others; long and lean muscles in his legs complemented the bulkier muscles in his chest and arms. I knew I'd never be able to look at him in his leather jacket and jeans again without picturing him like this, naked and strutting through his house.

Then I was treated to the front view when he came back out and walked to me. I swallowed hard and tried not to stare, but the man was so goddamned beautiful. He stopped at the edge of the bed and leaned down, placing both hands on the mattress.

"Wanna shower with me?"

I lifted my head once more from the pillow and felt my hair fall in a mess around my face. "I would love to shower with you, but I'm afraid I'm not ready to walk yet. So, go on without me." Just after I'd dramatically flopped my head down onto my pillow once more, I yelped as I felt his arms slide under me, flip me over, and then lift me from the soft heaven that was his mattress. I squealed as I wrapped my arms around his neck.

He walked to the bathroom, carrying me in his arms, a stupidly handsome smile across his face. He plunked me down in the shower, which was the most gorgeous walk-in shower I'd ever seen, right in the middle of a steaming hot stream of water. It was even more heavenly than his mattress.

I sighed as I let the water run over me and moved to wet my hair, closing my eyes, enjoying the moment.

"This is like every wet dream I've ever had combined into one."

I opened my eyes. Preston was obviously ogling me, watching every part of my body as the water cascaded over it. Then he moved into me, his arms coming to rest at my hips, and his mouth moving in toward mine. He kissed me gently, the beast I'd met earlier that morning apparently sleeping. This Preston was warm, sweet, and tender. If someone forced me to pick which Preston I liked better, I'd never be able to choose. Each one was sexy in their own right.

We kissed in the shower until I was wrinkled and then he washed me. Neither one of us tried anything besides stealing a couple of kisses, which I was thankful for. I didn't think I could take another round with him if the beast made an encore appearance. I wasn't too tired, however, to take in his glorious form as he rinsed the shampoo from his hair. Everything I'd admired about him the night before and even this morning, was only magnified and amplified by the water. The man looked good wet.

He led me out of the shower and handed me a towel.

"Is everything you own soft and fluffy?" I asked as I wrapped the towel around my shoulders. It might have been the softest towel I'd ever felt.

He chuckled. "I hope not."

"Seriously. Your pillows are like clouds and your mattress is the most comfortable one I've ever been on. And now the towels." I looked at him and smiled. "You like nice things." My smile grew wider at my realization. I thought about it for a moment and then other things started popping into my mind. His car—perhaps the nicest car I'd ever seen. His fancy leather jacket. The scotch. It all made sense. What single, thirty-something man had towels this nice? I brought it up to my nose and grinned when I smelled the fabric softener. He either hired someone who furnished his house with nice things and a maid who used fabric softener, or he totally enjoyed all this stuff. "Did you buy these towels? And the pillows?"

"Yeah," he said, wiping his towel through his hair, flinging water droplets everywhere.

"So, it's true. You like nice things?"

He thought about it for a moment. Then he shrugged. "I guess. Who wants scratchy towels?"

I shrugged back at him, smiling. Walking back into the bedroom, I looked around for my clothes, trying to remember which way they had been flung the night before.

"What are you looking for?" Preston asked as he walked back to the bed and climbed in.

"My clothes," I said as I walked around his bed.

"No clothes. Today, we lay around like naked, lazy people." He threw the comforter down, opening up the side of the bed he wasn't in, and then nodded me toward it.

"You want to spend an entire day naked in bed?" I didn't move from my spot, feet away from the bed. I knew if I got in I probably wouldn't get back out.

"Give me one good reason why not?"

"Well, I should go home, for one." I watched as his smile fell away and the muscle in the side of his jaw tightened.

"You're not going home. There's no reason for you to be there."

"It's my home. And Derrek is probably already wondering where I am."

"He's not," he said firmly.

"Preston," I tried to reason with him.

"I want you here, with me. Fuck, Lena. I was inside you not two hours ago and now you're just going to go running back to that life where you're unhappy and unsafe?"

"I'm not unsafe and Derrek can't know that I didn't go home last—"

"HE DOESN'T CARE IF YOU CAME HOME OR NOT, LENA!" Preston was out of his bed and yelling as he stalked toward me. "He couldn't care less what you do or whether you slept in your bed last night. He. Doesn't. Care. But don't let me stop you from running home to him." He was right in front of me, loud and angry, but I didn't feel threatened by his outburst. I was, however, confused by this new Preston.

"I'm not running home to him. I'm simply trying to manage the situation. You know what's at stake for me, Preston. You and me. We're the only ones who know what happens if he finds out I've been with you. But the only person it will affect is me. I thought we were on the same team."

"This isn't a team. This is some sick and fucked-up game you signed up for seven years ago that you can't imagine not winning."

"What would you do if you were me, huh? You'd let your wife fuck some other guy and then walk away with *nothing*? I highly doubt it. I didn't sign up for this. I was forced to play this game, and I'll be damned if your ego is going to cause me to start my life over from scratch. I'm entitled to what's mine."

"And what about me? Aren't I entitled to what's mine?" He closed the distance between us and his strong hands wrapped around my shoulders as he hauled me to his chest. "You're mine, remember?" He brought his face so close to mine our noses lightly touched. "You made that decision. You gave yourself to me, and now you're mine and I'll be damned if I let what's mine walk out the door."

In the matter of a millisecond, his lips were on mine and my hands were on his chest, trying to push him away, but one of his hands wrapped around my waist and the other cupped my cheek and even though the kiss started urgently, it melted slowly into desperation.

His hands pulled at me as if he was afraid I was going to float away. So I did the only thing I could think of and held on to him. I held on to him just as hard as he held on to me and eventually we found ourselves in that bed again, only this time we weren't fucking each other, or even having sex; I was simply letting him hold me.

I fell asleep on top of him, still naked, only covered by the soft blanket, one of his hands cupped around the back of my neck.

I woke up to his kiss pressed against my forehead.

"Hey," he whispered when my eyes looked up to his.

"Hey," I said, laying both my hands on his chest under my chin. "Are you still mad at me?"

"I was never mad at you," he said as he tucked a lock of wayward hair behind my ear.

"Well, all the yelling gave me a different impression."

His eyes bored into mine for a moment and then he sighed heavily. "Listen, I didn't mean to snap like that. I've just watched him ignore you, treat you poorly, undervalue you, and when you were just going to walk out to go back to him, well, it rubbed me the wrong way. I'm sorry. I shouldn't have yelled and I definitely shouldn't have yelled at you, but I couldn't let you leave."

"I wasn't *going back* to him. Nothing about my marriage has changed in the last twenty-four hours, Preston, but I am still married and I can't let him know what's happened."

"He's not at your house. He didn't go back to your house last night, either. Your alibi is still intact."

"Maybe I should hire someone else to handle the investigation," I said softly. I watched as that muscle in his jaw started twitching, and I braced myself for angry Preston again.

"Not happening."

"I feel like you're too involved, like whatever is going on between us is going to cloud your judgment and make things difficult." I pushed up off his chest and rolled to his side, pulling the blanket with me, keeping myself covered. "There are two very drastically different components to my life at the moment, and I feel like it might be better to keep them separated."

"I'm in this, baby, whether you like it or not. You can hire someone else if it makes you feel better, but I'm going to get you the proof you need, and I'll get it faster than anyone else you can find on Google."

I could see in his eyes he wasn't listening to me, that he wasn't going to just let things lie and let me take care of my own business. "I just think maybe you're too close to it."

"I've never been so close to anything in my life and I'm not about to let someone else handle what's mine. I've got this, Lena."

I sighed, exasperated, not entirely sure where to go from there or what to expect. So instead of stressing myself out about things I couldn't control, like Preston, I decided to curl into his side and let him figure out what the next step would be.

Chapter Four

Turned out, the next step was actually pretty amazing. We stayed in bed and naked all of Saturday and then all of Sunday.

I'd never felt more cherished or taken care of. I was treated to breakfast in bed both days and many hours of the most incredible sex I'd ever experienced. Preston was a sensational lover. He was generous but needy, intense but soft, domineering yet giving. He was the yin and yang of sex and I reveled in every minute of it. I could never be completely sure which side of him I was going to get, but I wanted to experience them all, so I followed his lead and let him take me wherever he wanted to go.

Part of me letting him take control was giving in to him when he insisted. He'd requested I not sleep at my house any longer and instead was to stay with him. I compromised by saying I'd only come over late at night after I was sure Derrek wouldn't be coming back to the house. This compromise was accepted after I agreed to let Preston pick me up and be my escort.

On Monday morning, Preston had me pressed against the tiles in his walk-in shower, gliding in and out of me at a ridiculously slow and leisurely pace, as if we had the rest of our lives to be with each other. The water was raining down on the wall next to us, its warmth cascading down the wall and flowing around me, keeping me warm even as Preston's mouth moved over every inch of my skin.

His finger found my clit and the slow pace at which he pumped in and out of me coupled with the fast flicks of his finger brought on a quick and powerful orgasm. My cries echoed throughout the shower, only to be joined by his groan as he followed me into climax.

This had been my life for the last forty-eight hours – Preston finding any way he could to make me come, whether it be fast, slow, sweet, or dirty. He could do it all and he did it well. This time, though, his leisurely pace wasn't a sexual maneuver, wasn't a calculated move. He was literally trying to stretch our time together, trying to delay the inevitable. Trying to suspend reality and pause the day. Soon, he'd be driving me back to my house and we'd both have to work. Even though we'd found a new reality together, it didn't change the reality that we both had jobs to get back to.

Even as the Lotus pulled up to the curb a few houses down from mine, I felt his tension. He didn't like dropping me off at the house I shared with Derrek and he hated the fact that he had to let me walk from this distance. But we both knew he couldn't just pull up in my driveway. Not yet, at least.

"I'll be here tonight. Eleven." His words sounded harsh, but I knew he was just unhappy with the situation. "If you hear from him, anything at all, I want to know about it."

I nodded, looking at him, watching his jaw muscle twitch. I leaned over and placed my hand against his cheek, trying to soothe him. I kissed his jaw tenderly, then moved to his lips, trying to tell him with a kiss that I was just as upset to walk away from him as he would be watching me walk away. I was grateful for the darkly tinted windows in that moment, knowing none of the neighbors could see our exchange. When I pulled away, he looked less tense, so I considered my tactics a success. I gave him a smile I hoped wasn't too sad, then reached for the door handle. Before I got the door all the way open, his hand was on my arm, turning me toward him.

"Lena, remember, trust me," he said, his tone serious and worried.

I nodded. "I trust you," I replied, trying to convince him. Because, truly, I did.

"I regret nothing about what's happening between us," he said, his sentiment catching me off guard.

I thought about his comment for just a moment and then smiled – a real smile this time – and said, "Neither do I." I got out of his car and walked to my house, wondering what anyone would think if they could see me in that moment.

I was wearing Preston's clothes even though they barely fit. His gray sweatpants and a t-shirt, no bra and no panties, and my flip flops. I'd put his clothes on that morning, wanting to take part of him with me. I held on to the waistband of the sweatpants to keep them from falling down and the neck of the t-shirt kept sliding off my shoulder, but the clothes smelled of Preston, so I was more than happy to wear them. I was anticipating getting into the house, where I could bunch the shirt up around my nose and take in his scent without embarrassing myself in front of him.

As I pushed the front door closed behind me, I heard the unmistakable sound of his Lotus driving away. I frowned slightly before I could stop myself, but then pressed his shirt against my nose and inhaled, loving the spicy scent of him. I made my way up the stairs and walked into the bedroom, catching a glimpse of myself in the mirror that hung on the wall near the closet.

The first thing I noticed was that I looked a mess. My hair was wild and crazy and there were dark circles under my eyes. When I moved closer to the mirror to inspect my reflection, I saw that although I looked tired, I looked sated. My eyes were clear, my cheeks rosy, and my lips full and swollen. I looked exactly like someone who had spent the weekend in bed having sex.

Even though I'd taken a shower with Preston that morning, my hair was obviously enraged and it needed a do-over, so I went into the bathroom to turn on the shower. I peeled off Preston's shirt, smelling it one more time, and then folded it, along with his sweatpants, and laid them neatly in my pajama drawer.

I stepped into the shower and let the water run over me as my mind wandered to the fantastic weekend I'd spent with him. So many images flashed through my mind – some of them sexy, some of them sweet, and some of them downright filthy. Each one made me smile and as I lathered up the shampoo in my hair, I thought of ways I could repay him for such a wonderful weekend.

"Lena?" I heard Derrek's voice and stilled instantly. I hadn't heard him come into the house or into the bedroom and was completely caught off guard. There was no hiding from him though; he knew I was here.

"Yes?" I called out.

"Are you almost done? I need to shower before work."

"Uh, yes. Just give me a moment." I put my head back under the water to rinse the shampoo out. Suddenly, the shower curtain was thrown aside and Derrek stepped into the stall behind me, completely naked. My hands went immediately to cover myself, my mouth gaping open at him. "What are you doing?" I shrieked, eyes narrowing.

"Come on, Lena. It's not like we haven't showered together a million times before."

"Derrek, you know it's different now," I said. I went to step out of the shower but felt him grip my upper arm, keeping me where I stood. He pressed me up against the wall of the shower and the chills ran down my spine, fear coursing through my veins. This was the exact opposite of how I felt when Preston had done the same thing not an hour before. "Let me go," I said, with as much conviction as I could manage, but even I could hear the fear making my voice shake.

"Where did you go when you left the gala?"

"I wasn't feeling well, so I left."

"Yes, but where did you go?" His hand squeezed tighter around my arm and I tried to wiggle free from his grasp.

"Derrek, you're hurting me."

"I checked the records from the alarm system. It shows someone came home that night and deactivated the alarm, set it again when they left, but then no one came home again all weekend." His eyes were wild and looking straight into mine. "Where were you?"

"I went to Samantha's house," I cried, finding the lie came to me quickly.

"All weekend?"

"I was sick and she didn't want me alone. She knew *you* wouldn't be here." His grip tightened on my arm and his body pressed into mine. I cringed, looking away, trying not to let my body shiver in revulsion caused by his skin touching mine.

"You should have told me, Lena. I would have come home to take care of you." His voice dropped low, and in years past it would have turned me on instantly. A month ago, even, had Derrek joined me in the shower, pressing his naked body against mine, I would have welcomed him and a chance to save our marriage, but now it was a lost cause. It took all my strength not to yell and scream at him that I knew the truth, I knew he was cheating and I had moved on as well. I bit my lip to keep the admission inside, but holding Preston's name inside me hurt almost worse than the grip Derrek had on my arm.

"Where were *you* all weekend, Derrek? Surely you couldn't have been at work this whole time?"

"Of course I was. I have spent the last seven years building this life for you, for us, and you couldn't be more ungrateful."

"I didn't want this life. I wanted you. I wanted the man I married, the man I fell in love with. But somewhere along the line he went away, abandoned me. So, excuse me if you're not the first person I call when I need someone."

"Who is the first person you call then, Lena?"

"Sam." My answer was quick, but I knew my eyes were darting back and forth between both of his. I was never a good liar and I was sure he didn't believe me.

"I wonder what Sam would say if I called her and asked her how she'd spent her weekend."

My heart rate sped up at his words. He couldn't get to Sam before I had a chance to talk to her. "She'd tell you exactly what I have. Now, please, let go of me so I can go to work." I wrenched my arm away from him and held in a sigh of relief when he let me go. I dashed out of the shower, grabbed my towel, and proceeded to get ready for work the fastest anyone ever had in the history of man. I was dressed and heading for the door before Derrek had even left the shower.

I nearly ran to the garage door, hopped in my car, and peeled out of the driveway before he could catch me or make me stop. When I was a mile or two away, I pulled into a parking lot and found a spot, parked my car, and let out a loud breath.

Then I had a breakdown.

My heart was pounding, hands shaking, breaths coming faster and faster. I grabbed my phone and called Sam.

"Hello?" she answered.

"Have you heard from Derrek?" I asked.

"Lena? What's wrong? Are you okay?"

My terrified voice had given me away. "Did Derrek call you?"

"No. What's going on? Where are you?"

"I'm on my way to work. I was at home and Derrek showed up asking me where I had been all weekend." I took in a staggering breath, trying to get all the words in my brain to make their way out of my mouth. "I told him I was with you all weekend. Please, Sam, *please*, if he calls you I need you to tell him I was with you. Tell him I came over Friday night, and stayed until this morning."

"Of course. Whatever you need. I'll do anything, but you have to tell me what's going on."

"I can't right now. But I will. I promise. But remember, if Derrek calls you, please tell him what I told you."

"You're scaring me, Lena."

"I'm fine," I lied. "I'll be okay." I sighed and wiped a tear that had escaped. "Can I call you later? I need to get to work."

"Of course. Any time. Be safe, okay?"

"I will, and thank you for everything."

We hung up and I put my car in drive, continuing my drive to work.

A few hours later, after countless sideways glances at my appearance and a few comments from concerned co-workers, I took my lunch break in a private conference room and called Preston.

"Sweetheart," he said in greeting. It sounded as if just saying that word was a relief to him, as if it was a release.

"Preston," I countered, suddenly very close to tears. "I don't think I can wait until eleven to see you." Perhaps I sounded needy and insecure, but that was exactly what I was feeling at the moment so it was useless to hide it.

"What happened?"

"Derrek came home this morning while I was getting ready for work."

"Shit."

I didn't really know what else to say, but just speaking those words to him was already making me feel better.

"Did he touch you?" Preston's voice was hard and deep. He felt very far away and I knew if I told him the truth about what had happened he would snap. I didn't want him turning into a loose cannon if I could help it.

"No," I lied.

"Don't lie to me, Lena. Don't you fucking cover for him."

"Preston," I whispered. I shouldn't have called him. "I'm sorry, I have to go."

"So you're choosing to protect him?"

"I'm not protecting him. I'm trying to protect you. I can hear how mad you are and I don't want you doing anything crazy. I can't win here, Preston. Either I tell you what happened and you fuck everything up with your temper, or I keep it all inside and Derrek wins again. I can't take this anymore."

"I'm coming to your work."

"Please don't. Everyone here already thinks I'm crazy with the way I showed up this morning. I just wanted to hear your voice. I thought maybe it would calm me down."

He was quiet for a moment and all I could hear were his rapid breaths, but with each passing moment, they slowed. Then, finally, he asked calmly, "Can I pick you up when you're off?"

I sighed in relief at his voice, soothing and warm. This was the Preston I'd wanted to hear from, the man I thought could make me feel better about the terrible morning I'd endured.

"I'd love that," I whispered.

Later I received a text message from Sam.

That fucker called me at work this morning asking how I'd spent my weekend.

What did you say?

I told him to go fuck off.

I laughed, a real, loud, therapeutic laugh. I felt more tension lift from my shoulders and smiled, looking down at my phone.

You just made my day.

Are you ready to tell me what happened between you two?

I sighed, because I really wasn't. I wanted to tell her, eventually, but I'd just managed to calm down and focus on my work.

Can we meet for lunch tomorrow? I just need a day to let my mind wrap around everything.

Sounds great. But call me if you need anything before then. I know you're going through a lot right now. I just want to make sure you don't push me out of your life.

Her words made me frown. I was going through a lot and perhaps I needed a little space to figure everything out, but Sam was my best friend and I couldn't imagine going through life without her.

I would never push you out, Sam. I need you more now than ever. Just bear with me for a little while. I will see you tomorrow.

See you then.

Chapter Five

That evening when I left work, Preston was waiting outside my building, leaning up against his Lotus, like every woman's *Sixteen Candles* fantasy. Arms folded over his chest, ankles crossed, sexy black leather jacket stretched over his shoulders; he looked just as I liked to picture him in my mind. I walked up to him with a smile on my face, a true miracle after the day I'd had.

"Hey," I said as I stopped a foot away from him. We'd spent the weekend in bed together, but all of a sudden, I was unsure how I was supposed to greet him, especially since we were in public. I was very much still married and still trying to appear the happily married person I'd always hoped I'd be.

"Hey," he said in response, the corner of his mouth perking up as if he could read my mind and knew all I really wanted to do was press my mouth against his and run my fingers through his beautiful hair. He jolted away from the car and opened the door for me, making sure I was snugly inside before closing it. I watched him walk around the front of the car and get in on his side. He started the Lotus, which purred like a cat looking for some affection, and drove out of the parking lot.

Once we were out of the lot and a few blocks away, he reached across the console and placed his hand on my knee, gently squeezing. I turned my head toward him, smiling shyly, thankful he'd made the first move to touch me. I still wasn't sure how we were progressing from our weekend together. I reached down to his hand, which he turned over, lacing his fingers through mine.

"I've got some news," he said as he expertly took a corner with only one hand on the wheel.

"Please let it be good news."

"It's not bad news, but not really good either."

"Okay, well, let's get it over with then."

He stopped at a red light and turned to look at me.

"The house he goes to? The one Jessica lives in as well? His name's not on the deed. It's just in her name. I was hoping he owned it and that could be some piece of evidence against him, but either she owned it before they started seeing each other, or he was smart and put it in her name. The car she drives is just in her name as well."

"Damn," I whispered. "What else can we look at?"

"I'm still trying to access bank statements to see if they share an account, but honestly, if the house is just in her name, I doubt he'd make a mistake like share a checking account with her. Other than that I can try to find small things, like electric bills, water bills, stuff like that, just to see if we can prove he lives there, but a piece of mail isn't necessarily going to hold up well in front of a judge."

"So you're saying the house was our best bet and we lost it?"

"All I'm saying is that the house isn't in play anymore." He accelerated as the light turned green, but he looked over at me briefly. "I'll find something, Lena. I promise." He squeezed my hand. "I've got a few more ideas," he said, not elaborating. I didn't push, either. I trusted him to do his job. I was instantly reminded that this was a job to him. I wasn't sure how I felt about that anymore. I'd hired him as a private investigator to help me make a clean exit from my marriage, but in the last few days everything had changed. Now, at least for me, it felt as if he was helping me escape my marriage for different reasons. Perhaps, I hoped, because he wanted to be with me, free from Derrek and his twisted ways. But, to be honest, I wasn't sure what Preston wanted after all this was over.

"Where are we going?" I asked, suddenly aware we were not heading to my house.

"My place."

"Preston," I began.

"This isn't up for negotiation, Lena. You're coming with me back to my house. We're going to have dinner and you're going to tell me what happened this morning."

"I need to go back to my house tonight."

"No. You don't."

I didn't bother arguing with him. I knew he'd never give in. Instead, I turned my head and looked out the window, watching the city pass us by as we headed into the hills to the west. As his Lotus wound through the tree-lined roads that led to his house, I started to feel tired, the events of the day obviously taking a toll on me. I yawned as we pulled into his garage and stifled another one as he led me into the house by the hand.

He walked me into the bedroom, the sheet and comforter still a mess from our weekend together, and walked me to the bed. He gently urged me to sit down and then knelt down and moved closer to me until he was just a breath away.

"I missed you today," he whispered, his eyes moving back and forth from my eyes to my lips.

"Preston," I started, wanting to tell him I missed him, too, wanting to talk about what was going on between us, but I was stopped when his lips closed the distance and pressed up against mine. It was the softest, sweetest, slowest kiss I'd ever had, and it both excited me, my pulse thumping harder and harder, and also made me sleepier. They were a strange kind of drug, his kisses.

"Lie down, sweetheart. Take a nap. I'll get dinner situated."

A smile twitched on my lips. "You don't cook."

He matched my smile and his hands slid up my thighs in a sweet caress. "I said I'd situate it, not make it. Do you prefer Chinese or Indian food?"

I leaned forward to kiss him and his hand moved to the back of my neck, taking the kiss deeper than I intended, but I wasn't about to argue with him.

"Chinese sounds good," I said against his mouth when the kiss finally ended. He smiled and kissed me quickly one more time before he stood up and walked out the door, flipping off the lights as he left.

I looked around the room and felt surprisingly comfortable. I stood and peeled off my work clothes, settling in the bed in just my panties and bra, loving the feel of his soft sheets against my skin. It didn't take long for me to drift away, surrounded by the scent of Preston as I pulled his pillow into my chest.

When I woke, it was to a gentle hand brushing against my cheek. My eyes fluttered open and I saw Preston's face leaning over me and his body next to mine. He was sitting on the edge of the bed, his hand pushing my crazy hair from my face. I stretched, much like a cat waking up from a long nap, and the way my muscles had been tightly coiled all day with stress, the stretching felt magnificent.

As I stretched out in Preston's bed, I noticed his eyes wandering down the part of my body not covered by the sheet. He was getting a pretty decent view of me in barely any clothing and I loved the way his eyes darkened and his tongue darted out to wet his lips. His finger came up and gently pushed the sheet further down, revealing that all I had on under the sheet were panties.

"Is dinner ready?" I asked with mock innocence. He narrowed his eyes at me and they blazed with lust. I thought it would be fun to tease him, but all I managed to do was turn myself on as well. As his eyes moved from mine, they ran down my body, leaving a hot trail as if he were actually touching me. I couldn't help but squirm under his gaze, feeling the heat from him move over me.

"Do you always wear underwear this sexy to work?" His eyes were still lingering on my body as he asked his question, and I felt goose bumps rise on my skin.

"I always wear nice things under my clothes." My voice was shaking slightly. I swallowed and tried to sound less like a scared little girl. "It makes me feel sexy if I've got something nice on under my clothes; like I'm keeping a secret no one knows about."

"Well," he said, his eyes moving back up to mine. "I know your secret now and I agree. It is very sexy." With no more words between us, he stood up and walked into his closet. Surprised by his hasty exit, I pulled the sheet up over my breasts, trying to cover the sight I thought he had just been enjoying. When he came out, he had something in his hands. He came back to the bed and held it out to me. I recognized the fabric and gave him a questioning look. He shrugged. "I stopped by your house earlier while you were still at work and picked up some of your things. I didn't want you to be uncomfortable while you were here and even though I'd love to stare at your body dressed up in satin and lace all fucking day long, it's not conducive to a productive lifestyle."

I grinned at him as I put the familiar nightgown over my head and threaded my arms through the short sleeves. There was a time, even just days ago, when him being in my house without me would have sent off all kinds of alarms in my mind. But now, to the contrary, I felt his urge to break into my house to get me the things that would make me comfortable sweet. He held his hands out for me, pulling me up to him, wrapping his arms around my waist.

"Damn," he said as he pressed his lips to the sensitive spot where my neck met my shoulder. My hands instantly found their way into his hair.

"What?" I whispered.

"I thought if I brought you the most modest piece of sleepwear I could find, it would make me want you less." I giggled and then gasped as his tongue flicked out to lick my skin. "Turns out," he said as he nipped at my neck, "it doesn't matter what you've got covering you, because I can still see every single inch of you in my mind. The nightgown is just teasing me, asking to be taken off."

"Preston," I rasped, his hands moving from my waist to my ass, pulling me against him, pressing his erection into me.

"You hungry, baby?" he said, as if he weren't currently pawing at me.

"Yes," I groaned. I was hungry for him. For us. For all of it. He gently bit my neck, trailed his teeth up to my jaw, and then traced the edge all the way to my chin, where he ended with a tiny kiss.

"Let's go eat dinner then." His hand found mine and before I could protest he was pulling me from the room and down the hall toward the kitchen. I followed without objection, but I wore a frown until I saw the smorgasbord of Chinese food waiting on the dining room table. "I didn't know what you liked, so I might have gone overboard and ordered a little bit of everything."

"You didn't have to do all of this. I would have been happy with some rice and crab puffs."

"I'd do anything to make you happy," he said, all playfulness gone from his voice. I turned and saw the lust gone from his eyes. The only expression he wore was one of earnest. I smiled at him, loving the way he chose to care for me.

"I'm beginning to realize that." I pressed my hand to his cheek, gently rubbing my thumb against his skin. I leaned forward and kissed him chastely. "Thank you for dinner," I said, my forehead pressed against his.

"You're welcome. Come on. Sit. Let's eat."

As we ate the Chinese food, which we'd never be able to finish because it could have fed an entire Chinese village, I realized there were fundamental things I didn't know about Preston. When we first met, he asked me quite a few questions about myself and I never really reciprocated because asking questions wasn't part of my job. But now, as I sat across from him at his dinner table in my nightgown, it became apparent there were things about him I wanted to know. Things a woman should know about the man she's sleeping with.

"Preston?"

"Yes, baby?" he said as he dropped a dumpling in his mouth from his chopsticks.

"Will you tell me about your family?"

He swallowed and took a sip of his water, but then he gave me a questioning look. "What exactly do you want to know?"

I shrugged. "I don't know. General stuff. How many siblings you have, whether you got along with them, if you see them often, if you're close with your mom and dad. Stuff like that." I took a breath, not realizing I would be nervous asking him about himself. "I just feel like you know a lot more about me than I know about you. I want to know you."

His eyes softened at my admission and a smile hinted at his lips. "I have two brothers and a sister." His smile grew wider. "A twin sister, actually."

"You have a twin?"

"Yeah. She's pretty great. You'll have to meet her soon."

"What's her name?"

"Piper," he said with a gorgeous, loving smile.

"Piper and Preston," I said, testing the name duo out. "Who's older?"

"I am, by three minutes. She's the baby of the family and she's got three older brothers. We made her teenage years miserable," he said, laughing.

"Does she live nearby?"

"She lives in New York City, actually. We moved there together after college, but when I wanted to leave the city to come back to Portland, she wanted to stay." He started to push his food around his plate with his fork.

"You miss her."

He shrugged this time. "I do, but I know she's happy there."

"Are your brothers local?"

"Yeah. They both work for my dad at his law firm in town."

"Names?"

"Parker and Patton."

I laughed. "So your parents liked the names with Ps?"

"Who? Pamela and Paul? Yes. They liked the P names."

I laughed louder this time. "Are you serious?"

"Perfectly," he said with a face made of stone, which only made me laugh louder.

"Well," I said through chuckles, "you'll have a big decision to make when you get married about whether to hold out for a woman whose name starts with a P."

"Oh, no," he said loudly. "I'm not putting my wife and kids through that. There will be no name alliteration happening." His gaze lingered on me for a moment and then he asked, "Do you have any siblings?"

"Nope. I was an only child. Well, sort of. I had a sister, but she died when I was very young. I don't even remember her."

"Oh. I'm so sorry," he said, sitting up a little straighter with my news.

"No, really, it's okay. I'm mean, it's not okay, but it was a long time ago. Like I said, I don't even really remember her. I just remember the idea of her, kind of."

"Do you mind if I ask what happened?"

"No, not at all. It was the Fourth of July and we were at a party a friend of my parents was throwing. Their house was near a lake and somehow Nadia wandered away and drowned." I sighed, remembering that day through the lens of my three-year-old eyes. "It was really tragic and, naturally, my parents took her death very hard. As I grew up, I dealt with the fact that my parents were really protective of me and terrified something would happen to me." I looked back down at my plate. "I'm sorry. This conversation got really depressing all of a sudden. I didn't mean to bring you down."

"Hey, it's fine. I'm really sorry your family went through that. I can't imagine…"

"I know. It's not something anyone should have to go through. We did, though, but I'm okay."

"So your parents kept you on a tight leash then?"

"Extremely tight. I couldn't even talk to boys on the phone until I was sixteen, let alone get in a car and go on a date with one. I was never allowed to sleep over at friends' houses and it took every trick in the book to finally convince my parents to let me get my driver's license." I stood up and took my plate to the sink and Preston followed me. He took my hand, led me into the living room and pulled me down onto the couch, setting me right between his thighs so my back rested against his front. I let myself relax into him, enjoying the warmth his chest was giving me, smiling as his arms wrapped around my shoulders, holding me to him.

"I'm sorry you lost your sister," he whispered into my shoulder, gently kissing me there. "But it sounds like you lost a lot more than just a sibling."

I nodded. "Perhaps." My mind was racing, not accustomed to thinking about Nadia and how her death affected me or my life. My little ploy to learn more about Preston had backfired and now I was lost in my head, connecting dots I'd never really seen on the same page before. "My parents, protective as they were, had a very specific plan for my life. They had a very clear and safe path laid out for me, and I never questioned them. I never once thought for myself or thought about whether or not what they wanted for me was what I wanted for myself."

"Do you think that's why you ended up with someone like Derrek?"

"Oh, I ended up with Derrek because it was exactly what my father wanted. There's no doubt about that. But it wasn't only his fault. I loved Derrek. The guy I met my sophomore year of college is not the same man I'm married to today. But my whole life, my father tried to manipulate me to do what he wanted. It all came from a place of love, but it was suffocating. I was sent to an all-girls school so I wouldn't get caught up with boys. I was forced to volunteer after school, which made it impossible to have a social life. My parents needed to know where I was and what I was doing all the time, and even though they were only scared of losing me, they ended up pushing me away."

I snuggled closer to Preston, letting my mind run away with me and allowing my mouth to speak the words I'd only ever thought before, never said aloud.

"When I met him and my parents found out who he was and who his father was, they made it easy for me to be with him. They gave me some slack, but they didn't really give it to *me*; they gave it to him. I was allowed to move out of the dorms my junior year, but only if I moved in with him. They allowed me to choose my major, but only because I could use it to work for either my parents, or his, one day.

When I graduated, they gave me enough money for a down payment on a house, but only if I bought the house with Derrek. They made me save the money until I was married and then gave it to him when we were ready to buy our first home."

I stiffened as I thought about the deaths of my parents and how every single part of my father's business had been left to Derrek. I had been a pawn in my father's game, only used to acquire the son he'd been longing for his entire life. A son capable and qualified to run his business. I'd been something he could bargain with, something he was willing to give up if it meant he'd gain a son.

My eyes closed as I felt Preston's lips gently move from my shoulder up my neck. He wasn't trying to seduce me; he was trying to comfort me. He was listening, so I kept talking.

"Throughout my marriage, I constantly asked for things from Derrek, but it was never a decision just made by him and me, it always involved our parents. Like having a baby. I wanted a baby so badly. I wanted to have children young. I wanted to be that young, beautiful pregnant woman who still had enough energy to run around with a five-year-old. I wanted to be a grandparent young enough to have sleepovers and take my grandkids to the park." I felt that familiar prickling in the back of my throat and knew I was close to tears.

"Now, I'll be lucky to have kids at all." I paused and took a deep breath, still trying to fight off crying. "Every time we spoke about children, he kept talking about 'The Plan'. He and my father had a plan, a big plan apparently, and kids didn't fit into 'The Plan' right away. He always told me 'later,' but I'm pretty sure he wasn't ever going to give me children."

That thought was sobering. If I hadn't found out about his secret life, if I hadn't decided to move on, he might have denied me children forever. At least now I had a chance.

"You never just went off the pill?" Preston murmured the words against my cheek, his hand brushing over my bare arm.

I laughed. "It wouldn't have worked. He never trusted me and always used a condom." I turned so my cheek was resting against his chest. "It's okay. I'm better off this way. I'm glad I never made a child with him, then I'd be tied to him for the rest of my life."

"You've got time," he whispered in my ear.

"I know," I replied, just as quietly. My heart rate spiked as I formulated my next question. I thought about not asking it at all, but wanted desperately to know the answer. With my fingers trailing faint circles along his forearm, wrapped tightly around me, I asked quietly, "Do you think you ever want to have children?"

He didn't answer right away and I couldn't feel any change in his body to my question, but I held my breath waiting for his answer.

"Someday," he breathed against me, and my whole body felt lighter, as if he'd thrown me a life jacket in the middle of a raging river. I knew if he'd said no, I would have made myself leave eventually. There was no point in being with a man who didn't want children – it was a deal breaker for me and it would have killed me to walk away from him.

"Someday," I whispered back. It wasn't any kind of promise from him, or even a suggestion, but it made my heart soar knowing I could spend time with him without worrying about *that*. I decided to change the subject and move on to something else. "Have you ever been married?"

I felt his head shake against me. "No. Never met the right person."

"Never even came close?" I pried.

"I had a few long-term relationships, and one really serious girlfriend, but none of them ever made me feel like I needed to cement our relationship, you know? I never felt like I couldn't live without them." I felt his tongue dart out and flip against my earlobe; my body shuddered in response.

"Oh," I managed. "That's too bad," I said, only because I was looking for words to fill the silence.

"Actually," he said as he brought his lips to the skin just below my ear. "It's fucking fantastic. If I'd married any of them, I wouldn't be here with a sexy-as-sin woman between my legs."

And just like that my breath was gone from my body. My veins zipped with electricity, and I was wet. His hands slowly slid across my chest and grazed over my nipples, which were taut points, stretching to meet his touch, aching to feel his hands on them. As he palmed my breasts, my hands fell to his thighs and I gripped him tightly, arching my back and pressing further into his hands.

I moaned and my eyes closed as his fingers teased me through my nightgown and bra.

"This might end up being my favorite piece of clothing you own," he said softly.

"Preston," I begged, writhing against him. He'd ignited something hot and electric in me and it was burning me from the inside out. "Please…"

Without warning, his ankles hooked around each of my legs, splaying them open, spreading me wide on his couch. Then his hands grabbed my wrists and pulled them up to wrap around the back of his neck.

"Lace your fingers together behind my neck, Lena."

I did as he asked me to, my chest moving up and down with my labored breaths.

"Now, don't move your hands from my neck. If you do, I'll find a way to bind you, baby, and I'd rather spend my time pleasing you than punishing you." His ankles moved even farther apart, spreading me even wider. His hands brushed down my body, starting at my wrists, smoothing down my arms and grazing over my breasts. Then he pressed the palms of his hands on my sides and spread them over my hips, squeezing me gently, his fingers digging into my skin.

He gripped my nightgown and pulled it up, urging me to lift my hips so he could get it all the way up and over my breasts. He didn't try to pull it over my head, but he did use it to cover my eyes, shrouding me in darkness. I shivered when I pictured what I must have looked like: splayed out on his couch, head covered, legs spread, breaths coming quickly.

I couldn't see anything, so my eyes closed and I tried to listen for cues as to what he would do next.

I felt his touch start right between my breasts. One hand slid down the center of my body, in the valley between my breasts and continued down to my bellybutton. My breath hitched as he played with the hem of my panties, his finger just ducking under the elastic and tickling the skin there.

"Do you want me to touch you, sweetheart?"

"Yes," I panted immediately, wanting his hands on me, *in me*, desperately.

His hand moved lower into my panties, just over the neat patch of hair on my mound. "Here?" he asked, and I could hear the smile in his voice. I shook my head back and forth quickly. He moved his hand down just a little more, still not close enough and I groaned in frustration. "Here?"

"No."

"Where, love?"

My heart stopped at his words. Stopped, then soared, and then thundered again. "Lower," I moaned.

"Show me," he whispered against my neck.

I bent at the waist, raising my hips up to meet his hand, guiding his finger to the right place – the place that ached for him. My hands behind his neck gave me the leverage I needed to move in just the right way, so that his finger slid right over my cleft and I sighed in relief. "There," I said, sounding terribly turned on and needy.

"Ah, I see," he said as he sunk his finger into me. I cried out, the invasion so beautiful and intense. His one finger came out of me and slid up to circle my clit and I came off the couch, back arching, fingers digging into the back of his neck. "Fuck, Lena. You're on fire."

"Help me," I cried, needing more from him.

"Always."

With that, he pressed two fingers back into me, pumping in and out, aggressively finding a rhythm that had me panting, squirming, and moaning, all while silently begging him to both make me come and never stop touching me all at the same time.

While his one hand plunged fingers in and out of me, his other hand freed a breast from my bra and began pulling and tugging on my nipple. The two sensations combined sent me into a dizzying tailspin, and I was lost in it all.

His thumb found my clit and he made slow, lazy circles around it, never touching it, just teasing it. My hips, again, searched for the friction my body so fiercely desired, grinding up against his hand, hoping to catch the right angle to send me over the edge. I felt him chuckle, which only made me more determined, throwing more vigor into my efforts.

Without any warning, he pulled out of me and took his hand from my breast, leaving me cold and frustrated. I groaned my displeasure, but still couldn't see anything to determine what was going on.

His hands came to mine and pull them over his head. My nightgown came up over my head and he pulled it up my arms and off my body. I left my eyes closed, not wanting to break the spell between us. I wanted him to be in control, wanted him to take charge. I wanted to trust him and give him everything. His ankles released my legs and he scooted away from me, leaving me for just a moment sitting on his couch with my hands in the air, feeling a little like an idiot.

When he came back to me, he pressed his hand against the skin between my shoulder blades and gently pushed me forward.

"On your knees, Lena," he rasped at me. My heart thundered in my chest as I maneuvered myself to my knees. My legs trembled with anticipation and apprehension, and before I knew what was happening his hands were on my hips, pulling me backward. Then his other hand was on my shoulder, pushing me down until my hands found the couch on either side of his thighs. I felt his fingers pull my panties to the side and then I felt his warm tongue glide over my opening.

I gasped, unable to keep my surprise quiet, but soon started mewling as his tongue found every spot inside me that begged for his attention. He kissed my pussy as if he'd waited to do it his whole life, ate me as if he'd been starved, and I cried out every time his tongue flicked my clit. I moaned and mewled as I rocked up against his mouth, wanting nothing more than to find that high he'd brought me to before. I felt precariously close to the edge and silently begged him to push me over, to find that spot that I knew would send me flying.

On one particularly sensitive pass of his tongue, I cried out and opened my eyes, unable to keep them closed through the jolt of pleasure, and I found myself looking directly at his erection tenting his jeans. Without thinking, I pulled open the button and undid the zipper, reaching into his briefs and pulling out his hot and hard cock.

Even though I still found myself on the edge of what would surely be a glorious orgasm, I couldn't resist the urge to put him in my mouth. I leaned down and slowly licked the head of his cock, relishing in the purely masculine smell of him and the salty taste of the pre-cum that waited for me. I placed the tip in my mouth and then took him all in, sucking him back as far as I could. I felt his leg tense underneath my hand and I felt him groan against my clit, the vibration of his voice adding another sexy dimension to our tryst.

I slid my mouth up and down, trying as much as I could to take him deeply and then swirl my tongue around his head, listening to him moan and using that to gauge what he liked most.

We devoured each other, neither one of us stopping for anything except staggered breaths and guttural moans. He found one particular rhythm, fingers crooked against the front wall of my sex, tongue flicking quickly over my clit, and the combination sent me rocketing into an intense and shattering orgasm. I came hard and fast, still recovering from the electric waves coursing through my body when I felt him slide out from under me, kneel behind me, and thrust inside.

I gasped, still sensitive from the orgasm I hadn't fully recovered from, and he cursed, all manner of four-letter words falling from his mouth.

"Fuck me, Lena. Shit. I love your pussy. Damn." Each word toppled from his mouth, was grunted out with gasping breaths.

I couldn't respond with more than a groan, still reeling from my climax, but I reached back to squeeze his thigh, hoping that relayed my mirrored appreciation. This wasn't flowery. It wasn't the sweet lovemaking we'd already had; this was rough, primal, and entirely base. It was dirty. It was hot.

Even though he caught me off guard, I still felt myself falling into the role, needing to participate. I started by gently moving my hips back to meet his thrusts, trying to match his rhythm. When my ass connected with his hips, we both cried out. My fingers dug into the arm of the couch, both from the bliss spiraling through me and trying to find purchase on something to keep me upright while I used my body to help Preston find his climax. I used the couch to push myself back onto him again, this time crying out from the new depths he reached inside of me.

"Christ, Lena," he growled.

We kept pace, each of us working to find that cliff we could both dive off together. His hands moved around my body, holding on to different parts, trying to get even deeper still. He gripped my hips, pulling me backward. One hand moved to my shoulder, gripping me, forcing me on to him. He even wound his hand through my hair, holding it firmly at its roots. That single act, feeling his hand woven through the length, using it to bring himself gratification, it was possibly the most erotic moment of my life – the most sexually fulfilling experience. It wasn't intimate – I couldn't even see his face – but it was. Weirdly so, in fact. His hands on me, my need to feel him in the deepest part of me possible; it screamed intimacy. I couldn't see his eyes, but I didn't need to in order to know what they looked like in that moment. They'd be dark and glassy, and they'd be focused on me.

His speed picked up and I worked to match him. When I felt him grow even harder inside me, when I heard his breaths speed up, then stop all together, I knew he was close. I pushed my ass back toward him again, but when I felt him seated in me fully, I added a swivel to my hips and ground back onto him.

He groaned, expelling his breath, but picked up his speed even more, keeping a punishing pace.

We continued this pattern a few more times, each thrust pushing both of us up that hill, until finally I found my release, only spurred on by the sound of his. His loud grunt coupled with a guttural moan was all I needed to follow him into bliss.

Chapter Six

I woke the next morning to my alarm with no arms wound around me, no warmth enveloping me, and no Preston to be found in the bed. I opened my eyes and listened for the shower, but heard nothing. Rolling onto my back, images of the night before flashed through my mind. Preston's ankles spreading my legs. His hands touching every part of my body. His mouth. I rolled back over and groaned into the pillow.

I was in trouble.

Every part of my body was sore from use. Sore from enjoyment. I'd be lying if I said I didn't love it, didn't love feeling as if every time I moved for the rest of the day I'd feel a reminder that Preston was deep inside me the night before. That he'd used my body to make himself come. That he'd brought me to my peak over and over again.

I was definitely in trouble.

I managed to climb out of bed and head to the bathroom, each slightly painful step another reminder. I hoped a hot shower would loosen me up, bring me a little relief. I found a note on the bathroom counter and I smiled as I picked it up.

You looked so beautiful sleeping, and so tired, too. I couldn't bring myself to wake you. Please make yourself at home. There's coffee in the kitchen and some fruit or muffins for breakfast. Your keys are on the counter in the kitchen, and your car is parked out front. I expect you to come home to me tonight. I'll be waiting.

I smiled because he had thought of everything. My smile never left until I found myself at my desk, trying to focus on a job that was quickly losing its appeal. I'd taken this job because it allowed me to use my business degree and because it was close to home. Derrek's company had also done work with the company I worked for, so it seemed like a good fit when I'd started right out of college. I'd worked hard, climbed the ladder, made strides, but with everything in my life up in the air, I found it difficult to harness the drive to do the work I was tasked with.

My phone buzzed in my top drawer and I pulled it out to find a text from Sam.

Still on for lunch today?

I typed my response immediately.

Definitely. Want to meet at the food trucks?

Sounds great! See you there!

When I came upon Sam at the food truck driveway, a smile took over my face and my cheeks bunched up for the first time since I left Preston's house. I walked toward her with open arms and she opened hers to me and took me in, just like she always did. We hugged and then backed away from each other, but her hands never left my shoulders.

"You okay?" she asked, her face strained with concern, a large wrinkle forming between her eyebrows.

I nodded and smiled sincerely. "Nothing a plate of noodles won't fix." She turned to stand next to me and threaded her arm through the crook of my elbow, propelling me toward our favorite Yaki Soba noodle truck.

"I've been craving these damn noodles, too."

We grabbed our plates and found an open table, sitting across from one another.

"All right, woman. I think I've been more than patient. Now it's time to spill. What's going on?"

I took a deep breath in and then thought about where in the world I was supposed to start my story. I decided that perhaps the best place was the beginning.

"Friday night I went with Derrek to a charity gala." I hadn't even gotten through an entire sentence before Sam started making fake gagging noises. I smiled at her open disgust for my husband. "Everything was fine until he introduced me to his mistress." I paused for dramatic effect.

"He. Didn't." Sam said, noodles suspended in midair, halfway to her mouth.

"He did. Her name is Jessica Fahey, and she most definitely knew I was her boyfriend's wife. She loathed me." I shrugged. "Honestly, it was kind of fun meeting her, because I totally got to fuck with her. I even asked her if she wanted to try on my wedding ring."

"You. Didn't."

"I did," I said with a smile. "Anyway, I was a little pissed off he'd been so brazen and practically shoved his mistress in my face, and when I excused myself to go to the restroom, Preston pulled me into a closet."

Sam's eyes widened, but her fork continued to her mouth. "Then what happened?" she asked around the noodles in her mouth.

"Things of a sexual nature." My eyes drifted down to the fork twirling on my plate and I could feel my face start to heat.

"No!" She gasped.

I went on to tell her all the sordid and fantastic details of our weekend together, giving her the specifics a woman only shares with her best friend. The kind of toe-curling details one has to make sure no one else is eavesdropping on. The particulars which made Sam fan herself with her napkin. Details that made us both blush, that made me ache to get back to Preston even more.

"Shit," was Sam's response.

"Indeed."

"Okay, so why did Derrek call me yesterday and freak out on me?"

My face fell as my mind fluttered to what had happened in the shower. "Derrek knows I never came home over the weekend and I needed an alibi. I told him I was with you." I looked up to meet her eyes, which were filling with rage as she put two and two together. "Thank you for covering for me."

"What did he do to you?"

I shook my head. "Nothing like you're thinking. He was just angry. I managed to get away. Preston won't let me go back."

"Good for him," she said firmly. "Even if he hadn't fucked you senseless all weekend I'd like him." All I could do was nod in agreement. "So what's the plan, then?"

"He said I'm not to go back to my house. He packed a bag for me and brought all my stuff to his house, and he says he's going to find a way to prove Derrek's cheating. He's on a mission, it would seem."

"Well, Jesus. I wonder why the hell it's taking so long."

We were both startled by the sound of my phone ringing in my purse. I saw it was Preston and answered with a smile.

"Hey," I said sweetly.

"Hey, babe. You busy?"

"Just having lunch with Sam."

"Well, I have news. But it's bad news, unfortunately. I was looking into Derrek's bank accounts, hoping to find some trail between him and Jessica. I found the accounts he has with you, but I couldn't find any others. I thought that was strange, considering how much money the company makes. I expected IRAs or 401Ks, investment accounts – anything. But I found nothing."

"So, you're saying he doesn't have an account with her?"

"Right. But there's more."

"Great," I said with mock enthusiasm.

"Since I couldn't find another account for him, I started looking into yours. You have hardly any money, Lena."

My brow furrowed in confusion. "That's not true. There's money in there."

"There *was* money in there. When's the last time you checked your balance?"

"Uh, a while ago," I stammered. Sam's face became worried and she stopped eating her noodles.

"Well, *a while ago*, Derrek started moving money directly from your savings account into an offshore account in the Cayman Islands. But this started a really long time ago. Nearly five years ago."

"What?"

"Yes. He's slowly been siphoning all your money out of the bank. But, I'll give you three guesses as to whose name is on the account I found in the Caymans."

"Jessica," I seethed.

"You're not only sexy as hell, but you're sharp as a tack, sweetheart."

"So he's taking my money and putting it in an account for *her*? That asshole."

"I don't know what he's planning based on what happened yesterday, but if I were you, I'd get to the bank and open a new account. Get what you can into a new account with just your name on it."

"How much money is in the offshore account, Preston?"

"Lena, just go to your bank, please?"

"Tell me. I deserve to know what he's giving to his whore."

"Baby," he whispered, sounding like he was in pain. No, that wasn't all of it. He sounded like he was in pain because *I* was in pain.

"Okay," I whispered back, just wanting to hang up the phone and deal with it. "I'll see you after work."

"Drive straight to my house afterward. I'll be waiting for you there."

"Okay," I said again, not able to find any other words to give to him in that moment. I heard his phone disconnect and sighed as I put my phone back in my purse. I looked up to Sam and instead of feeling sadness or shock at what was going on, I was a little annoyed. "Derrek's stealing all our money and giving it to Jessica."

"Excuse me?" Sam said, coughing on her diet Coke.

"Yeah. I'm living in a real-life movie. Derrek is transferring all our money into – get this – off-shore accounts in the Cayman Islands. Like he's in the mob or something." Annoyance was slowly making room for anger. "Derrek is a trust fund baby who wouldn't know the dangerous side of a gun if it was pointing at his forehead. Who the hell does he think he is, trying to be all James Bond with our money?"

I stabbed at my noodles, taking out my rage on my undeserving lunch. Sam and I finished eating and she walked me to my car.

"Do you want me to go with you?" She looked concerned, her eyebrows raised, worrying her bottom lip between her teeth.

"No," I say calmly, shaking my head while looking at the ground. This was slightly embarrassing. It was hard for me to imagine the way I must seem to Derrek. He must have thought me the most moronic, gullible, idiotic person alive. He probably laughed at me with Jessica behind my back. Every time he made a transfer from our accounts into hers. I could picture them, sitting on a cozy couch, her snuggled into his side, a fire roaring in the fireplace of their sin shack of a house. They were both holding flutes filled with champagne and a thoroughly trained golden retriever rested at their feet. Perfect.

"I just want this all to be over," I say with a sigh. "I don't want to keep feeling like the last seven years has been one, big, elaborate joke." Sam pulls me into a hug, but I don't move to hug her back. I just lean against her, taking the support she's offering. After a few moments, I pulled away and rubbed the crease I knew appeared between my eyebrows when I was stressed, struggling to keep my composure. "I have to go to the bank."

"You're going to go now?" She twisted her wrist to look at her watch. "Don't you have to go back to work?"

I shrugged. "I honestly feel like work is part of the charade I've been living. Whenever I'm there I feel useless and unhappy." I take in a deep breath. "It's hard for me to feel like I belong anywhere right now."

"I hate to bring up the obvious, even more so as it's bad news, but if you leave Derrek and you have nothing, you're going to need that job, Lena."

Shit. She was right. I exhaled, trying not to let tears escape with my breath. "You're right. I know you're right."

I squared my shoulders and stood up straight. "I just need to evaluate what's important right now."

"Keep your eye on the end, okay? There's a light at the end of the tunnel. This won't go on forever. Hopefully Preston will find what you're looking for."

"Here's hoping," I said as I gave her the weakest smile I could manage.

We parted ways and I decided to go back to work, taking Sam's words to heart. She was right: I would need my job when all this was over. I'd be a divorced woman and I'd need to provide for myself.

I managed to make it mostly through the work day, but did leave slightly early to make it to the bank before it closed. A helpful and friendly woman brightly informed me that my husband had, in fact, taken all of our money out of our account – all but twenty thousand dollars. I quickly opened a new account, transferred all the remaining money out of our joint account, and left the previously smiling woman with a pitying and sympathetic smile on her face. I guessed it wasn't every day the sad, forsaken wife came in and asked for the paltry remains of her previous life.

I was a little more than grumpy when I finally arrived at Preston's condo. I was floating around in a swimming pool sized haze of self-pity and aggravation. I parked my car in front of his garage, realizing it was the first time I'd driven myself to his house. I'd walked up to his door, primed to knock, when the door opened just before I made contact with my fist.

"Hey," Preston said to me as he pulled the door open. He had a hesitant smile on his face, as if he was happy to see me but expecting me to be less so.

I walked straight to him and wrapped my arms around his waist, pressing my face into his chest, taking in the scent of his aftershave and the feeling of his muscled body against mine. It was soothing to have him pressed to me, gave me a moment of relief, as if for just that one moment I could forget everything else going on. When his hands wove their way around my back and settled, pressed flat against me, just above the swell of my bottom, the calm came over me even more.

"Hi," I mumbled against him and I felt his chest rumble with soft laughter. When one of his hands came to the back of my head and slid all the way down my hair until he cupped my neck, I simply melted against him. He gave my neck a gentle squeeze, a possessive mark, and my arms instinctively wrapped tighter around him.

"I love that you came home to me," he whispered, his breath fluttering through my hair. "It feels good, yeah?"

I nodded, my cheek mashing harder into him. "Yeah."

Chapter Seven

Even though I'd had the day from hell and I didn't feel like going anywhere, Preston convinced me to go with him to dinner. He asked me to wear a dress, something nice, and I had to admit getting dressed up and putting myself back together did lighten my spirit. I felt beautiful and sexy sitting across the table from him at Lux, an up and coming restaurant in downtown Portland.

He'd ordered me a vodka martini and his neat scotch was slowly spinning as he manipulated the tumbler with his fingers. I still shivered when I heard the words, "Scotch, neat" fall from his mouth. Watching the amber liquid wet his lips was equally as arousing and I deduced he knew this fact as his eyes met mine over the rim of his glass as he slowly sipped.

"Was there anything left for you at the bank?" His words caught me off guard and I deflated a little. Pulled down from my climbing high, dragged back to reality. He put his glass back down and resumed spinning it slowly as he looked up at me.

"There was," I sighed. "But not much."

His glass stopped spinning and I watched as his fingers lost their color, white overcoming them as he squeezed the glass, anger apparent on his face.

I reached for him, letting my fingers wrap around his. His grip loosened and then he turned his hand and captured my fingers in his.

"I want you to move in with me. Permanently. I want you to come home to me every day, Lena."

My eyes widened at his words. I tried to take my hand from him, but his grip tightened and his eyes bored into mine.

"Preston," I began, but was cut off by him.

"Don't say no." His voice was insistent, assertive. Even though he was asking for something I couldn't give him, the way he asked – no, demanded – lit a fire inside me to which I was becoming accustomed. It was a persuasive elixir of possession and need, and it was exclusive to Preston. "I know all the reasons you have to turn me down."

I opened my mouth to respond but his free hand came up to stop me and my jaw snapped shut again.

"It's too soon. You're coming out of an extraordinarily bad marriage. We haven't known each other long enough. You need to be on your own for a while." He paused and his eyebrows pulled up. "Have I missed any?"

I shook my head.

"Now listen to the reasons you should give yourself over to me, take me up on my offer, and be a good girl, Lena." His hand left mine and I felt my bottom lip pull into a pout for just an instant before I could rein in my tell. He didn't need any more fuel for the fire he was slowly stoking. He left my hand cold, but his fingers found his mouth, his index finger running over the slight stubble above his lip. I swallowed hard, imagining that stubble running along my upper thigh, and felt my sex start to throb between my legs.

"One: I don't believe in God, per se, but I do believe in fate. I believe there's a reason I'm the one you've decided to help you end this. Is it bad timing? Sure. But when's the last time anyone was ready to find something as fantastic as we are together and it was just handed to them? Never. The best things happen when it's least convenient. Two: I can help support you while you sort out your marriage. I know it's not optimal, and I know you don't *need* anyone's help, but I can make it easier for you. I'd like to make it easier on you." He paused and took another sip of his scotch, swallowing slowly. "My third reason is my most compelling: I want you, Lena. I've never wanted anything more than I want you, and I'm willing to do anything to have you. I'm hoping you'll trust me to make this decision for us."

What he said was nuts. It was crazy. It was every bad idea I'd ever had, wrapped up in a bow, and put under the crazy tree. But it'd been years since someone had wanted me. And even though I knew it was a reckless decision, I couldn't admit I wasn't swayed by his words. I couldn't tell my heart to stop pounding in my chest, couldn't make my pulse stop skipping around, and couldn't keep the corners of my mouth from tipping up and even more, I didn't want to.

I could see the unease come over Preston when I didn't answer right away, and he began fidgeting with his glass again.

"I can't give you everything he gave you, can't provide the same kind of life he could, but I'm hoping you're looking for something different."

My hand instinctively found his again, trying to ease him slightly.

"Preston," I whispered, suddenly acutely aware we were having a supremely private conversation at a table in the middle of a swanky restaurant. "Look at me." His eyes found mine and I saw the worry in them. His apparent vulnerability tugged at my heart. "I'd be lying if I said I knew exactly what I wanted, or where I think I'll be in a month, or a year. But I do know that being with you has been the highlight of the last few years. Even in the wreckage that is my life," I couldn't help the small laugh that escaped me, "you've been able to give me something I've been lacking for so long, something I've always wanted."

"You haven't given me an answer."

"I don't have an answer."

"That's not good enough."

I shrugged. "It's the best I've got for now. I can't give you something I don't have, and I don't have any assurances. All I know with complete certainty is, I'm here with you right now and there's nowhere else I'd rather be."

Preston didn't move for a few moments and I felt my breath stall, afraid I'd lost him by not agreeing to his proposition. The panic that swelled within me was palpable, and I instantly wanted to take my words back, grab them right from the air and shove them back in my mouth. In fact, I opened my mouth to take it all back when he finally moved, only to grab his tumbler and throw back the rest of his scotch. He winced as he swallowed but then his gaze found me yet again.

"Lena." His voice was harsh and removed. Usually when he said my name, something inside me liquefied.

This voice made everything tense up. "I want you to walk to the ladies room, remove your panties, keep them in the palm of your hand, and then come back out here to me."

His words shocked me, but they also excited me. The memory of being panty-less in the storage closet at the gala flashed through my mind and I remembered how exhilarating it felt. I saw this man, someone who I couldn't say I knew, really, but also *did* know. I knew how he worked, how he operated, and how, most of the time, he was transparent. He was always up front with me, always telling me exactly what he wanted and so, even though I couldn't agree to some exclusive relationship where we lived together and pretended as if everything were normal and not the fuck-up my life actually was, I could give him this.

Without a word, I scooted my chair back, stood slowly, and headed toward the back of the restaurant. I found the restroom with little difficulty and thanked the bathroom gods for a single room with a lock on the door. I didn't want to have to worry about another woman seeing me peel my underwear down my legs from the stall next to me.

With the black lace bundled up between my fingers, I rested both hands against the sink and looked at myself in the mirror, trying to figure out if I recognized the woman staring back at me. It was the same face I'd always seen, but she had a glint in her eye that was new. A glow to her skin she'd never had before. She was excited about something; and far be it from me to deny myself the one person who could make me come alive again.

I took a deep breath and closed my fingers around my panties, trying to be sure no piece of errant lace peeked out and shouted to the entire restaurant what I was up to. I also pulled down on my dress, which now seemed quite a bit shorter than it had when I left Preston's condo. The respectable just-above–the-knee hem now seemed like an expressway to my most private of areas.

Walking back to our table, my eyes flitted over everyone in the room, waiting for someone to notice I wasn't wearing underwear and point it out to everyone else. When I came upon our table, I noticed Preston had moved my chair to the very edge of the table, right on the corner, and he was sitting close to the corner as well. I managed to sit down, smoothing the hem of my dress down over my ass as I did, trying to make sure no one got a free show, and I noticed our elbows were touching; that was how close our chairs were now situated.

Preston watched me sit, a satisfied grin gracing his face, making his handsome rating skyrocket. When my hands smoothed over my ass, I saw his eyebrow quirk, his grin growing. My heart fluttered thinking about his eyes on my ass.

He cleared his throat and held out his hand, his eyes boring into mine. I gave him a questioning look. Obviously, I wasn't going to hand him my panties out in the open.

He simply snapped his fingers and laid his open palm out again, waiting for me to deposit my underwear.

"Preston," I whispered with annoyance, leaning a smidge closer to him.

"Sweetheart," he answered, looking expectantly at me.

I quickly placed the panties in his hand and forcefully curled his fingers around them, hoping no one nearby could tell what they were.

His eyes lit up when the lace hit his skin and I saw his fingers grinding into his palm, feeling the fabric. Then I watched, horrified, as he placed them in the front pocket of his suit jacket, a tiny bit of black lace peeking out, taunting me, like a dirty, erotic pocket square.

Just then our waiter brought our meals and my heart stopped while I waited for him to notice my underwear. Waited for him to catch on to us, realize our dirty game, and throw us out with our heads bowed in shame. But he didn't bat an eyelash at us. Didn't notice a thing. It was then I realized I was being paranoid and I was likely going to have to play along with Preston's game.

"Calm down, Lena. You're practically trembling in your chair and even though I like to see you tremble, I usually like it to be caused by me making you come, not because you're about to have a heart attack. No one knows what we're up to."

I took a deep breath in as I closed my eyes. He was right. I could eat a meal with no panties. No big deal.

I opened my eyes, picked up my fork, and brought a bite of risotto to my mouth. I stopped, mid-bite, when I felt Preston's warm hand on the chilled skin of my thigh. I tensed, waiting to see where his hand was headed, but I also shivered in excitement, goose bumps rising up on the skin of my arms. His touch did magnificent things to my system, caused so many wonderful nerves to go haywire. When his hand rested between my thighs, I pressed them firmly together in an effort to maintain some boundaries, but sighed in relief. I loved his hand on me, but could hardly enjoy my meal if it wandered where it wasn't allowed.

I continued to eat, as did Preston, and we shared trivial conversation. We spoke about our day and asked questions you would usually ask on a date with someone you were trying to get to know. At some point, I had to laugh to myself, finding humor in the fact that we were doing everything backward. I was married. He'd just asked me to live with him, and I'd just asked him where his favorite vacation spot was. I also had to smile because even though it was backward, it wasn't wrong. In fact, it was the most *right* conversation I'd had with a man in years. Our situation was strange, uncommon, and perhaps a little dramatic, but the way I felt for Preston was anything but wrong.

My breath caught again when his hand slid farther up my leg, now brushing the hem of my dress. I grabbed my water, taking a sip, the muscles in my legs becoming strained from holding my knees together. His hand squeezed the fleshy part of my thigh and he leaned over to me, his face just inches from my ear.

"Open up for me, Lena," he whispered. I could not move my eyes from my plate, afraid if I met his gaze I'd give in to him. I wanted to give in to him, wanted to feel his hand slide up my leg and into me, but not here. I worried my bottom lip between my teeth and shook my head slightly.

My body was starting to betray me: my pulse was thrumming through my veins, my skin flushing with excitement, my sex becoming slicker with every second his hand begged for entrance. My body wanted what he was offering, of that there was no doubt, but the rational part of my brain was still in control – mostly.

I exhaled a breath I wasn't aware I'd been holding and my shoulders sagged when I felt his thumb making soft and slow circles on my sensitive skin just under the hem of my dress, silently asking me to do as he wanted, to let him in.

When I finally relented, gave in to him, a whimper escaped my lips as my knees fell apart. My muscles rejoiced as the stinging stopped, but new, more powerful sensations were flooding my system with every inch he gained up my thigh. His skin grazing along mine tickled in the most arousing way, prickled with the promise of pleasure, and the anticipation was nearly a physical being sitting at the table with us, it was that powerful.

I finally became brave enough to lift my gaze to him, only to find he was paying no attention to me above the table. He had no interest in conversation anymore or even to glance my way. The farther up my leg his hand roamed, the quicker my breaths came and the faster my heart thundered in my chest. I reached for my water glass, pausing at my lips as one of his fingers lightly grazed the length of my sex. Just barely and just enough for my eyes to flutter closed.

They immediately snapped open when I heard the waiter ask Preston if everything was fine with our meal. Simultaneously, Preston slid one finger inside me while answering the waiter with a, "Yes, everything is fantastic. Thank you."

I was paralyzed with the fear we would be caught, but also frozen from the thrill of feeling him inside me, feeling something very private in this very public place.

The waiter smiled and walked away, leaving us to presumably enjoy our dinner. I looked at Preston and he picked up his fork and continued to eat his pasta, his finger still pressed fully inside me.

He swallowed and then said, "Your food is getting cold, sweetheart."

"You want me to eat while you finger me?"

"No, I want to give you an experience you've never had before. I want to watch you writhe and squirm and sweat, all the while fearing someone will catch us." He moved his finger out, but then pumped back in again, this time with two. My hand slapped down on the table, palm open, making an obnoxiously loud "thwack". A few people turned their heads toward us, but turned away when they saw nothing of consequence.

"Preston, please," I said quietly as his fingers retreated again, this time coming forward and circling my clit.

"Tell me what you want, Lena."

His question was tied together with so many layers of meaning I was lost between them. Did I want him to stop finger fucking me in public? Maybe? Did I want to be with him in the way he was asking? Probably. Did I want to take the plunge to make these things happen? No. Not right now.

"You can't do it," he whispered as his fingers dove back into me, this time pumping back and forth in tight, swift blows. "Until you're absolutely sure what you want, I'm going to take what I need from you." He leaned toward me, pressing a kiss to my cheek, and from anyone else's perspective in the restaurant I'm sure it looked innocent enough, but then his mouth moved to my ear and he whispered, "I'll do whatever you want, Lena. You just have to let me know."

With that, his fingers reprised their slow thrusts while the heel of his palm began a firm, circular grind against my clit. I was thoroughly wet and only getting wetter. If I listened closely enough, I could hear the sounds our bodies were making from rubbing against each other and even though I knew, soon enough, others might start to hear, I couldn't bring myself to care.

I started to daze, one hand gripping the arm of my chair, the other wrapped around my water glass as if I were about to lift it to my mouth. In and out. Around and around. He was slowly building me toward an orgasm that would surely have me screaming the roof off this high-brow, classy restaurant.

In an effort to control myself, I lifted the water glass to my lips and sipped the water slowly. Preston shifted, his fingers sliding in even farther, then he curled his fingers, hitting an elusive bundle of nerves head-on, causing me to moan into my water.

I clamped my legs closed, trying to stave him off, trying to stop what I knew was inevitably unstoppable. Even with my knees locked together he still managed to continue to finger me at the dinner table. My clamped legs seemed to actually just keep his hand right where he wanted it. My life was compounding at that very moment. Everything was colliding and I had no control. The only thing I could do was let Preston lead me. Trust him to show me the right way.

In an instant, I put the water glass down, grabbed the cloth napkin from my lap, and tried as gracefully and inconspicuously as I could to groan into it.

I came ridiculously hard and surprisingly quietly. With my release came the relaxation which freed Preston's hand from my pussy just long enough for him to lift his hand and suck his fingers into his mouth, never breaking his gaze from mine. Even coming down from a shattering orgasm, even just after coming in a room full of strangers, I was still ridiculously turned on by his blatant sexuality, and would have climbed on top of him had we been in a different setting.

We didn't say another word to each other until we left the building. The longer we sat at the table, him ignoring what had just happened, the longer my emotions had to advance from being sated, to confused, to full of rage.

He held my coat up for me and I shoved my arms through the sleeves violently, then I took loud and hard steps through the restaurant, my heels clacking along the tile floor, until we were out on the street and I was walking at a fast clip.

"Hey, Lena, wait." He sounded like every other man I'd ever heard try to deal with an angry woman; like frustration mixed with fear. He didn't know how to handle me angry.

"Wait for what, exactly?" I shouted back to him.

"Wait for me. Look," he said, jogging up next to me. His hand wrapped around my arm, stopping me, and he turned my body to face him. "I'm sorry."

I narrowed my eyes at him. "No, you're not."

"Well, not one hundred percent, no…" His voice trailed off and I yanked my arm free.

"Ugh. Just take me home, Preston," I said as I continued to march down the street. He caught up, keeping pace with me but not reaching out to touch me.

"You're not going back to your house, Lena."

I sighed loudly, realizing even though he thought I meant I wanted to go back to the house I shared with Derrek, I'd really meant his condo. It figured that when I was really angry with him I'd have a Freudian slip.

"Fine, we'll go to your house, but you're sleeping on the couch." I turned the corner and entered the parking garage where he'd parked his Lotus. I made it to the elevator and the doors opened for us immediately. Once inside we stood at opposite ends of the car and while I maintained my best angry face, when I stole glances at him, he still looked confused and a little distraught.

The elevator doors opened and I walked out, heading right for the Lotus.

"What is it you're angry about, exactly? It seemed like you enjoyed yourself in there." He yelled across the parking structure, his voice echoing throughout.

"Enjoyed myself?" I turned on him, my dress flaring up around my knees, hair fanning out.

"You came hard, sweetheart," he said with a smug grin.

"Don't 'sweetheart' me, Preston. You did that to me even though you knew I didn't want you to."

Suddenly, he was right in front of me, pressing my back against his car, his front pressing into mine.

"You can be angry at me any day, Lena. You can throw your cute as fuck tantrums and stomp around, throwing your sass around like it weighs a ton, but don't ever insinuate that I forced you to do something you weren't onboard with."

"I was uncomfortable," I managed, even though I was sure my voice was too small to be heard.

"Good. You've been comfortable for far too long, from what I can tell. I wanted to make you uncomfortable, I wanted to show you that sometimes it's okay to trust me." As his words fell from his mouth, his eyes softened, as did his grip on my waist. One hand came to cup my cheek and his gentleness caught me off guard. "I would have stopped if you'd told me, if you'd even said anything remotely close to no. But you enjoyed it and that's okay, Lena. In fact, it was amazing. Watching you fall apart, knowing no one else in that room knew what I was doing to you. It was hotter than fucking anything I've ever seen before." His thumb moved back and forth over my cheekbone, his tenderness melting the residual anger I felt just moments before. "Are you upset because it happened, or are you upset because it felt good to let me be in control?" His face came close and his forehead rested against mine, waiting for me to respond.

"I've been lost for so long, Preston. It's scary to all of a sudden be front and center, experiencing things for the first time with someone new." I inhaled, trying to find my next words. "And I did like what you did to me, after I got over the initial shock of it all. I'm sorry if I insinuated it was forced, it wasn't. Highly discouraged, perhaps," I said, a smile tilting the corner of my mouth upward.

"I'm not going to hurt you."

"That's not a promise you can make to me."

"Perhaps not. But I can make it to myself. All I've ever asked you for was your trust."

"And my panties," I giggled, finally feeling the pressure of our argument falling away.

"Lena, I'm serious." His other hand came up and both were now on my face. "If I know you trust me, and you know I'll always protect you, then there's nothing else to discuss."

I looked him deep in his eyes, which always reminded me of chocolate, trying for the life of me to make the right decision. Trying to decide the course of my life in a parking garage, pushed up against a man's car, who had my panties tucked in his front pocket.

I leaned my forehead against his again and brought my hands to his chest. "Don't make me regret this."

"Regret what?" he said, his voice full of hope.

"This. Us. Moving forward, together."

His eyes lit up and his mouth found mine. He wasted no time taking the kiss deep, his tongue taking wide and delicious sweeps through my mouth. He growled as his hands moved down to wrap around my neck and his hips pressed into mine. I was reminded, again, that I wasn't wearing panties.

"Not here," I whispered against his lips, having met my limit on exhibitionism for one night. He kissed me again, softer this time, less needy. When he pulled away, there was a handsome smile on his face that made him look younger somehow, as if my agreeing to living with him had altered him.

"Let's go home, then." His smile only grew with his words.

"Let's," I agreed.

Chapter Eight

The next morning, I was awoken by the vibration of my cell phone from across the room. It was still in my purse, which had been flung to the floor before I had been flung on the bed. I hadn't been allowed to leave the bed for hours after, as Preston made it his mission to make me come as many times as possible in just as many positions.

I was surprised the phone wasn't dead, but ambled slowly to my purse to see who had the nerve to bother me so early. It was a text from Derrek.

Meet me at the house at eight am. Come alone and tell no one. Your future hangs in the balance. Make the right choice.

When I walked into the house, I knew Derrek was there. I could feel his smarmy presence making the air in the house dark and dank. I placed my purse on the hall tree by the door and took my jacket off, laying it over my purse.

"Lena, is that you?" Derrek's voice echoed through the house as if it were empty. It wasn't, of course, all our belongings were still there, but the house *was* empty. There was no family living there any longer, no warm feelings, and no life. It was just a very expensive storage locker for all the physical representations of a life we were both desperately trying to leave behind.

I didn't answer him but I did follow his voice. I wasn't surprised at all when it led me to his office. When I saw him sitting at his desk, for the slightest moment I was struck with how handsome he looked. He'd always appeared powerful to me, always seemed as if he was in charge, and I knew that had attracted me to him. But just as quickly as my mind noticed the things about him I found appealing, it was remembering all the things I'd learned in the last few weeks that made my stomach roil. On the outside, he looked like the perfect package, but on the inside, I knew he was rotten.

"Lena, I'm glad you got my message and decided to meet with me." He steepled his fingers in front of his face, his eyes roaming up and down my body, taking me in. I held back a disgusted shiver; his lingering glare making me nauseous.

"What do you want, Derrek?" I asked, not trying to hide my annoyance at being beckoned by him.

"Take a seat. I think it's time we had a real discussion." I held his glare for a moment, not sure I wanted to follow any instruction he threw at me. I decided, however, that I wanted this 'discussion' over as soon as possible, so I moved to sit in the club chair opposite his desk. Once I was seated I laced my fingers together and set my hands in my lap.

"Lena," he started, leaning back in his chair. "I've had a lot of fun over the last couple of weeks playing this game with you, but I think it's time it came to an end. Although, now, I wish it weren't the truth, I married a smart woman and I am tiring of watching you play dumb. The game was entertaining in the beginning, but it's becoming a burden, so I suggest we end it. Now."

I blinked at him, not letting my face give anything away.

"I'm not really sure what you're referring to, Derrek."

"Really? You're still going to play dumb? I would have pegged you differently. Surely you want to tell me off, give me what-for. I know you have things you want to say to me."

I still kept quiet.

"Fine. Have it your way, although my way would have been much more fun." He pulled a sheet of paper from a folder sitting on his desk, flipped it around, and slid it toward me with a pen. "This is a contract explaining that you agree to a divorce, leaving me everything, and you will not contest the divorce proceedings or file any further suit to gain any monetary or physical belongings gained during our silly, pathetic excuse for a marriage."

I took a deep breath in and held it. If I let it out, so many words and insults would come with it.

"Furthermore, it states you still agree to the hundred-thousand-dollar penalty for the adultery you committed many, *many* times over the course of our marriage."

"You're more delusional than I previously thought if you, even for one moment, think I'm going to pay you a hundred grand. *You* cheated, Derrek. You have a whole other family waiting in the wings. You strung me along for years."

"Where's your proof, darling?"

"Fuck you."

"No, thanks. We've tried that and it was lacking, terribly."

"You're crazy. You've got just as much proof as I do. Call your lawyer. We'll deal with this in court." I stood up and moved to the door, my hands shaking with anger.

"Lena, you don't want this to go to court, trust me. You might not have proof, but I do. Damn good proof, too."

I turned back to him sharply, my hair whipping around my shoulder, and saw him slide another paper across his desk toward me. I walked to the edge of the desk and picked up the paper, flipping it over.

My eyes focused on the photograph and my heart stopped. It stopped, then it leapt back into action, thundering in my chest, aching and pounding. My hand came to my mouth as it fell open, and I collapsed back into the chair. My hand shook and the picture trembled. My lungs burned, begging me to breathe again.

I was looking at a photo of Preston and me on the first night I'd spent at his house, after the gala. It was a black and white photo, grainy but still visible, and it was outstandingly damning. I was on his bed, on my knees, my hands grasping the slats of his headboard. Preston's hand was curled around my shoulder, his other hand rested at my waist, and his eyes were looking down, watching his cock slam into me. His mouth was open and he had what looked like wonder painted across his face as he looked at our bodies joined together. My head was tilted back, mouth gaping, and I knew the instant this picture was taken, I was crying out in complete ecstasy. Derrek had a picture of me mid-orgasm, with another man. In another circumstance, in another life, I would look at this picture and think it beautiful. But in this instant, it was ugly. It represented something ugly.

"What do you want?" I gasped, my eyes still not leaving the photo.

"I want you to leave, with nothing, and I want you to struggle for the rest of your life trying to pay me what you agreed to. I want you to think of me every day and obsess over the fact that I ruined your life."

He'd reached a new level of crazy.

"Or what?"

"This picture goes viral and if you think this is the only one I have, you're even more stupid than I could have ever imagined. I have *hundreds* of pictures of you being a filthy whore, and no judge would ever look at these pictures and believe you to be some jilted wife."

"And if I sign your paper, if I give you what you want, then what?"

"I forget you ever existed."

I thought about my life, thought about everything I'd been fighting for in the last weeks, and everything I'd put Preston through. Suddenly, I understood what he'd been saying all along. It wasn't worth it. Certainly now, when not only was I on the chopping block, but Preston too, the only sane thing I could think to do was to give it all up. To surrender.

"Fine." I said, walking back to the chair, clutching the picture. "But I want all the photos you have, and anything else incriminating."

"I don't want to look at your filth, Lena. You can have it all." He pushed the paper toward me again, along with the pen. I picked the pen up in my hand and took in a deep breath. This was exactly the ending I was trying to avoid; the ending I didn't think I deserved. The only comfort in all of this was knowing even though I'd lost a lot, I still had Preston.

I exhaled, and my hand swiped the pen along the line, and I signed the name I hated. *Lena Bellows*. I didn't want to be her anymore. The very first chance I got I would change my name. I didn't want to be connected to Derrek in any way.

As soon as I signed the paper, he slid another one my way, which he had signed, and I signed that one, then folded it up and squeezed it tightly in my hands.

"Here," Derrek said as he slid an SD card across the desk. "All the pictures are on that card. There was no other evidence, no videos or anything like that." Derrek smirked, placing his steepled fingers over his lips. "Truly, Lena, if you'd been even one tenth of the whore with me as you were with him, this might have played out differently. These pictures showed me a wanton woman I've never met."

"Perhaps, if you were one tenth of the man Preston is, I would have been more receptive," I said snidely.

"Oh, right!" he said, snapping his fingers, as if he'd just remembered something important. "That's the other piece of this puzzle."

"What are you talking about?" I was tired of listening to his voice and just wanted to leave and have this be over with.

"The other part – even more evidence you're a stupid whore." Derrek laughed out loud, his head falling back against his chair. "I'm sorry," he said between chuckles. "It's just too good."

"Just spit it out, Derrek."

"Preston, your lover, the man you've given everything up for, the man who you think you're going to spend the rest of your life with?" Slowly, an evil and wicked smirk grew on his lips and his eyes began to sparkle with excitement. "He works for me."

His words felt like a wrecking ball slamming into me. My breath stopped, my heart exploded, my veins ran dry because there was nothing pulsing through me except pain. Derrek was looking at me as if he'd just won the most important game he'd ever played.

"What?" I rasped, impressed I'd managed to say anything at all.

"I've had your phone bugged for years, darling. I was just waiting for the moment when you'd finally decided you'd had enough. When you called that firm for a consultation with a private investigator, I knew about it before you'd even told them your name." He laughed again and my mouth closed, then opened again, like a guppy. I felt tears welling in my eyes, my throat stinging with the need to cry, my body aching for the release I knew sobbing would bring. "I called the firm right back and told them their services wouldn't be needed, and I sent Preston in with one goal: to seduce you."

"No," I breathed.

"Yes, dear, and you took the bait just as I knew you would. You lasted, what? A week? You dug your own grave here, Lena."

"I don't believe you."

"Think about it," he said, suddenly sounding angry. "In the beginning, that first week, what did Preston really do for you? Nothing. He brought you along for a stakeout, for Christ's sake! What kind of private investigator would do that? He flirted with you, was inappropriate, and *pursued you*. He was on my payroll, doing a job for me."

My mind went back to that first week with Preston, thought about all our encounters, and the pieces started to fall into place: him telling me not to call him at the agency, the fact he knew my last name before I'd ever given it to him, he knew where I lived. He tried to convince me it was because he was a P.I., but really it was because he worked for Derrek, knew everything about me already, and had been fooling me from the beginning.

I felt the bile in my stomach start to make its way upward and I stood, desperate to make it out of that house, frantically trying to escape what seemed to be the inescapable. I'd given myself to a man who was working against me from the beginning. I'd fallen in love with an imposter and ruined my chances at making something for myself.

I ran for the door, grabbing my purse and jacket as I left, ambling out of the house on a sob. I couldn't see for the tears streaming down my face, couldn't hear for the pulse thundering in my ears, and I had no idea what happened when I ran into something hard. It gripped me, and wrapped its arms around me, and it smelled familiar.

Preston.

Once my mind registered who was holding me, I wrenched myself from his arms and pushed him away with more force than I'd ever used on anyone.

"No!" I screamed. I sounded, even to my own ears, like pain. There was no other word. I was the embodiment of pain. "Don't you touch me!"

"Lena, sweetheart," he started.

"Fuck you! You don't get to call me that!"

"Please, just listen to me."

"I'm done letting *men* ruin my life. Done letting men control me. I trusted you, that's the one thing you ever insisted on and I did it. I did exactly what you wanted. I trusted you and you fucked me over. Fucked me in so many ways, I can't even begin to list them all."

"No," he said, taking a step toward me. I stepped away from him and glared, making it clear he wasn't to come near me again.

"Answer one question, Preston. Just one. Do you work for him? Were you hired to seduce me? To trap me in exactly the future I was trying to escape?"

"Lena..."

"ANSWER ME!"

He sighed and I saw all the conviction leave his body. His shoulders slumped, his eyes lost their light, and he ran a hand through his hair. I knew his answer before the words even left his mouth. "Yes."

My hand shot out, faster than I'd ever moved before, and the crack my palm made against his face as I slapped him was the most satisfying sound I'd ever heard. His face slammed to the side with the impact of my hand and then I heard my own sob ring out.

"Fuck you, Preston. You're worse than he is."

I dug in my purse for my keys, got in my car, and drove away from two men who both had a hand in ruining my life. I had no idea where I was going, but I knew there was nothing left for me there.

END OF PART TWO

Part Three

PRIVATE
Getaway

Chapter One

An incessant buzzing, accompanied by an irritating beeping, pulled me out of a dead sleep, which had only been brought on by vodka and chocolate. I groaned, but rolled over slowly, blindly reaching around for my phone. When my fingers finally found it, I peeped one eye open, painfully, but all I could see was the dark veil created by my raven hair. I used my hand to sweep it aside and managed to swipe my finger over the screen of my phone, bringing it to life.

I winced from the bright light, but managed to silence the alarm that was blaring throughout the room. I tossed the phone onto the nightstand and rolled back over, ignoring the aching in my muscles and the jackhammer in my head.

That was the fourth morning my alarm had woken me up. It was a residual alarm left over from my previous life. It used to be the alarm that would remind me every morning to take my birth control pill. It was now the alarm that reminded me to not drown in my current pool of self-pity and hatred. I didn't have any birth control pills to take. I, in fact, didn't have anything with me aside from the clothes on the floor I'd been wearing when I fled from my life, the groceries I'd thought to buy before I'd checked into this motel, and my purse.

I was a mess. I'd been in this bed for the majority of the last four days and I felt it. Up until now, I'd not felt the need or want to change my situation. I'd wanted to stay in bed forever, sleep as long as the vodka would let me, and try desperately not to deal with the catastrophe I'd left behind. But I hadn't left it behind; it seemed to have followed me here and was now seeping back in. Reality.

Reality was a bitch.

I groaned again as I moved off the bed, flinging the scratchy comforter off my body, and swinging my legs over the edge of the mattress.

"Holy fucking crap," I whispered to nobody but myself. I rubbed a hand over my face, my nose crinkling up at the gross condition of my skin. I needed a shower. More than I needed anything ever, I needed a shower.

I ambled through the small motel room and found the bathroom. Switching the faucet on, I waited for the water to heat. When it was as hot as I could stand, I pulled the stopper up and watched the water fall like rain.

I climbed in, letting the harsh, hot water pelt me, stinging all the way down to my feet. I went about the business of washing the grime from my body. The tiny bottles I'd had the thought to buy at the grocery store weren't enough to last very long, but it was enough for now. As I washed my body, I held my cries in. I'd managed not to cry up until now, and I didn't intend to ever cry over Derrek or Preston. But I couldn't stop the tears that penetrated. They were tricky and sneaky, and had found ways to fall from my eyes multiple times since I'd walked out on Derrek, but I wasn't crying. Not ever.

Once dried off, I cringed as I put on the dirty clothes I'd come here in, silently cursing myself for not having the presence of mind to at least grab a new package of underwear. I'd never gone without underwear before – well, except when Preston had asked me to – but now, if ever, was the time.

Once dressed, I checked out of the motel and sat in my car, having no idea where I was headed. I hadn't thought of a plan past the parking lot, but I was determined to make a change.

I started my car and headed toward the nearest Target.

I had my new carry-on bag filled with new clothes, more tiny toiletries, a few pairs of comfortable shoes, and a paperback book I'd grabbed when the cover caught my eye, and I was near a panic attack.

I was standing in front of a giant screen, taller than I was, listing all the flights leaving the Portland International Airport that day. My mind reeled, trying to pinpoint a destination. It shouldn't have been a big deal, shouldn't have been the monumental decision my mind was forcing it to be. I knew I needed to leave, to get away, but I couldn't nail a location down. *Anywhere was better than here.* My mind wanted to attach a bigger meaning to wherever I ended up, like I should be going someplace that would scream independence and a new start, but some other part of me also wanted adventure and excitement. I wanted to go someplace I'd never been, to hopefully start living a life I'd never lived.

Unfortunately, at the moment, anywhere international was out of the question since, as I'd run from the house, I'd not thought to grab my passport. That left only domestic destinations until I could get a new one.

I had my driver's license and twenty thousand dollars. Hawaii suddenly sounded like the perfect place to start a new life.

Just thirty minutes later, I was booked on a flight and waiting at my gate. I pulled my phone out of my purse and turned it on, ignoring the influx of messages I'd ignored for four days. I did, however, send one. To Sam.

Hey. I just wanted to let you know I am okay, but I'm not going to be around for a while. I can't tell you much more, but I'll be in contact.

I hit send and my heart broke a little because I couldn't tell her everything I wanted to, couldn't tell her what happened with Derrek, what happened with Preston, and why I was leaving. And I knew she'd freak out at my vague text. But I also knew she couldn't be the one person who knew where I was – I couldn't do that to her. The less she knew, the better.

**I'll text you in a few days when things have settled down. Just know I'm okay and I love you. **

I saw a new text arrive from her, but I couldn't bring myself to open it, knowing it would just be questions I couldn't answer. So I walked to a garbage can and threw the phone away. I was officially and absolutely cut off from my old life entirely. And even though I was glad some parts were over and gone, other parts, I knew, would haunt me for a very long time. Even an ocean couldn't make me forget the things my heart wanted to hold onto. But I was hoping warm sand, beautiful sights, and a new life would help me heal and move forward.

Chapter Two

It had been three weeks since I boarded that plane to Hawaii, and even though I was far from healed, I was at least starting to put the pieces back together.

I'd never been to Hawaii before and so when I'd gotten off the plane in Maui, I'd had no idea where to start. First, I asked my cab driver to take me to the beach. When I'd first set foot on the beautiful sand, I'd taken my first deep breath in days. I could feel the air seep into my lungs, offering something I'd been lacking for years – life. I was breathing in new life.

After I'd sat on the beach for an hour or two, I walked until I found a motel that looked safe and inexpensive. I was smart enough to know Hawaii was expensive, but I also knew if I didn't watch my money, it would be gone long before I'd accomplished my task of, well, finding a new life.

Luckily, the motel had vacancies and wasn't too pricey. I paid upfront for a whole week and then asked the woman helping me where the best place to buy some groceries would be, and how to take the bus to get there.

"You're all by yourself?" the woman asked, hesitantly. She was a round woman, probably in her fifties, and I assumed she was a native as she looked everything like a born and raised Hawaiian woman would look in my mind. She was soft and warm and beautiful. Her dark hair was flowing freely around her shoulders, graced with just a few strands of silver laced throughout. Admittedly, if she'd been a man and asked me the same question, I would have lied and made up a story about my husband waiting in the car, but something about this woman left me feeling like she couldn't hurt a fly if she tried.

"Yes. This is sort of an unexpected trip."

"What brings a girl as pretty as you to the island all alone? Surely there's someone who wants to keep you company."

I couldn't even bring myself to think of a lie for her, something to assure her I wasn't as lonely and pathetic as she was trying not to see me as.

"Nope. No one wants to keep me company."

She gave me a sad look, but then directed me to a small grocery store and told me which bus I could take to get there.

"If you ever need anything, I live just on the second floor in room thirty. If I'm not here, I'm usually there." She paused, giving me an encouraging look. "I'm a real good listener, if you ever need to talk."

I smiled at her because what she was offering was sweet. I held my hand out to her. "My name's Lena."

"I'm Rose," she answered with a wider smile.

"It's nice to meet you," I said as I let go of her hand. "And thanks for the directions."

"Anytime," she replied, and I got the feeling she wasn't only talking about the directions.

This room was nicer than the one I'd gotten in Portland. I put my bag down on the bed and flipped on the lights in the attached bathroom. I saw my reflection in the mirror and instantly knew why Rose had seemed concerned about me. I looked just as torn up on the outside as I felt on the inside.

There were dark, plump bags under my eyes. My hair was in disarray, tumbled on top of my head in a dark nest of tangles and knots. My skin was pale, nearly gray. In other words, I looked like shit. I sighed at my appearance, but knew there was nothing more to do about it than sleep and eat.

Feeling more gross than anything, I hopped in the shower, hoping to wash away the grime of a day's worth of traveling. When I emerged from the shower, I didn't feel much better, but I looked it. The sun had set, and after a yawn, I decided it would be better to explore the island tomorrow in daylight than try to navigate a new area in the dark.

I flipped off all the lights and crawled into the queen sized bed, but only curled up on one side. I closed my eyes and tried to empty my brain, but just like the last few nights I'd spent by myself, my mind decided to torture me with images and memories of Preston. It was a nightly battle between my head and my heart. My heart remembered his touch, his words, and his body. I rolled back and forth, trying to get comfortable while I pictured Preston above me, slowly pumping in and out, while whispering sweet words of love and promises of a future together. My brain ached with the sound of Derrek's words floating around my head. Preston was hired by Derrek to ruin my life – and he'd succeeded.

Still, I didn't cry. I never let go of the control of my body, except for the tears that still slid silently down my face. That was something I couldn't control. In the dark, tears spilled. But I managed to keep it to that – just tears. No sobs. No hiccups. No wailing. I needed to keep something for myself, and control was the only thing I had left. I would give no more of my body to a man who hadn't wanted it to begin with.

For three weeks this had been my nightly routine: Go to bed with the intention of shutting my brain down, then give in to the relentless flooding of memories of Preston. I hated it, but I think I loved it more. It was sadistic and completely debilitating. Every morning I looked like I hadn't slept a wink, and in truth, I wasn't sleeping much.

But today I needed to look better than I felt. Today I had a job interview with a prominent marketing firm on the island. It was an entry-level position. I would be starting from the bottom and working my way up, but for once that was going to be a relief. Never had I worked for much of anything. I'd had a lot of things handed to me, and I was through with handouts. I wanted this job, but mostly because it would be the first thing I'd ever *earned*.

I took the bus downtown, dressed in the nicest outfit I'd purchased since I'd been on the island; something I bought especially for the occasion. I felt confident and attractive, and hoped I looked competent and approachable. I watched the amazing scenery pass by my window, still in awe of the beauty the Hawaiian Islands offered. It was, by far, the most breathtaking place I'd ever been.

The bus dropped me off at a stop just blocks from the building which housed the firm. The walk allowed me to work out some of my last minute jitters. I hadn't been through a job interview since I was just out of college, so I was hoping my skills were still intact and just lying dormant, waiting for the right moment to show themselves again.

Luckily, the woman I interviewed with seemed to take to me from the very instant we met, and forty-five minutes into my interview, I found myself shaking hands with the human resources manager and accepting a job offer.

I should have been ecstatic. I should have been overjoyed. And even though I was happy and a bit relieved, I couldn't grab a hold of the joy that was just out of my reach. The sorrow was still too thick to wade through and it clouded everything that might have brought me a smile in the past. When someone gets a new job, one they desperately need, excitement should be immediate. But I was morose.

With one giant "To-Do" ticked off my list, I settled into a large and comfortable recliner at the nearest coffee shop to browse the housing ads in the local newspaper. With an iced mocha by my side, I let out a sigh, and prepared myself for what I had always heard was an expensive housing market.

I did a general sweep first, looking at one-bedroom apartments or rentals, finding the results to be a little intimidating. I still had plenty of money saved from what I walked away with, but I wanted to be smart with my money, especially since I wouldn't be seeing a paycheck for at least another month.

"Excuse me," I heard a female voice say, and turned to see a woman looking at me with a pleasant smile on her face. "Hi," she said cautiously. "I couldn't help but notice you were looking at the ads for apartments."

I looked down at my newspaper with big, dark circles around the apartment listings I'd found. "Uh, yeah," I answered hesitantly.

"Oh, my gosh," she exclaimed, taking the chair right next to mine and setting her oversized purse on the ground next to her feet. "Isn't it ridiculous how much they want for a tiny little studio apartment? I mean, I knew Hawaii was going to be expensive, but I wasn't prepared for this kind of expensive, ya know?" She looked at me expectantly as she took a sip from her drink.

I nodded. "I agree, it is a little outrageous." I smiled at her because it seemed like the polite thing to do, but I wasn't sure what else to say, so I just went back to looking at my newspaper.

"Where abouts are you looking to move?"

"Um," I put my pen down, relenting to the fact that we were going to have a conversation. "I'm not sold on any particular area, just someplace not too far from my job since I'll be taking the bus for the foreseeable future."

"That's smart," she said, nodding. "I'm not looking in one area specifically either, just trying to find something I can afford." She paused, sipping again through her straw. "Where are you staying now?"

"In a motel."

"Oh, my gosh, me too! Isn't it horrible? The place I'm staying is decent, but I'm tired of sleeping in someone else's bed."

"I am too."

"I'm staying at a little motel not far from here. But the woman who runs it is so sweet. Her name's Rose and she has nearly become my surrogate mom since I got here."

My ears perked up at the mention of Rose. "You mean Rose at the Sea Breeze Motel?"

"Yes! Oh, my gosh, you know Rose?" she said excitedly.

I laughed. "I'm staying there too, and she *is* like a surrogate mother." I smiled now, a sincere smile, because Rose really was a lifesaver. She had come to check on me multiple times during the first two weeks I was there, making sure I wasn't wallowing all the time. Even though I'd never told her the reason I'd come to the island, she had been able to figure out it had to do with a man. She'd given me all the advice I'd expect a mother to give, although, Rose wasn't a mother.

"How funny. How long have you been there? I haven't seen you around."

"Oh," I said, waving a hand in the air, trying to dismiss her question, "I haven't been very social. I'm a 'stay in my room and watch reruns of *Friends* kind of girl."

"You sound like my kind of gal!" She held her hand out to me saying, "I'm Becky. I came here all the way from the East Coast in need of a serious change of scenery."

I shook her hand, still smiling, as Becky admittedly grew on me. "My name's Lena."

"Oh, pretty name! Is it European?"

"Russian, actually, on my father's side. My mother was Italian."

"Well, that explains why you're so pretty," she said with so much earnest. All I could do was mirror her smile. For just one tiny moment, her friendliness and openness made me forget everything bad that had brought me here. She was smiling and I was smiling, and an actual laugh bubbled up. An honest-to-goodness laugh. She was a breath of fresh air.

"Thank you, that's very sweet."

Becky's gaze on me was almost unnerving; it was so innocent. She looked as though she'd found a new best friend in me, like I was her newest shiny toy.

"Do you want to ride back to the motel with me?" Becky's eyes were soft and questioning, and I couldn't help but think that after everything that had happened in the last couple of weeks, a friend was something I shouldn't turn away.

"Sure," I replied, glad to have someone to share the ride with.

We talked non-stop all the way back to the motel. I learned Becky was very close to my age, only older by a bit. We shared a passion for cooking, even if we both couldn't find the time to indulge. And since we both lived in a motel, cooking wasn't really an option.

Becky was friendly, bubbly, and an excellent listener. In fact, she listened almost as well as she chatted, and she was a chatter. When she spoke, it was nearly at hyper speed, as if she were afraid the words would melt away before she got a chance to speak them.

When we came to our stop, we didn't stop talking, just walked side-by-side all the way to the motel, ending up right in front of my door.

"Thanks for riding back with me," Becky said. "Room number six, huh? I'm in twenty-two, upstairs. I'd invite you up, but I'm pretty beat. Long day."

"Me too. Thanks, though, for introducing yourself. I haven't enjoyed myself this much in weeks."

"Well, what are you doing tomorrow? Want to hunt for apartments together? It would be better than doing it all alone." She looked hopeful and I honestly thought it would be much better to hunt for a place to live with Becky than alone.

"Sure. That sounds great. Wanna meet out here at, like, ten?"

Her mouth pulled up into a beautiful smile. "Sounds like a plan. See you later." She turned and I watched as she disappeared around a corner. I heard her footsteps up the stairs, and just took a moment to reflect, staring out at the beautiful scenery around me.

Today had been a good day. The first I'd had in weeks. Without provocation and for my own reasons, a smile spread across my face.

Instead of going into my room, I turned and headed for the sidewalk, leading toward a convenience store only a block away.

With the excitement taking over, I walked in and went straight for the counter, knowing the pre-paid cell phones hung on pegs right below. I'd eyed them before, knowing eventually I'd need one, but before now I couldn't bring myself to purchase one. I wasn't ready to talk to anyone, didn't know what I would say. But today I wanted to talk to my best friend.

I picked out a simple phone and paid, then nearly jogged back to my room. I opened the package and followed the directions for activation, and when the screen lit up, my heart sped up as well. I dialed her number carefully, making sure I hit all the right numbers, and then I put the phone to my ear, breathing rapidly.

After a few rings, I heard her voice and my smile grew tenfold.

"Hello?" She was confused by the unknown number, I assumed. I took a deep breath and responded.

"Hey, Sam," I whispered.

"Who...? Lena? Is that you?"

"Yes, it's me."

"Lena, oh, my God! Where are you? Are you okay?" She immediately started crying, and to hear her speaking through tears wrenched at my heart. My eyes welled with tears and I cried as I answered her.

"Sam, it's so good to hear your voice. I miss you. So much."

"Lena," she cried again. Then we both sat on the line crying, and I wished I could hug her.

"I'm sorry I haven't called. I'm sorry."

I heard her sniffle and the crying tapered off. Then I laughed as I heard her blow her nose so loudly it was comical.

"Where are you?" she asked again. I wasn't sure I should tell her where I was, not yet at least.

"I'm safe," was the only response I could think of.

"Where?"

"Sam, it's not important."

"Are you okay?"

"Yes. No. I don't know. I'm fine. I'm doing all right. But no, I'm not okay. I don't know if I'll ever be okay."

"Where are you?"

"I'm safe."

"Lena, this isn't funny. Tell me where you are."

"Sam, I can't. I will eventually, but not today. I'm sorry. Can we just talk? I've missed talking to you."

She sighed loudly, but in her breath I heard her acquiescence. "What do you want to talk about?"

"I got a job today," I said, smiling.

"A job? Are you planning on staying wherever you are?"

I shrugged. "I don't know. All I *do* know is that I can't live off twenty thousand dollars forever."

"Come home, Lena." Her words were soft and pleading.

"I can't be in Portland, Sam. I just can't."

"Derrek's gone." Her words hit me like a freight train.

"What do you mean he's gone?"

"I mean, he's gone. Disappeared."

"Disappeared?"

"Yeah. Him, Jessica, their girls. Gone. The police are investigating, seeing as how he abandoned his company and no one knows where he is, but it's just, I don't know, like a missing person's case. It's all really confusing."

"It doesn't matter."

"Doesn't it?"

"Not really. It doesn't involve me at all."

"Perhaps not, but I'm sure the authorities would like to speak with you about it. You were probably the last person to see him before he disappeared."

"Perhaps, but I'm not coming back for that. I'm not hiding, Sam. If the police want to find me to ask me questions, they will."

I heard her sigh again and knew she was accepting that she wasn't getting anywhere with me. "What is your new job?"

I smiled a little, silently thanking her for moving on. "I got a job at a marketing firm. I'm starting at the bottom, but I'm okay with that. I just want something that, for once, wasn't handed to me."

"That's great, Lena. I'm glad you're getting what you want."

"I miss you though," I said softly. "I made a friend today, and she was so nice and warm. And even though I was so happy to have met her, she just made me miss my best friend. So that's why I called."

"Well, I'm glad you did. I just wish I knew where you were. I'd come see you. Like, hop on the next plane just to see your face, Lena. That's how much I miss you."

Those words, even the suggestion of seeing her, was almost enough to make the words fly out of my mouth, almost tell her where I was. I wanted to see her so badly, wanted to tell her everything, but I needed more time. "You have my number now though, so feel free to call me whenever," I said with a little sadness.

"I will. Take care of yourself, Lena."

"Okay."

I heard the line disconnect and hung my head. That phone call did not go as I had planned. I called her because I wanted to hear her voice, wanted to tell her I missed her. But by the way she sounded toward the end of our conversation, it seemed I might have pushed her even farther away. I stared down at the cheap phone in my hand, and my fingers, trying to have a mind of their own, floated over the keys that would dial Preston's number.

Sharp pain shot through my chest at the thought of his name. I had tried to not think about him for three weeks, and sometimes that was nearly impossible. When I had this phone in my hand, knowing I could dial his number and possibly hear his voice in just seconds, it was heartbreaking. I could call, listen to his voice, and hang up, like some sorry teenager pranking her crush. I didn't allow my fingers to make that damaging decision and I put the phone back in my purse.

Hearing Preston Reid's voice would surely end me. And if his voice didn't kill me, it would just anger me. I was very in tune with my emotions, enough to know I harbored a lot of anger toward him. And rightfully so, in my opinion. What he'd done to me was unforgivable, not that he'd asked for forgiveness. I'd imagined many scenarios where we'd come face-to-face and all he ever said to me in my made up encounters was, "Looks like you should have left him when you had the chance." Then his face would spread into that beautiful smile and he'd say, "But the fucking sure was fun."

Yes, even in my daydreams he was an asshole. Only, my daydreams battled with my memories because in my memory he wasn't an asshole at all. Well, not in a bad way. He was confident and brash, but he was also infinitely caring, protective, and gentle. The only unkind words he'd ever said to me were out of frustration for the situation I was in.

I shook my head, trying to break the conflicting thoughts. I had to remind myself that Preston Reid had played me. He'd taken money from my husband to bury me in lies and deceit. Any remaining thoughts or memories that painted him as the man I'd fallen in love with needed to be erased, abolished. I couldn't let myself remember the way it felt when his traitorous hands were on me. Couldn't think about how my heart had fallen for every poisoned word he'd said.

No.

I had to keep moving forward.

So that's what I did.

Chapter Three

The next morning, I met Becky outside my room at ten. We walked back to the same coffee shop we'd met at the day before, but instead of a newspaper, we used her smart phone to look for listings.

"I knew Hawaii was an expensive place to live, but this is a little daunting," she said, taking a sip from her latte.

"Yeah, I know what you mean. Some of the single listings are a little scary. I don't mind living alone, but when I think of what kind of place I could get for fifteen hundred dollars back home…" My voice trailed off as I thought about the tall apartment buildings in Portland.

"Where are you from?"

"Oh, uh, Portland, Oregon." Her question had caught me off guard. In fact, most everything caught me off guard these days. It was hard to trust people because I'd learned that I obviously was a terrible judge of character. I wasn't sure I wanted to share personal information with her.

"I've heard great things about that place," she said with a smile, then turned back to her phone. "Oh, here's a good one. It's close to the bus line, utilities included, new carpets, and walking distance to the beach! And it's in the area you wanted, too." She looked back up at me. "Wanna go check it out?"

"How much is the rent?"

"Fourteen."

I sighed. But then I straightened my shoulders. It was time to bite the bullet. I didn't want to live in squalor, so I was going to have to pay a lot for an apartment. Hopefully, once my paychecks started coming in, it wouldn't seem like such a burden. "I guess we have to start somewhere."

"Great! Let's go."

Thirty minutes later, we found ourselves outside a building that looked like it housed about ten individual apartments. It looked cozy. I imagined everyone who lived there knew each other's names and borrowed cups of sugar from one another. They kept an eye out for their neighbors and baked them cookies. I could use something like that in my life.

A very round, short, balding man met us out front.

"Hi, I'm Becky and this is Lena. We called about looking at the available apartment."

"Sure thing, ladies. This way," he said, motioning to the building behind him, walking toward a small staircase at the side. Once upstairs, he let us into an apartment and my eyes took in the empty dwelling.

It was beautiful. It had a ton of natural light, it was clean, and it embodied the cozy feel I'd picked up from the building on the outside. I walked into the living room and looked out the big picture window and all I saw was blue: blue sky and blue ocean.

"Lena, this place is perfect."

I smiled at Becky because she was right; it was gorgeous and perfect. There had to be some sort of catch. I wandered down the hall, which led to the bedroom. It was spacious and had the same beautiful view as the living room. I looked through the rest of the apartment, not finding anything to complain about. There was even a washer and dryer in a little closet right off the bathroom.

"I'm a little surprised. Is there something I'm missing? Why is this place even still available?"

The man shrugged. "I just listed it yesterday. They do tend to go fast, though."

"Lena, if you don't take it, I might have to," Becky said with a friendly smile.

"You're both looking?"

"Yeah, we both just moved here."

"Well, this is the only one bedroom I have available, but there's a two-bedroom unit just next door. Nearly same floorplan, just an extra bedroom on the back end. One bathroom. That one has furniture in it you can use if you'd like. Rent's twenty-two hundred."

Becky's eyes got big as she turned to face me. "That's only eleven hundred each!" She turned back to the landlord. "Can we see the two bedroom as well?"

"Sure," he said with a shrug. I followed, but my shoulders tensed and I got an empty feeling in my stomach. I didn't know Becky, and I thought it was a little strange that she wanted to share an apartment with me. I could be a serial killer for all she knew, or she could be one.

We walked next door, and sure enough, the two bedroom was just as beautiful as the one. It did have some furniture: one couch, a coffee table, a queen-sized bed in each bedroom, and some end tables. It wasn't much, but it was more than I had in the world. Becky was practically jumping up and down with excitement.

"What do you think, Lena?"

"Are you sure you really want to live with someone you just met?"

She laughed a little and then smiled. "What's the difference between living with you or living with someone I meet on craigslist? I need a roommate, regardless of who it is, and you seem way more normal than some of the people I'm sure post their vacancies on the internet."

She had a point. I had considered meeting people from the internet and looking for a roommate that way. This, meeting her just yesterday and now looking for a place to live together, just seemed a little too convenient. However, my mind started focusing on the price. My brief research had shown eleven hundred dollars for a place this nice, with a washer and dryer, this close to the ocean, was a steal.

"I don't know…"

"Want me to agree to a background check? Want a drug test?" She asked the questions, but it was obvious she was joking. "Lena, honestly, if you're uncomfortable, I get it. It's just a really great deal. If you don't want to room with me, I'll just get the two bedroom and look for a roommate myself. But I'd rather just room with you. You're the first friend I made on this island."

She watched me as my mind sifted through all my options. The financially smart decision would be to room with her. And I *did* like her.

"Okay, let's do it." Then Becky did start clapping and jumping up and down in her spot. "When is this one available?" I asked the landlord.

"It's ready now. I'd just need first and last month's rent, and the security."

"I'm good with that." I turned to Becky. "You good to go?"

"I'm golden," she said with a smile that was so big and bright.

So we both filled out the paperwork, wrote checks for our portion, and he gave us keys.

The next day, after I'd brought all my clothes to the new apartment, along with the small amount of personal belongings I'd acquired in my three weeks on the island, I walked into the living room to find Becky looking out the big window.

"It really is beautiful here," she said, not taking her eyes off the ocean. I'd only known her a short time, but this was the first instance where I heard anything but bubbly sweetness in her voice. She sounded introspective and a little sullen, almost as if the beauty she was referring to wasn't just the scenery.

"Yeah, it is," was my response, but it seemed inadequate. Her mood had me worried.

Then, suddenly, she turned to me with the smile I was becoming accustomed to and said excitedly, "I bought a TV and it's being delivered in a few minutes. I thought we could have a roomie movie night and christen our new pad."

And just like that, she was back to normal.

"That sounds awesome."

That evening, one of the things I learned about Becky was that she was the kind of girl who, when packing her things to move to the other side of the country, brought her *Friends* DVD collection with her.

"It goes where I go," she said with a laugh as she loaded the first DVD. We'd spent a few hours watching Ross pine after Rachel, eating take-out, and munching on some popcorn I'd purchased for the event. We even had some cheap, girly beer. I was enjoying myself, and loved getting to know Becky better, but the whole situation made me miss Sam, too.

"So," Becky said, throwing a piece of popcorn in the air and then catching it in her mouth. "Why did you leave Portland?"

"I needed a new beginning. A fresh start."

"That's the impersonal response you give to the girl you just met at a coffee shop," she said, sounding almost insulted. "Tell me the real reason." She was looking straight into my eyes, like she genuinely wanted to know, and more so, she seemed like she cared about my answer. For the first time in weeks, I was compelled to tell someone else about my ruined life back in Portland.

"I was married, am still, in fact. At least I think so. I haven't signed any papers. Anyway," I exhaled, pushing out a breath and pulling my hand through my hair, trying to build up the nerve to say the words. "I was in a bad marriage and made some bad decisions. My husband found out and took everything from me. It's actually pretty complicated."

"He didn't, like, hit you, did he?"

"No, he didn't hit me, but he wasn't a very good husband."

"Well, what were your bad decisions?"

"I had an affair."

"Hmm."

We were both quiet for a while. She was probably thinking I was a horrible person, but my mind was torturing me with images of Preston and all the times he'd pretended to care.

"So, what happened with the guy you had the affair with?"

"What do you mean?"

"I mean, why aren't you with him now?"

It took me a moment to formulate my answer, but I finally settled on, "He didn't want me after all."

"I find that really hard to believe."

"Well, that's the funny thing about good liars, they're easy to believe."

"Obviously I don't know the situation, but I would venture to guess he's torn up that you're not with him."

She was looking at me with concern, her eyes soft and imploring.

I sighed. "You're sweet, Becky, but he's not thinking about me. He probably hasn't spent one second thinking about me since I left."

"Impossible," she stated firmly, as if it were a fact she was sure of.

I smiled at her because, really, I appreciated her kind words, but thinking about Preston just made my heart hurt that much more.

"I think I'm going to head to bed."

"You don't want to watch any more *Friends*?"

"Maybe tomorrow." I climbed off the couch and started walking toward my bedroom.

"Lena," Becky called from the living room.

"Yeah?" I stopped in the middle of the hallway and turned back to her.

"Do me a favor? Don't give up on him. That guy back in Portland. Just," she paused and bit her lip, "don't give up hope yet."

I laughed, but it was a sad, pathetic laugh. "Becky, in order to give up hope, I would have had to have some to begin with. And I didn't. There was never any hope for Preston and me. It was over before it began, and he's probably somewhere tricking someone else into believing his lies."

"Well, I hope someday you find out you're mistaken," she said sweetly, like she really wanted what she was saying to be true.

"Goodnight, Becky."

"Night, Lena."

Weeks passed and life started to take on a new "normal." I started my job, easing my way into a new position, trying to learn as much as I could and impress the people working around me. There were a few women who I worked with who seemed friendly and had extended invitations to me to hang out after work for happy hour. I always declined, telling them I had plans already, but in reality I wasn't sure about letting new people get close to me.

Sam and I spoke on the phone every once in a while, but even though I missed her terribly, I could never bring myself to fully open up to her. There was a clear division in my mind between my old life and my new life, and I couldn't fully convince my head to let Sam into the new.

Becky was the one constant in my life that brought me a sense of familiarity and routine.

She got a job on the island working for the newspaper in advertising. We both had a regular nine-to-five job and so, after a week or two, we started to resemble an old married couple. We'd both come home from work, eat dinner, and then hang out in the living room either watching TV, reading, and sometimes she talked me into playing games.

After our first delve into personal topics, she never really pressured me for any more information. Also, she wasn't very forthcoming about herself either, and that was totally okay with me. We could spend time together and not have to talk about our pasts. In fact, it was encouraged.

Every morning I got up early to run. I still found it cathartic and craved that time when my mind emptied out and I let myself simply *be*. Plus, nothing beat running on the beach in Hawaii. I ran without music, simply listening to the sound of the waves crashing onto the shore, the sounds of the sand moving beneath my feet.

There were always other people out running and there was a polite courtesy amongst us runners to just nod as we passed each other, if looking at them at all. Most of the time, I tried to keep my eyes on the sand or out at the horizon.

This morning, however, another runner had other plans.

He jogged toward me and I saw him coming. I veered toward the water, trying to give him enough room, sticking to my side of the 'road,' staying to the right. But instead of a polite nod, he gave me a bright smile. I smiled back, instinctively, but then looked down to the sand. Then I noticed he slowed and stopped jogging about twenty feet in front of me. I slowed, not sure if I was supposed to stop as well, or if I should start jogging in the other direction. Before I could decide, he spoke.

"You run every morning." He smiled as he said the words and there was something familiar about him that I couldn't quite pinpoint.

"Yes." It was a sort-of answer to his sort-of question.

"You should take a break. A day off every now and then. I see you every morning and wonder why you aren't ever tired."

I tilted my head to the side, squinting my eyes at him. "If you see me every morning, that means you run every morning. Perhaps you should take your own advice." I pushed off and made it past him when his hand grabbed my arm.

"I'm sorry," I heard him say as I wrenched my arm from his grasp. I turned on him and his hands were up as if he were surrendering. "I wasn't trying to be an asshole." He took a step toward me and I took one back. "What's your name?"

I narrowed my eyes at him.

"Well, my name's Ryan. I just thought, since we both run on this beach every morning, maybe you'd like a running partner."

"I run alone."

"I noticed." He just stood there, staring at me, waiting for me to say something else.

"I don't need a running partner."

"Everyone runs better when they do it with someone. You need a partner to push you, take you out of your zone. You'd get better results."

I put my hands on my hips, letting my annoyance take over. "I don't run for *results*. I run to clear my mind, to find clarity, to let my brain breathe for a minute."

"Well, we could still run together. I like to run with a partner better, and you're the only one I've seen who I think could keep up with my pace and be reliable."

"You've been scouting me?"

He chuckled. "I suppose. Come on. It's just running."

"I'm just going to continue to run on this beach. I can't control what you do." I turned and continued to run down the beach, and only a small smile came across my face when Ryan took up pace next to me.

We ran like that, side-by-side, for another mile or so, and then I sharply turned around, heading back the way I came. I heard him laughing, but after a few moments, he was at my side again.

When I made it back to the path I normally took to get from my apartment to the beach, I stopped and placed my hands on my knees, taking in deep, ragged, breaths. Perhaps Ryan was right, running with him had pushed me.

"Can I run with you tomorrow? Same time, same place?"

His words caught me off guard, echoing the same words Sam and I had always said about our coffee shop.

"Are you all right?" he asked, noticing the shocked look on my face.

"Yeah, I mean, yes. I'm fine." I shook my head, trying to rid my brain of thoughts of Sam. I straightened my shoulders and looked him in the eyes. "I run every morning at the same time. I can't control when and where you run."

He chuckled, and again something familiar yelled at me from the very back of my mind. "Okay, I'll see you tomorrow morning then." With that, he turned and ran back the way we'd come.

"Hey," I yelled after a few moments. He turned and continued jogging backward, his smile still plastered across his face. "My name's Lena."

He gave me a small salute and then turned back around, disappearing along the horizon.

Chapter Four

For a week, every morning, Ryan met me where the path met the sand and we ran. For the first two days, he didn't say a word to me, just followed my lead, running along next to me. I could tell every once in a while he picked up his speed, causing me to run a little faster to keep up. When I was ready to go back, I'd just turn around and he'd follow suit. No questions, no conversation, just running.

On the third day, when I came upon him, he was on the phone. I awkwardly tried not to listen to his conversation, seeing as how I didn't even really know him, so I started running without him.

A few minutes later, he caught up with me, out of breath from sprinting.

"Sorry about that," he rasped as he came to run beside me. "That was my sister. She's the baby in the family, so when she calls, I answer. Lord knows what kind of trouble she can get herself into."

I didn't turn to look at him, but I did answer. "Is everything okay?" I don't know why I asked; it didn't matter to me one way or another. Except, it kind of did. I didn't know him, but I sort of cared if something bad had happened to someone in his family. I could see him from the corner of my eye as he turned to me with that brilliant smile again.

"She's fine. Just chatty."

With that, we picked up our quiet running routine. We ran and ran. I almost forgot he was there, that is, until all of a sudden I heard him swear and then the unmistakable sound of someone's face slamming into sand.

I stopped and turned to see him, sure enough, face planted in the sand.

"Oh, my God, are you all right?" I ran back to him as he started to pull himself from the sand.

"Yeah," he groaned, sand falling from his mouth as he spat it out. The sand was stuck to the entire top half of his body, getting plastered to him from the sweat he'd built up from the run. He looked like a legitimate sand monster and I couldn't help the laughter that bubbled up in my throat.

And then I was laughing.

And laughing.

Laughing so loud and so hard I had to sit down, holding my belly.

Laughing until there were tears running down my face.

Laughing for so long I must have looked crazy.

Laughing until it became apparent to me that I was no longer laughing at Ryan and his sand covered body, but laughing as a release, laughing at what had become of my life, where I'd ended up.

"I'm sorry," I said through hiccups as I started to come down from my hysterics.

"You're a little wacko," Ryan said, not hurtfully.

I turned my head to look at him and noticed he'd taken a seat on the sand right next to me. Most of the sand was wiped from his face, except for the granules stuck in his bushy eyebrows. This was the first time I'd allowed myself to really look at him. Sand aside, he was an attractive man. Dark eyes, dark hair, strong jawline. I also noticed, even though he'd run without a shirt every day, that he had a magnificent body. In a normal circumstance, a woman would look at his chest and it would cause all kinds of fluttering to happen. I would take in his muscled body and find myself attracted to him. Any hot-blooded, straight woman would.

But I didn't and I was more than okay with that.

"That's the first time I've laughed in months. Like, really, honest-to-goodness laughter."

"If I'd known I just had to eat some sand to break you open, I would have done it sooner."

I thought about his words for a moment. "Well, I don't think it would have worked before now. It's time, I think."

"For?"

I shrugged. "Time to pick myself up and dust myself off."

"You and me both," he said, laughing.

"Maybe you more than me," I said, smiling.

"Just because I can't see your sand, doesn't mean it's any less important than mine."

His poignant words washed over me and I embraced the friendship I had built with him, even without speaking much.

"Feel like getting a smoothie? There's a place right off the beach a few hundred yards up. I usually go there after I run. Get some protein in my system."

I looked over at him with a smile that I hoped was friendly. "I didn't bring my wallet with me."

"Tell you what, your first smoothie is on me." He stood up and started brushing the sand off his body, even though it was a futile effort. Then he held both his hands out to me. I looked up at him before I placed my hands in his, then he hoisted me up so fast I almost lost my balance.

When he let go of my hands, I couldn't help but notice the lack of electricity he left me with. I didn't feel any of the sparks just by touching him that I had with Preston. He didn't light me up, my heart was still beating at its normal pace, and I was left breathing evenly. It was then I realized I might not ever feel the butterflies in my stomach again, might not ever feel hands on me that branded me with their heat. And if I thought I'd been depressed over the last month or so, I was sorely mistaken. A new wave of darkness washed over me with these thoughts and I had to hold back the tears.

But I shook it off and turned back to Ryan. "A smoothie sounds great."

I ordered some raspberry concoction that probably undid all the calories I'd worked off on my run, but it tasted fan-fucking-tastic. Ryan was more responsible and had gotten a spinach, kale, coconut smoothie with a protein powder boost. Watching them pour it into his cup had made me gag. He smiled at me, though, and held up his Styrofoam cup for me to tap mine against.

"To falling in the sand," he said, his eyes twinkling with a smile on his face.

"To getting back up after you've fallen," I responded, thumping my cup against his. Ryan took a deep suck off his straw and I watched the green sludge make its way up and into his mouth, and I couldn't help the grimace that stretched over my face. "Does it taste as terrible as it looks?"

He shook his head. "It's not that bad." He shrugged. "I've had worse." Just then, I heard a beep coming from his pocket and he shifted as he reached inside and grabbed his phone. He didn't bring it to his ear, but tapped away at the screen, so I assumed he was texting someone.

"Sister drama, again?"

"Huh?" he asked, looking up at me. "Oh, no," he laughed. "Boyfriend drama."

"Oh," I said instinctively. "Oh!" Then his words dawned on me. It suddenly made perfect sense to me why there'd been no flirty vibes from him. This realization made me feel exponentially better about spending time with him. I did not need a man to complicate my life. "He's not a runner?"

Ryan laughed loudly at my question. "No. No, he's not a runner. He's in great shape, but he'd rather do something extreme like snowboard or rock climb. Running on the serene beaches of Hawaii isn't really his idea of a good way to spend time outside. Plus," he said just before he took another sip of his torture drink, "Chance lives on the mainland."

"The mainland?"

"Yeah. You know, that big chunk of earth where the other forty-nine states are located?"

"Ah ha. The mainland. Right." I sipped on my blissful raspberry smoothie. "Doesn't it suck being so far away from him?"

"Yes, but business calls. I've only been here for a few weeks and I'm hoping I can go home soon."

"Where's home?" I asked, feeling more comfortable with him by the minute.

"All over, actually. I have hideouts everywhere," he said, not looking at me, but instead staring at his cup. "How long have you lived here?"

"A month or two. I'm a transplant."

"What made you uproot?"

I stared at Ryan for a moment, trying to figure out why I got the feeling he already knew the answer to his question. "Needed a change in scenery and I'd never been here before."

He nodded but didn't say anything in response.

"I have to head home," I said as I stood. Ryan's eyes followed me, but he made no move to stand.

"Well, I guess I'll see you tomorrow morning."

We both just looked at each other, neither one of us saying anything, and I found myself wishing I could read his mind.

"See you then."

That night, Becky surprised me by not coming home until late, and although she didn't owe me an explanation, I was curious as to what had kept her out.

She walked in looking frustrated, sighing loudly as she dropped her purse onto the couch then plopping down next to it. I put my book down on my lap and looked over to her.

"You okay?"

She sighed again, then looked over at me. "Things just aren't going as they were supposed to. My plan is unraveling."

"What plan?" I'd never heard her talk about a plan.

She didn't answer right away, but I sat patiently waiting for her to open up to me.

"There are things in my life that I regret. I've made mistakes. Part of coming out here was to make up for some of those mistakes. But, I also wanted this to be a new start, a new beginning. And I keep trucking along, doing what I think is right, but I also feel like nothing is happening the way it's supposed to." She sighed loudly again. "I'm tempted to throw the towel in." She looked over at me and her eyes went from frustrated to sad. "There are just things I want to make right, but it's not panning out the way I wanted to."

"What is it you want to make right?"

She paused, swallowed, and then stood up. She walked from the couch and went into the kitchen, opening the fridge and grabbing a can of soda. "It's not important, Lena. It's not my place to say anyway."

"Yeah, but if you're upset about something then you should be able to talk about it with someone."

She was looking down at her soda, using her finger to flick the tab on it, refusing to meet my eyes.

"I *have* been talking to someone, trust me. It's just..." She took another drink, draining the soda in one long draw. Then she tossed the can in the recycling bin under the sink. "I can't talk to you about it."

Before I could even formulate a response, she headed down the hall and disappeared into her room. I heard the door shut and I just gaped at the spot in the kitchen she'd just vacated, mouth wide open in shock. Becky had never, not once, been that short with me. She didn't seem angry, but she did seem upset. Frustrated. And it seemed as though part of her frustration was with me. And I had no idea what in the world had gone wrong.

I picked up my book and tried to continue reading, but my mind was drifting back to Becky and what she'd said. What wrongs did she want to make right? And why in the world couldn't she talk to *me* about them? Just when I thought I'd reached a point of frustration strong enough to inspire me to march down the hall and knock on her door, I heard her yelling from inside her room. She was obviously in a heated discussion with someone and her voice was carrying right into the living room.

"Listen, I know you're trying," she said, "but I can't do this much longer." There was a pause. "It's not fair to anyone." Pause. "You have three days to get your shit together."

I didn't hear any more yelling coming from Becky's room. In fact, I didn't hear from her for the rest of the night. Becky and I found ourselves in this living situation in a funny way – almost like fate. Right place, right time. But even though we're roommates out of convenience, over the last month, I thought we'd become friends. I didn't want to lose the only person I'd befriended since I'd been here. And what the hell was happening in three days?

I went to bed hoping I'd hear Becky get into another yelling match with whomever was on the other end of her phone call just so I could eavesdrop and do a little more investigating of my own.

Chapter Five

I ran with Ryan for the next three mornings, just like we had the week previously. There were no more instances in which he made me nervous or gave off any weird vibes. In fact, after his sand-eating incident, things between us were pretty friendly. We chatted as we ran, well, as much as we could while running in the sand.

I told him about my roommate and her weird tantrum followed by her strange phone call. He listened, but didn't really have much advice to offer. He chalked it up to "woman issues" and then changed the subject.

On that third day, the day for which Becky had thrown down the gauntlet to her partner in arguments, I didn't see her before I left the apartment to run and figured she was going to be gone for work before I came back home, so I wasn't expecting to see her. I was, however, curious as to whether the other person on the phone with her that night had come through for her and abided by this three-day timeline.

As I was walking up the stairs to my apartment after my run, I caught a dark head of hair out of the corner of my eye. The hair was attached to the head of a man whose back was to me, and whose leg was currently being lifted over the seat of a motorcycle.

All the breath was forced from my body, as if the sudden hollowness of my stomach couldn't allow any extra room for oxygen. I knew that hair.

The hair was suddenly covered up by a helmet, and that action made my eyes frantically move over his entire being. My hand came to cover my mouth as a strangled sob escaped my lips. Just below that helmet was a black leather jacket, wrapped around a man's body that I would recognize anywhere.

Preston

I moved to the top of the stairs just as the motorcycle roared to life. The rumbling of the engine shook me, stopping me in my tracks. I watched as this man expertly balanced on the bike, removing the kickstand, and then pulled out of the parking lot before I could get any closer. I watched the bike drive away and then I turned, darting toward my apartment.

I put the key in the lock with shaky hands, making it a hundred times more difficult. When I finally made it inside, I ran directly to my room and found my phone on my nightstand. I entered the phone number that I'd never forget and then brought it to my ear, listening to the line connecting.

I heard Preston's voice, but it was his voicemail message and it hurt too much to listen. I wasn't even sure what I would have said had he answered. Everything at that moment was instinctive, gut reactions to what was happening around me. I had all these puzzle pieces, but I couldn't fit them together with my mind.

Why was Preston here? Why hadn't he contacted me? Was he here to see me? To hurt me? To find me and take me back to Derrek? There were so many variables, so many things that could be happening, and I couldn't remember ever feeling that out of control.

I tried to call Becky, just in case he'd stopped by the apartment before she'd left for work, but she didn't answer either.

I sat down on my bed and hung my head between my knees, trying to drag in calming breaths. My mind was second guessing itself. Maybe it wasn't Preston. Perhaps there was another man with a black leather jacket riding around Hawaii whose body called out to mine on a primal level. I raised my head up and flopped back onto the bed.

I couldn't imagine spending a day at work with all these thoughts flittering through my mind, but the reality was I was new in my position and couldn't risk missing a day. I forced myself off the bed and made my way to the bathroom to get ready for work.

To have thought I could spend a day working while I had visions of Preston riding a freaking motorcycle in paradise was ridiculous. More than once I was caught by a co-worker in a daze and my productivity was atrocious. Not only was I mentally consumed with reasons and ideas as to why Preston would even be in Hawaii, my body was like a drug addict who'd just broken their sobriety – I was craving a fix.

I made my way home from work and just wanted to go inside and open a bottle of wine. As I approached my apartment door, I could hear Becky's voice softly coming through the walls and I was immediately relieved I wouldn't be alone. But then I heard a man's voice and my heart started to beat faster in my chest.

Again, my shaky hand inserted the key into the lock and when I got the door opened, I was confounded by what I saw in my living room.

Becky was sitting on the couch and on the other side was Ryan. I didn't even bother stepping inside, I just gave them both curious looks and let my mouth flop open and then snap shut, much like a guppy. I couldn't even string words together to make a sentence.

"Lena, why don't you come sit down," Becky said as she patted the cushion next to her. Ryan didn't say anything, but eyed me warily.

I couldn't explain why I did what she asked, but I had nothing better to do than listen to what she obviously had to say to me. I placed my purse on the floor by the door and walked slowly to the couch, sitting next to her, my head moving back and forth as my eyes jumped from Becky to Ryan.

"How do you two know each other?" I finally managed to speak as the most obvious question came forth first.

"We've known each other a while," Ryan said.

"Yeah," Becky countered, looking directly into my eyes.

"But how?" I whispered. I had a feeling whatever they had to tell me was going to change everything I'd built here in Hawaii. All I'd worked for here, the effort I'd put into moving on and making a new life for myself was going to come crashing down around me with their words.

"He's my brother."

My eyes bounced back and forth between the both of them as my eyes bulged. "Your brother?"

"Her older brother," Ryan added.

"Why didn't you tell me your brother lived here?" I asked her.

"It's a long story, Lena. I promise I'll tell you everything. I just need you to promise you're going to hear us out. That you're going to listen to us before you make any rash decisions about what we tell you." Becky was looking at me with pleading eyes as she spoke.

"What is this about?" I whispered.

"Lena, you have to promise," Becky urged.

"Fine, I promise I'll listen."

Becky's eyes moved to Ryan and she nodded at him slightly, then leaned back against the couch.

"Lena," Ryan started, "we were sent here to protect you." He paused and looked at me as if he expected me to bolt at his words. I looked at him blankly, waiting for him to continue. "She's been here longer than I have and sought you out, made sure you roomed with her so she could keep an eye on you. I came a few weeks later, just to make sure I could cover you when she couldn't." He looked over at Becky and she nodded slightly again, seeming to corroborate what he was saying.

"And you're brother and sister?" They both nodded at my question.

"Only," Becky said hesitantly, "my name's not Becky and he's not Ryan."

"Wait, what?" My eyebrows scrunched up and my forehead wrinkled in confusion. "Why would you lie about your names? And who sent you here?"

"We knew if we told you our names, you'd know who we were and not want anything to do with us," the man whose name I no longer knew answered.

"So, what's your name then?" I asked him.

"I'm Parker."

"And I'm Piper."

My stomach bottomed out at their admissions and my heart nearly flew from my chest.

"You're Preston's brother and sister," I said quietly. Much quieter, in fact, than I wanted to say it. I wanted to scream at them. "Why are you here? Why did he send you?" Surely Preston was behind this, but I couldn't fathom why.

"He wanted me here with you until he could be the one with you," Piper said softly.

"And I came a few weeks ago because, even though he was trying to make his way back to you, it was taking him longer than he anticipated." Parker exhaled loudly. "He just wanted to make sure you were safe."

"Why?"

"Well, that's really his story to tell."

I looked down at my lap to where my hands were laying. I was wringing my fingers together so hard my knuckles were white. I flattened my palms on my thighs and rubbed them on the fabric of my pants down to my knees, trying to calm the nerves that had come over me.

"He's here, isn't he?"

Parker nodded. "He's next door in my apartment."

"Your apartment?" I exclaimed. My body tensed immediately, warring with itself. My nerves came alive, knowing he was so close, but my body fought the urge to run to him, to be with him again.

"He moved into the apartment we first looked at," Piper said.

"Are you serious?" I couldn't believe what she was saying. "Why the hell would the two of you uproot your lives to do this? To be my roommate," I said, gesturing at Piper, "and to go running with me?" I said, looking to Parker.

"Again, we can't tell you the whole story," Piper started, "but it's my fault we're all in this mess."

"And he's our brother. Once he told me what you mean to him, I couldn't *not* help him."

"What I *mean* to him? He lied to me! He ruined everything! He thinks he can send his little sister and big brother in to clean up his mess? What an asshole." I stood and started pacing around the living room. How dare he? How *dare* he! I let out a frustrated breath.

"He's not asking us to clean up after him. He wanted us to make sure you were all right until he could make it to you himself." Parker's voice was soft and I knew he was trying to calm me down while also trying to protect his brother.

"This is all one big farce," I whispered. "If he wanted me, or wanted anything that you've said in the last five minutes, then why didn't he just come for me himself?" My heart ached at my own words. Even though he'd ruined everything, it still hurt that he never came for me. Each day that passed without contact, without hearing his voice or feeling his touch, it was just as painful as hearing that he'd been involved with Derrek from the beginning.

"That's his story to tell, Lena," Piper said, her voice equally as soft as Parker's.

"So what now?" I said as I unconsciously wiped an errant tear that had streamed down my face. I didn't want to cry. I hadn't cried in so long. And even though I knew eventually the dam would burst, all the tears I'd held back would eventually seep through the cracks in my walls and the flood of emotions would crash through me, I didn't want this to happen because of Preston. I didn't want to be surrounded by strangers, because that's who Piper and Parker were to me: strangers. They weren't the people, the friends, I thought I'd gained since being here; they were people, pawns, placed in my life to manipulate me.

"Well," Piper said, the word drawn out slowly, "if you'd like to speak with him, he's waiting next door to talk to you."

I scoffed at her words. "I have to go to him? After all he'd put me through, I have to go to him?"

"He doesn't want to force you to do anything you're not comfortable with," Parker said cautiously. Obviously, they could tell I was dangling precariously from a ledge, about ready to drop into a chasm of all kinds of crazy.

"Oh, he doesn't want me to be *uncomfortable*?" I asked with snark dripping from my voice. No sooner had the words left my mouth than I turned and yanked the front door open, my strides long and hard as I made my way next door, heading for the apartment I had been in a month previously.

Without pausing, or even thinking anything through fully, I grabbed the door handle and forced the door open. Luckily, it was unlocked, so my dramatic entrance was just as I imagined it, doorknob crashing against the wall and all. I was breathing hard, shoulders rising and falling with my angry breaths, when my eyes fell upon Preston's face for the first time in nearly two months.

He was sitting on a couch, his elbows propped on his knees, his head bowed, resting in his hands. The first thing I noticed was his dark hair and how messy it was, pointing in every which way. When he heard me explode through the door, his face snapped up and I was immediately drowning in the darkness of his eyes. He looked surprised, bewildered almost. As if he was seeing something he hadn't dared to believe existed before.

His face was pale, his eyes tired, and there were dark bags under them. He looked as if he hadn't slept since possibly the last time I saw him. He had a light beard, which was not something I was used to. If he didn't look like he'd been hit by a truck, I might have admired the way the beard magnified everything manly about him.

I tried to fight the urge I had to run to him and try and fix him. I reined in the need to hold him, reminding myself how his affection for me was simply an act, something he was paid to fabricate. The battle inside me was deadly and

I still wasn't clear which side would end up winning. But, to his credit, I saw a battle going on inside of him too.

He stood, almost immediately, and started to make his way toward me, but I held up my hand.

"No," I said, more forcefully than I knew I had the capacity for. He halted in the middle of the living room, looking at me with eyes that begged for something.

"Lena," he pleaded. His voice, caressing my name, crashed through my veins, igniting the spark inside of me that had been smothered for so long. He looked as though only I had the ability to save him from drowning; he was waiting for me to throw him a lifeline.

"You don't get to say my name. You don't get to talk to me. You *ruined* me, Preston. You took the trust you *begged* me for and you threw it away like it was garbage. I don't know why you're here, or why you sent your family after me, but I want you to leave, now. Leave now and never contact me again. I may have been desperate enough to end my marriage to fall for your lies once, but I am not stupid enough to subject myself to you a second time." I took in a deep breath. "Find some other poor housewife to manipulate."

I turned to leave, but before I even made it one step, his hand wrapped around my arm, and then I was spinning back toward him. My black hair swung around, my mouth gaped open in surprise, and my shriek caught in my throat when I saw his face up close.

He looked absolutely tortured. Broken. Fractured.

"Please don't leave before I get a chance to tell you everything."

"You don't deserve anything from me, and I'm not going to listen to your lies anymore."

"I never lied to you," he growled.

"Oh, really? So all those times you let me believe you worked for me, that you were helping me, those weren't lies, Preston? That wasn't you *lying* to me?"

"I worked for Derrek until the very moment I saw you walk from your car into that bar. The instant I saw you, the moment my eyes found you, all my loyalty was to you, not him. Christ, Lena," he paused and ran his free hand over his jaw, his other hand still clamped around my upper arm, "I saw you and my world changed color." He moved infinitesimally closer to me, just a tiny step, and my damned breath stuck in my throat, my heart skipped a beat. Traitors.

"You can't sweet talk your way out of this. You still lied. You still gave him what he wanted." I closed my eyes and turned my head away from him, knowing that soon all the sobbing I'd kept at bay for months would break through my walls. If he kept talking, if he kept standing so close to me, I wouldn't last much longer.

"I had nothing to do with those photos, Lena. I swear." His voice had turned angry, but only his voice. His hand was still firm around me, but not painful.

"For some reason, I don't believe you," I said icily. I pointed my chin up and opened my eyes, meeting his straight on, feigning strength.

"Every reason you have to be angry with me is valid. You're right to be upset. But every wrong you think I committed was done in an effort to help you. Everything I did, I did for you, sweetheart."

My last string to sanity snapped at his endearment. My arms wrapped around my belly and I folded in half, crying. He let go of my arm only to crumple to the ground with me as I cried. He tried to comfort me, tried to wrap his arms around me, but I wouldn't let him, crying out "No," and pushing him away. I sat on the floor, crying into my arms, and he sat next to me. I could feel his need to touch me, could feel his desire to hold me, but I wouldn't let him.

We stayed like that for a while. Perhaps a half hour. And I cried until I didn't feel like I had any energy left in me to put out. In the end, I was just a puddle of a woman, hiccupping and trying to breathe normally, in the middle of his floor.

Finally, he moved to get up and I heard him enter the kitchen, then the faucet turn on, and a few seconds later, he was kneeling next to me with a glass of water and some pills.

"Ibuprofen," he said.

I sat up slightly and took what he was offering. The cold water felt blissful as it ran down my throat and spread throughout my belly.

"Please, come sit on the couch." I looked up to him and noticed his eyes were rimmed with red and I realized he'd been crying too. Not sobbing, like I had been, but crying quietly beside me. He held a hand out to me, a hand to help me up from the floor, but it felt like so much more. I reached for it and sighed when our skin met.

He pulled me from the ground in one fast movement. Gasping a little at his strength, I was reminded of how powerful he was, and had to tamp down the wave of lust that rode through me. It was hard enough to not be turned on simply by the memory of him, but the sight of him in front of me, the feel of him against my skin, to be handled by him again, was too much. I pulled away from him and moved to sit down on the couch. I took another sip of water and closed my eyes.

"Please let me explain," he whispered from the other side of the couch. "If it's the last thing I ever say to you, I want you to know the truth."

I couldn't really argue with him. I wanted the truth just as much as he seemed to want to share it. I just didn't know if I was ready to hear it. Listening to him tell the story of how he lied to me over and over again would surely break me open even more so than I was already.

"It hurts too much."

"I'm so sorry, Lena."

I let a pause linger between us, my eyes still trained on the glass in my hands.

"That helps," I said sincerely. And it did.

"Let me help more. Let me explain."

"I don't know if I can hear that tonight. I think I need to go home and go to bed."

He didn't say anything right away, but I could feel him tense. He didn't want me to go without explaining himself.

"I've been fighting for you for the past two months, Lena. I know it doesn't seem like it. I know how it must look to you, but every day I've fought for you. I'm not going anywhere. You need to hear the truth and if it's not tonight, it'll be soon."

I lifted my eyes to meet his and said with as much strength as I could muster, "You can't tell me anything I don't want to listen to, Preston. You lost your chance to explain anything to me when you lied." I paused and took in a deep breath. "If I feel like listening to your excuses, I'll let you know. But until then, leave me alone."

I put the glass on the table and then left the apartment without another word, surprised he didn't try to stop me or ply me with more words. I opened the door to my apartment and saw Piper and Parker sitting right where I'd left them.

"Oh, look," I said with snark, "more liars." I walked past them, not waiting to listen if they tried to argue with my assessment. Even though it was more than obvious I'd been lied to by both of them for the duration of my time knowing them, I didn't think they were dangerous. I was sure they did everything out of love for their brother, so I didn't bother making them leave. It wasn't worth the energy.

Chapter Six

After a night a fitful sleep, I woke when sunshine was suddenly filling my room. I heard the curtains being pulled aside and the warm, bright sunshine fall upon my face. I groaned and brought the blanket up to cover my head.

"Time to get out of bed, lazy ass."

I immediately flung the blanket off me when I heard her voice. "Sam!" I jumped out of bed and ran to her, wrapping my arms around her shoulders, hugging her like I never had before. "What are you doing here?" I asked into her hair.

"I figured you could use a friend right now."

I sighed with relief because she was so spot on. But then I tensed. She knew. She knew what was going on, which meant one of the three liars had told her.

"Don't be mad at me, Lena," she whispered, wrapping her arms around me. "We all did what we thought was right."

"Not you too," I mumbled.

"I'm sorry."

I let out a groan and pulled away from her. "Well, what exactly are you sorry for?"

We both sat down on the edge of my bed, our knees pulled up so just one leg hung over, facing each other. "I'm sorry it took me two months to come visit you. That's one thing I shouldn't have listened to him about. I'm sorry you had to go through all of this alone. But, honestly," she paused, taking in a deep breath, "I knew if I came here, I'd never be able to lie to your face and I believe in Preston and what he's doing, what he's done. So I didn't want to risk ruining it. Not for the selfish need to see my best friend."

"I thought you pulled away because you were mad at me. It was as if every time I called, you were upset with me for leaving you."

"I was never mad at you. I totally understand why you left. I would have too. It was just better for me to not talk to you for a while, to let him do his thing."

"And what thing is that?"

"He has to be the one to tell you. He at least deserves that."

"Ugh! Why is everyone protecting him? He lied, Sam. He begged me to trust him and then he lied."

"You're right, and you have every reason to be upset, but do yourself a favor and just hear him out."

"What if what he tells me just breaks me even more?"

"It won't," she said with a surprising amount of certainty in her voice. "He might be able to put you back together."

"Did you fly all the way out here just to tell me you're on his side?" I asked my question with a pout, but regardless, I was glad Sam was there for any reason. I'd missed her more than I realized.

"I'm on your side, always."

"Well, I need to run before I can even think straight. Want to come with me?"

"I just took the red-eye over an ocean," she said with a raised eyebrow.

"Okay, point taken. Wanna take a nap on my bed?"

"I knew we were best friends for a reason."

Sam changed into some comfy clothes and crawled into my bed as I put on my running gear. I left the house and made it to the beach. The sky was still watercolor hues of red and orange. It looked like a painting and I took just a moment to breathe in the clean air and appreciate the fact that I was, in fact, in paradise. If there was anywhere to have some sort of quarter-life crisis, this was the place.

With a little bit of the weight lifted from my shoulders, I began my run, again seeking that place where my brain could empty out and let clarity seep in. I needed clarity more in that instant than ever before.

I don't know why I was surprised to see Parker jog up next to me at our usual spot, but I was. I guess I figured that since the jig was up, there was no need for him to run with me anymore.

"Hey, Lena," he said easily as he fell into pace beside me.

"Parker," I replied, coolly.

"Good to see you out and about. I was worried you'd close up and hide in your apartment. Or even worse, run."

"I am running."

"I meant run away, like you did before when you left Oregon."

"Excuse me?" I snapped, stopping in my tracks. "I didn't run away from anything in Oregon. There was nothing left there to run away *from*."

"Except Preston."

"You're delusional," I said as I started to run again, only this time I went faster.

"Just promise me you'll at least listen to him, Lena. Give him a chance to explain."

"For crying out loud! How is every single person I know on his side? Do you know what he did to me? Did he tell you he did the exact opposite of what he was supposed to do? That he lied to me? That he made me believe he was working for me when, in fact, he was working against me?"

"He wasn't against you. Please, you just have to listen to him."

"Why does it matter so much to you?"

"Because he's my brother and, even though this might be hard for you to see right now, he's never cared for anyone like he cares for you."

I scoffed. "Well, yippee. How did I get so lucky to be the one he cares about so much he lies and manipulates me?"

"Lena…"

Parker was pushy; I could give him that.

"Fine! I'll let him explain, but if I listen to him and ask him to leave and never speak to me again, you all have to leave me alone. It has to end when I say so."

"Deal," he said without hesitation.

I looked over at him and slowed my pace until I was stopped and Parker was facing me. "You really believe in him, don't you? You think he's going to explain himself and I'm just going to fall all over him again?"

"I just think he deserves the opportunity to explain his side of the situation. And you deserve to hear it, too."

I couldn't argue with him. I did deserve to hear what happened. I just wasn't sure I wanted to know.

"Can I run by myself now?" I kicked some sand, feeling a little like a petulant child. "I'd like a few minutes alone to get my thoughts in order."

"Sure," Parker smiled. "And thank you, Lena."

"He really cares?" The question slipped from my mouth before I even realized I'd thought it. It tumbled right out in the open and my heart stopped, waiting for the answer.

"I don't think 'cares' is a big enough word to wrap around how he feels about you." His voice was soft and careful. It was also honest. I could tell he believed what he just said, and for the first time in months, I let myself believe too. But just a little and only for a moment. Then I tamped it back down. There was no one who was going to protect me except me.

After over an hour of running, I made my way back to the apartment and purposefully took the back staircase to avoid walking past the apartment containing Preston. I'd listen to him as I'd promised Parker, but it didn't mean I wanted him to see me all sweaty and sandy.

When I entered the apartment, Piper was sitting on the couch with a mug in her hand. She looked as if she was waiting for me. She opened her mouth and I immediately held my hand up to stop her.

"Parker already got to me. I told him I'd listen to Preston, so you can save the diatribe. I've been converted."

She smiled at my words. "I knew Parker would get his point across."

"Yeah, well, he can be pretty convincing when he wants to be."

"He's a lawyer," she said with a shrug.

"You know what? I'm pretty sure I knew that. Dammit! I shouldn't have let him corner me."

"It'll all be good, Lena. I promise."

"Well, just because I agreed to hear him out doesn't mean you're off the hook. You lied to me too," I said as I walked into the kitchen to get a glass of water. It surprised me in the moment when I realized I wasn't really upset with Piper. Or Parker for that matter. They didn't hurt me with their lies. If anything, they were a distraction when I was in such a dark place and they helped me. I couldn't be mad at them for that. But I could give them both a hard time about it. I took a long drink of cold water and then looked back to Piper.

"I'm sorry. I know I lied to you, but really, I was just trying to make sure you were all right. Preston didn't want you all alone."

I let her words sink in and took them for what they were worth: a sister doing a favor for her brother. She wasn't trying to hurt me, or harm me, she was just making sure I wasn't sad and alone. I pushed off the edge of the counter I'd been leaning against. "I know. It's all right."

She looked relieved at my words. "You know, Preston asked me to come out here and watch over you, but he never asked me to be friends with you. I wanted to be your friend that first day we met. I never lied to you about the important stuff. I'm exactly the person I portrayed to you."

"Ha. Except for that one important fact of who your brother is." I dropped my tired body onto the couch next to her, leaning my head back on the cushion.

"Well, I got the impression that if I told you I was his sister, you would've run in the other direction."

"You would've been correct," I said with a smile. I heard a door open down the hallway, followed by footsteps. Sam came around the corner, hair a mess, eyes half closed.

"Your phone keeps vibrating," she said as she walked toward me with her arm out like a zombie, handing my phone to me.

"Piper, this is my best friend, Sam."

Sam and Piper had identical, guilty looks on their faces.

"Let me guess, you already know each other?" I asked, rolling my eyes. They both exchanged small smiles with each other and then gave me identical shoulder shrugs. "Shut up."

"We met in Portland before I came out here," Piper said sheepishly.

"Of course you did." I didn't even have the energy to let that bother me. "Anything else I should know about?"

Again, Piper and Sam exchanged looks.

"I don't think so," Sam said.

I looked down at my phone and saw a text from Preston.

Please tell me I can see you today.

I sighed and tried to ignore the part of me that was secretly excited to see him again. I hadn't been able to really look at him the night before.

Meet me for coffee in two hours.

I sent him a link to the coffee shop I'd met Piper in and then looked up to my two friends who were eyeing me with expectant looks on their faces.

"I'm going to have coffee with him," I said reluctantly. I stood up from the couch to get ready and shook my head, half in exasperation and half in amusement, when Piper and Sam gave each other a loud high-five.

I sat in the far corner of the coffee shop watching the door nervously. I arrived thirty minutes early, wanting to arrive before Preston to avoid having him buy me coffee. I needed this meeting to be nothing like a date. I didn't want him thinking I'd agree to see him and we would immediately fall back into that wild, passionate affair we'd had before. No. I needed to maintain the upper hand, needed to be the one in control of the situation. I knew the instant I conceded the control, Preston would take it and I'd never get it back. I took a deep breath in, trying to ignore the goose bumps spreading over my skin at the thought of Preston wielding control over me.

I heard the tinkling of the bells that hung over the door to the coffee shop and my eyes landed on Preston as he entered. I was instantly reminded of the first time I'd seen him when he came into Bartini. He wore his amazing black leather jacket, dark jeans faded in all the right places, but this time he had on his Converse. I ignored all the live wires coming back to life throughout my body, all the prickling of attraction, all the tightening of muscles that itched to be touched by him.

He didn't bother stopping at the counter to order a drink. He marched right toward me, our eyes never losing each other. He stopped when he was just feet from me and I just sat there, staring at him.

After a few silent but tense moments, he spoke. "Mind if I sit?"

I shook my head and he pulled the chair out across from me and sat. It was then I noticed that he held a motorcycle helmet in his hand. *It was him on that bike.* "How long have you been in Hawaii?"

"Just a week."

"You've been here a whole week?"

He nodded, saying nothing.

"Well," I sighed. "You're here for a reason, I imagine."

"You know why I'm here."

"I really don't. All I know is I came here to get away, to start over, and I find myself surrounded by you and your immediate family."

"I need to tell you the truth. To explain to you what happened. You made the decision to leave without all the pertinent information."

"Because you lied to me the entire time we were together!"

"That's only sort of true," he said as he shifted in his seat. "The things I didn't tell you were only to keep you safe, Lena. And I always intended on telling you the truth. I never imagined I would wake up one day and you'd be gone."

"Well, that's what happens when you take someone and their trust for granted. You lose it all."

"I'm here to win it back." His voice was firm and low, and I was proud of myself for reining in all the reactions my body wanted to have to his words, merely fluttering my eyelids.

"Start from the beginning, Preston."

Chapter Seven

"Six months ago, Piper called me. She was frantic. She had been dating a guy, Caleb, for a little over a year. She'd never brought him home, but the whole family knew of him and we also knew they were pretty serious. But Piper was living on an actress' pay in New York City, so we understood why flying home to Oregon to introduce her boyfriend to her family wasn't a reality for her."

"Piper's an actress? That explains a lot," I muttered.

The corner of his mouth perked up and I watched as he pushed his amusement down. I watched that part of his mouth, the part that was aching to smile, as he continued to talk.

"So this Caleb guy, turns out he was a huge asshole. Piper will tell you he didn't start out that way, but he eventually just went down the wrong path. Regardless, he's a douchebag." He shifted in his chair again, obviously upset by thinking about Piper's ex. I made a mental note to talk to her about him later. "He got into online gambling and that led to him seeking out bookies and making real live bets with some pretty dangerous men." Preston's hand came up to rub his chin, his new beard still there, making a grainy noise as his hand moved over it. "Well, he did okay for a while, but he was a dumbass and eventually he started getting in over his head. So much so, in fact, that he ended up betting all of Piper's savings and losing it."

He shook his head. "Piper should have known better, should have kicked him to the curb, but she let him stay on the condition he started a treatment program. He told her he would get help, and it seemed like he was. He went to meetings. Had a sponsor. Everything looked like it was improving."

I saw a muscle in his jaw start to twitch and the hand resting on the top of the table clenched into a hard fist.

"One day a man shows up at her apartment and beats the crap out of her."

I gasped and my hand flew to my mouth. "Oh, my God," I whisper. Piper was so small and sweet and lovable. Who could lay a hand on her?

"Yeah. It was pretty bad. My parents got the call in the middle of the night that she was in the ICU. I flew out there with them to see her. She was a mess, but after a day or two, she woke up and, amazingly, made a full recovery. Well, nearly. She's still emotionally damaged, as one would be." He cleared his throat, bringing a fist to his mouth, and I wanted so badly to wrap my arms around him in that moment. "But she's so strong."

"Preston," I whispered, not really knowing what to say. I couldn't imagine what it would be like to watch your twin sister fighting for her life in a hospital bed.

"Anyway," he continued, powering through. "Once she woke up and told us what happened, I found Caleb and beat him within an inch of his life." The steel with which he spoke those words chilled me. "Piper said someone came to their apartment looking for payment. Said Caleb owed this guy twenty grand and he took part of the payment out on her. So I found Caleb, kicked his ass until he could barely talk, got the name of the person he owed the money to, and then I kicked his ass until he was barely breathing." He paused again, this time tapping his fingers on the top of the table. "I'm not one-hundred-percent sure he lived, but I'm assuming he did because I haven't been able to find a death certificate for him. And no one's come to look for me yet."

I didn't really know what I was expecting Preston to say to me, but this story definitely wasn't on my short list. I was a little taken aback by all the new information. "You might have killed him?" I asked, my voice small and quiet.

He shrugged. "It's possible. I wasn't concerned at the moment with sparing him, but I didn't intend to kill him. I just wanted to do to him what his loan shark had done to my sister."

I nodded like I understood, but I didn't. I couldn't relate to what he was saying at all. I was shocked and surprised and caught off guard. I'd seen Preston protective and forceful, but I'd never seen him violent.

"Anyway, I found the loan shark and made an arrangement with him. He'd forgive the debt, to which my sister was linked to through her sleazy boyfriend, and I would be in his pocket. It was a good deal. He had no idea who I was, or any real proof that I could be of any help to him, and could have told me to fuck off, but he took the bait. I gave him all my information and was told he would be in contact when he needed my assistance. It just so happened that he liked the idea of having his hands reach all the way to the West Coast. Stroked his ego, so to say."

He took a deep breath in then let it out and I watched as some of the tension that had appeared when he was talking about Piper release.

"Funny thing about mobsters and people of that nature, they trade favors like picks in the NFL draft. So eventually I was approached by Edgar."

My mind raced trying to place the name. I'd heard it before.

"He's the guy who followed us in his car after the gala. He cornered us in the alley," he supplied when he noticed I was trying to put the pieces together.

"Right," I said, remembering the round guy who'd known who I was even though I had no idea about him.

"Turns out, Derrek and Edgar were buddies. Edgar owed Derrek, for what I'm not sure, but when you made that call to the private investigation firm, you set everything in motion. Derrek wasn't lying when he said he'd been waiting for you to make your move. And," he continued, "if it's any consolation, I didn't work for Derrek I worked for Edgar."

"It's not," I said quickly, even though I was still a little confused about the specifics.

"Well, I got a call from Edgar and he told me I was to meet my mark, you, and my job was to get you into bed."

My stomach rolled at his admission and I knew he could see the unease in my eyes. He reached across the table to take my hand, but I quickly slipped them below to my lap. My defenses went up automatically. "Well, congratulations. Mission accomplished." My voice was shaky, emotions coming out that I was desperate to keep in.

"Lena," he said softly. "I watched you walk into that bar and I couldn't for the life of me understand why any man would want to give you up, would want to jeopardize you in any way. Then I met you, got a taste of your sass, learned how incredibly smart you were, and I knew instantly I was fucked."

Just like the first time we'd met, his use of that word sent unwanted, yet delicious, jolts of electricity to the core of me. I trembled and hoped he didn't notice.

"This is all very interesting, but I'll remind you that you did, in the end, jeopardize me. You fucked me. In every sense of the word. So, tell me, why are you here now?"

"Because you're mine."

"No, I'm not."

"Lena, you're mine until I decide otherwise. And right now, you need to hear the rest of what I came here to tell you."

I couldn't think of a response and was still trying to recover from him voicing his possession of me, so I decided to stay quiet.

"You have to understand the position I was in, Lena. I wanted you. More than I've ever wanted anything in my life, I wanted you. I wanted to save you, to be with you, to help you. But I also wanted to give myself to you. I wanted everything with you. But, it wasn't that simple. I could have told Edgar to fuck off, could have just snatched you up, shown you everything you've been missing in your sorry excuse for a marriage with Derrek, and it was damn tempting to do it. But if I didn't play my cards right, Piper would be right back where she started. I had to protect her, but I couldn't just let you go.

"It would have been so easy to just take the job and seduce you, but I knew I'd never be able to walk away. So I had to figure out a way to keep you while still keeping Piper safe. It just turns out that Derrek and Edgar were a little smarter than I gave them credit for."

"What do you mean?"

"Those pictures you saw? The ones of us together?"

I swallowed hard. "Yeah?"

"Those were supposed to be taken at your house. That was the deal. I was supposed to sleep with you in your bed. Derrek had cameras in there for weeks just waiting. That's why I insisted we leave. I wasn't going to give him the ammunition." He rubbed his hand over his bearded jaw again. "So I made sure we never had sex in your house. Do you remember? You remember how I made sure we left?"

"Yeah?"

"You remember how, right before I slipped into you, I made you tell me you wanted it?"

My heart simply stopped at his words. I'd thought about him and I together that way a lot over the last couple of months, remembering the way we were together, how possessive and domineering he was, but also how tender and sweet he could be. But even with all the nights I laid awake thinking about him, I hadn't recalled that moment until now.

"I couldn't tell you just then how important it was to me that our being together was your decision, but it was. I needed that. Needed you to know that, in the end, you wanted it just as bad as I did. You *wanted* me."

"You said if I chose to be with you, it would be only you from then on. You said you'd protect me and keep me safe."

"That's all I've been focused on doing since you left."

I scoffed.

"You handed pictures of us, *together*, right to him. Pictures of you buried inside of me. I was mid-orgasm in that picture. And you just gave it to him." Tears threatened, my breath hitched, the heartbreak of his betrayal bubbling over inside of me.

"I did nothing of the fucking sort," he snapped, leaning over the table toward me, his hand slapping its surface loudly, jarring me.

I wiped away the tear that had escaped. "Your credibility is shot, Preston. That photo came from your house. How else did he get it?"

"That night – the first night we were together – that's the reason Edgar tailed me and cornered us in that alley. Once I took you from your house, he knew I didn't do it his way; that I wasn't going to. So, he sent someone to my house to plant that camera there. Edgar was stalling me so Derrek could still get his proof. I was never going to give him what he wanted. I would never do that to you. I never knew the photos or videos existed. I've never seen any of them."

I was losing a battle I'd been fighting for weeks. I wanted to believe him so badly. I wanted to believe that he'd never meant to harm me, or cost me everything. I wanted to believe everything he was saying.

But he'd lied to me.

And I wasn't sure how big or small that was; how significant or insignificant. Surely, if he was lying to me to help protect his sister, I could forgive him that, right? But that would mean I'd have to believe him – have to believe the whole story – from beginning to end. I'd have to believe he felt our connection as deeply as I had. That he cared about me. That he was hurting without me. That he'd come after me.

He must have sensed my wavering, must have picked up on the fact I was getting lost in the possibility of believing him, because he moved toward me.

As if in slow motion, his chair slid across the floor and his thigh was pressed up against mine. The warmth of his hand wrapped around the back of my neck, holding me firmly, pressing his fingers into me just enough to make me gasp. My eyes slowly closed, as if using my vision would be sensory overload coupled with the feeling of his touch on my skin. Then his nose moved over my cheek, nuzzling me, stopping when his lips were pressed against the shell of my ear.

"I can't be apart from you anymore, sweetheart," he said so quietly, it was barely a whisper. "I love you, Lena. You have to believe me when I say it was always you." His breath pushed up against the skin of my cheek, sending shivers throughout my body. "Everything I did, I did for you."

"I want to believe you," I said, bringing my hand up to cradle his face, eyes still closed, not caring that anyone in the coffee shop could be witness to our private moment. "But if I let you in again, if I choose to believe you and I'm wrong, it'll break me. You'll break me."

"Please let me take you somewhere. I don't want to have this conversation in a coffee shop." His thumb was brushing up and down the side of my neck and all I could do was nod. He stood and held his hand out for me. Placing my hand inside his warm, strong one was like curling up with my favorite blanket. It was familiar and reassuring.

He led me outside to the motorcycle I'd seen him on days before.

"That was you," I murmured.

"Huh?" he asked, reaching into a compartment and pulling out another helmet then handing it to me.

"I saw you on this bike the other day. I saw your hair and your leather jacket and knew it was you, but convinced myself I was just wishing you here or something."

He gave me a sad smile and then pulled the helmet over his head.

"I didn't know you could drive a motorcycle," I said, pulling on the helmet.

"I looked into having my Lotus shipped over here, but it was too costly, especially since I wasn't sure I'd even get you to agree to talk to me." He swung his leg over the bike and I nearly went cross-eyed. He looked sexy behind the wheel of his Lotus, but he was sinful on the back of a bike.

"Climb on." His words could have stopped my heart, could have liquefied every part of my body, but instead, they sounded tense and worrisome.

"You're sure you know how to drive one of these?"

"Lena, you can trust me."

Suddenly, I wasn't just going on a motorcycle ride, now I was making a decision as to whether or not I trusted him. I wanted badly to climb behind him and let him lead me wherever he was going, but hesitated for just one moment. I ran all the facts I knew through my brain, tried to weigh what I knew against what I felt, and the scale tipped just slightly toward him. In truth, the last pebble to fall on his side was Sam. I knew Sam wouldn't be here, encouraging our relationship, if he wasn't trustworthy.

I followed his example, having never been on a bike before, and swung my leg over the back. I found that as soon as I lifted my feet from the ground, gravity slid my body down the seat until I was snuggly pressed up against Preston's back. His hard legs and hips fit against the inside of my thighs. I laid my hands tentatively on his waist, but he grabbed my hands and wrapped them around him.

"Hold on tight."

My lungs snapped shut with his words, my mind instantly picturing Preston behind me as I was on all fours, open and waiting for him, right before that damned picture was taken of us. I squeezed my arms around him, both trying to hold onto him safely, but also to push all the humiliating thoughts from my mind of Derrek seeing those photos.

He smelled incredible. The scent that was simply Preston mixed with the unmistakable smell of his leather jacket was enough to force my eyes closed as I breathed him in.

The bike suddenly jolted forward, moving into traffic, and I yelped, unprepared for the movement. His hand came off the handlebar and rested against mine clasped to his chest. He ran his hand over mine a few times, soft and gentle, before putting it back on the handlebar. I relaxed as the ride went on, getting use to the unfamiliar feeling, leaning into turns and being so vulnerable to every car on the road.

It occurred to me about ten minutes into the ride that Preston was an excellent motorcyclist, and he must ride often to be that proficient at it. I began to relax and enjoy the scenery passing me by. I hadn't thought to ask him where we were going, but I didn't worry about it. I was willing to go wherever he wanted in that moment.

We left the city proper and started to ride away from the commotion. The road we were on wound up the hills of a volcano in the middle of the island.

On one straightaway, I watched as Preston took his hand from the bike and placed it high up on the outside of my thigh, giving it a firm squeeze. The touch was simple but meant so much to me. It was thankful, as if he were glad I was with him in that moment. It was regretful, as if he were sad this was the first time I'd been on the back of his bike. But it also felt possessive, as if he were just reaffirming that I was, indeed, his. All I could do in response was snuggle in closer to his back and let my hands roam a little freer across his chest, pull myself into him further.

After about an hour, he pulled off the main road and onto a gravelly path that led to what seemed like an unofficial lookout. Obviously, many people came here to admire the view as indicated by the pieces of litter along the edges of the area.

He flipped out the kickstand with his foot and I unwound my leg from the bike, eager to stand and take in the view. I pulled the helmet off and a smile spread across my face. The view was absolutely breathtaking. Blue ocean met blue sky, wispy clouds far off in the horizon, and white waves crashing onto the shores below.

I turned, a smile still stretching my cheeks, like I hadn't smiled in weeks, to find Preston leaning against the seat of his bike, ankles and arms crossed.

"Don't you want to come see the view?"

"I like the view from here just fine." He smiled as he spoke, but it wasn't the brilliant smile I wanted to see. "Come here," he finally said, the darkness back in his voice. I walked to him and stopped a few feet away. "I did a lot of talking back there. Is there anything you want to say to me?"

His question caught me off guard, but I thought about it for a second. Then I shrugged. "Why weren't you just honest with me from the beginning?"

He sighed heavily and ran a hand over his bearded face. "Looking back, that might have been the better choice. But just because I lost my mind when I saw you that first day, didn't guarantee you felt the same way about me. I guess I figured if I could get you out of your marriage unscathed,

I'd done my job." He paused and looked me in the eyes. "I wasn't planning on falling in love with you, Lena."

"That's the second time you've said that today," I murmured.

"What?" He looked puzzled.

"That you love me."

"I've said it to you in my mind a million times." He stood, pushing off his bike, moving closer to me. "I've said it silently to you while you've slept next to me." He took another step toward me, leaving just half a foot between us. "I've said it out loud, praying you could hear me an ocean away."

"I feel like I'm on a roller coaster," I whispered, looking down at my hands, wringing them in the space between us. "For weeks now I've cursed you, hated you for how you betrayed me. Then, you just show up, and you seem to have an explanation for everything. And I want to believe you, Preston, I do." I took in a breath, bracing myself. "I want to believe you and go back to the blissful place where you and I were exploring what it meant to be 'us,' and let you in all over again, but I'm scared."

"I know," he said as his hands reached gently for my face. My first instinct was to pull away, to keep a safe distance from him, but I couldn't move. He brought his hands up to my jaw, fingers curled, the back running along my jawline and down my throat, leaving a warm tingle in their wake. My eyes closed again and I swallowed, trying to keep down everything his touch evoked. Then, his fingers opened and slid around to the back of my neck, his thumbs resting on my cheeks, pulling my face even closer to his. "I want you to trust me," he said softly. "But I know I have to earn that back from you. But please, tell me you'll give me that chance. Let me show you."

I could feel his breath on my lips, could smell him all around me, and feel his hands on my skin. Then, suddenly, I was touching him too. My hands tentatively rested on his chest and he took in a small but audible breath at my touch.

"Please, sweetheart," he begged. It was as if he was asking for everything: to forgive him, to love him, to be with him, to let it all go and move forward. I couldn't answer him, didn't have all the resolutions he was looking for, but I could kiss him. So I moved my lips just close enough to his to feel the warmth of them. Then, like I'd given him the first ray of light in a dark room, he took my mouth and showed me how sorry he was.

It wasn't a soft kiss. It wasn't a slow kiss. It was a desperate kiss, as if he were afraid I was going to change my mind at any moment and he was trying to soak up as much of me as he could before I came to my senses. But my senses had fled and left me alone with this man and his mouth.

It was a hungry kind of kiss, the kind of kiss that was vocal. I could hear him kissing me, all the growls and groans. I didn't need to worry about breathing because, somehow, the kiss was breathing for me.

His hands were still on either side of my face, holding me to him, turning me every which way, trying to reach every part of my lips with his. My fists gripped his jacket, then blindly found their way to the zipper, pulling it down and finding his shirt underneath. I slid my fingertips down his torso, remembering every ripple of corded muscle, every ridge. When I reached the hem, I slipped my hands beneath it and started my journey back up his stomach, this time feeling his warm skin against mine.

He spun us around, one hand coming to my back, and he pressed me down to sit on the seat of his bike, straddling my knees.

Then, he shifted gears unexpectedly and I was floating. His mouth was a whisper upon mine and he feathered his hands down my neck, along my jaw, teasing my collarbone.

All the times Preston and I had been together, he'd been all manner of lovers. The first time was hard and rough; the release of all the tension we'd built between us. The second time was sweet and slow; a celebration of finding one another. But this, *dear sweet Lord*, this was divine. He was worshiping me, giving thanks, and each kiss was a prayer. Each kiss seemed almost breakable, so fragile, and it was perhaps that moment, in that kiss, I realized how sorry Preston actually was.

The reverence with which he touched me, the gentleness, it broke something inside of me. The dam I'd built, the wall I'd erected, and it came crashing down. Each tender kiss from him was like a wrecking ball to my defenses. Tears started streaming down my face, but for the first time in months, they were a mixture of sad and happy tears.

A sob broke free against his mouth, and then his hands gripped my hips and he hauled me up against him, lifting me off the ground. My legs went around his waist without a single thought, and then he sat the bike so he was balancing on it and I was straddling his lap. His hands moved upward, moving over my back, curving over the top of my shoulders, pulling me down to him even more.

I cried against him and eventually my face found the crook of his neck and I let everything out I'd held on to so tightly since that day when I thought my world had fallen apart. He let me cry. He held me, rubbed every part of my body available to him with his large, strong hands. He whispered to me, trying to calm me.

"Shh. Baby, please."

His voice was shallow and broken, hurting along with me.

"I'm so sorry."

I could hear the sorrow in the low timbre of his voice.

"Everything is all right now."

I believed him.

When I'd finally exorcized all the emotions from my body, I pulled away and looked at him. He looked just as wrecked as I felt with worried eyes and creased brow. I cupped his jaw with my hands and spoke softly to him.

"I forgive you." I shook as I spoke the words. I wanted him to hear me say it, so I said it again, louder this time. "I forgive you, Preston."

"Lena—"

"No, let me finish." I took a breath and trudged forward, staring into his eyes, watching the worried look from his face slowly disintegrate. "It was shitty that you lied to me." I watched as he opened his mouth to speak, but I narrowed my eyes at him. "But, I understand why you did it." My thumbs brushed over the peaks of his chiseled cheekbones under his beard and a smile crept across my face. "And if I didn't love you so much, I would probably hold it against you forever."

I watched as the understanding moved over the features of his face as he realized what I had said and what it meant. His hands slid down my back, coming to my sides just over my ribcage, his thumbs just brushing the sensitive skin at the underside of my breasts through my shirt.

"You have no idea how much I've missed you, how many times I stopped myself from getting on a plane and just coming for you. You'll never know..."

"It's okay," I said, my forehead pressed against his. "I wasn't ready for you. If you'd come any sooner, I probably would have turned you away. I was pretty mad at you for a while."

"I'm sorry."

I pressed my fingers against his lips, effectively stopping any more words he tried to speak. "I know, and it's over. No more apologies." I ran my index finger along the length of his full bottom lip, then I moved down and took it into my mouth.

The heat was back and it came through me like wildfire. The sweet kisses from moments ago, and even the mournful ones we'd just shared, all gave way to the raging heat coursing through me in that moment. The kiss erupted and so did my self-control. I found myself gripping him, wrapping my legs around his waist tighter, trying to bring myself closer.

Even though the horizon was orange and pink with the sunset, the sky just overhead had turned purple with clouds. Suddenly, we were in a downpour with rain falling from the sky, washing away everything from the last two months. All the anger, the sadness, the heartbreak; it all was rinsed away by the warm rain.

"Please let me take you home," Preston rasped against my lips. I knew what he was asking, knew he didn't just want to drive me to the apartment. My heart sped up at the thought of being with him again, letting him see me vulnerable again. But then I remembered what it was like to give myself to him.

When I was with Preston, when I gave him control over my body and let him have his way with me, it was the best form of escape. I didn't have to think about anything when I was with him, and I definitely never worried about a thing. It would be nice to disappear for a while, only concerned with Preston and what he was doing to my body.

He gently bit my lower lip, tugging on it, pulling it through his teeth. Shivers exploded all over my body, shooting directly to my core, heating me instantly.

"Yes," I breathed, bringing his mouth back to mine, tasting the rain water running down his face. "Please." He kissed me thoroughly, but then I was picked up and plopped down on the ground next to the bike, a little dizzy from the kiss and the movement. He pulled his leather jacket off and wrapped it around me.

"Put this on, sweetheart." My heart soared at his words. I slipped my arms through his jacket as he climbed on the bike, pulling the helmet over his head. I mounted the bike behind him and did the same. I wrapped my arms around his waist and held on tight.

He navigated the winding roads back down the mountain, the rain pelting us for nearly half the time it took to get home. The rain was warm – something a native Oregonian had to get used to over time – but the wetness combined with the air whipping past us made every part of me cold.

By the time we arrived back at the apartment, I was shivering and my teeth were chattering. He parked the bike and took me by the hand to his door, opening it, and ushering me straight to the bathroom.

He reached into the shower and turned the faucet on, then turned back to me and immediately started taking off my layers of soaked clothes. I was too incapacitated by the cold to argue or stop him, but I wondered why he wasn't freezing as well. He'd given me his coat and his tee shirt was soaked through, clinging to every contour of his chest. I found myself just staring at how each muscle moved, each one rippled in acquiescence as he moved about the bathroom, shedding me of my clothes.

By the time he had me in my bra and panties, I regained a little use of my brain and started to pull up on his shirt, trying to help him get warm too.

His shirt peeled off his skin with a slurping noise and then made a wet plop as it hit the floor, water droplets splattering all around it. I reached for the button of his jeans, threading it through, then pulling the zipper down, all requiring my full attention. When I looked back up to him, his eyes were on me and somehow, even though I would have thought it impossible, the chocolate of his eyes was even darker.

He toed off his shoes and socks, never breaking eye contact, then walked backward, carefully climbing into the tub, watching me all the while. He held his hand out to me and I didn't hesitate to join him inside the shower.

The water rained down on me and I sighed loudly, the hotness stinging against my cold skin. I closed my eyes and leaned my head back, running my hands through my hair as the water ran down it. Preston's mouth was on my neck and immediately a different kind of heat come over me. His mouth worked against my pulse point and his hands slid around my ribs to unclasp my bra. He pulled it off my arms and threw it over the top of the shower, the sound of it hitting the floor outside making me smile.

My smile was short-lived as it disappeared the instant Preston's fingers slid between the fabric of my panties and the cold skin of my ass. The combination of his lips on my throat and his hand grasping my ass forced a moan through my lips, and my head to fall back even farther still. My hands found his forearms, sliding smoothly up and over his biceps, feeling the taut muscles twitch beneath my touch, straining as he grasped at me.

I pulled away slightly to look down between us, relishing the sight of Preston Reid, completely wet, hard, and in black Calvin Klein boxer briefs. His cock pushed against the fabric of his briefs and I wasted no time moving to rid him of them. My hands moved into his underwear at the front of his body, then slowly slid around his waist and I enjoyed feeling all of him. My hands ran over the roundness of his ass as I pushed his underwear down his body. I moved down, dropping to my knees as his underwear hit the floor of the shower. He lifted each ankle one at a time and I freed him, tossing the underwear aside.

I looked up and was greeted by the sight of Preston's magnificent cock straining forward, arching toward his belly. All I heard was the pelting sound of the water hitting my back, running down the drain, and the heavy sounds of his breaths, pulling in and pushing out. I placed my hands on his thighs and then met his eyes. His gaze was so intense; it caught my breath in my throat and I had to remind my lungs to function, force my eyes to blink, make my pulse keep a steady, if not racing, rhythm.

I reached up and gripped his shaft, tugging gently downward so the head was pointing toward me, then lifted my eyes to meet his.

"Is this all right?" I asked, tentatively.

"Fuck, sweetheart, yes."

I stroked my hand up and down his cock slowly, taking a few moments to appreciate it up close. I'd never seen a more perfect dick. His was thick and long, cut, with one pulsing vein running down the underside. I moved forward and used the tip of my tongue to lick the underside of the head and a hiss echoed through the shower. As I swirled my tongue around the very tip, I heard him groan and saw his head fall backward.

"Don't fucking tease me, Lena. Put me in your mouth."

"Yes, sir," I said, smiling.

He'd been very careful with me all day, soothing me, caressing me, talking sweetly to me. But now I was being reminded of the very reason I fell in love with Preston – because he knew what I wanted and made it happen. And right now, I wanted his cock in my mouth.

I opened and slid my mouth all the way down his shaft until I wasn't sure I could take him any deeper, then used my hand to make up the difference, stroking him up and down as my mouth took long, sucking drags over him.

"Fuck," he groaned, leaning a hand against the wall of the shower, then taking his other hand and pushing the hair out of my face, which had been moved there by the water from the showerhead. "You look so perfect like this, sweetheart, with your mouth wrapped around me."

"Mmm," I mumbled my response, and as my voice vibrated against him his eyes rolled back and his head leaned to the side.

His taste was addictive and manly. Clean. When he started to taste more of salt, I knew he was getting closer, so I picked up my pace and moved my free hand from his thigh to his balls, rolling them in my palm. I squeezed them, then tugged gently while sucking hard on the length of him, pulling him slowly out of my mouth.

"Shit, shit, shit. Lena, baby, stop." His hips jerked back from me, pulling himself out of my mouth completely, and his hands were pulling me up to my feet. "Christ," he said, running both of his hands over my hair, pushing the water out of my face. Then he dipped, sliding my panties down my legs, leaving them in a pile on the floor of the shower. "I've been away from you for two months. I'm not about to come in your mouth the first time we're together again." He stood and his hand moved down, grabbing my leg behind my knee, pulling it up above his hip, and he pressed me back up against the wall.

I could feel him hard between my legs, just at my entrance, and my hips instinctually tilted forward in offering, wanting him inside me desperately.

"Preston," I whispered. I needed him but couldn't get the words to form.

"Shh shh, I know." His other hand came up to cup my breast, his fingers lightly brushing over my nipple, tugging gently. Then, suddenly, his mouth captured my breast, pulling and sucking on my nipple, eliciting a guttural groan from me. I was panting as I slid my hands over his shoulders, then dug my fingers into him when his teeth bit into my flesh, sending sharp, painful pangs through me, only to be soothed immediately by the warmth of his tongue. "God, I've missed your body, Lena," he said against my skin. His hand left my breast and traveled down my belly, finding my cleft. He didn't hesitate one second and slid a finger inside, both soothing and aching, creating an inferno.

"*Please*," I begged him.

"I thought about you every second of every day. And your body was one of the things I thought about the most. I couldn't get you out of my head. Couldn't forget the way your pussy felt against my fingers, the way it gripped my cock when you came, the sounds you made when I finger-fucked you like this in that closet." He looked into my eyes, slipping another finger into me, curling them both, and making me whimper. "Tell me you thought about me too."

"Yes," I agreed, immediately. I'd do anything he wanted, just as long as he never stopped touching me.

"Tell me what it was like to be away from me." He widened his stance in the shower, giving himself more leverage to push his fingers even deeper into me, using more pressure on the spot that drove me absolutely crazy.

I looked into his eyes and I knew he was hurting, needed reassurance that he wasn't alone in his feelings for the last two months.

"I was broken," I cried. "Shattered." I breathed the words out and nearly saw the weight lift off his shoulders. It was what he needed, to know I was just as lost as he was while we were apart. That without him, I was in pieces.

"I'm about to fucking fix you." His hand was gone in an instant, and then, suddenly, I was full. He thrust inside of me, just once, with such force I cried out, wrapping my arms around his shoulders and holding on. He pushed into me and then stilled, deep inside. We were both still, the only movement our breaths, and I was simply remembering what it was like to feel like all of him fit inside of me perfectly. I was so deliciously full, stretched exquisitely over him, and it was the most glorious feeling.

"No no no," I said, panicked when he started to pull out. "I'm not ready. Just, let me…"

"Shhh," he hushed me, swiping the hair off my face again. "I've got you." Then he pressed a sweet and soft kiss against my mouth. His tongue swept slowly over my lips and I opened for him, welcoming him in, tasting him. As he kissed me, he slowly lifted my other leg and I wrapped them both around his waist, letting him pin me against the wall completely. He pulled away, but only far enough to speak, his forehead still pressed against mine. "I'm going to move now, okay?"

I nodded, thinking I was ready for it, but gasped when he pulled out just slightly. My nerves were shot, every fuse inside me blown, all the synapses firing all at once. I was so keyed up; I could feel my impending orgasm just waiting for me, mocking me, teasing me.

He was moving so slowly; it was agonizing. He pulled out, then slid in, dragged back out. I could hardly take it any longer.

"Please…faster…"

He sped up his thrusts, building a tempo, drilling into me, his mouth finding every surface available to assault, his hands gripping my thighs, supporting my weight.

I was hanging on the edge of my orgasm, keening against his throat, trying desperately to find the release my body was thirsting for.

"Lena, fuck, you're so sexy. Reach down and touch yourself. Make yourself come." I didn't need any more instruction than that. My hand found its way between us, and feeling him sliding in and out of me was almost enough to throw me over the cliff, but my finger started circling and a loud moan escaped me.

"Oh, God…"

That orgasm would forever be remembered as one of the best in the history of orgasms. It was the kind of orgasm that made every muscle in my body constrict right down into my belly, and then, as if on cue, they all exploded in a synchronized burst of sensation that could have blinded me. It was a toe curling, lung seizing, nail scratching, unadulterated, fucking fantastic orgasm.

Preston pumped into me throughout the entire experience, prolonging it, making it that much better, kissing my screams away. When I'd settled and stopped trembling, he leaned away from me and slowly placed my legs back down, feet firmly planted on the floor.

"I want you in a bed, sweetheart. This was hot, and I definitely needed to get inside of you, but I can't touch you the way I want to like this, can't be as close to you as I'd like."

"Okay," was the only thing I could come up with as a response. He kissed me again, deeply, before he led me out of the shower. He took a towel from a shelf and started at my shoulder, running it down the front of me, moving down my belly. The towel wasn't anything special, pretty typical in fact, but it made me remember the towels at his condo back in Portland and how they'd been so soft against my skin.

"You didn't bring your expensive towels with you to Hawaii?"

A grin spread over his face. It was a playful grin, almost boyish, and it was beautiful. "No, but these will do for now. We can have something to look forward to when we go back to Portland."

My stomach bottomed out at his words, my mind automatically going into overdrive. I hadn't thought about going back to Portland. Ever. I wanted to be as far away from that place as I could get. The thought of following Preston back there sent me into a panic. He must have noticed my face freeze and eyes widen because he was instantly in front of me with his hands cupping my face.

"Hey, hey, Lena, it's fine. We don't have to think about that right now. It was stupid of me to say that. Please, baby, don't get upset."

"I don't know if I can ever go back there."

"I know. I understand. Don't worry about it."

"I came here and built a life. I started over. I made it, on my own, for the first time in my life. I can't go backward, Preston."

"Lena," he said, grabbing my shoulders firmly, looking me right in the eyes. "I would never make you do anything you didn't want to do. We don't have to figure this out right now. Right now, I just want to be with you and I don't really care where, geographically, we are." His grin snuck back onto his face and melted my panic a little, and my breaths evened out.

"Okay," I sighed.

He took my hand and led me back into the bedroom. Sitting on the edge of the bed, he pulled me to stand between his legs, his hands sweeping over the skin of my thighs, goose bumps trailing behind his fingers. He leaned forward and laid soft, wet, open-mouthed kisses along my belly.

"I know I've said this a lot today, but I really missed you, Lena." His eyes met mine and I'd never seen them more sincere than in that moment.

I swallowed and brought my finger up to run through the hair just above his ear. "I spent a lot of my time trying not to think about you at all." My hand dropped down so that my palm was flush against his cheek. "But that doesn't mean I didn't feel your absence. I did. I ached for that person I fell in love with, but it hurt so much because I didn't think it was real."

"The way I feel about you is the most real thing I've ever experienced."

I moved to place one knee on the bed next to his hip, then lift my other to do the same, straddling him. His hands smoothed over my skin, moving from the front of my thighs to the back, then both of his hands were molding to my ass, pulling me closer into him.

"Show me," I said quietly just before I kissed him.

He kissed me endlessly, or so it seemed, and his hands were everywhere, roaming every inch of my skin. When he moved to lift me, I let him lay me out on the bed, feeling his magnificent weight press me into the mattress and his mouth rained kisses all over my face, neck, and chest. The urgent, filthy mood we'd established earlier was gone, and we were swimming together in a pool of lust and affection.

When he finally slid into me, we both let out matching groans. His hands moved my wrists above my head, linking our fingers together, holding me down, and his face curled into my neck.

"God, I love you, Lena." He nearly choked on the words; they were so full of emotion.

"I love you too," I managed, just as overcome as he was.

From that point on, there were no more words; we didn't need them. His mouth spoke to me in kisses, his body communicating with panting breaths and tensed muscles. I conveyed my pleasure through touch, urging him on with whimpers.

His body prayed to mine, worshipped it. I'd never experienced sex in a way that left me so emotionally vulnerable than I did with Preston. Every move he made was a promise to me. Every time his mouth met my skin, I could feel his intentions, understood the meaning behind the movement even without him telling me. We were both wrapped up in using our bodies to connect, to impart our love.

When he came, I was on my side, legs splayed open, him behind me, with his hand wrapped around my jaw, pulling my mouth to kiss as he switched between biting my lip and sucking it into his mouth between thrusts. He sighed into my mouth as he came, trembling. He didn't pull away at first and we just laid together, connected, breathing heavy, lost in the reality of us together.

When he finally moved away, he kissed my temple as he pulled out.

"Stay there, sweetheart."

He came back a minute later with a warm washcloth and ever so gently ran the cloth between my legs. I was moved by his tenderness, but still squirmed at the intimacy of the act. When he finished, rather than walk back to the bathroom, he bundled up the cloth and threw it in the general direction of the door, then joined me under the covers, pulling my back to his front. He splayed kisses along my shoulder blade, and twined his fingers with mine, pressing our hands against my belly.

"I can't imagine it gets any better than that," I said quietly.

"Hmmm," was his response and my eyebrows rose.

"Hmmm? You've had better than that?" I was a little embarrassed, immediately thinking the most intense sexual experience of my life had only been mediocre in his eyes.

"God, Lena, no." He was laughing. "You just immediately got me thinking of all the chances we'll have to top it." His free hand pulled my dark hair off my neck so he could kiss me there. "That was, by far, the best I've ever had. Making love with you, well," he sighed. "It defies words."

I couldn't help the blush that spread into my cheeks. Then I giggled. I giggled, and then I snapped my mouth shut, or tried to. My mouth wouldn't close all the way for the huge smile on my face.

I was happy. Ridiculously, gloriously, exceedingly happy. I hadn't been happy like that in years.

"Thank you for coming for me," I rasped, the laughter suddenly gone from my voice. I brushed my thumb across the skin of his hand, using the motion to distract myself from all the post-coital emotions that were surfacing. "I don't think I would have ever gone back for you. I didn't think there was anything left for me there."

"Shh. Let's not think about what could have been. I want to focus on what *is*. And we're here together, right now. I'd like nothing more than to sleep with you in my arms and wake up to your beautiful face, because honestly, up until a few hours ago, I wasn't sure I'd ever be able to do that again." He kissed my shoulder blade again. "And I'm very much looking forward to it."

"Okay," I whispered, turning my face into the pillow, smiling as Preston's arm pulled me even closer to him.

Chapter Eight

The next morning was like a dream. I woke to his warm hand resting possessively over my belly, immediately smiling, liking the way he wanted to claim me even while sleeping. I turned my head toward him, sneaking a peek at him while he was unaware, and was treated to the view of his body, face down, and sprawled out on the bed naked from the waist up. The one hand that wasn't on me was laying right underneath his cheek, resting between his face and his pillow.

He was beautiful. And mine.

I rolled toward him then, pressing my lips to the shoulder nearest me, and then his arm tightened around me, pulling me in, urging me closer.

"Good morning," he garbled through his sleepy fog.

"Morning," I whispered against the skin of his bicep.

His hand wandered over my bare skin, coming to rest just above my ass, where he trailed light fingers in the curve of my back. Then, slowly, he rolled over, his hand remaining on me as if he were afraid to lose contact, but coming to rest on his back. "You feel perfect here, in my arms, in the morning. You're soft and warm."

I moved so my hands were resting on top of one another on his chest, my chin propped up on them, looking him in the eye.

"You look pretty good too," I said, smiling. He leaned forward and pressed a small kiss to my lips.

"I think," he said as he rolled his massive body over mine, giving me no choice but to roll to my back and look up at him, "we should take a shower." He placed a kiss on the hollow of my neck. "Then we should get dressed." His mouth moved down my chest, pausing to kiss me between my breasts, stopping my breath, speeding up my heart. "Eat breakfast," he said with a smirk as his mouth moved even lower to my belly, making me squirm. "Then, we should probably go check in with everyone else." His mouth moved even lower still, making me gasp when his breath feathered over the sensitive skin between my legs.

My hips tilted up toward him, wanting the contact, needing his touch.

"Sound good, sweetheart?"

Panting, I looked down to him, meeting his gaze over the rising of my breasts with each breath.

"I'm not going anywhere with you until I feel your mouth on me."

His eyebrows shot up, obviously surprised by my demand.

"You're the boss," he said with a grin. Then his mouth disappeared entirely.

An hour later, we walked into my apartment to find Sam, Piper, and Parker all sitting around the kitchen table.

"Well, look who's decided to come up for air," Parker said before we even got the door closed. I immediately blushed, but Preston's hand at my back urged me forward. Suddenly, Piper jumped up from her chair and darted toward Preston. I moved to the side, trying to not get run over, and watched as Piper launched herself into her brother's arms.

He took her in, wrapped her up, and the two of them swayed back and forth in their embrace.

"I've missed you," I heard Piper mutter into his neck.

"Hey, Pipe, it's okay. I'm here." His voice was tender and I was reminded why all of us were here to begin with; because Piper had been in danger and because Preston had protected her. It was moving to see him hold her, a protective big brother. Although, I imagined their bond went even deeper than that. Twins always seemed to be closer than normal siblings.

When she finally pulled away, she made sure to turn away from everyone, but I couldn't miss her wiping away the tear that had fallen down her face. I was both equally touched at the emotion she was showing toward her brother and surprised to watch their interaction. I looked back to him and his face was pained, matching hers.

Piper made it back to her seat and Parker gave her a smile, ruffling her head as she sat. Preston walked to the table and shook Parker's hand, then slapped the back of his shoulder.

"Thanks for vacating the apartment last night. I hope you didn't have a hard time finding a place to crash."

Parker laughed. "No problem. I stayed here on the couch. In fact, we had a great time."

I made my way to the table, taking the only available chair, sitting next to Sam.

"Hey, sunshine," she said to me with a smile.

"Hey. Sorry I disappeared."

"Listen, the three of us have been working like dogs to make sure last night happened," she said motioning between herself, Parker, and Piper. "This is what we wanted; the two of you together."

I smiled hard, but I blushed harder. It was unnerving thinking about all our friends and family plotting to get us back together, all of them knowing we'd spent the night reuniting. Sam placed her hand over mine.

"Are you happy?"

My eyes glanced to Preston and his smile was so radiant and beautiful. I couldn't help the corners of my mouth turning up to match. I looked back to Sam and nodded.

"Good. Then mission accomplished." She patted my hand again, then went back to eating the muffin that sat in front of her. Suddenly, I was starving. I stood up and went into the kitchen, searching for a muffin like Sam's, but was halted when Preston pressed his front to my back, sweeping my hair from one shoulder, and planting a kiss right on my neck. I shivered, his kiss awakening every nerve in my body.

"Do you want a muffin?" I asked, trying to keep our interaction PG for everyone else's benefit.

"A muffin sounds fantastic." I tried to ignore my mind's insistence that he was being dirty, and simply grabbed a muffin and put it on a plate. I turned and the friction caused by my front running along his chest caused my heart to speed up and my nipples to harden instantly.

"Haven't you had enough sex yet? After last night and this morning, I would think you needed to recharge a little." I tried to press the small plate between us, but he wasn't budging.

"Have you had enough of me?" he asked, feigning insult. He took the small plate from me, but just to place it on the counter behind me. Then he moved in, both hands pressed to the counter, caging me in. His head moved slowly until his lips were pressed against my ear, and any space between us had been eaten up by his long hard body pressing into mine. "I only got to enjoy you for a few nights before circumstances took you away from me." He moved down and pressed small kisses along my neck, teasing me. "So, forgive me if I want to get as much of you as possible."

"Okay," I whispered, afraid if I spoke too loudly everyone in the dining room would hear how needy I was. "But, not in front of everyone."

"Hmmm," he growled in my ear, his voice so low and gravelly, my body pressed into his even more. But then he gave me what I wanted and pulled away, but not before placing a very quick, chaste kiss to my lips. Then he took his muffin and sauntered back to the table and I was jealous of his ability to look completely unaffected.

I turned back to the counter and took a few deep breaths, steadying myself before I returned to the table, taking my seat again.

"So, what's the plan now?" Sam asked, looking first to me and then to Preston.

"Well, now that you have everything under control here, I should probably head back home," Parker said.

I looked to him, saddened by the idea of him not being around. "Who will I run with?"

He laughed and then took a sip of his coffee. "I'm sure Preston wouldn't miss an opportunity to see you running on the beach. And hey," he said, lifting his hand in the air, gesturing toward me, "if you ever make it back to Portland, we can run together there."

I frowned. Parker was a great running partner.

"Don't look so sad, sunshine," Sam said. "I'll run with you while I'm here."

My eyebrows shot up. "You're staying?"

"Listen, I didn't come to Hawaii to stay for a few nights. I took a couple weeks' worth of vacation I'd been saving up. I mean," she said, placing her hand over mine, "I hope you don't mind if I stay a while."

"Oh, my God, of course not!" I was nearly bouncing up and down in my seat, so excited by the thought of getting to spend some real time with Sam. "What about you?" I asked, turning to Piper.

She shrugged. "I have nowhere else to be." She said the words with a smile, but the overwhelming emotion was sadness. I got the feeling that for the month we'd been living together, she'd been shielding me from the troubles she was facing, keeping her emotions inside. I hated how she'd been hiding things from me and I wanted to make her open up.

"What about you? What are your plans?" Sam asked, her eyes locked on Preston.

He looked to me and smiled. "I'm wherever she is," he said, nodding in my direction, his eyes focused on mine. My heart fluttered at his words, warmed by the idea of him being near for now.

"One last run? For old times' sake?" Parker asked me.

"Love to."

It was hours later. Parker and I had gone on one last run, all the while he tried to convince me not to give up on Preston.

"I know it's great right now, the reunion high is so perfect, and it's probably hazing out all the bad stuff that hasn't found its way in yet. Just promise me, when it does, when all the bad finds the cracks and seeps back in, you'll believe in him and trust him enough to give him a chance."

I was watching the sand move beneath my feet as I ran, feeling my feet sink in, then pull out, muscles burning with each step, breath panting. Listening to Parker was mesmerizing. It was so abundantly obvious he had every bit of faith in his brother.

"I promise," I said through heavy breaths. It was such an interesting experience for me to watch Preston's brother and sister go to bat for him, to have such unwavering faith in him. I found myself looking out to the ocean and wondering what kind of sister Nadia would have been. Would she have flown to Hawaii to make sure I was all right? Would she have seen how bad my marriage to Derrek was and tried to help me?

I'd never really felt the loss of my sister. Later in life, I knew the way my parents raised me was influenced by their loss, but I'd never considered what I missed by not having a big sister around.

"He's lucky to have you and Piper," I said, just loud enough that I knew he heard me, but still quietly. It always seemed sacrilege to speak over the sound of the waves of the ocean.

"Patton loves him too. He's just less available to drop his entire life to help at the moment. You'll meet him eventually."

I gave him a smile and we continued our run.

Afterward, Parker found a flight, packed his bags, and took a taxi to the airport. It was sad saying goodbye to him, and I'd obviously become more attached to him and his friendship than I realized. But I knew I'd see him again; it was inevitable.

"Remember what I said," he whispered into my ear as he hugged me goodbye. "Have faith in him."

I nodded, smiling against his shoulder as I hugged him. "I will."

Later that day, after everything had settled down, all four of us found ourselves on the beach. Sam and Piper were in the water, sitting together with the water lapping around their legs. Preston and I were laying on towels, soaking up the sunshine as it slowly made its way toward the horizon, the day nearly gone.

I sighed in contentment, thoroughly enjoying the relaxation the last hour had afforded me.

"I can't believe that in the two months I've been in Hawaii, this is the first time I've just laid on the beach. I might not ever go back to work. I might lay out like this every day of my life until I shrivel up like a raisin."

"I'd definitely sign up to watch you lay around in a bikini all day, every day." Preston turned his head to look at me and gave me his sexy smile.

"Deal," I said, laughing. "You'll still love me when I'm all wrinkly?"

"Sweetheart, I'm going to love you forever, no matter what. The sooner you get that through your head, the better off we'll be."

"Deal," I repeated, but this time I leaned toward him to give him a kiss. His hand slid behind my neck, holding me to him, and he deepened the kiss. In fact, he took it much deeper than I had intended and I found myself lost in his lips, lost in the way his mouth moved against mine, how possessive it was, and how much I liked being possessed by him.

My skin was warm from the sun, but hot from the way his tongue caressed mine, the way his fingers dug into the tender flesh of my neck. His other arm wrapped around my waist, pulling me to him, but he also rolled over me, pinning me into the sand between our towels.

His hand grazed the skin just above the back of my bikini bottom, fingertips sliding just barely into the elastic. My heart trampled in my chest, and even though we were on a public beach, in broad, albeit dwindling, daylight, I couldn't bring myself to stop him. His hands felt too good on me. Thankfully, his hand didn't roam any farther and I trained my focus on letting him kiss me.

My mind swirled with the feeling of him over me, his mouth taking everything from me: my breath, my voice, my ability to think clearly.

"Lena," he finally rasped against my mouth, after what seemed like hours of making out on the beaches of Hawaii.

"Yeah?" I said, my hand raising up to run through his hair.

"I think we should go back to the apartment."

I laughed at his to-the-point statement. Nothing sexy about the way he said it, but sex was all he implied. I kissed him through giggles, then laughed even harder when he pouted.

"I've only just come up for air. I've hardly spent any time with Sam." I trailed my hand down from his hair to his cheek, trying to soften the blow of my tiny rejection. "We can go back to the apartment when it's time for bed."

He rolled off me and motioned toward where Sam and Piper were still sitting in the waves. "They wouldn't notice if you left. They're entertaining themselves just fine."

"That's not the point."

"I see my plan to get everyone here to force you into listening to me is backfiring. You're using my own weapons against me," he said as he pressed his mouth into my neck, biting me gently.

"We have plenty of time to spend together, don't we?"

He pulled back, suddenly looking very serious. His hand started at my forehead, then moved down my dark hair, twining through the strands, gently tugging when he got to the ends. "Yeah, sweetheart, we do."

"How long before you think you'll have to go back to Portland?" I asked the question even though I didn't want to hear the answer. In my perfect world, Preston and I would stay on this island forever, giving not one care about what happened back in Oregon, not letting anything taint the perfection we'd found in each other. But I knew that was an unrealistic daydream. I knew eventually we'd have to sort our shit out.

"I'm not on a timeline, Lena. I know how you feel about Portland, but we don't have to go back there. We don't have to stay here either. I can be a private investigator anywhere. The only thing I need is you. So, what do you want to do?"

I looked at him, looked into the beautiful chocolate eyes I'd lost myself in so many times before, but would never tire of seeing. Looked at his new, hipster beard, running my hand along his jaw. Then I looked at his mouth, the mouth that was so expressive. He was always smiling, or smirking, or grinning, or even pouting. I leaned forward and pulled his bottom lip into my mouth, tugging just hard enough to get a low growl from him before I let it loose.

Before I could answer, before I could tell him pretty much what he told me, that all I wanted for now was to be with him, the location ultimately unimportant, his mouth opened again.

"I want you to know, though, Lena, the two months we were apart, I wasn't just sitting around."

I inhaled deeply, my hand still resting on his cheek, his eyes not meeting mine.

"I know you were here, trying to move on with your life, trying to forget everything that happened with Derrek, and I totally respect that. I could go the rest of my life and never see his face again and I swear nothing, well, almost nothing, would make me happier."

His words were scaring me, my heart was thumping rapidly in my chest, and I could only imagine what he was alluding to.

"But I couldn't let him get away with it, Lena. I couldn't. I also couldn't come here without something to offer you, something to help prove I was, and will always be, on your side."

"What are you saying, Preston? What did you do?"

His eyes snapped to mine, and I'd never seen him so worried. His eyes were almost frantic, looking back and forth between mine, as if he were afraid he'd never look into them again.

"I found him. I found Derrek."

My body snapped to attention. "What?"

"I found him."

"How? Where? Wha—"

"It was the only thing I could think of to do that would prove I was never working for him. Not after I saw you."

"What did he say?"

"I didn't approach him. Haven't gone anywhere near him. I didn't know if that was something you would want."

"What I would want?" I was nearly speechless, not able to wrap my mind around the fact that Preston had found him.

"Sam told me he disappeared."

"He did. Right after you left, he bolted. But you were gone, and you didn't want to be reached. So, I did the only other thing I could think of. I hunted him down, determined to make him pay for what he put you through. I spent six weeks trailing him, following any lead I could find. When I finally was sure I'd nailed him, I couldn't do it. I needed you more than I needed him, and I didn't want to do anything that might take me farther away from any chance I had with you."

"You could have nailed him? What the hell does that mean?" My pulse was pounding, the very last thing I wanted was for Preston to go to jail, and I had no idea what nailing someone entailed.

"Nothing major, just, you know, confronting him, trying to find some sort of information to convince him to give you what you deserve."

"I don't need anything from him anymore," I said firmly.

"I know, baby," he said, his hand coming up to my face. "But you deserve so much more than what you walked away with. He not only took what you earned in that marriage, but he took everything your father worked for too."

He wasn't telling me anything I didn't already know. I'd given up thinking about everything Derrek had taken from me, mostly because I didn't feel like there was anything to be done about it. I'd signed every document he'd ever placed in front of me – and put in the position again, I'd do the same thing. Every time I made one of those mistakes, I'd done it out of love for someone. It wasn't my fault that Derrek ended up being a complete bastard and took advantage of me and the love I had for him. And it wasn't my fault that some asshole beat the crap out of Piper and Preston was forced to agree to ruin me before we'd ever met.

No, these problems were all Derrek's fault.

Suddenly, there was a fire inside of me. I was angry. More angry than I could ever remember being, and there was only one person responsible for the rage.

Preston was here, offering me the opportunity to find Derrek and get back everything he'd taken from me.

"You really think you can find him, you could find something to persuade him to give me what's rightfully mine?"

Preston's eyes never left mine. "All I know is that if it's what you want, I'll die trying to make it happen."

I looked at him, focused on his eyes, and I knew what I had to do.

"All right," I said firmly. "Let's find him."

END OF PART THREE

Part Four

PRIVATE

Property

Chapter One

There were few things in my world that could beat a morning cup of coffee on the beach in Hawaii. However, watching Lena jog toward me in rather small shorts and a sports bra ranked higher than any other luxury. I tried to ignore the fact that she was jogging with my baby sister, focusing more on the stretch and coil of the taut muscles in Lena's legs. Sam was also jogging with them, albeit reluctantly, but my feelings toward Sam also bordered on brotherly.

Lena was the first woman in years who made my blood run hot. She was also the first in years who I felt could match me in intelligence, humor, and—most importantly— in the bedroom. It wasn't even that Lena was overtly sexual—she wasn't. She was conservative in most areas of her life, including her body. I considered myself supremely lucky to be privy to what she covered up with clothes. I would forever be grateful that at the end of the day, she was in my bed, telling me about her day, and letting me turn her inside out with pleasure.

I'd never been with a woman before who inspired me to find every single part of her body that could make her writhe, to spend as much time as possible using my mouth, hands, and cock to get her off. A woman so perfectly made to fit me, it was as if we were pieces of the same puzzle.

Being away from her for two months as I tried to find something to offer her, something to convince her that I wasn't the man she'd been led to believe, was torture. I was sure she'd come to Hawaii and, inevitably, some other man would try to fill up the part of her heart I'd left empty and I'd lose my chance to rectify our situation. Piper had been my saving grace in those early weeks. That critical time when, in most other situations, I'd try to fix the problem immediately. I knew Lena needed something more, something I'd have to dig to find.

Piper owed me nothing, but insisted on going to Lena and being my eyes when I couldn't be there myself. Parker had always been the brother to swoop in and save the day, and I'd been grateful when he'd decided to head to the island to help Piper. Parker had a life back in Oregon, and his departure was harder on Lena than I'd anticipated. She'd bonded with him in the small time they'd been together, but I was happy they'd connected. I planned on keeping Lena in my life for a very long time, so her relationship with Parker was a tick in the pro column.

I smiled as all three girls approached me. Lena's eyes locked on to mine.

"You've certainly become an early riser since you've come to Hawaii," Piper said, her breath slightly labored. She knelt down and placed her hands on her knees, taking in deep breaths.

My eyes were still locked on Lena, but roamed down her body. "I'd never really had a reason to get up early before. But there are some sights in Hawaii you have to wake up early to appreciate."

Sam took clomping steps to join the group and then collapsed on the sand, not appearing to care that the sand would stick to the sweat covering her body.

"I," she said, then dragged in a deep gasping breath. "Am never," she rasped out before she took another breath. "Jogging again." She was sucking in air as if she'd been trapped under water, deprived of oxygen.

Lena smiled at her friend, but looked back at me. "She's used to jogging on a treadmill," she said, her voice light and happy, finding joy in simply being with her friends, and me, I assumed.

"Ah, yes," I said, sipping my coffee. "Running in the sand is a different exercise altogether."

"That's not exercise," Sam growled from the sand. "It's torture." She rolled to her side and stood up slowly, still breathing a little heavily, brushing sand from her body. "The devil endorses beach jogging."

"Dibs on the shower!" Piper sprinted past Sam, laughing, as she ran toward the apartment building the four of us were currently staying in.

Lena laughed but Sam's eyes narrowed at the disappearing Piper.

"She's going to regret that," Sam said.

"You can use our shower," Lena offered.

Sam's hands, which were still brushing sand away, stilled and her eyes darted from Lena to me. "It's all right. I'll wait. Besides, it looks as though he's about to eat you alive." Sam nodded toward me and I tried to hide my grin. Sam had proven to be one of my biggest advocates in the last few weeks, and I appreciated her complete and unwavering support. She also was exceptionally good at making herself scarce when I needed to be alone with Lena.

Sam winked at Lena and then limped off the same way Piper had gone. Lena turned her smiling face to me and tilted her head to the side, her grin spreading. "Are you going to eat me alive?"

I walked to her, pulling her against my body, feeling the heat from her sweat-slicked body pressed up against mine, my hand sliding up her back to cup her neck just below her raven ponytail. "Only if you're a really good girl," I said quietly, my lips at the shell of her ear. I felt her shiver and myself harden. Knowing the effect I had on her was the biggest turn on.

It had only been a week since I'd made my presence known to her. Just seven days since I'd laid my whole story out, hoping she would believe me, that she would give herself to me again. And in those seven days, after she had accepted that I never betrayed her the way she was led to believe, she'd been nothing but eager and responsive. She wanted me just as much as I wanted her.

My tongue darted out and pressed against the tender skin just under her ear. The salty taste of her caused a low groan as I imagined how the rest of her tasted. I felt her hands both come to rest on my forearms, then slide slowly up my shoulders.

"If you weren't holding that cup of coffee, I'd ask you to carry me upstairs right now," she whispered, her breath hot on my ear. My hand moved up, grabbing hold of her ponytail, pulling it down and forcing her eyes to look into mine. I dropped my cup filled with coffee to the sand and pressed my now free hand to the swell of her backside, pulling her in to me, letting her feel my erection.

"Be careful what you wish for, sweetheart," I muttered, just before bending down and capturing her with my arms, and turning to carry her up the stairs. She immediately started squirming, laughing and mildly complaining as I climbed the stairs with her in my grasp.

"Preston, this is ridiculous," she laughed, kicking. Lena was a strong woman. She ran regularly and took care of her body. But compared to me, she was slight, and she stood no chance against my arms when they wanted her close. One hand reached out and opened the door to my apartment and once we were inside, I used a foot to slam it shut, wasting no time walking back to the bedroom.

"I missed you when I woke this morning to an empty bed," I said after I laid her down and covered her with my body. She was breathing hard, but it wasn't from her run; it was her body reacting to mine.

"I didn't want to wake you," she whispered. "You looked so peaceful."

My eyes ran over her face, trying to read her expression. I'd had a hard time being away from her since I'd come here. At night, my body wound itself around her, my arms and legs sought her out, making sure she was next to me while I slept. She'd probably wanted a few minutes alone; a few minutes where I wasn't claiming her with my hands or holding her to me in my sleep.

My eyes roamed over her face, trying to read her expression, trying to figure out where her head was at. Lena had always been forthcoming with me, never shied away from telling me what I wanted to know—sometimes I just had to ask.

"Is it difficult to be around me so much? Would you rather go back to staying in the apartment with Piper?" Ever since we'd reconciled, she'd been staying with me in the apartment Parker had originally taken. Sam and Piper were staying in the two bedroom. I'd ambushed her. Shown up when she thought she'd gotten rid of me forever, and I'd practically held her captive since. I knew I was clinging to her, knew I was keeping her close, trying desperately to make up for the two months I had been away.

Her brow furrowed at my words and confusion became evident in her expression.

"Why would I want to move back into that apartment? I want to be with you." She sounded convincing. In fact, she sounded almost a little offended I'd asked.

"We've been together almost every spare moment since last week. I just want to make sure you aren't feeling smothered or in need of some space."

"I had two months of space that I didn't want to begin with." Her hands moved around my waist and up my back, urging me closer to her. "I want to be with you. It was just a jog."

She was right, I was being paranoid, but I would give her anything she wanted. I pressed my lips to hers, kissing her lightly, not entirely finished with our conversation.

"I just want you to be happy," I said, my mouth just a breath away from hers.

"I'm happiest when I'm with you," she breathed, her words making me lighter somehow. We'd met in a very unconventional way, started a ridiculously unconventional relationship, and then everything had gone to shit. She'd been convinced I was the worst man on the planet and there were times I worried her mind was still tainted with those thoughts of me—consciously or not. But I exhaled a sigh of relief at her words, my forehead falling gently to meet hers.

"Same goes, sweetheart."

"Preston?"

I lifted my head to look at her. "Yeah?"

"One of two things needs to happen here. You either need to take my clothes off me and follow through with your threat, or I need to take a shower."

A slow smile crept across my face and I leaned back so I was sitting on my ankles, her legs spread out around me. Her body was flushed from her run, a pink hue stretching from her chest up her neck. She bit her bottom lip, waiting for me to decide what I would do with her. To her. I reached behind me to grasp her ankle, bending her knee and pulling her foot in front of me. I removed her shoe and sock, then placed her foot back down and did the same with her other leg. She squirmed a little each time I removed her sock and I assumed she was ticklish, storing that information away for another day.

Once her legs were bare, I bent lower and put my mouth on the skin just below her sports bra, my tongue darting out, eager to taste the salt on her skin. She hummed as my mouth moved lower, stopping just above her shorts. Goose bumps broke out over the soft skin of her stomach and I smiled against her, my mind drifting back to the first time I saw her body and knew she'd be mine.

***

When I'd purchased my baby, my brand-new jet-black souped-up Lotus, I'd imagined myself in lots of scenarios. Sure, I was a private investigator, but the job was less glamorous than one might imagine. I spent more time tailing old married men than gangsters or criminals. The color of the car came in handy at night, but I had to be creative to utilize the speed and sexiness of it. I might have been guilty of happening upon street races or driving recklessly late at night, just to feel like I was using the car to its full potential. But sitting outside of a bar, waiting for some poor unsuspecting woman, was only made better by the car I was sitting in.

This wasn't my usual job. No. I had always kept my professional and private lives separate. No need mixing the two and creating unnecessary messes. But I'd do anything for Piper. Even if it meant seducing a woman. Even if it meant having my picture taken while I was inside of her— job's terms, not mine. It was a very specific job. Not just "sleep with the target." No, it was unusually more in-depth than that. More like, "sleep with target in her own bed, allow photographs to be taken in which it's obvious and undeniable that sexual intercourse is occurring, deliver images to target's husband." What kind of man wants that type of explicit photographic evidence?

As if I couldn't get more confused about why a man would want someone to *purposefully* sleep with his wife, she appeared in front of the bar and I was speechless. Her long, black-as-night hair was tied up high, but still hung to the middle of her back. The knee-length skirt hugged her slim thighs as she walked toward the doors, and her sky-high heels made what I could see of her legs look fucking fantastic.

As she reached to pull the door open, she turned toward my car, her eyes scanning the sidewalk, and I knew—from that instant—my life had just been hijacked by a woman I was hired to ruin. Never before had I felt such instant ownership over anyone, but she belonged to me. The way she put herself together, the way she tried to portray herself to the outside world, was a juxtaposition to the softness of her face. Her outfit, so stark and cold, hell, even her hair was tight and unobtainable. But her face, it was searching for something, longing and hope prevalent in her expression. She needed someone to help her and I'd be damned if it was anyone but me. In that moment she became my exclusive property.

Chapter Two

I woke to the sound of the front door opening and then closing, and my body shot up from the bed, my instincts taking over. I reached for the gun in the drawer of my bedside table, my fingers nearly on it when I heard Piper's voice.

"Preston," she shouted, "are you here?"

I shut the drawer and sighed heavily as my hand ran over my face, my heart pounding. I looked at Lena; she was still asleep. Usually I'd marvel at her ability to sleep through the ruckus, but we'd spent hours earlier wearing each other out in bed, so I understood how she was dead to the world. I stood up, grabbing my jogging shorts from the floor where Lena had thrown them after taking them off me, and pulled them on before heading into the living room.

"Preston?" Piper called out again just as I entered the room.

"Shhhh," I hushed her quietly, my finger to my lips. "Lena is sleeping," I said, walking past her into the kitchen and flipping the switch on the coffee maker.

"It's the middle of the afternoon," she said, her voice teasing. I could hear the smile on her face, and could tell by the tone of her voice she knew we'd been in bed all day and Lena was sleeping off sex.

I turned toward her. "And your point is?"

"I don't really have one," she said, laughing. "Just giving you a hard time." She came up next to me and took the coffee from my hands, finishing the task for me. Piper had always been louder than I was, more expressive, more forthcoming. I was the quiet one, the one who was thoughtfully silent. Most of the time, at least when we were younger, we were thinking the same thing, our minds always on the same page, but she was just more vocal about everything. There were advantages to being a twin, but those came with disadvantages as well. Even so, I wouldn't trade her for the world. Having a twin was like having a built-in best friend for life.

"What have you and Sam been up to? Did you beat her to the shower?" I leaned back against the counter, crossing my arms over my chest.

Piper let out a loud and humor-filled, "Ha!" and continued to prep the coffee then reached into the cupboard to grab two mugs. "She couldn't have beat a snail. She was literally crawling to the apartment." She put the mugs down, closed the cupboard door, and then turned to face me. "I know you and Lena are deep in the honeymoon phase of being reunited, but I'm starting to miss you both."

Piper's brown eyes met mine and I couldn't ignore the sadness I saw there, the loneliness. We'd spent a year or so apart—her in NYC while I was in Oregon—but separation for us was never easy. And now, not being separated physically but having my time taken away from her, well, I could understand how she felt. We weren't children, we could handle our emotions just fine, but there was something special about being a twin. Another dimension of connection that I was sure regular siblings didn't feel. I missed my brothers, but not the same way I missed Piper.

I opened my arms to her and she wasted no time stepping into my embrace. I wrapped my arms around her shoulders and felt her sigh against me, relaxing into the hug. We stayed that way for a long moment, then she pulled back and resumed her stance across the small kitchen, watching the coffee drip into the pot.

"How long will you and Lena stay here?"

My hand came up and rubbed the stubble on the underside of my chin. "I don't know. As long as she wants, I suppose. I'm not in any hurry to leave and she's the one who's made a life here." I shrugged. "If I want her to stay with me, I've got to make it easy for her. She deserves at least that."

Piper nodded. "She's lucky to have you," she said with a smile, even if it was a little sad. I tucked her sadness away in my mind, wanting to help, but not knowing what I could do for her. I'd done everything I could think of, everything in my power, and it seemed like her happiness going forward was in her own hands.

"How long will you stay here?"

She shrugged. "Sam has invited me to stay with her in Portland. You know, just until I can get back on my feet."

In the two months I was separated from Lena, Sam had been an invaluable ally to me. Sure, at first she'd literally tried to maim me, but after I convinced her I had been set up and only wanted to help Lena, she'd come around and become a friend. "Sam's great."

"Yeah," she said.

"You know Parker would take you in, or even Mom and Dad. You could even stay at my place. I'm not sure when I'll be back, but you'd have privacy there." And I could keep track of her using the surveillance equipment that'd been installed.

She shook her head. "Parker is almost as overprotective as you are and would make my life hell if I lived there. And you know how Ma is. She'd try to set me up with all of her friends' single sons, she'd start forcing me to go to all of her social functions—it would be embarrassing. Besides, I get along with Sam. Plus, I think she feels a little lonely without Lena around all the time anymore."

I'd never force Lena to go back to Portland, but if she could get past the idea that Portland held all the terrible memories of Derrek, I feel like there was a lot of *good* there, that we could be happy there again.

"Lena has to be comfortable wherever she is and I won't force her to go back there if it's not what she wants."

"No, of course not," Piper said quickly. "I guess I just wish all the good parts of my new life could all be together. You and Lena, Sam, my independence," she said with a small grin. "I know I came here to help you keep tabs on her, but I really care about Lena."

"I know, Piper," I said. "And she knows it too. She'll miss you when you leave."

She smiled at my words, but the smile didn't reach her eyes. "Can we all do dinner tonight? Maybe one of those fun luaus? I know Sam really wants to go to one before she leaves and it would be great to spend an evening all together."

"I don't see why not. Sounds like fun." I gave her a smile and then stepped forward to pour some coffee into my waiting mug. I poured Piper's too, and then reached into the refrigerator and handed her the creamer I knew she wanted. When both our coffees were just the way we liked them, we walked silently onto the attached balcony overlooking the ocean. It was just early afternoon, but the heat was already making the air muggy. We sat down next to each other and looked out to the ocean. My hand found hers and we sat in silence, just content to be near each other.

After nearly thirty minutes of silent contentment, Piper finally asked the question I knew had been burning in her mind since she walked into the apartment.

"Do you think we'll ever be together again, like, in the same state, for good?"

I gave her hand a squeeze before pulling mine away, using both hands to bring my coffee mug to my lips, trying to piece together an answer for her.

"In a perfect world Lena would choose to go back to Portland and we could all be in the same city. But I don't know if she'll ever want to go back, and I'm not willing to pressure her about it." I took another sip, still not looking over at Piper, knowing her face would be sad yet strong. "If I were her, I probably wouldn't want to go back there. I have to support that if I want her to stay with me."

"Do you remember being young and being captivated by magnets? Remember how they either stuck together with so much force you could hardly pull them apart, or they repelled each other and you couldn't get them to touch if you tried?"

"Yeah," I said, quietly.

"For most our lives we were stuck to each other, Preston. I knew if I turned around you'd be there. I could feel your presence all around me, supporting me, backing me up. It was something I could always count on. But, suddenly, one of us flipped over and now it's as if we're pushing each other away."

"I'm not pushing you away, Piper. I could never do that." I'd never heard her talk this way, never gotten this vibe from her at all.

"No," she said, turning her head away from me, pretending to look out to the ocean as she used the hand farthest from me to wipe her cheek, trying to hide her tears. "But, we're going in opposite directions, and it feels more permanent now than it ever did before."

I knew my little sister was trying to come to terms with the fact she wasn't the only important woman in my life. I also knew it had nothing to do with how she felt about Lena. Piper loved Lena—of that I was sure—but this was the first time I'd ever let my future depend on someone else and Piper was feeling the gravity of the situation.

"You're always going to be my twin sister, my *baby* twin sister. My relationship with Lena isn't going to change that and she wouldn't want it to; she loves you. I'll always be here for you in any way I can." Piper still wouldn't look at me, but I could tell there was more than one tear to wipe away when her hands brushed over her face. After a few moments, she finally turned to look at me, her face red and blotchy.

"I'm so happy you found Lena," she said, smiling weakly through tears. "This is just the first time I've felt truly alone in a while."

"You're not alone, Piper."

"I am, Preston. I am alone, and as sad as I am right now, I know that being alone is what I need. I am one hundred percent, completely aware of the fact that I need to work on *me*." She took in a deep breath and then sighed it out loudly. "It's just hard to think about being separated from you again *and* being on my own."

She was right. In all our years together, since birth, she'd never been on her own. She was either always with me or with a boyfriend. I hadn't realized it until she'd said it, but it was true. And based on her last relationship and how it had ended so disastrously, she didn't need to be jumping into another one any time soon.

"I don't really know what to say," I admitted. As much as I felt the need to protect her, to keep her safe, I knew that with Lena was where I was supposed to be. Lena was who needed me the most. Piper needed to find herself.

"Just tell me I'll be all right and that you'll never be too far away," she said, looking exactly half sad and half happy, as if she were torn completely in two.

"You're going to be fine, Piper, and I'll always be here for you."

"You're the best big brother ever," she said, smiling more, true happiness pushing out the sad.

All I could do was return her smile, hoping she found herself sooner rather than later.

We both turned our heads back toward the apartment when we heard movement from inside. I watched as Lena's slender body walked out of the hallway and into the kitchen. She'd put on some sleep shorts and a tank top, looking sexy and sleepy all at the same time.

"Lena's up," Piper said, not taking her eyes off her for a moment. When she finally looked back to the water, she wiped her face with her hand, making sure she had gotten rid of all the residual tears, then took in a deep breath, stood, and walked into the apartment. I followed, still worried about her but unsure how to help.

"Hey, Piper," Lena said with a genuine smile. "Where's Sam?"

"She's probably still in a puddle on the floor of the shower," Piper answered with a smirk. Lena laughed and the sound of it made the hair on my arms stand up and the beat of my heart pick up as well. Her dark hair was loose and it fell down almost to her waist in carefree waves. I shook away the image of her naked back, my hand running up her spine while my other hand grabbed hold of her hair, pulling her back onto me.

She turned back to the cupboard, opening the door to pull out a mug, and I walked up behind her, pressing my front into her back, loving the way my now hardening dick fit nicely up against her backside. She yelped a little, surprised by my sudden proximity, then laughed again as she pulled all her hair to one side of her neck.

"Sleep well?" I asked, just before I pressed my mouth against the skin of her neck.

"Mmm. I slept very well. Until I woke up and you were gone." She accommodated my lips on her skin, never moving away as I trailed my mouth up to her ear, then back down to where her neck met her shoulder.

"Miss me?" I mumbled, purposefully scraping my stubble against her, loving the way her breath caught from the friction.

"Something like that," she said as she pressed her ass further in to me.

I bit down, a little rougher than I intended, but knew my point had gotten across when she gasped. "Careful, Lena," I said quietly into her ear, then licked the spot I'd just bitten.

"Would the two of you knock it off?" Piper's voice interrupted my thoughts of Lena's ass against my cock, and thinking about my sister just in the next room calmed me down quite a bit. Lena turned her head and smiled at me right before she pressed a small kiss against my lips. Then she poured coffee in her mug and took it to the table, sitting across from Piper.

"What's with the midday nap?" Piper asked, a smirk still stretched across her face.

"I was tired," Lena answered before she took a sip of her coffee, trying to hide a smile behind her mug. I walked to the table and took the chair between them.

"Piper wants to go to a luau tonight."

Lena's face lit up with a bright smile. "That sounds amazing. Great idea. I've never been to one before, but always wanted to go."

"Great, now we just have to convince Sam."

"Sam will go. It's right up her alley—attractive shirtless guys playing with fire? Done deal."

The girls laughed and I was glad to just sit back and watch them interact. Piper had never disliked any of my girlfriends. In fact, she'd become friends with many of them and that was important to me. I wasn't interested in dating anyone who didn't get along with my twin sister. But I wasn't *dating* Lena. I wasn't trying to woo her, wasn't even trying to see if she fit into my life. She was mine and my life was now wherever she was, and it was of paramount importance for Piper to like her, to love her even. So to see them laughing, and to know that for two months they'd built a friendship without me in the picture was something that brought me a lot of peace.

"Well," Piper said, taking the last sip of her coffee, "I'll go pick Sam up off the floor and tell her to get ready for an exciting evening." She walked to the sink and deposited her mug, then walked to the door, stopping and turning to us once it was open. "I'll make the arrangements and let you guys know what time it starts, all right?"

"Sounds good. Talk to you later," Lena said with a smile.

Piper gave me a warm smile and a wink. I winked back, glad she was leaving with a smile on her face and the tears she had shed earlier seemed to be gone. When the door closed behind her, my eyes went to Lena. She sat quietly at the table and looked to be lost in thought. I let the silence settle, content to just look at her, fresh-faced and comfortable.

"I love that you get along with my sister," I finally said, my eyes still captivated by her ease and beauty.

She looked at me, her gaze meeting mine. "Piper saved me when I first got here. I don't know what I would have done without her. Even though I know you sent her, she was and still is truly a great friend." She paused, considering her next words. "I need good people in my life. Besides Sam, who's the best, I've been surrounded by people who didn't care about me or my happiness for most of my life. I was lost in the shadow of my sister and then used as a tool by my father to climb the corporate ladder. It's good to finally feel as if the people in my life don't need me for anything, but want me for everything."

"Come here," I said, crooking a finger at her, needing her close to me. She smiled shyly, but stood and walked to me. I tried not to notice how tiny her shorts were, failing miserably as my eyes were drawn to the expanse of the creamy skin of her thighs. When she stopped in front of me I spread my legs wider and tapped my knee, signaling for her to sit. She obeyed, sitting sideways on my lap and wrapping her arms around my neck.

I placed my finger under her chin, lifting her face just slightly so I could look her in the eyes.

"I need you for everything," I said, not looking away. "I want you for everything, too."

"Everything?" she asked, an air of vulnerability in her voice; she was obviously asking more than a rhetorical question. Her tone worried me, but I didn't flinch, didn't let my concern show on my face at all.

"Everything, Lena. I want it all."

Her face pulled down and I let my finger fall away. She took in a deep breath and I could feel her steel herself.

"There's something I should tell you, then."

I reached up to her face, my hand moving over her cheek, threading through the hair at the nape of her neck, gently gripping it there. "I'm here. What is it?"

"After that morning in front of my house back in Portland, after Derrek showed me the picture of us, after I thought everything in my life had fallen apart around me, I just kind of shut down."

I felt my stomach drop and my grip on her tightened. I hated knowing she'd been hurting without me, because of me. Hated thinking of her all alone, thinking she'd lost everything, when in reality, I'd never let her go. "I'm sorry, sweetheart, for everything."

"Shhh," she said as she gently put her thumb over my lips, effectively shushing me. "You've got nothing to apologize for. I know why you did what you did, and I'm glad you did it." She inhaled again, her eyes darting between both of mine. I got the feeling she was trying to tell me something and she was afraid of how I would react. I could tell she was nervous, feel that she was tense beneath my hands. "I left my house that morning and went straight to a hotel. I didn't have anything with me, including," she said softly, her eyes falling away to her lap, "my birth control pills." She sighed heavily, obviously lighter once the words left her. "I haven't taken them since that day."

I took in her words, processed them, then looked at her, trying to gauge how she felt about her admission. I knew how Lena felt about children. I knew we'd been sleeping together nearly nonstop for a week and neither of us even mentioned condoms—we'd never used them in Portland. I also knew her husband had denied her a family but then started one with someone else, stringing her along for years with promises of babies down the road. Promises he never intended to keep. I imagined she felt guilty for not telling me earlier, but I also thought she might feel hopeful about the situation.

I pulled her face to mine, gently kissing her, feeling her relax against me. Her arms came back around my neck and I breathed her in. My free hand roamed up her back, feeling her soft skin under her tank top, loving the way she pressed further in to me.

"I'm sorry," she whispered when the kiss broke. "I should have told you sooner."

I knew she wanted words from me, but I had none.

I wrapped my arm around her waist and stood, letting my other arm catch beneath her knees, and carried her to the bedroom, kissing her the entire way. When I sat her on the bed, her eyes looked worried, but I could do nothing besides kiss her again. I wanted to reassure her, wanted to ease her fears, but needed to do it with my body.

My knees rested on the bed on either side of her hips, straddling her. She raised her arms as I lifted her tank top over her head, tossing it on the floor. Her dark hair fell over her breasts, her nipples hard and peeking out through the strands. Her chest was moving up and down rapidly with her breath, and a flush was starting to cover her throat and cheeks. My hands cradled her face and my mouth found hers, kissing her insistently. She moaned and my cock jumped at the sound.

She leaned back, lying fully on the bed, and my body ached to cover hers, to feel her beneath me. Just as eager as I was, she lifted her hips and removed her shorts. Her hair fell away from her body, uncovering her breasts. I sat up again, looking down at the beautiful woman who, even after I'd lied to her, chose to believe in our love and give herself to me again. And not only that, but chose to let me give her everything in return. I was in awe of her.

My hands started at her waist, caressing gently up her stomach and over her full breasts. I watched as her chest rose and fell, her breath shuddering, eyes closing, mouth opening. When she pushed her breast further into my palms, I knew she was aching for me too.

I wrestled with the urge to give our bodies what they craved, or feed our souls what they needed. In the end, I decided to go with both options.

I sank into her, our bodies connecting, both of us groaning as sensation took us over. I brought my face directly level with hers, our eyes searching each other's, bodies pressed together, and breaths intermingling.

"I want to have everything with you," I managed, even if it was just a strangled whisper. My voice was gone somewhere, definitely overtaken by the enormity of the moment I was sharing with her, humbled by the idea that she would give me the gift of being the person she made her children with. It was almost too much for me to process. So, instead of thinking and analyzing, I kissed her.

I kissed her as I brought us both to a place where nothing that had happened in the last two months mattered, where our pasts were forgotten, and our future was painted in bright lights.

When we came, we came together, eye to eye, mouth to mouth, and everything in the world ahead of us.

Chapter Three

I walked alongside Lena, holding her hand and listening to Piper and Sam commenting on the abundance of shirtless Hawaiian men. Every once in a while Sam threw in a comment about a particularly nice "rack" she admired on a woman, and then all three girls would silently admire said breasts, longing for their own bodies to be improved upon.

This was one thing I hated about women in groups—they constantly and openly compared themselves to other women, and then degraded themselves because their bodies were different. Also, they usually immediately disliked any woman who had a physical trait they lacked, or perceived themselves as lacking. I had heard Piper many times admire a woman's ass, in that weird jealous way they do, then assume the woman was a bitch because she had what Piper wanted.

As a man, did I admire a beautiful body on a woman? Sure. But it was going to take more than a nice ass to keep me interested or make me want more than just a look. I'd tried to tell this to Piper time and time again, trying to make her realize any man worth her time would fall in love with her because of who she was and her body would be a bonus.

The whole thing was stupid as fuck as all three women next to me were beautiful and turning heads themselves. Women were their own worst critics.

We entered the luau through an arch covered in brightly colored flowers and foliage, all native to Hawaii. There were two women at the entrance who placed leis over our heads and said "Aloha" with bright smiles. There was loud rhythmic drumming and the smell of the food was intoxicating. I felt Lena's small hand capture mine, threading her fingers through my own, and I looked over at her to see a bright smile painted across her face. She was excited.

"Lena, they're giving hula lessons over on that lawn," Sam said, turning back to us, looking just as excited.

"Would you like to take a hula lesson?" Lena asked me.

I leaned closer to her, making sure my lips were pressed softly against the shell of her ear, knowing my words would cause her heart rate to speed up. "No, but I'd really love to watch you learn." At my words, I felt her lean in to me and pull up her shoulder, as if she were trying to capture me and keep my mouth as close to her as possible. Then she turned her face and kissed me. I pulled our clasped hands closer, bringing her body against mine, and brought my other hand up to gently cup the side of her face.

Lena's mouth was almost as unpredictable as she was. Sometimes her lips were soft and gentle. Other times her kisses were curious. She'd used her mouth to convey so many things to me, so many emotions, I was constantly trying to read her thoughts through her lips. Was she needy? Angry? Scared? Happy? All could be told through her kisses. In that moment her lips told me, as they moved slightly against mine, that she was happy and relaxed. When she pulled away she gave me another breathtaking smile, then headed toward a woman in a floral bikini top and grass skirt who was giving hula instructions.

All three girls approached the teacher and then after a few words were exchanged, formed a line facing in my direction. I found a chair at an empty table not too far from the stage and sat, content to let my eyes wander over Lena as she learned the traditional dance.

I watched as her hips swayed from side to side, enjoying the visual and also appreciating that I could imagine what that swaying looked like without the flowing skirt made of grass. I'd have to convince her to show me the dance later, only naked. Thinking of Lena's body without clothes immediately woke up my cock, which, admittedly, wasn't ever fully asleep when Lena was around anyhow. I saw her delicate hands and fingers make tiny yet distinctive movements, trying to tell a story with the motions. I heard her laughing with Sam and Piper and the whole scene left me feeling more whole than I'd ever felt before.

Lena's eyes met mine as she laughed and it was as if something broke my chest open and squeezed my heart. She was absolutely everything I would ever want. As long as I had her I would never want for anything. And I *did* have her—every part of her. She was mine just as much as I was hers.

Minutes passed as I watched her hair get caught in the breeze, her skirt fluttering around her soft knees, her hips moving to the beat of the music. I was interrupted by the vibration of my phone in my pocket, and when I saw who was calling I felt my heartbeat falter and my lungs seize up.

The past week with Lena, since I'd revealed myself to her, had been better than I could have imagined, and there were only a few people on the planet who could mess everything up. One of those people was calling me. I swiped my finger across the screen and brought the phone up to my ear.

"Edgar," I said, trying to sound irritated and bothered, not wanting him to know his call had made me nervous. "I wasn't expecting to hear from you again. Ever."

"Preston, I know you must be thrilled to talk to me. I hadn't expected to ever hear your voice again either, but things change."

"What things?" I asked, shifting in my chair, growing uncomfortable. I'd worked off my debt to Edgar. Derrek had gotten exactly what he wanted in the end, and that was all that was required of me. I owed nothing to Edgar.

"We have a common interest—a problem that's gotten out of hand—and I need your help."

"What common interest?" I asked the question, but I knew the answer. There was only one reason he would be calling me.

"Derrek Bellows."

I tried not to physically cringe at the mention of his name. Lena's eyes were still drifting to me every once in a while, between laughing and smiling with her friends, and I didn't want her to know I was on the phone with someone potentially dangerous, someone who could snap his finger at any number of people and make life difficult for us. Sure, I was a private investigator, but I wasn't dirty. I didn't deal with crooked cops or gangsters. I worked with lawyers and regular citizens. I checked public records, for Christ's sake. I could follow a mark, I could bug a phone, and I could become invisible if I needed to, but it wasn't my first choice to deal with crooks.

"The last tail I had on Derrek he was sitting pretty in the Caribbean with his mistress, sitting on a shit load of money."

"That's my money he's sitting on."

"Oh?" I tried to sound apathetic, but he'd piqued my interest. Edgar wasn't the biggest fish in the sea of crooks, but he had some big fish friends, and I knew you didn't want to end up on his bad side. I didn't want to be in his pocket any longer, but I knew it was better to appear to be his ally than to fuck him over. Then you'd be swimming with a whole different kind of fish and your shoes would be made of cement.

"Seems our Derrek thought he could pull a fast one on me. He was in deep with me, and because we had a good history I'd given him a little leeway. He took that inch of rope and hung himself with it when he decided to split town, taking my money with him. Abandoned the business and no one seems to have any answers for me."

I sighed heavily. "What can I do for you, Edgar?"

"Call me Eddie, please," he said, his voice a little too pleasant.

"Lay it out for me, *Eddie*," I acquiesced.

"Simple. I need you to find Derrek, and I need you to kill him."

My heart stopped. Instantly. My jaw muscles tensed as I ground my teeth.

"I'm not a hit man. I'm a fucking private investigator. I don't kill people. You've got the wrong guy."

"Funny. I seem to remember the reason you were even brought to me was because you beat the living shit out of someone in New York. He was minutes from death, or at least that was what I was told."

My foot started bouncing, jumping with irritation. "That wasn't a job. That was just me doing what I had to do."

"Well, consider this something you just have to do."

"I'm cleared with you, Edgar. I paid my debt. I'm free and clear."

"You may be free and clear, but Derrek isn't. And if I'm not mistaken, you're involved with his wife."

Whatever fear I'd been feeling before, it hardened in my veins and ran cold through me at the mention of Lena. My eyes darted to where she was still swaying her hips to and fro, laughing with Sam and Piper. "Leave her out of it," I spat, immediately feeling the protective urge to keep her as far away from this mess as possible.

"Listen, I don't want to hurt anyone besides Derrek. He knew what he was doing when he took off with my money. I just need you to find him, kill him, and get me what's mine. That's all. Then I'll forgive every debt against you and your new love."

I wanted to argue with him, wanted to point out that neither one of us was indebted to him, but I knew it was pointless. If I didn't do what he wanted, he'd just come after me or, worse yet, Lena. The best course of action I could take in that moment was to let him believe I was on his side, to stay in his pocket.

"What's the timeframe?"

"You know, I'm not in a huge hurry. If I had to choose between having the job done fast or the job done right, I'd pick right. So, bring me my money and Derrek Bellows' death certificate, within a reasonable amount of time, and everything will be kosher."

"And how much money does Derrek owe you?"

"Five million."

"Five million dollars?" I asked, half shocked anyone had that kind of money to loan to someone, and half impressed Derrek had managed to weasel that much money out of someone.

"If it were less, I'd probably let him disappear and write the whole thing off as a bad investment. But Derrek knew what he owed me and decided to stiff me anyway. He'll pay for that and it'll cost him his life."

"And you don't have anyone in your band of criminals who'd be better suited for murder?" My tone was probably more sarcastic than it should have been, but I couldn't help myself. It was bizarre that he was asking for my help with something I knew very little about.

"Preston, the man with the most at stake is the right man for the job. And that's you. I expect to hear from you when you've gotten my money and Derrek Bellows is no longer breathing."

The click on the line indicated that Edgar had hung up, and I was left in a somewhat shocked state. I put my phone back in my pocket and tried to force a look of disinterest on my face, wanting to come off as anything but worried. After a few minutes of my brain zipping through a million scenarios in my mind, all of which ended badly, the girls appeared at the table, startling me. Lena took the chair closest to me, sitting down so that our shoulders brushed, and then placed her hand on my thigh, gently squeezing. It did little to calm me, but did offer some relief from the thoughts running amok in my mind.

"Who was on the phone?" she asked, innocently curious, smiling at me as if I were the brightest light in her life.

"Parker," I lied. Her eyes lit up, her smile growing even wider, making my lie sink even more heavily in my gut. I never wanted to lie to Lena again, not after everything we'd been through, not after all the lies I'd already told her.

"How is he?"

"He's doing fine; just wanted my opinion on a case he's working."

"Well, the next time you talk to him, be sure to tell him hi for me."

"Will do, sweetheart." I leaned in and pressed a kiss against her lips, hoping she couldn't sense my unease, hoping it was just the same as any other small and gentle kiss I'd given her. I could feel the difference, feel the desperation in my body, but hoped she couldn't.

We stayed through the luau, the girls enjoying the show, the food, the dancers, the fire, the whole experience. But I was winding tighter and tighter, my eyes darting around the darkness looking for any signs of imminent danger. I was, perhaps, being paranoid, but Edgar had threatened Lena and I was on high alert. I knew, realistically, I had some time before Edgar would go after her, but just the thought of her in danger awoke some dormant animal inside of me that had been sleeping for the last week.

The only thing that kept me grounded and a little bit sane was knowing this time I was here to protect her. She wasn't hundreds of miles away trying her damnedest to keep away from me, she was sitting next to me, her fingers entwined with mine. I had her, and I wasn't going to let anything happen to her.

Chapter Four

The girls were laughing as we walked down the beach on the way back to our apartments. Sam and Piper were commenting on the bulging muscles most of the men in the luau possessed, while Lena was laughing along, all the while holding my hand as we made our way home. They'd had more than a few drinks with dinner and were all smiles for the evening, but with one question, their moods all deflated.

"When do you think you'll go home?" Lena asked Sam.

Sam let out a big breath, sighing into the night. "I bought my plane ticket this morning. I leave in a week."

With the moon as her backlight I could see Lena nodding, her bottom lip trapped by her teeth. Then I heard her take in a breath. "So, we've got one more week to spend together in paradise."

"I'm going to fly back with her," Piper added, and Lena's hand tightened around mine.

"Really?" Lena asked, her voice shaky and weak.

"Yeah. I think it's time for me to go and figure out what to do with my life. Hawaii is nice, it's beautiful, but it isn't home. I've got to go home. I've got to get my head on straight and life figured out."

"I understand," Lena whispered. "I'm just going to miss you both."

"Preston will be here to keep you company," Sam said, her voice teasing. "I'm sure he won't let you get lonely."

Lena let out a small bubble of laughter. "I guess that's true, but it's just not the same. I'm going to miss my girls." At that point, Lena's hand left mine and I watched as the three slightly drunk girls wrapped their arms around each other in a group hug, swaying and stumbling in the sand, but ultimately staying upright as they embraced each other. I stood back and let them have their moment, smiling at how much they seemed to genuinely care about each other. Women seem to form bonds, strong bonds, quickly. They could become best friends with someone almost instantaneously, and remain loyal for a lifetime. But, they could also turn on you even quicker. Men were much more reserved and cautious when it came to trust and friendship. I gave my friendship to very few people, and even then, they were men I'd known for years.

When the girls dispersed, Lena made her way back to me, her eyes a little sadder than before. The three of them were quiet until we'd made it back to the apartments, then they made plans to lie on the beach the next afternoon, all three agreeing that a morning run wasn't on their to-do list.

We walked into our apartment and I flipped on the lights, heading directly to the kitchen to bring Lena a tall glass of water and some pain pills. She quietly sank into one of the chairs around the table.

"Wanna talk about it?" I asked as I grabbed a glass from the cupboard.

She looked back at me and gave me another sad smile. "I'm just going to really miss the girls. I've never been far from Sam, besides the first two months here. And I love Piper, but I'll be honest, it makes me a little jealous that the two of them will be living together while I'm all the way across the ocean." She dropped her face into her hands and groaned. "Ugh. I sound like an annoying child." She took another deep breath and her eyes met mine once more. "I'm mostly just sad." She paused again. "Sam's always been around, and when she wasn't I had Piper." Her face turned into an adorable pout and her eyebrows scrunched up in the middle. "Now I won't have either of them."

"Babe, come here," I said, trying not to laugh at how adorably drunk she was. She stood and wasted no time ambling into my open arms. I ran my hand down the back of her head, loving the feel of her silken hair against my skin. "Everything's going to be all right." I let her lean in to me for a while before prodding further. "You know I'll support you in whatever decision you make, sweetheart. And if you want to stay in Hawaii I will, gladly. But I'll follow you anywhere." I felt her tense a little in my arms and I knew what was going through her mind. "Do you have any friends or relatives anywhere else? Do you have any place else you can go where there would be people you could rely on?" She shook her head against my chest.

"The only family I have left is in Russia and I haven't seen them since I was a small child. Any other friends I had were friends of Derrek's." She slumped further against me and I hugged her closer. "You're all I have."

Her words, although they meant the world to me, left her feeling less, left her lacking. She needed her friends just as much as she needed me, but wasn't allowing herself to be close to them. I wanted so badly to just shake her and tell her to go back to Portland, that I would keep her safe and far away from the memories of Derrek, that she didn't have to punish herself this way. But I knew she needed to come to that conclusion on her own. I knew Lena, and I knew the decision to be in Portland needed to be hers alone, so I didn't push. I couldn't help but wonder when Lena would take something for herself. She'd spent years in a marriage of giving and giving up, and did nothing but sacrifice for others I resolved in that moment that I would try to help her realize that she deserved to take what she wanted, that she deserved the same happiness anyone else did.

"Everything is going to be all right. I swear. If I'm all you have then I'll be all you need." I leaned back and pressed a kiss against her forehead. "Will you drink this water for me and take these pills? I need you to sober up a little so we can have a conversation."

"Is everything all right?" she asked anxiously.

"Yeah. Just do this for me and then get ready for bed and I'll meet you there after I shower."

She nodded then tipped up on her toes, trying to reach my lips with hers—always failing since I was so much taller than her. So I smiled and leaned down to meet her, accepting the way her lush lips pressed into mine, the way her meek and shy tongue asked gently for permission to enter, then took more from her than I had anticipated when my tongue took a few wide sweeps through her mouth.

I pulled away, not wanting to take the kiss further, needing, instead, to clear the air between us.

"Go, babe. I'll meet you in the bedroom in a bit."

She smiled, turned away from me, and made her way down the hall. I scrubbed my hands down my face, trying to build up some nerve to have a discussion with Lena that could really go one of two ways. I made my way to the bathroom and showered, distracted, trying to piece together what I would say to her, how I would tell the woman I loved I was being forced to kill her husband.

I stepped out of the shower, confidence at an all-time high, convinced I was going to march into the bedroom and tell her the truth, tell her about Edgar and Derrek, and everything would work out for the best. I wrapped a towel around my waist and marched into the room, only to be stopped in my tracks by the sight of Lena kneeling on the bed.

Her black, luscious hair was falling down her back, her knees were spread, and her hands rested on her thighs. She was wearing what looked like a short lace dress. It obviously wasn't made to wear in public and was more of the bedroom variety of dress, but it was absolutely sexy. The lace did nothing to hide the brownish-pink color of her nipples, nor the fact that they were hard and straining through the lace itself.

"Fuck me," I mumbled, still standing in the doorway.

"That's the idea," she responded, her voice deep and sultry. She lifted one hand and crooked a finger at me, and I'll be damned if my feet didn't move of their own accord. I couldn't have stopped myself if I'd tried—which I didn't. When I made it to the foot of the bed, she lifted to her knees and her hands slid up my body, starting at my waist and trailing all the way up to my shoulders. Once she had a firm grasp on me there, she pulled me in closer to her. I watched as her mouth came to press a kiss right in the center of my chest, moving to one side, licking my nipple, then moved to the other side and repeated the attention on the other. Her lips moved up my chest and headed for my neck, leaving a trail of kisses. When she met the skin just below my neck she sucked and my knees nearly gave out.

"Lena, please, we need to talk." I groaned at my own words. Her hands moved down my sides then gripped the towel, pulling it from me, leaving me bare.

"We can talk, but we can only say dirty words."

I tried to keep my laugh in, but she was too goddamned cute. Lena was sexy all of the time, so watching her *trying* to be sexy was hilarious. "You don't know any good dirty words," I teased. If she was offended, I couldn't tell. She continued her assault against the skin on my neck, her words coming out between kisses, licks, and bites.

"Dick," she whispered.

"Sweetheart, dick is a nicer way of saying cock. Cock is the dirty word you're looking for." My hands came to her waist. I loved the way the lace looked on her, but I didn't like the way it felt on my hands. I wanted her skin.

"Fuck," she whispered again, sounding more determined. I could admit, hearing the word come from her, raspy and vibrating against my skin, was definitely sexy.

"Closer." I surprised her by climbing onto the bed. It made me taller than her again so her lips were forced from my neck. I wrapped my arm around her waist and pulled her to me, I wound the other hand in her hair and pulled back so her eyes found mine. "Try again."

"I want to feel your cock in my pussy." Her eyes never left mine as she bravely said words I'd never heard her utter before, but her breath faltered; she was obviously affected on a base level.

"Oh yeah? What else?" My pulse raced, wanting to do everything she suggested and more. I pulled her hair a little harder, but then moved forward, forcing her to lie on the bed. I grabbed both of her hands and pinned them above her head.

"I want to feel your hard cock pound into me from behind, and I want to feel your hand pulling my hair, all while you tell me what it feels like to be inside me."

Well, holy fuck.

"Is that so?" Apparently, if Lena got a little drunk, her inner minx came out.

She nodded, her eyes glassy, a sexy grin gracing her lips.

"I'm pretty sure I can manage all that." My cock was begging to give her exactly what she wanted and I'd given up trying to deny her when she started whispering dirty words in my ear. I reached down and grabbed the bottom of her lacy dress, pulling it up and over her body while she wiggled, giggling. As the black lace passed her magnificent breasts I stopped to take one into my mouth, never willing to pass up an opportunity to admire their perfection. She had the kind of breasts my dick wanted to live between.

She groaned quietly as I took one of her nipples into my mouth and sucked hungrily, her lip trapped between her teeth. I moved away and continued to pull off the lacy garment, then took a moment to let my eyes take in all her beauty as she lay naked in my bed, her black hair fanned out around her, creamy skin just barely pink with arousal. When she reached between us, grasping my cock and stroking me up and down, I knew she was done waiting.

Her hand moved over me like silk and every muscle in my body tensed at the sensation. Nothing felt as fantastic as having Lena's hands on me. I placed my fingers just at the edge of her entrance, and all my breath left me at the wetness there.

"Jesus, Lena. You're soaked." She groaned, more loudly this time, as I slid two fingers into her, loving the way her body accepted me, the way it seemed to be waiting for me. I moved my fingers in and out of her at a bruising pace, neither one of us looking for slow or smooth. She wanted it rough and I intended to give her everything she wanted. Always. Her hips bucked up into my hand as she cried out. Apparently, slightly drunk Lena was also louder. Hearing her cries only made my cock jump and throb harder. I leaned down and grabbed her breast with my free hand, squeezing roughly, and then my mouth covered her hard, tight peak.

With every thrust of my fingers, I not only heard her arousal climbing, but I could feel her warm slickness. She was nearly to her peak. Still with two fingers plunging in and out, I used my thumb to circle her clit and watched as she exploded like a firecracker. Hips bucked, mouth opened, eyes closed, and I watched as she lost herself in the sexual euphoria I got so much pleasure out of giving her. Watching her fall apart at my hand was one of the most singularly arousing things to witness.

I didn't wait for her to come all the way down before I grabbed her hips, flipped her over, pulled her ass up, and plunged into her.

"Fucking Christ, you're so tight. I love slamming into you while you're still clenching. It feels fucking amazing."

I reached forward and wrapped my hand in her hair, just as she'd asked, pulled back gently and watched as her back arched and ass tipped up, fitting me perfectly. I continued to pound into her, loving the sound of her cries with every thrust. A ball of heat erupted in my spine, shooting forward, and I knew I wasn't going to last much longer. I gripped her hair more tightly, pulled her back harder, impaling her with significant force and speed, listening to her guttural moans and incoherent words. When she collapsed onto her forearms, her pussy gripping me with more force than ever before, I knew she'd come again, and I followed right behind her.

We both collapsed, panting, trying to catch our breath, each on our respective sides of the bed. When I finally felt as though my heart wasn't going to gallop away, I turned, wrapped my arm around her waist and pulled her toward me. When she was secure against me, her back to my front, I brushed her hair aside and kissed her temple. I heard her exhale a shallow breath, then she settled into her spot, snuggling down.

"Love you," she murmured, which I understood as her telling me goodnight.

I smiled, as if I could help it, and whispered into her ear, "I love you too, sweetheart."

I sighed as she drifted off to sleep, resigned to having our much-needed conversation the next day. I smiled to myself as I vowed not to let her distract me with hot, drunken sex again.

Chapter Five

The next morning, I didn't waste any time getting Lena to listen to everything I had to say. I woke up early, brewed coffee, cut up some fruit, and set it all out on the balcony. Then I gently woke Lena, asking her to meet me for breakfast overlooking the ocean. A few minutes later, when she joined me, I let myself drink her in. Her face was soft from sleep, her hair pulled up high and piled atop her head, and she'd put on one of my button-up shirts. She looked delectable, but I couldn't let myself get distracted.

She came up beside my chair and leaned down, pressing a kiss against my lips, then sat down next to me, taking a sip of her coffee.

"It's gorgeous out this morning," she said, her voice still raspy and fucking beautiful.

I smiled in response because I knew if I opened my mouth some cheesy bullshit about nothing comparing to her beauty would fall out of it, and I would mean every word.

"Do you remember how every night, back in Portland, I would sleep in my Lotus outside your house to make sure you were safe?"

She looked confused by my question; I had obviously started a conversation she wasn't prepared for. "Um, yeah."

"I need you to remember that. I need you to remember that, since the day I met you, I've done everything I could to keep you safe. Remember that, and trust me. Can you do that?"

"You're scaring me, Preston."

"I'm not trying to scare you, sweetheart, but I do have something to tell you and it will go more smoothly if you just keep that in mind—that I've always been focused on you and your safety and your happiness."

She nodded, her expression a little hesitant.

"Yesterday, at the luau, I took a phone call."

"Right, from Parker." Her face paled and I watched as she became instantly panicked. "Oh my God, is he okay?"

"Parker is fine, but it wasn't him on the phone. It was Edgar." I waited as my words sunk in and watched as realization came over her face.

"The man who tailed us the night of the gala?"

"Right."

"Why would he be calling you? Isn't he the man you were working for when we met? I thought Derrek got what he wanted and all that was over?"

"Well, it turns out Derrek got what he wanted, but Edgar didn't. Derrek was in deep with Edgar and owed him a lot of money. When Derrek disappeared, he did so before he paid Edgar back. And now Edgar wants his money."

"Sucks to be Derrek," Lena said just before popping a strawberry in her mouth, chewing with more force than necessary. I tried not to smile at her sass, but I lost that struggle, my mouth curling upward. Fuck, she was perfect.

"It does suck to be Derrek, but that's not really news. News is, Edgar wants me to find Derrek." Lena stopped chewing, her eyes locked on mine. When she moved again, it was to speak.

"I thought you knew where Derrek was."

"I did know where he was—a week ago. I haven't kept up any investigative work since I've been here. I could probably find him again, and there's also the chance he hasn't moved at all. But that's not all Edgar wants."

"What else?" She sounded nervous.

"He wants me to kill Derrek." I didn't know how else to put it to her, didn't know any other words to say. It was blunt and to the point, but I figured she needed it that way. Needed to know exactly what was happening. Exactly what we were facing.

"Kill him?" Her voice was shrill and scared.

I nodded in response. She remained quiet for a few minutes and I watched her profile as she looked out to the ocean. She blinked and she breathed, but she did nothing else. Finally, she turned back to me, her eyes worried.

"If I ask you a question, do you promise to be completely and one hundred percent honest with me?"

"Yes," I answered instantly.

"I'm not kidding, Preston. I need the truth, even if it changes everything. I need you to give it to me."

"Ask me."

"Have you ever killed anyone before?"

"Never." My answer came immediately and with force. I pushed the word out as if it weighed a thousand pounds. I needed her to believe me, needed her to realize that not only was I telling the truth, but also that killing people wasn't something I did. I turned toward her and made sure she was looking me in the eye before I continued. "I am not a thug, a gangster, or a mob boss, Lena. I am a clean, law-abiding private investigator. I got caught up in *one* questionable job to protect my sister. One. And that job led me to you, so I can't regret it. But I am not crooked. I promise you that." I sighed, feeling some tension leave my body with my words. "I might have killed Piper's ex, I wouldn't have cared at the time if I had, but that was different. That was me protecting my baby sister. He lived. But I've never killed anyone. Not for the job and not for any reason."

"Okay," she whispered. I reached my hand out and wrapped it around the back of her neck, pulling her over to me, our bodies stretching out to meet each other's, my forehead gently touching hers.

"You believe me?"

"Of course I believe you," she whispered gently.

I sighed out my relief. Of course she believed me. I pressed my mouth to hers, kissing her just barely, then let her go, resting back into my chair. "I'm not going to kill Derrek." I looked over at her just in time to watch her nod. "Edgar wants him dead, but we'll find a way to work around that."

"Do you think if Derrek gives Edgar his money, he'll leave him alone and let him live?"

"I honestly don't know. My instincts tell me no. Edgar may not be the most prominent boss out there, but he's still dangerous and definitely means business."

"Wait," Lena said, new worry and panic filling her voice. "If you don't kill him, won't Edgar then come after you?"

"Let me worry about Edgar, sweetheart."

"Where was Derrek the last time you tracked him?"

"Caribbean."

"Do you think he's still there?"

"I don't know. He moved around a bit at first, then landed there and didn't leave for a few days before I found him, but that doesn't really mean anything. He could be anywhere."

"I assume that means you'll have to go wherever you end up finding him."

I sighed. "Yeah, these aren't the kind of conversations you have with someone over the phone. I have to go wherever he is."

Lena turned to look back out to the blue sea. "I want to go with you," she nearly whispered, her words so light and soft, almost as if she were afraid to say them, afraid of how I would respond.

"You know I never want to be away from you, but this isn't safe."

"I need to go with you."

"I need to know you're safe, Lena. I need to do my job without worrying whether or not you'll get hurt."

"And I'm supposed to just stay here and wonder whether or not you're safe? That isn't fair to me. That will drive me insane."

"What if you went to Portland and stayed with Parker?"

"I am *not* going to Portland. Not now. Not yet."

"Portland, with Parker, is the safest place you could be right now, Lena. The only place where I would know someone would be watching out for you."

"And who would be watching out for you? Edgar? Derrek? What if Parker came with us?"

This was not an angle I'd considered. Parker was someone I could always count on, and I had used him before in my work, but not in this way. I had never asked Parker to help me with something so fundamentally and obviously illegal. I didn't want him knowing anything about what was going on. I couldn't implicate him that way. "He can't know what I'm up to, Lena. That would mean, if I were caught, he'd be an accomplice. I can't do that to him."

"Now you think you're going to get caught?" She was almost to the point of panic. Her face was pained, eyebrows arched toward the sky, hands gripping her thighs, and I swore I could see her pulse beating in her neck.

"Lena, baby, Derrek isn't dangerous. He's got money, but that's all. He doesn't have contacts—and even if he did have any, he's abandoned all of them, gone dark. I'm not planning on getting caught. But if something were to go wrong, I wouldn't want you and Parker there. It's just not worth the risk."

Suddenly Lena stood and took two quick steps, standing right in front of me. I couldn't help it when my eyes roamed down her body, landing right where my white shirt ended and the smooth skin of her thighs began. Before I could reach out and touch her, like I ached to do every time she was within reach, she knelt between my legs and I was taken by a whole new visual.

"Listen, Preston. I know you're used to getting your way, and you're used to people bending to your every command, but you forgot to take one thing into account."

"And what's that?" I asked, too mesmerized by the image of her mouth and lips so close to my cock.

"I refuse to be away from you. Especially if you're going to find Derrek. We decided, together, we were going to find him. So, I'm coming with you."

I could have argued with her, could have fought with her all day and all night, explaining all the reasons I didn't want her to come. When we'd decided to find him, it had been on our own terms, for our own reasons. This was different. This was dangerous. If Derrek knew we were coming for his money, coming for him, coming to finish whatever Edgar had wanted done before Derrek had so conveniently disappeared, he wasn't going to welcome us with smiles and handshakes. But I couldn't argue with her. Not when she was in front of me, half naked, asking to be near me, her mouth so close to me, so lush. There was also the fact that I did, always, want her with me. So, in that moment, I decided it would be pointless to argue, and better to just give in and let her think she'd won.

"Okay," I said softly, raising one hand to run the backs of my fingers along her cheek and down to her chin. Her eyes closed and she leaned in to my touch. "Come here," I said softly, opening up my body, signaling her to come closer. She stood and curled her body onto my lap, her cheek resting high on my chest, ass right where I wanted it, knees curled up. I held her, feeling how small she was in my arms, and knew I didn't want to be without her. So she would come with me.

"Will we bring Parker?" she asked, sounding hopeful.

I shook my head. "He needs to be in Portland for Piper. She'll need someone to be there for her as she tries to put her life back together."

Lena was quiet for a moment and then lifted her face to look at me. "Are you sad it won't be you who'll be there for her?"

I knew Lena was amazing in many ways. I loved her for a variety of reasons. But in that moment I loved her because she *knew*. She knew, without me having to tell her, that it would be difficult to be away from Piper. I pressed my lips to her forehead, mumbled, "Yeah," against her skin. She sighed deeply, then inhaled a big breath.

"I'm sorry my estranged husband is causing so many problems for you."

It hurt me to hear her apologize for him. His actions were not her fault.

"Soon, hopefully, we'll find a way to get him out of our lives for good."

"When do we leave?" she asked on a sigh, her eyes wandering out to the ocean, peaceful and blue.

I kissed her brow again. "We should probably leave when Piper and Sam leave."

"That doesn't give me any time to give notice at my job."

Silence hung between us.

"I'm sorry," I whispered. She'd worked hard to build a life before I showed up, and now she was being forced to leave it behind. It was important to her that she'd done something on her own for once, without the help or influence of anyone else, and I knew she would be sad to leave it at all, let alone on bad terms. That's just the kind of woman Lena was.

"In the end, when everything is sorted out, it'll all be worth it, right?" She looked up to me, searching my eyes for an answer.

"Right," I promised, knowing I had no right to make that promise to her.

"Parker, I need your help with something. And fast." I had snuck back up to the apartment, leaving all three girls on the beach, sunning themselves, soaking up as much Hawaiian sun as they could before we all left paradise. With my phone to my ear and my eyes on the girls, I quickly called my brother.

"What is it?"

"I need you to draft up divorce papers between Derrek and Lena. And I need those papers to indicate that Derrek gives up everything in the divorce. The house, the cars, and gives her all but two million dollars."

"What? Why? He isn't going to agree to that."

"He won't have a choice."

Parker was quiet for a moment, then spoke. "What's going on?"

"Nothing you need to be looped in to. I just need those papers drafted, and I need them faxed to me when you've got them." I dragged in a deep breath. "Piper's coming home and I need you to look after her."

"Where are you going?"

"Lena and I are going to find Derrek." I heard Parker sigh, and knew what his next words would be.

"Do you think it's wise for Lena to go with you? Perhaps she should stay here with me as well."

"Lena doesn't want to be in Portland. She might never be in Portland again. She wants to be where I am, and honestly, I want her with me, too."

"It sounds like shit's going down, Preston. It doesn't sound safe and it doesn't sound like you've really got it under control."

"I need something else. And this might be more difficult for you to get a hold of, but you're the only person I can ask." I took in a deep breath, knowing I was about to ask something of him I never imagined I would, knowing it would probably change our relationship and the way he viewed me. I could see no other way to get from point A to point B. There was a piece missing, and Parker was the only person I could think of who could provide us that missing link.

Chapter Six

The four of us had flown into Seattle, working around Lena wanting desperately to not have a layover at the Portland airport.

"The last time I was there I was completely broken. I don't really want to go back there," she'd told me in a whisper one night as she lay sprawled over me in bed.

I didn't need any more convincing than that, so we flew into Seattle and Parker had no problem meeting us there for dinner. Parker and Lena hugged tightly when they reunited and, again, I was filled with gratitude, grateful he was there to support Lena when I couldn't be.

We had dinner at a restaurant inside the hotel Lena and I were staying at that night, waiting for our morning flight. It was a sham of a dinner; the girls were pretending not to be sad, even though the grief of separation was weighing down the very air we breathed. Parker and I were trying to be sensitive to their situation, but all three of the women were shredded, knowing they'd be saying goodbye again for who knew how long.

When we could extend dinner no longer, the girls reluctantly stood and headed toward the lobby of the hotel, Sam already wiping tears from her eyes.

"Be safe," Piper said as she wrapped Lena in a hug. My heart pounded just a little harder seeing the two women who meant the most to me in the world embrace. I'd give up everything for either one of them, and something felt right when I saw them together.

"Don't be a stranger," Sam said, still crying, as Lena hugged her. Lena was surprisingly quiet, and I assumed it was because she was afraid if she spoke, she'd just end up crying. Everyone took in her silence and didn't press her. When she hugged Parker though, the two of them exchanged words in hushed whispers, quietly enough I couldn't hear.

I hugged the girls, kissed Piper on the cheek as she murmured the same "Be safe," to me, then hugged me again a little more tightly. I tried not to look in her eyes as we pulled apart; didn't want to see the pain I knew would be lighting them up.

I shook Parker's hand and clapped him on the back, stilling when he leaned in and whispered to me, "Once you get settled in the hotel room, meet me down here alone." I nodded as I pulled away, knowing exactly why he wanted to see me.

After Lena had given the girls another round of goodbyes, I took her hand and led her back to our room. I could see her holding back more tears and as the doors to the elevator closed I pulled her to my side and kissed the top of her head.

"Everything will be all right, Lena. I promise." She nodded slightly as her arms squeezed my waist tighter. The doors opened on our floor and we walked, still wrapped in each other, to our room. I led her straight to the bathroom and started filling the bathtub with warm water. I turned back to her and could hardly stand her tear-streaked face. "Turn around, sweetheart." I pulled the zipper of her dress and watched as the fabric floated down into a pool around her feet. I reached back up and unclasped her bra, watching it too fall to the ground, leaving her nearly bare. She bent at the waist and slid her panties off, then, with the grace of someone so accustomed to wearing them, took her high heels off without a single totter.

She turned back to me with not one single piece of clothing marring her body, nothing to shield her from me at all, and with sadness in her eyes, asked me, "Will you join me?"

I framed her face with my hands, saying, "In a little while, love. I'm going to get some ice and settle in for a minute. But then I'll join you."

She leaned forward and pressed a small kiss to my lips, and I fought every urge I had to pull her in closer, to take her mind off her sadness by making her feel good again. But I managed to watch her pull away and slowly dip her perfect body into the steaming water, then I turned around and walked out.

I found my brother exactly where he'd said he would be, and to say he looked worried would have been a massive understatement. He looked nervous and uncomfortable.

"I will never, not ever, do this for you again. So you better make sure you get this right the first time, Preston. I know you'd go to the ends of the earth for Lena, and I'll do anything I can to help you, but this," he said, slamming a sealed manila envelope into my chest, "is outside my comfort zone."

I grabbed the envelope and breathed out a sigh of relief.

"You don't know how much I appreciate this. It's all there?"

"Everything you asked for is in that envelope. This *cannot* come back to me, brother. You have to find a way to end this."

"Trust me," I said, looking my older brother directly in the eye. "I've thought this through and this is the only way we all get what we want, and everyone gets what they deserve."

"You better be right," he said firmly, his face a mixture of concern and apprehension. Then he clasped my shoulder and brought me into a hug, forceful and startling. "Keep her safe. And keep yourself safe too, Pres. I need you both to be okay when this is all done." After a few hearty claps on the back I pulled away, trying not to let my surprise at his worry show on my face. I was trying to be stoic, to show him I had everything under control.

"We'll be fine."

In response, Parker reached out his hand, and I shook it.

"Call me if you need anything." He paused, my hand still clasped in his. "I mean it."

"I know, Parker. I will."

With that, he turned and walked toward the exit of the hotel, head bowed.

I let out a harsh sigh. It was official. We were on our own. We were on our own and about to attempt something insanely dangerous and very illegal. But as I'd told Parker when I asked for his help, I didn't see any other way out.

The only thing I could see, the only thing my mind would let me focus on, was Lena. I needed to keep her safe. Needed to ensure that, come what may, she was through the storm and safely on the other side of the destruction. Out of harm's way. In my arms. So, the very next day we would depart on, without a doubt, the most important trip of our lives.

The next morning, after a short flight to Toronto, we found ourselves on a much longer flight taking us to Athens, Greece.

"You know what sucks?" Lena asked, her head leaning against my shoulder as her hand lay in my lap, fingers laced through mine.

"What's that?"

"The entire time we were married I begged Derrek to take me to Europe. Greece was one of the top places I wanted to see. But we never went. And now that I get to go, now that I get to see the beautiful country I've always wanted to visit, I won't even be able to enjoy it." She pressed her cheek closer to me and I gripped her hand a little more tightly. "And more than likely, after we leave, I won't ever want to go back."

My heart pounded, jaw clenched, thinking about Derrek still taking things from her. Still managing to impact her and her happiness. Even after setting her up, leaving her with nothing, demanding everything from her, he was still able to reach her, still able to affect her. I tried to regulate my breaths, tried to calm down, but she must have felt me tense because her free hand came up to gently cup my cheek.

"It's okay, Preston. I don't need Greece." She pulled back, her hand still on my face and her eyes looking into mine. "I don't want anything from him anymore. You give more to me than he ever did." She leaned in and pressed her mouth against mine, then pulled away and rested her head against my shoulder again.

She hadn't asked many questions about Derrek and Jessica; never inquired as to what they'd been up to in the last three months. I wouldn't tell her the truth. Wouldn't tell her that it looked like they'd been on a dream vacation, traveling the world. I couldn't figure out whether he was stupid and actually taking his little family on a trip around the world, or if he was running, trying to stay one step ahead of anyone who might have been looking for him. Once I'd found his trail it hadn't been hard to track him.

I knew he wasn't a criminal mastermind, but he wasn't completely dense. He had to know people were out to get him, had to know if he stayed in one place long enough he'd have company.

Three days ago, when I'd found him in Athens, I knew, based on his record, he'd be there for at least a week, perhaps two at the most, so we had a good chance of finding him. So that's where we'd headed.

The flight was long, but it was also nice to have seventeen hours of uninterrupted time with Lena. Time where, even if she was asleep against my arm, there wasn't any outside influence. We watched a movie, did a crossword puzzle together, read books. It was almost as if we weren't on our way to find her ex-husband who'd ruined her life. Almost.

When we touched down in Athens it was just dusk, although my body had no idea what time it was or which way was up. Everything about my system was disrupted.

Lena, on the other hand, was exhausted. She resembled a zombie going through customs, and could hardly keep her eyes open to take in whatever sights of Athens we could see in the darkness.

When we arrived at our hotel, I checked us in and helped Lena to our room, steering her directly to the bed where she promptly climbed in and fell asleep almost immediately. I hadn't mentioned to her our hotel was the same hotel in which I thought Derrek was staying. I didn't think she needed that information. I thought, instead, she needed a night of uninterrupted sleep during which she wasn't worried about the other people staying there.

When I was sure she was fast asleep, I quietly made my way out of the room and headed downstairs to the bar. When I spotted him sitting on a stool, tumbler in hand, alone, I couldn't decide if I was surprised I'd been right, or worried for the exact same reason. He was here, in front of me, and now I had a real decision to make. Did I approach, and possibly alter the course of all of our lives, or try to find some alternate solution I hadn't come up with yet? I'd spent every waking moment since Edgar called me trying to find another way for Lena and me to get past this problem, but I could see no other way.

I took in a deep breath and pushed forward, never having taken steps which felt heavier or more weighted than those few steps to the bar. My hands rested on the cold wood and I caught the eye of the bartender just a few feet away.

"Scotch. Neat."

The bartender nodded just as I saw Derrek's head turn toward me. Then I watched with anticipation as his eyes widened in shock, mouth gaping open, then closing, quite like a fish. I watched as the bartender placed a tumbler in front of me and poured the amber liquid two fingers deep. He slid it toward me and walked away as I brought the glass to my lips, my eyes never leaving Derrek's.

"How did you find me?"

"Derrek, I'm a private investigator. It's my job to find information people are purposefully trying to bury." He blinked but didn't respond, although I could practically see the wheels spinning in his head. "You did a decent job covering your tracks, but not good enough." I put the glass down and sat on the stool next to him.

"I'm not going to lie—I'm pretty impressed you found me."

"I've known where you were for weeks now. I wasn't going to do much with the information unless Lena wanted me to, but other people forced my hand in this case."

"You're here with Lena?" His eyes darted around the room, looking for her.

"Don't be a fucking idiot. You won't be seeing her until I say so and only if she wants to see you." I turned toward him, my eyes narrowing, my pulse pounding in my neck. "Let's get one thing straight. The moment you hired me to seduce her was the moment you lost her. Forever. She's mine now and you don't get to look at her. You don't get to speak to her. You don't even get to breathe the same air as her."

"Why are you here, then?" he rasped at me.

"Edgar sent me."

I watched as the blood drained from his face and little beads of sweat appeared on his forehead and right above his lips. He looked ill and a not-so-small part of me enjoyed watching the fear physically affect him.

"Edgar not only wants his money, he also wants you dead."

Derrek's eyes widened and his Adam's apple bobbed as he swallowed hard. He turned back to the bar and drained his drink, then lifted his glass at the bartender, signaling he wanted another.

"Looks like hiring you to seduce my wife might have been the biggest mistake of my life. Or, rather, tangling myself with Edgar was." He sighed and took a gulp of his refreshed drink, then ran his hand through his hair, obviously nervous and frustrated.

"Let me ask you a question. Why didn't you just pay Edgar off? You got more than enough money when you ran, why didn't you just give him his money?"

He sighed heavily. "I don't expect you to understand my decisions, uh, Preston, was it?"

I caught the small smirk pull up the corner of his mouth as he took another sip and refrained from putting my fist directly into that same spot with so much force he'd fly from his stool.

"You know my name, asshole. You also know that I could make one phone call and you'd be dead by morning. Probably dead right next to your woman and your children. So, from here on out, choose your words wisely." I moved close, closer than I wanted to be to him, but I needed to make my point. "I'm not a murderer; even if Edgar ordered me to kill you, I don't have it in me. Lena doesn't want you dead either, which both confuses me and makes me damn proud of her. You gave up the best woman you'd ever have, but lucky for me, I was there and made her mine." I looked around to make sure no one was eavesdropping, but moved even closer still, my mouth just a hair's breadth from his ear. "I might not want you dead, but I've got no problem telling Edgar where to find you. But, if you'd shut your goddamned mouth for just one minute, I'd tell you how we can all get out of this situation with our lives and the people we love."

Chapter Seven

When I woke, it was to the feeling of Lena's hands running softly along my chest. Starting right above my navel and moving up, trailing all the way to my shoulder, then down to start the journey over again. Her cheek rested on my other shoulder and my arm was wrapped around her waist. I pulled her closer and buried my nose in her hair. I loved the smell of Lena's hair in the morning. That scent could wake me up for the rest of my life and I'd be a happy man.

Then her hand moved lower still and I was happy for another reason entirely.

"Good morning, sweetheart," I whispered, pressing the words into her hair as her hand moved lazily over me.

"I've decided," she said teasingly, smiling up at me, "just because we're in Greece for unpleasant reasons doesn't mean we can't have a pleasant morning."

"I like the way you think," I said, smiling, lifting my hips and pressing my now solid cock right into the warmth of her hand.

"I like the way you feel," she answered, just before she sat up and hiked a leg over my waist, straddling me, and effortlessly sliding me into her. I watched, unable to look away, as Lena rode me, slowly rocking back and forth. Her raven hair tumbled down her back, her head tilted to face the ceiling, eyes closed in obvious ecstasy. She unhurriedly used my body to bring herself to orgasm, and just listening to her cry out my name nearly had me following. I managed to grab hold of her hips and pump up into her, over and over, forcefully and at a punishing pace, quickly finding my release just before she crumpled on top of me.

I turned my face back into her hair, my hands running up and down her spine, feeling her breathing slow. Eventually, I rolled her onto her back and slipped out of her, watching her mouth open slightly at the feeling of losing me. I trailed the backs of my fingers down her cheek, trying to soothe her before I had to tell her what had transpired the night before.

"I met with Derrek last night." The words slipped past my lips and I watched as her expression moved from relaxed and happy to confused and angry.

"What are you talking about?"

"After you fell asleep, I went downstairs to the bar and he was there. So I spoke with him."

The anger drained from her face, her features softened, and she moved closer to me by just a bit.

"So, he's here? And he knows I'm here? What did he say?"

"He didn't have much to say, love. I made it pretty clear that he wasn't to speak your name, and I just explained the situation. He knows Edgar is after him and pretty upset he took off with his money. He also knows we have a solution for him."

"Did he agree to your plan?"

"I didn't tell him yet. I told him we'd meet this morning." I paused, watching her face give away all the emotions she was feeling as she took in the new information. "I wanted to give you the opportunity to talk to him, to tell him what needed to happen." I searched her eyes, hoping she would give me a clue as to what she was thinking. I knew Lena didn't love Derrek anymore, hadn't for a while even before I came into the picture, but he was her husband. She'd spent many years with him and I'd be a fool to think there wasn't at least one small part of her that cared what happened to him. "I know I spoke with him last night without you, but I wasn't even sure he was here." My hand found her face again, trying to offer her something soothing, something warm and gentle when I knew there must have been so many thoughts racing through her mind. "I needed him to know that I wouldn't allow him to hurt you, see you, or even think about you without my permission." She leaned her cheek into my touch, which only intensified the possessive feelings that were growing inside of me.

"He needed to know you're mine now: my life, my responsibility, my property. I own you. Just as much as you own me, Lena. I just needed to make that clear to him before I let him see you again. I'm sorry if that upsets you."

She shook her head just slightly, bringing her entire body to lie right next to mine. "That doesn't upset me. I *am* yours. I never belonged to Derrek the way I belong to you."

I knew it was true, even before she'd admitted it, but no words had ever been more beautiful coming from her mouth. I leaned forward and kissed her, my hand moving from her cheek to the back of her neck, holding her firmly to me, giving her everything in that kiss. I pulled away just far enough to speak.

"So, you'll come with me then?"

"Of course. He needs to understand this is his best option. I can reason with him, I think."

"All right, then."

I watched her roll away from me and walk naked to the bathroom, then I heard the water start to fall from the shower. I closed my eyes and prayed I wasn't making a mistake, hoped I wasn't walking the most precious possession I had into a trap.

Two hours later, we'd walked through the iconic and somewhat ancient streets of Athens. The streets wound through the village, slowly descending toward the water, where boats lined the marina. Some small boats, some enormous boats, and most falling somewhere in between. Lena and I, hand in hand, came upon Derrek standing exactly where I'd told him to meet us. His back was to us as he looked out over the water. The sounds of our footsteps alerted him to our arrival, and he turned just as we approached him. When his face came into view, I felt Lena's hand grip mine more tightly.

"I see you made the smart choice to meet me here," I said, coming to a stop just feet from him. The blue water behind him, glittering and beautiful, was a stark contrast to the dark circles and bags underneath his eyes.

"Yes, well, I didn't really see another option." He glanced at Lena and my gut clenched, watching as his eyes roamed over her body from head to toe. Luckily for him, he didn't look longingly at her, just seemed to be taking inventory. "Lena," he said to her in greeting, coldly, and I felt her stiffen beside me.

She nodded in response, but said nothing. I pulled her a little closer.

"You look well," he said. Again, not in a way that made me think he was admiring her, but just making an observation. Before I could cut in and redirect the conversation, she responded.

"Two months in paradise will do that to a person." Her words were short and powerful. I got the feeling she wanted him to know that life without him was better for her, that she'd been able to move on and find happiness even after he'd tried to ruin her.

"Yes, well, isn't that what we're all after? A little piece of heaven?" His arm swung out to motion around him, to show us that we'd invaded his paradise and that he wanted us out. "Now, tell me what you want from me so we can get this show on the road. Jessica doesn't know where I am, or that you've come to force my hand. I'd like to get back to her and the girls before she gets suspicious."

"Already lying to her?" Lena's voice rang clear and sharp amidst the sounds of the marina—water slapping against the sides of boats, birds calling out overhead, sails being filled with wind.

"I'm here because your *boyfriend* basically threatened me last night and that's the only reason. The instant either one of you insinuates that my relationship with Jessica is anything in comparison to the sham of a marriage I had with you, this conversation will be over. The way you feel about Lena," Derrek said to me now, pointing a finger in my direction, "is the same way I feel about my family. Threaten them and you'll never see me again."

"Well, I won't threaten you, but I will tell you if you don't cooperate and take the help I'm offering, you probably won't live to see your girls start school. And I can't guarantee Edgar will spare their lives either. This isn't a threat, Derrek, this is reality. The choice is up to you."

All three of us were silent for a moment as he contemplated his next move. There was a part of me that hoped he walked away, hoped that Edgar came looking for him and delivered whatever punishment he thought his money was worth. Another part of me, the part that loved Lena and wanted her safe and sound, was silently begging him to trust me, to let me help him, even if he didn't deserve it.

"As much as we all want to be rid of each other, we're basically all in the same boat, and we're all looking for the same resolution: to be done with Edgar forever. And each other." I let my words sink in, my gaze holding steady with his.

Derrek took one more pause then sighed loudly. "What's the plan, then?"

"First," Lena started, and I watched Derrek's expression move from indifference to surprise as he realized she was running the show, "I'm going to need you to sign divorce papers. And those papers officially transfer most of the money you took from our marriage back to me." Derrek moved to argue, his mouth popping open almost instantaneously, but she didn't let him get a word in. "Don't worry, I'm leaving you enough to start a new life with your family, but I'm taking most of it, and I'll pay off your debt to Edgar."

That last bit surprised him, and I could see him mulling it around in his mind, trying to fit the pieces of the puzzle Lena and I had built together.

"Why would I give you all of my money and trust you to pay off Edgar?"

"You won't have any other choice," she replied, her voice cold and flat. Derrek moved from foot to foot, his nerves giving his uneasiness away.

"Why wouldn't I have any other choice?" His voice was low and teetering on the edge of scared and nervous.

"Because, Derrek. You'll be dead."

Chapter Eight

It took Derrek about a minute to think about the deal Lena was offering him, even though she wouldn't elaborate. But after that minute he decided he needed to bring Jessica into the discussion. Lena didn't miss a beat and agreed, which only made me admire her more. The idea that she was willing to have a civil, albeit strange, conversation with her husband's mistress only made my affection for her grow.

Derrek called Jessica and we all agreed to meet at the bar of the hotel after Jessica arranged for childcare for their girls.

Lena and I sat at a table, she with her vodka martini and me with my scotch, and my hand rested firmly on the fleshiest part of her thigh. For just one moment I was irritated by the pants she was wearing, wanting my hand to be on her skin, to feel the heat radiating off her, but my thoughts were cut short by the sight of Derrek and Jessica walking into the bar, hand in hand. I had never met Jessica, but her face gave all her feelings away; she was scared, nervous, and trying like hell to appear the exact opposite. The most prominent thought circulating through my mind was that she couldn't hold a candle to Lena. She was nothing in comparison. I couldn't help but wonder how Derrek could leave someone like Lena behind in favor of Jessica. The quandary was short lived though, because it didn't matter why he'd left Lena. She was mine now. His loss was my ultimate and phenomenal gain.

Lena didn't stand as they approached our table, so I followed her lead and remained seated as well.

"Lena," Jessica said in greeting as she pulled a chair out and took a seat. "I'd say it was nice to see you, but honestly, I'm a little irritated by your appearance in Greece, so I won't insult you by lying."

"Funny. You didn't have a problem lying to my face about sleeping with my husband and ruining my marriage." Lena's verbal jab was sharp and hit its target dead center. I watched as Jessica scrambled for a response, but Lena wasn't waiting for her and just continued on. "I'm not here to fight with you, Jessica. In fact, I'm here for something quite the opposite." She reached down into the bag sitting by her feet and pulled out the manila envelope, sliding it across the table to where Derrek had sat next to Jessica.

"It's simple, Derrek. You sign these papers, we fax them back to the US, to Preston's brother. When the money is transferred and safely received in my account, you'll get the other manila envelope in my bag that guarantees your safety along with the safety of Jessica and your girls."

"What's in the other envelope?" Jessica asked.

"That's not up for discussion," I interjected. We needed to maintain the upper hand and giving them too much information too early wouldn't be wise.

"You expect me to gamble my future on some mystery envelope?" Derrek's voice was growing irritated and angry.

"This isn't a game," Jessica added.

"You're right. This isn't a game. This is life and death, I'm afraid," I said sharply, trying to show them I wasn't trying to play with them at all. "I want out of this mess just as much as you. We've all got something important to us on the line. This isn't a gamble; this is a way out. For all of us."

"I've never given you any reason not to trust me," Lena said, her voice a little softer than before, her eyes focused on Derrek. "I gave you, arguably, the best years of my life. My youth. Possibly my only chance at having a family. But I never lied to you. I'll remind you, you're the one who got us all into this mess. Be a man for once in your life and make the right decision."

Derrek took the envelope, opened it, and his eyes moved over the pages of the document. He flipped through it, taking his time examining the fine print, then put it down on the table, bringing his eyes to Lena's again. "You expect me to give you everything besides two million dollars? You think I'm going to just hand everything I've worked for over to you?"

"The way I see it," I said, slowly turning my glass of scotch in my hand, "your negotiations are with me from here on out. From what Lena's told me, most of your money came from the merge of her father's company with yours. You got most of your wealth directly from your marriage to her. She deserves *all* your money for what you put her through, so walking away with two million and your lives is more than you deserve."

"How are we supposed to live our lives with only two million dollars?"

"That's not my problem to solve," Lena stated coolly. "However, if you'd prefer to keep all the money you've practically stolen from me, I'm sure it'll come in handy when Edgar comes for you. Although, I'm not sure if he makes the effort to find you he'll let you live."

Jessica looked at Derrek with legitimate fear in her eyes and it occurred to me that perhaps he hadn't been very forthcoming about all his dealings with Edgar. I watched as she mentally put two and two together, watched as she considered what Lena had said, and saw the moment she realized the lives of her children were more important than money.

"Sign the papers, Derrek," Jessica said, her words harsh and angry. He sighed loudly, but then pulled a pen from his jacket and signed the documents, and slid them across the table to me. I felt Lena relax against me just a little when the papers were in my hands and I could only imagine the relief she was feeling at that moment. For once, she'd won a battle against him. For once, she was going to get what she deserved, something that was taken from her. If I hadn't been sitting across the table from her now ex-husband, I would have turned and kissed her gently, showed her exactly how much I understood what those papers meant to her.

I pushed the papers in front of her, and handed her my own pen. She took it from me, smiling, and signed her name next to Derrek's for the very last time without hesitation. I put the papers back in the envelope, making sure the clasp was shut, and looked to Derrek.

"I am going to fax these to our lawyer, and once everything is finalized I will be in touch. Do not leave Athens. If you leave without seeing this plan through, Edgar *will* find you and there won't be anything for me to do to save you or your family." My eyes darted to Jessica and I saw the fear in her eyes as she nodded slightly. She understood the severity of the situation.

"You want us to just sit around waiting for you?" Derrek asked, sounding annoyed.

"I'll remind you that I'm the one with the plan. If you follow my instructions everything will be fine. You have my word."

"Your word means shit to me." Derrek's voice was angry now, and a red flush was moving over his face. He was coming to terms with the fact that I'd outsmarted him, that I'd accomplished the exact opposite of what he'd originally hired me to do. I'd ruined him. Or so he thought.

"How you proceed is entirely up to you, but I can assure you that trusting me is your best bet. I won't try to convince you. I've told you everything I am willing to share; the choice is up to you. Regardless, I'll contact you when it's time for the next move." I took a cell phone out of the bag. A burner phone. Some cheap piece of crap that I knew couldn't be traced. I slid it across the table to him. "Until then," I said as I stood from the table and pulled out Lena's chair. I took her hand gently and led her out of the restaurant, noticing that she never once turned her head to look back at what she was leaving behind.

We walked silently through the hotel to the front desk where I inquired if they had a fax machine I could use. We were led to a private office and left to our own devices. I pulled out my cell phone and called Parker. He answered with a hopeful voice.

"Hello? Preston?"

"It's me."

I heard him sigh in relief. "I've been waiting for your call. I thought I would hear from you yesterday and when I didn't I started to worry."

"Sorry to worry you. We've been trying to acclimate ourselves and also working on Derrek."

"How is Lena?" His tone was even more concerned when he spoke her name. His protective older brother persona extended to Lena and I was never more thankful for the way he cared about her. It made my next move so much easier.

"She's doing as well as can be expected." My eyes moved to her as I spoke and she gifted me with a small smile. It wasn't the gorgeous smile that reached her eyes, but it was the small troubled smile I'd grown accustomed to recently. She was worried, and a little bit sad as well. I opened my free arm to her and she came to me instantly, wrapping both her arms around my waist and pressing her cheek against my chest. "I'm going to fax you the divorce papers. I need you to get them processed immediately, and get the money transferred as soon as possible. We need to rush this."

"I'll do what I can. The money shouldn't be a problem, a day or two at the most. But it might be a few more for the divorce to be finalized."

"Just do what you can. And Parker?"

"Yeah?"

"Thank you."

There was a long silence, but finally he responded with, "You know I'd do anything for you and Lena."

"Yeah."

"Tell her I say hello."

"I will."

"I'll let you know as soon as everything is finished."

"All right."

We hung up and I tore myself from Lena's arms to fax all the paperwork to Parker. When everything was sent I was left with a sense of anxiousness. We were back to waiting. Back to being in limbo, in flux, where anything could go wrong. I wanted desperately for this part of the plan to come together, to happen without a hitch, simply because Lena deserved that much. But it was also important that the next piece of the puzzle fall into place effortlessly as well. And now there was nothing to do but wait. I hated not being in control, not being the one making things happen. Feeling the control slip from my fingers made me jumpy.

I felt Lena's arms wrap around me from behind, felt her breasts push into my back, and it caused my whole body to relax. Just the presence of her body pressed against mine was enough to alleviate some of the anxiety, but I needed more. Needed more of her.

I placed my hand over hers, then trailed my fingers up her arm, watching as goose bumps spread over her skin. "I'm going to take you upstairs and the first thing I'm going to do is use my mouth on you until you beg for more." I felt her breasts push against my back with more force as she drew in a breath, not expecting my words to be so sexual. "You're going to be filled, sweetheart."

"That sounds like a challenge," she whispered, her mouth pressed right between my shoulder blades.

I gripped her arm and pulled her around my body, pressing her ass against the edge of the desk in front of me. I used my finger to bring her chin up, looking right into her surprised and wide eyes. "You think I can't make you beg? I'll eat you to the point of explosion, then ease away, making you crazy, making you beg me to fucking finish you."

Her hand came up to my face, her gentleness a stark contrast to the fire I felt nipping at me. "You can do whatever you want with me, Preston, and I'll give you anything you need." My eyes searched hers frantically, wondering how I'd managed to find and capture a woman who could read me so perfectly, understood exactly what I needed and handed it to me in ways I could never expect from anyone else. "You don't have to take anything from me, as I'll always give it to you freely," she said, running her hand from my cheek to the back of my neck. "But if you need it that way, if you need to be in control, I'll give it up to you. I'll let you take everything."

I dropped my forehead until it just touched hers, and breathed in her scent, eyes closed, hands roaming up and down her back.

"I just want to get lost in you," I whispered, all pretense of control just a haze above our heads.

She nodded, but after a few moments said quietly, "I'll allow you to get lost in me, so long as you promise to let me find myself in you."

I kissed her without thinking, kissed her for knowing exactly what I needed and giving it to me, and for being more than I could ever have imagined. I pulled away from her and took her hand, leading her to our hotel room, where I was lost and she was found.

Chapter Nine

"Well, babe. I'm a millionaire." Lena tossed her phone onto the bedside table and let out a loud and heavy sigh. It had been two days since Derrek signed the papers and, apparently, Parker had managed to get the funds transferred rather quickly. I sat on the edge of the bed, a towel wrapped around my waist, still wet from my shower, and she bent her legs until they curled around me. She was quiet—had been since our encounter with Derrek. She seemed thoughtful, pensive, and I tried to give her the mental space she needed to dig through her thoughts.

At night she gave her body to me, but during the day she was distant.

Her gorgeous dark eyes were focused on nothing, glazed over with the musings of her mind. I could almost see the wheels spinning, hear the gears turning. Eventually, her eyes found mine and she gave me a small smile.

"Are you all right?" I could have been more specific, could have asked her a million more detailed questions than that: do you regret taking the money from him? Are you upset that you're getting a divorce? Do you wish things had turned out differently? Is the money worth the upset?

But I didn't ask those questions because the possible answers scared me. I was willing to live my whole life not knowing the answers to those questions because if she gave me the wrong answers, the answers that meant she'd realized this was all a mistake, I couldn't find a way to live without her. No. I'd rather ask the easy questions.

She nodded and gave me a weak, "Yeah."

I brushed my hand over her forehead, pushing the dark hair off her face.

"It's okay if you're not. It's okay if you're upset." And it was. However she was feeling, it was okay. She deserved to feel every single emotion the whole situation evoked from her. I just hoped my heart could survive them.

Lena sat up a little, resting on one elbow. "I *am* upset. But I'm all right." She sighed again, but I didn't take my eyes off her. I wanted her to know she could talk to me, tell me anything.

"Do you want to talk about it? I'm gonna be really honest right now; your silence on the matter is freaking me out a little."

She sat all the way up, holding the bedsheet to her breasts, and leaned forward, pressing her lips to my shoulder. "I guess I'm just trying to figure out how I let my life get so out of my control." She propped her chin on my shoulder, her breath skating over the still-damp skin of my neck, working through more thoughts before speaking again. "I feel very conflicted," she finally stated, her eyes moving upward to catch mine. "Like, I wish I had never met Derrek; wish I'd never dated him, never married him, never spent all those years of my life, wasted, with him. But, if I hadn't given up so much to him, I never would have found you."

"That's a pretty big sacrifice." *And I'm not sure I'm worthy of it.*

She sighed and leaned away from me, dragging a hand through her long hair. "It wasn't a sacrifice. I guess, in reality, I didn't give anything up; it was taken from me."

"You know I want to give you everything, right?" I heard the words before I was even sure I'd been the one to say them. Of course they were true. They were the kind of truth that existed beyond everything else. I hadn't even formed the words; they just were. "Everything you think you might have lost, or given up, I want to be the one to give it back to you." I turned toward her, my body shifting to face her, my hands coming to rest on either side of her neck.

She nodded, as much as she could with my hands gently gripping her neck, but her eyes still found mine with a question in them. Her voice was a gravelly, quiet whisper when she said, "I guess I'm just not sure why."

"Because you've given everything to me." She shook her head, pulling away from my hands, looking down at her lap, still covered in a white sheet. "You're not broken, Lena. I'm not here to fix you. You don't need my help and you certainly don't need me to bring you back to life—as you demonstrated by taking off to Hawaii on your own. I'm not trying to swoop in and make everything easy for you. I want to walk through the hard times with you, I want to celebrate every exciting milestone *together*. I want to be with you, forever, and to share a life with you. But in doing so, I plan on making sure you get every single thing you were afraid you'd never have with him, because you deserve them." I pulled her chin up with a gentle finger and pressed a kiss to her forehead. "You deserve to be a mom, to be a wife who's *cherished*. And I want to be the lucky husband who gets to spend his life making sure you're happy, safe, and fulfilled."

"I want to give you all that too," she whispered.

"When all of this is behind us, we'll figure everything out. Together."

She nodded then pressed one hand to my cheek while she kissed the other. "I'm gonna go take a shower."

I watched her disappear into the bathroom, then raked my hand down my face as I sighed loudly. I wanted nothing more than to get Lena to a place where there wasn't constant upset. She deserved peace. A normal life with normal issues.

I picked up my phone and dialed Parker, unaware and frankly uncaring of the time difference. He answered, sounding alert and awake.

"Preston, I was just about to call you."

"Tell me you've got good news."

"I do. I pulled a few strings and had a judge sign the divorce papers. So, it's official."

I let out a silent sigh, and my hand went through my hair as I exhaled. "Lena received the money too."

There was a long pause. "Sounds like everything's in order, then."

"Yeah."

"Preston," he said, his voice pleading, "you don't have to go through with it. There has to be another way."

"This is the only way that ensures Lena is out of the mess for good. I don't want this to touch her ever again."

Parker sighed, and I could hear the torment in the groan he released. All he wanted to do was protect us, but we were out of his reach, both literally and figuratively. We were in too deep, and he was standing on the shore waving a life vest that could never save us.

"I'll let you know when it's over. Everything will be all right." I wasn't sure who I was trying to convince more, him or myself. There was a very good chance that everything would definitely not be all right. I'd never attempted anything like I was planning with Derrek. But Lena's safety and future happiness was more than enough of a motivator to get it right.

"If I don't hear from you by midnight your time, I'll call the local authorities. I'm serious, Preston. This ends today, one way or another."

"I know. I'll call you."

"Good luck."

"Thanks." *I'll need it.*

I ended the call with Parker and sent a text to the phone I'd given to Derrek.

Meet me at the Marina at 2 p.m. Bring Jessica and the girls.

At two p.m. on the nose, I watched as Derrek walked down the planked walkway of the marina, one hand holding Jessica's, the other supporting the small blonde girl on his hip. Jessica's free hand held on to the older girl's hand. They looked like the perfect family, on vacation, about to enjoy a relaxing boat ride. They were all wearing white linen, sandals, and hats. I couldn't have planned it better myself. It was the perfect set up. It was almost ironic.

"Derrek," I said as he approached.

"This is a very strange place for a rendezvous," he said, his voice dripping with disdain.

"There's a method to my madness." Just as my words left my mouth Lena appeared at the end of the walkway, and for a moment, I lost the ability to speak.

She looked the part as well. Too well. Her incredible body was adorned with a black bikini, her hips covered by a sheer black sarong that did absolutely nothing to hide the perfection of her curves. The sandals she wore laced up her calves and made her legs look endless. As she got closer, she pushed her sunglasses up, making her soft hair fall to the sides of her face, then flow behind her shoulders.

She smiled at me, her eyes never straying from mine, and walked straight to me, wrapping her arms around my neck, pressing her breasts against my chest. My arm slid possessively around her waist, as I knew Derrek was getting a fantastic view of her perfect ass. He swallowed hard and I knew he'd taken her in, seen exactly what he'd once had and lost.

"Hello," she said sweetly when she pulled away, not removing her arms from around me.

"Hello, sweetheart." I watched her eyes soften at my endearment, then she turned to face the man she was ready to leave behind.

"Derrek. Jessica." That was her greeting to them, and it was cold. She did, however, give a small wave to the little girl at Jessica's side, and I wasn't surprised when the child's face lit up with a smile and she waved back.

"What are we doing here?" Derrek asked, irritated.

"We're here to go boating," I said deadpan, fully aware that my answer was snarky and frustrating.

"Cut the bullshit," Derrek snapped.

"Lena and I are going to rent a boat. You and Jessica are going to rent a boat. We are going to meet about seven miles southeast of here. You can follow me."

"First you tell me what's going on."

"No. We're doing this my way. You either rent this boat and meet us in the water, or the first call I make is to Edgar. I'll remind you that you no longer have enough money to pay him back." Derrek thought about his options, but in the end, the choice I gave him wasn't really a choice. I turned, my arm around Lena's shoulders, and proceeded to the small building to rent a speedboat.

Forty-five minutes later Lena and I were shooting through the water, cutting through the ice-blue waves, wind whipping past us. Lena was smiling and so was I. Even though we were about to try and pull off something completely crazy and illegal, it was hard not to enjoy the ride. Lena looked back toward the shore, Athens disappearing in the distance, and I couldn't help but admire the picture she had painted for me. Long tanned legs crossed, black bikini covering enough to be appropriate, but leaving enough skin available for me to peruse that my thoughts were anything but. Her hair was captured by the wind, flowing behind her in a wild mess that looked both beautiful and free. Perhaps she felt free. Perhaps she had faith enough in me to understand that this would be the last hour of her life where she'd have to worry about Derrek or the mess he'd made. I couldn't help but smile bigger thinking I'd given her the happiness and freedom painted across her face.

Once we'd reached our destination I slowed the boat to a full stop.

"I know you've wanted to keep the details to yourself, and I understand why, but I'm really curious as to what we're doing way out here." Lena was sitting on one of the benches that lined the side of the boat, her hair no longer blowing in the wind, but her face a little pink from it.

"Derrek and Jessica are about to get lost at sea," was my only response and Lena, God love her, accepted it with a nod.

When their boat pulled up near ours, obviously a little behind, not wanting to take theirs at a full clip with little girls on board, Derrek's face was both worried and irritated.

"Okay, we're here. Now tell me what the hell is going on."

"First thing's first. Jessica and the girls need to board our boat."

"What?" The rage in his voice was clear and loud, and I completely understood.

"Listen, Derrek. I give you my word that everything will be all right. But you've got to trust me here. I want nothing but for this to be over with." I picked up the rope I'd pulled out of the supply hatch and raised my eyebrows at him, waiting for him to comply. I knew he would—he had no other choice. He held his hands out and I tossed him the rope, then we gently pulled until our boats were side by side.

Jessica climbed aboard first, then slowly, Derrek passed the girls over to her. Lena held her hands out, offering to take the smaller girl from Jessica. She hesitated for just a moment, but then handed the tiny girl to her. Even though she was holding the love child her ex-husband created while cheating on her, Lena's face lit up and she made it her mission to make the little girl smile amidst all the uncertainty and chaos.

Once all three were safely aboard, I looked to Derrek.

"You see that island just south of us?" I pointed to the horizon, where one could see the outline of an island in the distance.

"Yeah…." Derrek's answer trailed off as he tried to put together all the pieces I was giving him.

"The east side of the island is just a rocky cliff. I want you to take your boat around the island and then point it directly at the rocks. Max the speed out. You need to be going fast enough to wreck that boat beyond recognition."

"What?" Jessica practically yelled, but then calmed immediately when both her children began to panic too.

"You want me to crash the boat into the side of that island?" Derrek's voice was both scared and unbelieving.

"Yes. I want you to aim the boat at the rocks, but jump into the water about five hundred yards out. We'll come and pull you out of the water."

"That's crazy. I could die."

"That's the idea."

Derrek stared at me, eyes wide, until I saw recognition cloud them over. "You want me to fake my own death." It wasn't a question, but a statement.

"Not just yours. The registrar at the marina thinks your whole family is on that boat. They'll find the boat, but they won't find your bodies. They'll think you all died in the crash and your bodies were lost at sea."

"This can't be the only way," Derrek said, his voice wavering somewhere between angry and scared.

"This is the only way where you disappear, but are still breathing. Edgar wants you dead. Thinks I'm here to kill you, in fact. But I can't do that. Even with how much I despise you, I can't kill you. But I will tell him where you are." I paused, letting everything sink in for him. "If you do this, if you crash this boat and disappear, I will pay Edgar off and tell him you're dead. You'll be free to start a new life, and I'll make that a possibility. But if you don't, it's over."

Derrek's eyes flashed to Jessica's, and she looked just as shaken as he did. After everything that had happened in the last few days, I was shocked this had come as some sort of surprise to them both. If someone were after Lena and myself, if we were being hunted, and someone offered me an out, I'd take it without hesitation. It would hurt, but I'd put my past behind me, leave my family, leave my life behind, to ensure Lena was safe and with me. I watched his gaze move from Jessica to the faces of his daughters and I knew the moment when he made the decision.

"You promise you can make us safe?"

I leaned forward and looked him in the eye, trying to impart as much urgency and passion with my words as I could. "If you're not safe, then Lena's not safe. There is nothing I take more seriously than her safety. You mean shit to me, but she means the world. I wouldn't gamble with her life."

Derrek's eyes jumped from Jessica to Lena and back to me. He took off his hat, ran his hands through his hair, and exhaled loudly. "Okay, let's get this over with." At his words, Jessica stood up and moved to the side of the boat, leaning toward him and kissing him with all the passion you'd expect a couple in love to share. My eyes darted to Lena, to see if their exchange caused her any pain, but she was happily cooing at the child in her lap, oblivious.

When Jessica and Derrek pulled away from each other, she sat back down and I watched as Lena ran her hand down Jessica's arm, comforting her. "He'll be all right," Lena said quietly as Jessica wiped a few tears from her cheeks.

"Okay," I said, turning back to Derrek. "Like I said, just aim for the rocks then, literally, abandon ship before you get too close. It'll probably explode and you don't want to be too close to the explosion." I heard Jessica muffle a cry at my words but Derrek just nodded. "Make sure your life jacket is on tight."

"Yeah, no shit," Derrek responded, with almost a laugh.

"We'll be out to get you as soon as it's safe for the girls," Derrek just nodded at my words.

"I love you," he said firmly to Jessica, but she just nodded in response, pressing her lips together to keep herself from crying. Derrek threw his end of the rope back into our boat and then took the wheel of his. We all watched as he pulled away slowly. Once he was a safe distance away, I took to following him.

We went at a slower clip, just far enough away to see him clearly. I was more than relieved to see that there were no other boats on the east side of the island. I hadn't expected there to be any, really; it wasn't an optimal spot for tourists. The west side of the island had all the beaches. I slowed the boat when he aligned his with the rocky cliffs. We stopped altogether and watched as his boat sped up, heading directly toward the rocks.

Jessica started whimpering as the boat approached the island, and eventually turned her head away, unable to look any longer.

The boat was starting to get a little closer than I would have liked. "Jump, Derrek. Jump, damn it," I whispered. My heart started pounding harder; he was getting too close. Finally, I watched as he jumped from the boat, saw the orange of his life vest hit the water. Then just seconds later the boat hit with an impressively loud crash into the rocks. As I suspected, the boat burst into flames; the sound of the explosion was much louder than the crash, and the whole event was hard to look away from. Flames licked the sky, black smoke poured from the wreckage. Surely, if anyone had been aboard, they'd be dead on impact.

I pushed our boat forward and as we neared the crash site, the air was hot with the fire. I saw Derrek in the water, his life vest bobbing in the waves. As I neared it became clear he was moving, swimming away from the crash. I sighed in relief, glad to know he'd made it. I stopped the boat just yards from him and threw the rope out. He grabbed it and I pulled him in. After a struggle to bring him onboard, with lots of coughing and sputtering, he finally landed on the deck of the boat and Jessica flung herself on him, crying fully now, and very loudly.

Lena had both girls and tried to distract them, but we made eye contact and she gave me a small smile, obviously glad everything had turned out the way I'd planned.

"We've got to get out of here, now," I said urgently. "Someone on that island heard the explosion and I'm sure the authorities are on their way here. Derrek," I snapped, hoping to get his attention. When he finally looked at me from the deck of the boat, still coughing and breathing heavily, I nodded at the ocean. "Throw your wallet in the water. Jessica, you too." They didn't bother arguing or questioning me, which made everything so much easier.

After they'd ditched their personal items into the water, they sat on the bench, Derrek's arms wrapped tightly around Jessica. I aimed our boat back toward Athens.

Chapter Ten

I pulled the boat up to a marina that was much less popular, hoping there would be fewer people around to see us arrive. This marina was mainly used by fishermen, so when we docked, we got hardly any looks from the men cleaning their boats. Perfect. We walked down the wooden-planked walkway and I spotted the black SUV I'd hired.

"This is as far as we go," I said to Derrek. I handed him the manila envelope that contained the items Parker had managed to get for me. "In that envelope you'll find passports, IDs, and all the paperwork you'll need to leave the country under new identities. For all four of you. There is also paperwork that will lead you to a bank account I've set up in your new name that has the two million dollars we promised you, plus another fifty thousand to get you started."

Derrek took the envelope from me, looked inside, and then sighed. "You had this all figured out, didn't you?"

"Indeed," I replied. "Now listen, this is important. You are all dead. You cannot, under any circumstances, contact anyone from your previous life. You cannot come back to Portland, cannot even come back to Oregon. I'd say stay out of the US for a while, even. Am I making this clear? If you come back, you're dead. And so are we," I say, motioning to Lena and myself. Jessica looked more upset about this prospect than Derrek, and I guessed she might have been closer to her family than he was. For just one moment I wondered if she was regretting getting involved with him to begin with. She hadn't signed up for all of this. But then I looked at Lena, who was wearing a look of true compassion. She actually felt bad for them. Her open and enormous heart wiped away any concern I had for Jessica; she'd gotten herself into this mess and I'd done everything I could to ensure the man she loved lived. I couldn't feel guilty about it. Refused to feel guilty. "In that SUV there you'll find luggage with a few changes of clothes for each of you. The car will take you to the airport and I suggest you leave immediately."

Derrek reached out and I took his hand and shook it firmly. He nodded toward me, and it sort of looked like he wanted to thank me, but the words never left his mouth. Lena knelt and waved to the kids.

"Bye, girls. Be good for Mommy and Daddy, all right?" The two little girls nodded and smiled at her as she stood.

We stayed in place and watched as the four of them climbed into the car and drove away. When it was out of sight I heard Lena let out a giant, relieved sigh. I turned to her and saw the same relief written across her face.

"That was pretty intense," she said softly as she turned to me. "I'm glad everything went as planned. There were a million things that could have gone wrong."

I pulled her to me and wrapped my arms around her shoulders, smiling when her cheek came into contact with my chest.

"It was the only way I could think of to end this, once and for all."

"I get it. I just hope it worked."

"If they head straight to the airport, which is where I hired their car to take them, they should be on a plane before anyone really notices they're gone."

She exhaled loudly again and I buried my nose in her hair. "You're safe and that's all that matters." Her arms squeezed me a little tighter and her face pressed against my chest a little harder.

"Can we go back to the hotel now? I just want to lie in bed and try to forget this ever happened."

"Of course," I responded.

We spent the rest of the afternoon in the hotel room, showering and lounging on the bed, holding each other, trying to wrap our minds around what had happened just hours before. It wasn't until that evening when we turned on the television that we realized we just might have pulled it off. The reporter spoke in Greek, but there were captions in English running along the bottom of the screen.

The coastguard has confirmed a tourist boat that was rented by an American family has been found crashed just miles off the shore of Athens. The boat careened into a rocky beach, exploding on impact, and all four of the people on board, two adults and two children, are presumed dead. The coastguard is searching the nearby waters, hoping to find survivors, but based on the wreckage, I'm being told the chance of survival is slim.

Lena looked over to me. "It worked," she said, sounding astonished. "It actually worked." Her finger came up to pull at her bottom lip as she watched the television in fascination.

I stepped out onto our terrace and called Parker, knowing a text wouldn't give him any satisfaction. He answered sounding worried, his greeting rushed.

"Preston? Is everything all right?"

"Hey, everything is fine. It all went according to plan."

"I don't want to know any details. I'm just glad you're all right. And Lena?"

"She's fine too."

He breathed a sigh of relief and I knew he was slumping, all the anxiety leaving his body.

"Listen, I don't know where we're headed, or what we're up to next...." My words trailed off because I didn't know how to tell my brother I didn't know when I'd see him again.

"I understand, Preston. I get it. Like I said, I'm just glad you're both safe."

"I'll let you know as soon as we nail down some plans."

"Sounds good. Give your girl a hug for me."

"Will do."

We disconnected after our goodbyes and I took in a deep breath, trying to ready myself for one more phone call.

"Preston, I assume you're calling me with good news."

"Good news for you, perhaps, Edgar," I responded.

"Did you do as I asked you?"

"It's done. And I have your money for you."

There was a pause from Edgar's side of the line, then a booming laugh. "I knew you could do it." He laughed, a big whooping laugh, then chuckled until he could speak again without interruption. "You're a gem," he finally said. "I'll expect the money in my account by the end of the week."

"Then both Lena and I are cut loose, right? This is it, Edgar. We don't owe you anything ever again."

"I believe those were the terms. You get me my money, kill Derrek, and you're both off the hook. I'll forget all about you as soon as the money is in my account."

"You'll have it ASAP."

"It's been nice dealing with you." He paused and then asked one more question. "Was Derrek's death at least a little painful?"

I swallowed hard, hoping I could lie well enough to fool him. "Don't worry, he definitely suffered."

The evil laugh which emanated from him nearly made me hurl. I was glad I'd never have to see him again.

"Thank you for your patronage," he said, his evil laugh continuing. Then I heard the line go dead, and I relaxed against the railing, looking out to the picturesque Greek cityscape below me. I thought about everything that had happened in the last few weeks and suddenly I was overcome by so much tension leaving my body, I nearly collapsed. So much had been riding on this, so much of my life had been on the line, and it was finally over. I heard the French doors open and I smelled Lena before I felt her arms wrap around me from behind.

"Everything work out?"

My hand came up to smooth over hers and I sighed. "Yeah. Edgar bought it, really believes Derrek is dead. It's over." Before I knew what was happening she was in front of me, her dark eyes peering up into mine, her lips pulled up slightly at the corners.

"I know you did this for me."

My hands slid up her arms, loving the feel of her skin under mine. I loved watching her eyelids flutter at the sensation of me touching her. I cupped her cheeks and looked right in her eyes.

"Everything I've done since the first day I saw you outside that bar has been for you. Everything I do until the day I die will be for you. You're it for me, Lena. You're the reason I wake up each morning, the reason I'm standing here breathing. Whatever you need, just tell me, and it'll be my mission to get it for you."

She smiled and moved forward slightly until our noses touched. "What if everything I've ever wanted is standing in front of me?"

The corners of my lips pulled into my first genuine smile in almost two days. "Then that makes my job pretty easy." She laughed as I pressed my mouth against hers. I teased the seam of her lips with my tongue and, of course, she opened for me. She moaned against my lips and all I wanted was to pull her back to bed, to feel her beneath me and around me.

"Oh, wait," she said, pulling back and bringing her hand to her mouth. "I need one more thing." Her face was suddenly very serious, and she looked nervous. "I need you to look up how to say 'pregnancy test' in Greek so I don't sound like a bumbling American at the pharmacy."

I'd never experienced how truly empty and cavernous my stomach could feel before she'd said those words. My stomach dropped, my heart pumped ferociously, and my eyes blinked wildly.

"You think you're... You need a... How late..." I couldn't have completed a sentence in that moment if my life depended on it. I couldn't find the right words as one million of them were crashing through my mind faster than the speed of sound. She started laughing at me and brought her hands to my cheeks.

"Breathe, Preston," she said between giggles. "You're turning purple."

"You're pregnant?" I was impressed not only with my inference skills, but also my ability to put two words together. Three technically if you count the contraction.

"I think so," she said shyly. "Either that or I'm a week late for some other reason."

I picked her up, my arms wrapping around her waist, and I spun her around while hugging her to me. We were both laughing, and she was crying happy tears, and I couldn't think of another moment in my life where I'd been so ecstatic. When I finally put her down, I cradled her face and kissed her senseless.

"I think you're the only woman on the planet who could take possibly the worst day I've ever lived through and make it the best day of my life."

"Well, I'm glad you're excited," she said, smiling and wiping a few stray tears away. "But, Preston, I was totally serious. I need you to tell me how to say 'pregnancy test' in Greek."

I laughed and pulled her closer to me, feeling her heartbeat through her chest pressed up against mine.

"I'll give you anything and everything you've ever wanted," I said, my lips pressed against her hair. And I'd never spoken truer words.

Epilogue

Lena

I knew I only had a few minutes to accomplish my goal, and even though speed was not always a friend during sexy times with one's husband, in this situation, speed was imperative. I opened the door to our master bathroom slowly, so as not to make any unwanted creaking, then quietly peeled off my clothes and climbed into the shower.

It was always a struggle not to stop and admire my husband's beautiful body, even more so when soapy water was cascading down all the firm ridges and valleys of his muscular back. So it was no hardship on my part to put my hands on said gorgeous back and feel the hardened skin slippery under my fingers.

"Jesus, Lena. You scared me," he said right after he'd nearly jumped out of his skin.

"Hmm," I replied as I ran my hands around his waist, up over his ribs, then right back down again to find him hardening in my grasp. "But it's a good surprise, right?"

"Definitely." He spun in my arms and suddenly I was pressed up against the wall of the shower, his big hands under my thighs, lifting me and pressing me back. His mouth found mine and I groaned as my stomach flipped with his kiss.

Years.

Years later and his kisses still gave me butterflies.

I knew I would never tire of Preston, or what he could do to my body. I loved that he could still make me feel like a teenager experiencing my first love all over again. It was a quality I was sure you couldn't find in just any man. No. It was special to *my man*. And I wouldn't trade him for anyone else.

With one hand wrapped tightly around my waist, his other hand found my breast, kneading and palming it with gentle yet firm pressure, fingers pinching my nipple, eliciting more moans from me.

"I hate to be a buzz kill here, babe, but we don't have all the time in the world." I gasped again as his mouth found my neck, internally rolling my eyes because I knew his mouth would leave a mark there—it always did—but outwardly not caring because, well, I just didn't. If Preston wanted to mark me with love bites, I wasn't going to be the one to stop him. His parents sometimes avoided looking at me when I showed up with a hickey, and Piper always rolled her eyes, but I simply didn't care. Everyone knew how passionate we were about each other and sometimes I had the marks to prove it.

"What if I want to take my time?" His words were garbled against my skin, which felt awesome, but it also made me smile. He never wanted to be rushed when we made love.

"Well, you take all the time you need. I just put the baby down for a nap, but you never know when he'll wake up, so you might not get to finish, if you get what I'm saying."

"It's only really important that *you* finish, if you get what I'm saying."

I laughed. "That's sweet of you, but it's a big lie. You know just as well as I do that you need to get off just as much as me. It's been days."

That's right. Days. Preston had given me so much—everything, in fact—but he'd paid the price as much as any man does with small children. The sex was spread out and not the marathon exploits we had been used to pre-babies. Now, there were hurried quickies and stealthy shower escapades as we tried to not only orgasm, but connect on that level we'd thrived on for so long. Most nights, sex was off the table because we were both so worn out, so sex in the middle of the day while the baby napped? Yup. It was our new normal.

I just wanted to feel him inside me. To feel how perfectly he fit, to get that rush that always accompanied him, to feel the calmness and rightness that came along with sex with my husband. Oh yeah, and to come. That too.

At my words he put me down, my legs wobbly on the floor of our walk-in shower, and he kissed me hard before spinning me around.

"Bend over; put your hands on the wall, sweetheart."

Oh, hell, yes.

I did as he asked, aided by his hands on my waist, then his hand on my back, between my shoulder blades, gently pushing me down. When my hands reached out for the wall, his slid down my back, right along my spine, until he reached my backside, which he gave a gratuitous squeeze.

"Fuck, I love your ass," he said, still squeezing and groping. I smiled lazily, enjoying his praise. His hand moved lower and slipped inside me. "Jesus, Lena, you're soaked already."

"I'm just—" I stalled on a gasp as he explored. "Anticipating what's coming to me." His fingers moved in and out, slowly turning and stretching me. "God, I love your fingers."

"Not as much as you love my dick," he said with an obvious smile in his voice.

"True," I replied, also smiling. My smile faded when I felt his hardness pressing up against me, just barely there, but still making my heart skip a beat and my breath quicken.

"Do you want it?" he asked, rubbing the head of his cock along my entrance, teasing me.

"Yes," I panted.

"Tell me you want it," he demanded, his voice hard and ridiculously sexy.

"I want you inside me, Preston."

"Good girl," he said as he sank into me slowly. I groaned with every movement, loving the feel of him sliding into me, filling me, giving me every single inch of him. "You feel so fucking amazing, Lena. You always feel so perfect."

There weren't many words after that, just moaning and the sound of wet skin meeting with every pounding thrust. He let out a long hiss when he was close, as he tended to do, and reached around my waist and touched me to urge me over the edge with him. I came hard, as I tended to do with Preston, and loved the sounds he made as he came with me. It wasn't terribly romantic, it wasn't champagne and rose petals, but it was him and me, connecting, giving each other what we promised we would never again give to anyone else: ourselves.

I would take a quickie in the shower with Preston for the rest of my life over flowers and chocolates with anyone else. No contest.

He splayed kisses over my shoulder, his hands finding their way to my breasts, making me laugh. "Aren't you done yet?" I asked, laughing.

"Never," he said with so much sincerity it made my heart ache.

Eventually he spun me back around and gave me the slowest and deepest kiss, then we just proceeded to shower, making sure we took the opportunity to soap each other up.

Hours later, after the baby had woken up from his nap, we were pulling up to his parents' house for our weekly Sunday dinner.

It had taken me a while to decide that Portland was where we needed to be, or to believe I could even go back to Portland and be happy there. But, the truth of the matter was, our whole family was there. Well, Preston's whole family—who had become my family—and my Sam. When we found out in Athens we were indeed pregnant, the idea of raising a child without the support of everyone who loved us seemed not only stupid, but also unfair to all the people who loved Preston. I had lamented for my whole adult life my lack of family, so who was I to take Preston away from his? And the thing that sealed the deal was that

Preston would have lived somewhere far from them if it was what I wanted. He would have resigned himself to yearly visits and Skype calls, if he thought I would be happier anywhere else on the planet.

So, we'd moved to Portland when I was seven months pregnant and never looked back.

Piper opened her parents' front door and my little Nadia came bounding out, reaching directly for her father. He knelt down, scooped her up in his arms, and kissed the side of her head as she snuggled him.

"That one is a handful," Piper said as she hugged me. "We stopped at nearly every store in the mall that could have even *possibly* had anything princess related."

"Well, your first mistake was taking one of Lena's kids shopping. Nadia here inherited her shopping gene. I avoid malls like the plague," Preston said those words as he pressed his forehead right against Nadia's, making her giggle. I slapped his arm playfully, pretending to be offended, but laughing because he was pretty right.

"Daddy, Auntie Piper bought me this pretty princess dress and even a tiara. I was a good girl so she took me to get ice cream, even though I hadn't had dinner yet."

"Oh," Preston said, giving his twin sister the stink eye. "Sounds like Auntie Piper gets to take you home for a sleepover in that case."

"Really, Auntie Piper? I get to sleep at your house?"

Piper laughed. "We'll see, sweetie. First I need to snuggle your little brother." She took the car seat from my hands and almost ran away with it. I would have tried to stop her except I didn't mind not having to carry it and I knew I'd never be able to wrestle the baby from her. And once Preston's mother got hold of him, it would be game over for sure.

If Nadia was the princess of the Reid family, our son Devlin was the prince. He was beloved by all and could do no wrong. I happened to agree with their assessment so I never argued with anyone about it.

We walked into the kitchen and my eyes found Piper lifting Devlin from his car seat and pressing her nose into his neck and taking a long, gratuitous sniff.

"Oh, my God. My ovaries are firing like a freaking machine gun," she whined. "He smells delicious."

Preston's mother greeted me with a hug and I didn't miss how her eyes found my hickey. "How's my favorite daughter-in-law?" she asked, as she always did. Preston was the only child of hers who'd married a woman. Parker was married, but his husband was her favorite son-in-law.

"I am well, thank you."

"Yes, I can see that," she replied with a knowing wink. I tried not to blush but it was no use. I liked it better when she didn't comment on the hickeys.

"Oh! Happy Anniversary!" Piper whisper-yelled, as Devlin lay asleep in her arms.

"Thank you," Preston said, wrapping his arm around my shoulders and holding me close.

"Six years of marriage. That's pretty exciting," his mother said. "I still wish I'd been able to be at your wedding."

There it was—the obligatory guilt trip that we'd gotten married in Las Vegas with no one but Elvis as a witness. We endured it every year, and his family didn't mean any harm. They weren't trying to make us feel bad about it; they just genuinely wished they could have been at our wedding.

"Maybe when we hit ten years we'll renew our vows," I said. It was my automatic answer to their obligatory guilt trip. But I meant it—maybe we would renew our vows. I never got to throw a big party when I married Preston, and if there was anything worth celebrating, it was our marriage. Marrying him was the best decision I'd ever made and everything that had come after that day had been nothing short of perfect. He'd practically rescued me from the worst kind of marriage and given me something I'd only ever dreamt about. He was my knight in shining armor. Well, my knight in a shiny black Lotus, anyway.

"I'd like to say that we invited you to dinner because we wanted to spend time with you, but actually, we invited you so we could kidnap your children for the night. You've got the night off from parenting." Preston's mother was making shooing gestures at us and pointing toward the front door.

"Here," Piper said, holding keys out to us with her free hand. "Take the keys to my car. You've got reservations at Bartini at six, and a room reserved for you at the downtown Hilton. Happy anniversary."

"Wait," I said, still trying to catch up. "You're watching the kids for us? We're going on a date?" Devlin was only five months old, and we'd never left him overnight before, but my gut was telling me to take their offer and run off with my husband for a night of uninterrupted adult time.

"Piper is going to stay here with me to help take care of the kiddos; we'll keep your car with the car seats in case we need to go anywhere, and you two go and have a good time. If you come back before ten a.m. tomorrow morning I'll be very upset with both of you."

"Are you sure?" Preston asked.

"We're sure. You know Mom's got that nursery just waiting for some baby time," Piper said, gently rocking back and forth as all women tended to do unconsciously when holding a baby.

He looked at me and I looked at him, and I knew we were in agreement. We both walked toward our children and took turns kissing them both goodbye, and I shouted last-minute instructions to my mother-in-law before closing the door and walking to Piper's car.

Once we were both in the car and pulling away from their house I turned to Preston. "I feel like we just got ambushed, but in reverse."

"Yeah," he said, reaching over and taking my hand in his as we drove. "But it's a pretty sweet anniversary gift."

"Yeah. Hey, can I ask you a favor?"

"Anything," he said as he brought my hand to his mouth and kissed it.

"Can we go home first and get the Lotus?" Butterflies took flight in my belly at the thought of being alone with him in that car again. I very rarely ever got to ride in it, and he usually drove a more practical car to work.

"Just so long as you understand if I see you sitting in my Lotus, I won't be able to keep my hands to myself."

"I would never expect anything less."

"You know I'm gonna take what's mine."

"And I'll happily give you everything."

The End

Acknowledgments

The first thank you definitely goes out to every blogger who took a chance on this serial. I asked you all to trust me and read something blind, support something without knowing much about it, and you gave your support in spades. From the beginning, creating this story has been a roller coaster ride for me and I appreciate everyone who read it, blogged about it, posted about it, shared a teaser or a cover...I appreciate it all. THANK YOU!

The second thank you goes to my street team. You guys go above and beyond for me. I am so glad I have a group of ladies that I can go to for advice and to be completely neurotic around. Also, thank you all who beta read for me on this project.

Becca, Kelly, and Andrea for always giving me such honest and invaluable feedback. I trust you all implicitly with my words and thank you for your help.

To the READERS! Thank you for loving Preston and Lena. Thank you for every time you told me you were excited to read the next installment; your words of encouragement kept me writing and motivated me to give you the best possible product. I started this serial because the story was there and I loved the characters, but I finished the project because of the love and enthusiasm you shared with me for Preston and Lena (along with Sam, Piper, and Parker).

Special thanks to Sprinkles On Top Studios for creating such a lovely cover for this beast of a book!

More books by Anie Michaels:

~The Never Series~

Never Close Enough

Never Far Away

Never Giving Up

~The Never Duet~

Never Standing Still

Never Tied Down – Coming 2015

~Stand Alone Novels~

The Space Between Us

The Absence of Olivia ~ Coming 2015

Please feel free to follow me on any and all media platforms!

http://www.facebook.com/AuthorAnieMichaels

https://twitter.com/Anie_Michaels

Shoot me an email!

anie.michaels@gmail.com

Sign up for my newsletter to stay up to date on exciting news and new releases!

http://eepurl.com/-DPjn

www.ingramcontent.com/pod-product-compliance
Lightning Source LLC
Chambersburg PA
CBHW051513250626
47156CB00001B/80